Enthralled

Enthralled

Paranormal Diversions

EDITED BY

MELISSA MARR &
KELLEY ARMSTRONG

HARPER

An Imprint of HarperCollins Publishers

*To Smart Chicks everywhere,
we're grateful that the future is in the hands of so many
strong, clever, and wise girls and women.*

CONTENTS

Enthralled

INTRODUCTION

Most anthologies start with a theme. This one was a little different: it began with a tour.

Having done a few joint events, we decided that it would be fun to set up a multiauthor, multicity, author-organized tour. Touring is great, but touring with others is even better, both for us and for the readers. So with that in mind, we started talking to authors whose books we liked—books we thought our readers would like too. The response was so overwhelmingly positive that we didn't get very far down our wish list before the tour was full.

Nineteen authors visited twelve cities on the Smart Chicks Kick It tour. That sounds huge, but it still means we missed a lot of places and a lot of readers. We wondered how we could bring some of that tour experience to readers we couldn't meet. The solution? An anthology. We'd invite the authors from the tour to contribute a story—schedules permitting. As the 2010 tour got under way and we began inviting authors for 2011, we added two of them to the collection, as a sneak peek at Smart Chicks 2011.

Like the tour itself, the anthology needed a focus. We decided on journeys, trips—including diversions—in keeping with the tour idea. In some stories, the characters embark on actual road trips, getting from point A to point B. But there are other kinds of journeys, and you'll read those here too, as our characters find their paths and discover things about themselves and their places in the world. We hope you'll enjoy taking these trips as much as we are enjoying being on the road together.

From somewhere out here,

Kelley & Melissa

GIOVANNI'S FAREWELL
by Claudia Gray

Before I was awake or aware, before my heart began to beat, Cairo was there. We curled around each other in the womb, so much so that the doctors had to pry our limbs apart to deliver us. Until we were four years old, neither of us spoke; we each understood the other without words, and nobody else was as important. There were Mom and Dad, of course, but they always recognized our bond.

He served as my one constant in a life led on four different continents (to date), where instead of schools and suburbs (until a year ago), we'd been taught by various tutors, sometimes Mom's grad students, the different cities and cultures we lived in, or occasionally just books and our own curiosity. Last year, Mom took a visiting professorship at Georgetown, and for the first time in our lives, we were plunged into a "normal American high school"—the biggest culture shock of all. I adapted well enough; Cairo found it harder. We weren't like other kids, something he reveled in and I tried to hide. But even as I made new friends and Cairo withdrew into the background, the bond between us never wavered. We were two parts of one whole. Inseparable, forever.

Maybe that was why I tried too hard to hide from the fact that Cairo was . . . changing. Why I denied this new truth until it was beyond denying. Until our first trip to Rome.

"Okay, so, seriously, I don't get it." My friend Audrey painted her toenails baby-pink by the gleam of her iPod's flashlight app, so the chaperones wouldn't see we were violating the lights-out rule. "Toilets come with seats. Always. So why does every single freakin' restaurant and museum in Italy have toilets without seats? Do they, like, remove them just to be evil?"

Although the no-toilet-seats thing in Italy was annoying, I'd seen worse. My brother would've told Audrey so, explaining that we'd been to archaeological digs in Egypt and Syria where the only bathroom facilities were holes in the ground, and how different cultures look on different things as necessities or luxuries. I just said, "I know. It's disgusting."

And the truth was, Rome was kind of a disappointment.

Of all the places we'd lived and traveled, Cairo and I had never made it to Rome before. Strange, considering that Mom and Dad were archaeologists who specialized in the history of the ancient Roman Empire. But their work never took them, nor us, anywhere in Italy. Mom's research concentrated on Roman settlements in the Middle East, and Dad long ago gave up digging in favor of writing books. He was as serious about history as Mom, but his books still became bestsellers thanks to their flashy titles (like his latest, *Cleopatra: Eternal Temptress*). So we grew up hearing about how glorious Rome was back in the day. When the school announced the summer trip for Rome, we both wanted to go, and our parents were thrilled we'd finally get to see the city.

But once we arrived, I realized that I knew too much to enjoy this the way my new friends did. The Forum would have been glorious 2,000 years ago; what I saw when we finally visited it was a ruin not unlike ones I'd seen my whole life. Tour guides acted like the Colosseum was just the world's oldest sports stadium, instead of a place where thousands upon thousands of people and animals were slaughtered. Even the pizza wasn't as good as it was at Vincenza's in Falls Church. Instead of having some magnificent, enriching experience, I spent my days wondering which was hotter—Rome in July, or the surface of the sun.

A knock on the hotel room door startled us both. Audrey slid her iPod under the sheets. Mrs. Weaver called, "Ravenna? Are you awake?"

"Just a second." I threw off the sheet to get out of bed while Audrey tucked herself in and tried to look like she was sleeping. Despite the darkness of the room, I could see her mouth the words *What did you do?*

Nothing, I mouthed back, as though I had no idea what was going on.

But I did. I knew. With my brother, I always knew.

I cracked open the door to find Mrs. Weaver standing there in a pink plaid bathrobe she couldn't have wanted any of us to see. I said, "Is Cairo okay?"

She blinked, maybe in surprise that she didn't have to tell me what was going on. But she didn't ask any stupid questions. "He seems to have had . . . a nightmare or an upset of some sort. We've tried to calm him down, but—"

"He'll be okay. Just let me talk to him."

Mrs. Weaver led me down the long corridor of the hotel. Behind various doors, I could hear giggling or talking, everyone else breaking curfew to gossip or make out. As we reached the end of the hall, I saw Cairo's roommate, Jon, a jock assigned to room with him at random. I used to think Jon was beautiful with his carved muscles and white-blond hair—until I got to know him.

As I reached the door, Jon muttered, "Shut that freak up, will you?"

"Go screw yourself." Nobody got to call my brother a freak but me. Before Mrs. Weaver could scold us for that exchange, I went inside.

This hotel room looked just like mine, except that it had been trashed. The covers were crumpled in one corner, the sheets in another, and the mattress had been flung up

against one wall. Curled next to it, shaking, hands over his ears, drenched in sweat, was Cairo.

"It never stops," he whispered without looking up. My brother always knew it was me. "I can't sleep and I can't think. It never, ever stops."

"Shhhhh." I sat next to him, careful to keep us from touching. My presence soothed him, though, just as his presence did for me. Maybe it reminded us of the time before our memories began, when we knew nothing of the world but each other.

We looked like negatives of each other: both thin to the point of being bony, with big, dark eyes and too much blue-black hair to control, but me with Dad's pasty Irish complexion and Cairo with Mom's deep Indian skin tone. The two of us shared accents nobody could ever place, fluency in five languages, a sense of belonging everywhere and yet nowhere, and our ridiculous names (Cairo's for the place Mom and Dad met, mine for the city where they spent their honeymoon).

I always thought we would share everything. Then, a few months ago, these . . . episodes . . . began.

The signs were subtle, at first: Cairo would go very still and quiet, and his normally deep concentration would shatter to distraction. Nobody besides me could even tell something was really wrong, and even I was unsure exactly how to react. But slowly the episodes became longer. More intense. He would bolt from wherever we were, whatever we were doing, to isolate himself. His skin became sweaty and cool. Despite the lack of

any rational explanation for it, he acted like a guy in severe pain.

Between episodes, it was like nothing had ever happened. Which was maybe why he never talked about it, and why I never made him talk about it.

We hid it from Mom and Dad, always tacitly, never admitting even to each other what was going on. The first time, at school, we claimed Cairo's behavior was a reaction to some medication. The next few times at school he was able to cover by hiding in the guys' bathroom and accepting the tardies. The only time it happened at home, Dad was at the store and Mom was puttering around in the yard—I got him calmed down before either of them came back inside.

I didn't understand what was going on. I didn't like the fact that there was anything about Cairo I couldn't understand. Or anything that he didn't want to share with me.

That night, as we huddled together in his wreck of a hotel room, I decided to finally press for answers.

"What's going on with you?" No answer at first. "When you—when you get like this, what's happening?"

"I don't know."

"Tell me what you do know. What you feel."

He rocked back and forth, trying to calm himself. "I feel . . . what everyone else feels."

"Huh?"

Cairo breathed out raggedly. "Audrey's scared Michael has a crush on you. He doesn't, but she ought to be worried, because

Michael isn't really into her. He's just into her feet. Only the feet. He thinks about her doing things with her foot that I'm not sure are actually physically possible."

I tried not to picture exactly what Michael would want Audrey to do with her feet. "How do you know this?"

"I just know. Just like I know Mrs. Weaver kind of has a thing for Jon—"

"Ew." Mrs. Weaver was at least forty.

"She'd never do anything about it, but she fantasizes about Jon constantly. Tegan's afraid her parents are splitting up. Marvin's afraid he's gay, which he is. Lindsey hates herself—everything about herself. She goes through her whole body over and over, hair to bones to skin, and hates each part of it in turn."

I didn't understand why he was inventing stories about all of our friends, which was weird enough without it having this strange effect on him. All I understood was that I wanted to shake him to snap him out of it. Yet I knew, without being told, that any contact would feel like broken glass to him now—nothing but pain. "You don't know these things. You're imagining this weird stuff about people, and it's—messing with your mind. We've never spent a lot of time around kids our own age, and maybe it's just getting to you. It gets to me sometimes." *Never* like this, I thought but didn't say. "After this trip, we'll have some time to ourselves. We'll go hiking. Make some music. You won't be surrounded by people anymore."

"It's worse when I'm surrounded by them, but—it's getting

stronger. This new . . . ability." His dark eyes found mine, and in the dim light from the city beyond our window, I could see the glimmer of unshed tears. "Ravenna, I know you don't understand. I know because I know what you're thinking. What everyone's thinking. I can . . . I can read minds."

I didn't say anything. I didn't move.

He said, "You think I'm going insane, don't you?"

I hadn't—until he said that. His eyes were so intense, his belief in his . . . "psychic power" or whatever so absolute. I'd been worried before, but that worry kindled within me, blazing into fear.

Cairo had always been my other half. The second part of my soul.

If he was going crazy, I was being cut in two.

Terror made me angry, made me stupid. I pushed myself up to my feet, hands balled in fists by my side. "Stop it. Just stop it. You're not even trying to get a handle on yourself. You're making yourself crazy and you don't care what it does to you or to me. So spare me the guilt trip, okay? Get the hell over it and start acting like my brother again."

The look on Cairo's face—the total sense of betrayal there—I couldn't stand it. I ran out the door of his room and back toward my own. As I ran past, Jon whispered, "Freak," again, but I pretended I didn't hear.

"I wish your brother wasn't such a weirdo," Audrey said the next day. We stood, with the rest of our school group, in the gardens in front of the Catacombs of Saint Cecilia. Though it was still morning, the Italian sun beat down, sweat beading between my breasts so that I could feel my cotton sundress sticking to my skin. Tendrils of my hair that had escaped from their high, sloppy bun clung damply to my neck. "I don't mean that in a bad way. I mean, he's *different*, right? But so hot."

That was another of the ways in which my twin and I were not alike. No matter how much Cairo stood out from the crowd, girls always raved about how gorgeous he was. No matter how hard I tried to fit in, guys never seemed to agree with my mother that I was "growing into my looks."

At that moment, I was doing my best to be just one of the twenty schoolkids from Virginia—standing around, giggling at Jon's handstands on the grass, eating a lemon gelato from the stand across the road, and trying to catch the eye of one of the hot guys with the Italian school group also waiting for the tour.

Cairo, on the other hand, stood off to one side reading the 2,000-year-old Latin carvings in an ancient salvaged stone.

Of course, I could read Latin too—Mom and Dad made sure of that early on—but I had the sense not to flaunt it.

Cairo's shoulders were hunched over. His oversized black T-shirt hung off his slim frame. Though he was steady again, himself again—at least for the moment—I could see how alone he felt.

If I went to stand with him, let him borrow some of my "normal" for a little while, it would help. That was what I usually did. But Cairo had become . . . unstable. I couldn't say whether it frightened me more for his sake or for my own. I couldn't deal with that. Couldn't face it. Easier to remain there, to keep giggling even if I didn't pay attention to the jokes, keep flirting with guys who didn't notice me.

Except that one of them did.

"Where are you from?" The Italian guy closest to me gave me a bashful smile. He was probably the cutest boy there—curly hair, nice build, the longest eyelashes I'd ever seen on a guy. His clothes were unfortunate, a plaid shirt and stiff jeans that screamed 1970s, but maybe there was a retro craze in Italian high schools.

"DC." I wasn't sure that would translate. "America. Right outside Washington, DC."

"You are enjoying your trip?"

"Uh-huh." I wanted to ask him the same thing, but maybe he lived close by. So I kept it simple. "I'm Ravenna."

"Like the city in Italy? Very beautiful." This guy had an amazing grin. "I am Giovanni."

His accent was so warm, so sexy. JhoVAHNny. The name seemed to melt in his mouth. I felt a smile spreading across my face. "What about you, Giovanni? Are you from Rome?"

"Not living here now—"

"Come on, you guys," Michael interrupted, stepping between me and Giovanni. "Mrs. Weaver's calling the group." It was rude of him to do that, and I meant to apologize to Giovanni immediately, but something stopped me: I noticed that Michael was staring at Audrey's feet, and her painted toenails.

Coincidence. Had to be. She had just changed the polish color, after all. What if Michael had noticed that? Didn't we want guys to notice?

By the time I turned back to Giovanni, he was gone. His group must have been called too.

Scowling at Michael's back, I followed him to the gathering spot. A weary tour guide, going through his spiel by rote, explained what the catacombs were, the theories about why they existed, the need to be careful because these were built before modern safety standards, and how if anybody was scared of enclosed spaces or graves, they should speak up immediately instead of having a panic attack underground.

Cairo and I had been visiting tombs with our parents since we were old enough to walk. If he were next to me, we'd share a look and a laugh at the thought of anybody panicking down there.

But we weren't next to each other. The divide between us was still so new and so small, but if what I feared was true—if Cairo was losing his grip on sanity—it would only get wider. And it might last forever.

I couldn't think about it.

The blazing summer heat evaporated as soon as our group had filed only a few feet down into the catacombs. The underground chill always turned the day to winter. My friends began shivering; I had known to bring my embroidered shawl in my bag. Several steps ahead, I saw Cairo shrug on a hoodie.

Crudely carved fish and lambs dotted the bleak stone walls as we went farther and farther down. Since the tour guide was rattling off a lot of history my parents had already taught me, I fell toward the back, making room for my friends to hear better.

And, as it turned out, for someone else to fall in beside me.

"Hey." I felt that smile tugging at my lips again as I glanced over to see Giovanni walking downstairs by my side. "I thought you'd wait for the Italian-language tour."

"I have been here before many times." Giovanni's hands were tucked into his jeans pockets so that his elbows splayed out a little, revealing what broad shoulders he had. "I do not need to hear the tour guide again."

"Why come at all?"

"Have to."

"School trips suck." I sighed. Though this one was looking up all of a sudden. I wondered if Giovanni and I could meet up after—Mrs. Weaver would never have let me go on a date, but an espresso at the hotel café seemed possible.

"One thing is better this time." Giovanni's shy smile made this cold, dark, dead place feel warm and alive. "You are here."

I ducked my head, unable to meet his eyes any longer but unable to quit smiling. No guy had ever flirted with me before. Maybe it was something about Italian guys. Maybe it was something about Giovanni himself. But I felt totally sure he wasn't just playing me—that he'd never done anything like this in his life.

That made two of us.

We reached the very bottom level of the catacombs, catching up with the rest of the group—my friends were silhouetted by the naked bulbs that served as lighting down here. They stood just through a stone archway. Carved-out graves surrounded us, and I saw Giovanni glancing their way.

"No need to be nervous." I felt bold enough to tease him. "No dead bodies in there anymore."

"Nothing but dust, now." Giovanni's mournful expression reminded me what this place used to be. Now it had become a stop on the standard tourist routes, with school bus trips tromping through every day and a souvenir shop nearby. Once, though, it was a secret cemetery where people came to hide their martyrs and hope for miracles. I looked up into the dark chambers above us and felt a shiver that had nothing to do with the cold. What I felt was wonder—the emotion I'd been waiting to feel in Rome, but that had evaded me. Until Giovanni.

I smiled at him and whispered, "Thank you."

"Thank you," he said. "For finding me. I have waited so long."

"Waited?"

"No one sees me. Only you see me."

"Giovanni, we only just met—" I edged through the archway,

with a glance over my shoulder. I expected him to follow me, and he did.

What I didn't expect was for him to walk through the wall.

Straight through the stone wall.

I didn't imagine it. It wasn't a trick of the light. Giovanni really walked through the stone. "How did you do that?" My voice was too loud; I could hear the echoes in the stone chambers, and several people turned back toward me in irritation.

Audrey, in particular, looked put out. "Who are you talking to?" she muttered. "You've been ranting to yourself all morning. Did Cairo, like, infect you with weirdness?"

I pointed at Giovanni, who stood right in front of her, where she couldn't possibly miss him. He had an apologetic look on his face. Then I realized that our shadows were all outlined sharply against the stone wall—everyone but Giovanni's. The light shone right through him.

When our eyes met again, Giovanni nodded. "You are the only one who has seen me since I died."

I screamed because I couldn't do anything else, louder and louder, until someone turned out the lights.

What happened next—I couldn't say. To me it was only confusion. I must have fainted, because the next thing I knew, I was lying on the sun-heated grass outside, Rome's summer light nearly blinding me, Mrs. Weaver almost panicking, Marvin trying to get me to drink water out of his squeeze bottle. None of it made any sense until I saw my brother.

Cairo knelt by my side and took my hand. None of the instability I'd seen last night, or the insecurity I'd seen this morning, was visible now. Even when my brother had trouble being strong enough to take care of himself, he could be strong for me. "She needs to rest; that's all. Just put us in a taxi back to the hotel," he said. "I'll see that she gets some sleep."

Mrs. Weaver looked around, as if she wanted someone else to tell her what to do. But there weren't enough adults on this trip, and she had about another twenty minutes to get the rest of the group back on the tour bus for the afternoon trip to the Castel Sant'Angelo. That, plus Cairo's steadiness—his apparent recovery from last night's upset—must have convinced her. "Don't set one foot outside the hotel," she said. "When we get back at six, I expect to see both of you waiting for us."

"We will." I would have said anything to get out of there.

Only when Cairo and I were truly alone—me flopped in exhaustion across my hotel bed, and him sitting yoga-style on Audrey's—did we speak to each other. "What happened?" he said.

"I was talking to this guy, Giovanni, but . . . he wasn't real."

"What do you mean, not real?"

"He didn't have a shadow. Nobody else could see him. And he said—he said I was the only person who'd seen him since he died." I clutched the cover on my bed into a knot between my fingers. "That can't be real, right?"

Only after I said the words did I realize—I didn't have to tell Cairo the truth. I could've pled sunstroke or dizziness or something else and denied what had happened to me. But I never lied to him; it hadn't occurred to me to start now.

Instead of calling the nearest psychiatrist, Cairo remained by my side. He even smiled. "It all makes sense now."

"What makes sense?"

"Don't you get it? I wondered about this before, but . . . when it was just me, I couldn't be sure. Now I am. We're psychic."

"Psychic?"

"Or . . . talented, somehow. I don't know the right word for it. But I have moments when I can hear people's thoughts, and you can see the dead. We're twins; I guess it makes sense that if it was happening to me, eventually it would happen to you too. Maybe it's the . . . family inheritance. Something like that."

I wanted to tell Cairo to stop talking about hearing people's thoughts, just like I had the night before, but I couldn't, and not just because I had begun experiencing something even stranger. I wanted to go back in time to the night before and not be such a bitch to Cairo, to come through for him the way he came through for me.

Most of all I wanted to go back to the life I'd had just this morning, where fitting in seemed possible. If Cairo was right, then I would never fit in. My brother and I really were freaks, and we'd be freaks forever.

But down deep I knew, for certain, that I'd seen Giovanni.

"How can we be sure?" I said. "It could have been heatstroke, or . . . déjà vu, or something."

Cairo folded his arms. "Do you honestly believe that?"

"Can't you tell?" I retorted. If he wanted me to take him seriously as Mr. Mind Reader, he was going to have to offer more proof.

"When I can hear thoughts, I can hear all of them. When I can't, I can't," he said. He was bouncing on his heels, energized by the possibilities. "I can't turn it on or off, but lately I've started thinking there might be a pattern—but I'm not sure yet. Enough of that. Back to you. Ravenna, do you really think what happened to you was as simple as heatstroke?"

"No," I admitted. "But I need to understand what's going on before we try to diagnose ourselves because of a vision I saw in the catacombs."

He checked the time on his phone. "If we cab it out there, we can get to the catacombs and back before the others return to the hotel."

Breaking Mrs. Weaver's rules didn't bother me nearly as much as seeing Giovanni again. When I looked into my brother's eyes, I could see that he understood my fear.

I said, "I don't know why he appeared to me. What Giovanni wants."

"Neither do I. What was he saying to you?"

"Ordinary stuff." I shrugged. "Actually, I thought he was flirting with me. But I guess he was just excited that someone could see him finally." It had been nice, thinking some hot Italian guy was into me. I should've known something was up.

"Well, we'll go back. I'll be with you. I can't see the dead—not yet, anyway—but you won't be alone. And you can figure out for sure whether or not this is real."

"Thanks." It came out in a small voice.

Cairo gave me a look. "If this had happened to you first, instead of me? I wouldn't have believed you either. So stop feeling guilty. We have bigger things to deal with."

When we returned to the catacombs in the early afternoon, the summer sun had intensified until even the roads seemed to sizzle. Although trees grew on the grounds outside the tombs, shade didn't help much. My skin felt grimy with sweat. For a while we stood around where I'd first seen Giovanni that morning, but nobody appeared except a gaggle of blue-habited nuns awaiting their own tour.

"Maybe it doesn't happen every time," I said. "Maybe I can't predict when it happens."

"Possibly." Cairo wasn't ready to give up. "We should go back to the last place you saw him."

Nobody could walk down into the catacombs without being on a guided tour, so we had to buy more tickets. The seller said crisply, "The next English-language tour is in just over one hour."

Too long, I thought, to give us time to explore the catacombs and yet get us back to the hotel on time. "What's the very next tour?"

"French, in five minutes."

"We speak French," I said. *"Deux billets, s'il vous plaît."*

As we walked toward the gathering spot for the tour, Cairo said, "You wouldn't have admitted that yesterday."

"I wouldn't have admitted a lot of things yesterday." My long-cherished desire to look and act normal had so obviously died that there was nothing to do but let it go. If I could see the dead, "normal" was never going to happen.

We arranged ourselves at the end of the French tour. For the first little while, nothing appeared out of the ordinary—but as we descended the uneven stone steps toward the chamber where Giovanni had walked through the wall, my heartbeat quickened. It wasn't just nerves; it was like my body *knew* he was near.

When I walked back in, Giovanni stood there, as if he'd been waiting for me the whole time.

He looked so relieved to see me. Almost on the verge of tears. I thought I might cry too. Giovanni was more beautiful to me now than he was before—now, when I knew what he was, when he ought to have terrified me. But there was nothing scary about him. He was simply someone who had died—something that happened to everyone, eventually.

He was the proof that I was sane.

And he was the proof that Cairo and I really were twins

of the soul and always would be.

"You have come back," he said.

"Yeah. Sorry I panicked."

"He's here?" Cairo whispered to me, looking around wildly in pretty much every direction but the right one.

"You can't see him?"

Cairo shook his head. Whatever powers he possessed, they weren't like mine. Just as I had zero ability to read other people's thoughts. Our gifts were unique. Our own.

Giovanni looked even sadder. "You have told someone about me? He is . . . boyfriend?"

"Cairo's my brother. He's just trying to help." Glancing behind me to see if the French tourists were paying any attention to the muttering teenagers in the back—which, fortunately, they weren't—I took a deep breath. "Giovanni, I'm not sure how to ask this, but . . . you're definitely dead, right?"

He nodded, unconcerned; it was old news to him. "My school came here. I fell. My neck, it broke."

Maybe his clothes came across so 1970s because that was when he died. "Do you think you were pushed? Did someone murder you?"

"What? No. Not possible." Giovanni seemed utterly sure about this. "Rain was falling. The steps were wet all over. My feet went"—he made a hand motion that resembled the Nike swoosh.

"He says he wasn't murdered," I whispered to Cairo, who

shrugged. The only other sounds were the increasingly distant patter of the tour guide and the shuffling feet of French tourists walking away. I turned back to Giovanni. "Then why are you still here? I always thought . . . if spirits stuck around on earth, it was because they had some kind of unfinished business here." But what did I know? It had been only stupid TV shows and horror movies to me until a few hours earlier.

Yet Giovanni nodded. "One thing I never did on earth. One thing I always wanted to do."

Maybe he needed me to find his mother and tell her he loved her. Maybe I had to search for some long-lost friend. Or get revenge. Was I willing to get revenge for Giovanni for something that happened decades before I'd been born? Carefully, I said, "What's that?"

Bashfully, Giovanni said, "Never I kiss a beautiful girl. Never any girl, actually."

For a long moment, I thought I must have gone crazy after all. He couldn't have said that, could he? "You've hung around on earth for thirty years or so because you didn't want to go to heaven without kissing a girl?"

"You have got to be kidding me," Cairo whispered. I elbowed him sharply in the side; mockery wasn't going to help us.

Giovanni said, "I want this very badly. Please—maybe you would—maybe? You are most beautiful girl."

I didn't especially want my first kiss to be from a dead guy. If this was a sign of how my love life would go from then on, my already low expectations were going to have to drop even lower.

And yet . . . it was such a simple request. He wanted it so badly. He thought I was beautiful. He was so gorgeous; if I hadn't realized he was dead, I would have kissed him for certain. And Giovanni would always be the first guy who had ever flirted with me.

The tour group had moved significantly ahead of us now, but we could still hear them—still catch up if we had to, without getting lost down here. I told Cairo, "Can you give us a second?"

"For what? So you can kiss him?" To my surprise, Cairo—who'd been so unflappable through all of this—looked disgusted. "You don't know what that will do. He might, I don't know . . . suck your soul out."

"I don't think it works that way." How it worked, I wasn't sure, but I felt convinced that Giovanni wasn't trying to hurt me. "Remember how you know that Michael's always interested in Audrey's feet? That's how I know Giovanni isn't trying to hurt me."

Cairo considered this. "You can read his mind?"

Giovanni said, "Tell him I will not hurt your soul."

"It's not mind reading. It's just . . . if he were lying, I'd know. I feel sure of that." And I did.

The French-speaking guide had taken our group almost out of earshot. With a sigh, Cairo said, "Okay, I'm going ahead. Catch up when you can. And if anything weird happens . . . scream even louder than you did last time."

"All right." We tangled pinky fingers for just a moment, a quick sign of solidarity we hadn't shared since we were eight years old. Then Cairo walked off without a backward look. I knew it was his way of saying he trusted my judgment. The question was, did I trust my own?

I turned back to Giovanni, who still stood there, hopeful and sweet. He was so beautiful—big, dark eyes, long eyelashes, dimpled chin—that only one question came to mind: "How is it that you never kissed a girl?"

It turned out to be possible to blush after death. Giovanni flushed so that the catacomb around us seemed to turn a soft shade of pink. "Did not always look like this."

"What do you mean?" I shouldered my cloth bag and tried to stay focused. I hadn't brought my shawl this time, and I shivered slightly in the underground chill. "Did you . . . change or something? After you died?"

"After death, we look like we are meant to look. Not always in life."

I began to understand. This wish of his wasn't only about kissing a girl; this was about making up for the life he lost—not after he died, but before. "Show me."

Giovanni didn't want to, I could tell, but he obeyed. His beautiful face seemed to melt, the skin along the left side of his jaw crinkling and turning a vivid, meaty red. A burn scar, I realized. Giovanni's fall on the catacomb steps wasn't the first terrible accident he'd been in.

It wasn't so horrible, really—just a line along one side of his face—but I could imagine what most girls would've said about it. What Audrey would have said. If Giovanni had lived to be a little older, he might have met a girl mature enough to look past his scar and see the gentle, beautiful guy beneath. But he didn't make it.

"You see me now," he said, ashamed.

"I see you now." I stepped closer to Giovanni and put one hand to his face. I couldn't actually touch him—or so it seemed to me—but when my fingers appeared to brush his face, his lips parted slightly as though he could feel it. "I see all of you."

I lifted my face to his and closed my eyes. I felt his kiss not as a touch, but as a glow—warmth spreading through me, making me aware of my blood and my pulse, of everything that separated the living and the dead. For one moment, I knew more than ever before what it meant to be alive.

The kiss's end was like the snuffing of a candle—a little less light and heat in the world.

When I opened my eyes, Giovanni was beaming at me, his face whole and perfect once more, and slightly transparent now. "Thank you," he said.

"Is that enough?" I still couldn't believe that he wanted nothing more than one kiss.

Giovanni shook his head as he faded even further. "Nothing is enough. Nothing makes up for it. But . . . is something. Something beautiful."

"You're beautiful," I said, and he must have known that I meant it, because the last of him I could see was his smile.

I caught up to the French tour group, and Cairo and I managed to get a taxi to the hotel more than an hour before the others were due back from the Castel Sant' Angelo. We ordered a couple of coffees from the café downstairs and drank them in his hotel room, which had a view of the street below—crowded with little cars and motor scooters, both more tourists and just Roman people trying to get on with their day.

"We have to tell Mom and Dad about this, don't we?" I said.

Cairo sipped his cappuccino. "I think they already know."

"How could they know?"

"Ever since this started happening to me—I know we tried to hide it from Mom and Dad, but I always suspected they knew. Almost like they were waiting to see what would happen, you know? To see what I'd make of it."

"How would they guess you were hearing people's thoughts?"

He gave me a look. "They got married three weeks after they met, Ravenna. I always wondered about that, and now I believe we see the reason. You don't think they recognized something special in each other? Something unique? Just consider it. Everything they've discovered—stuff they found where nobody else even knew to look—and the way Dad's books all seem to be written like he was really there?"

Cairo was making some wild leaps—but I wasn't sure he was wrong about our parents. If they possessed these powers, did that mean Cairo and I had inherited them?

My mind was full of so many things, too many for me to

discuss them with my brother before our friends returned and we were once again surrounded by other voices, other thoughts. So I said the most important thing first: "I shouldn't have turned on you like that last night, Cairo. I'm really sorry."

"Thanks for saying that. But I mean it, Ravenna. I get why you didn't believe me. Why you were angry. You thought I was leaving you, didn't you?"

"Yeah."

"No such luck." My brother grinned at me over the rim of his paper coffee cup. "No matter how weird it gets from now on . . . we're in it together."

SCENIC ROUTE
by Carrie Ryan

"Where should we go next?" Margie sets the large atlas on the table, smoothing her hand over the worn cover. Her younger sister, Sally, shifts to her knees on the bench to get a better view.

"Mississippi?" Sally asks, tucking dirty-blond hair behind her ears.

Margie shrugs and fiddles with pages, swollen after getting wet in the rain. "Too hot right now. Besides, we'll be coming from the west here, under Canada. That's where we left off planning yesterday."

"Page fifty-seven, then," Sally says, leaning her elbows on the table.

Margie rolls her eyes as she flips through, letting the atlas open almost on its own volition. "You know, I really don't get your fascination with West Virginia."

"It looks pretty," Sally says, tracing her small fingers around the counties.

Neither girl has been there. Neither knows anything about it other than the contours on the map and the teaser entries from the guidebooks stacked along the front wall under the window.

Margie pulls the light closer and checks over her shoulder outside. It's full dusk, the summer days stretching late and dying slow. Greasy smoke chokes up from the lantern—almost all their oil is dirty, and dark patches stain the ceiling over the kitchen table from their evenings cramped over the atlas.

"So maybe we come in on the interstate here," Sally says, "but I think it would be more fun if we did the smaller roads after that. More scenic and probably less crowded."

Margie pushes a notebook across the table, sifting through the pages until she finds where they'd left off the night before. "You start writing it all down, Sal. I'm just going to check outside real quick."

Sally looks up at her sister then. It's almost silent in the cabin, just the sputter of the flame and the two girls breathing. "Why?"

"One last sweep before bed." Margie tries to keep her voice from fluttering.

"You already did the last sweep," Sally points out. A sliver of hair hangs limp and heavy across the side of her face, throwing her eyes into shadow.

Margie doesn't want to tell her that something outside keeps making her look up. It's the feeling on the back of her neck, like the tension before a thunderstorm—that quality of light spreading a sense of dread somewhere in your body left over from before humanity knew such things as language and science.

"Here." Margie squats by the small stack of books against the wall and flips through for the right one. "You figure out where you want to stop for dinner and if there's any sightseeing you want to do. Plan it all out, and I'll be right back." Margie sets the *Visitor's Guide to West Virginia* on the table and picks up the shotgun before stepping outside.

When she looks back, her little sister still kneels on the bench by the table. Her finger's stuck on that map, pointing at something too far away, which probably doesn't exist anymore anyway.

Margie never mentions to Sally that sometimes she just has to get away from the tightness of it all. In the beginning, just after the change time, she'd hated the outside, hated to leave the comfort of four walls and a roof, but now it makes her feel trapped. She's always judging the escape routes, figuring distance and the time it would take to cover it.

Their newest cabin sits on top of a mountain that's steep enough to keep the monsters away. There's a deep well, a gun cabinet stashed with crates of ammunition, a cistern of fuel oil, and a pantry brimming with canned food—enough to make Margie think that perhaps they have a shot at surviving all of this so long as it's just the two of them. They've lived here for most of the summer, so that now the fear's just a low humming noise in the background, like the sound of bees around a blackberry patch.

The first thing she did after Sally and she moved in, other than tossing the bodies over the cliff, was cut down all the rhododendron and laurel. She piled it in a circle partway down the mountain and in the gaps she strung old cans and bottles on twine to rattle if anyone—living or dead—came near.

That's why it doesn't make sense that something could be moving around outside. That's why she's jittery and pre-lightning-strike aware. If someone's on their mountain, it's not one of the monsters, and too often it's the living that end up being worse than the dead. She's seen it before when the bandits have come claiming supplies and people and shelter as their own. There's not enough safety in this new world, and too many people are willing to take what little they can find at any cost.

"I know you're out there," she calls, her fingers curled around the gun, holding it tight to her shoulder. She's lying—she doesn't know that anyone's really out there at all. She figures that if it's somehow a monster, he's already smelled her, so shouting won't give her away, and if it isn't a monster then she may as well have been shouting at the stars.

No one answers, which doesn't surprise her.

"I've got the place trapped," she calls out again. "You try coming inside and you might as well go blow your own head off."

Another lie—but nothing whoever or whatever is out there needs to know.

"Find anything?" Sally asks when Margie gets back inside.

"Skunk," Margie mutters. "Don't go out there stumbling around until I find him," Margie warns. "We don't need to smell things up again."

Sally crinkles her nose. Dirt mingles indistinguishably with freckles along the bridge. She yawns, long and loud.

"Bedtime," Margie says, pushing Sally toward the rope ladder up to the loft.

Once they're both curled up on the wide bed with just a sheet pulled over them, Margie says, "Tell me about this trip we're taking through West Virginia."

"There's this place there called the Paw Paw Tunnel—it took them more than a decade to dig," Sally starts to tell her. "First we'll have to stop by the town and eat at this place on a hill called Panorama at the Peak. It'll be a long walk from there to the tunnel, but the travel book says it's a must if you're visiting the area."

Margie closes her eyes. Her little sister smells like sweat and unwashed hair, but it's a sweet smell, familiar and steadying. Margie tries to sleep—she wants to sleep—but instead she just counts heartbeats. Outside it begins to rain, thunder tripping through the valleys around them. Sally's breathing falls into a steady rhythm, and in between lightning strikes all Margie can think about is someone being outside. Right now. Watching their little cabin.

She sneaks back down the ladder and crouches by the window, looking out at the clearing surrounding the house. Rain courses from the sky—a curtain of water blocking the outside world.

The storm rolls closer, lightning and thunder wrapping around each other and pummeling the mountain. In the bare seconds of light, Margie scours the clearing around the cabin, terrified of seeing something out there that doesn't belong.

Eventually, when her legs fall numb, she moves to the table, where the flashes of lightning illuminate the atlas and tattered notebook. The change time came when Sally was in third grade and Margie in tenth. Her sister's handwriting is stiff and careful, the letters showing the unsteadiness of her little hand as if she's still stuck in the before time that happened years ago.

Margie flips through the book: page after page of adventures and plans. Details of a path across the entire continent, as far as their maps can take them. It's to be the grandest road trip ever, according to Sally.

Margie wonders when Sally will figure it all out. Figure out the truth of their life.

Because it's the end of summer, another big thunderstorm rolls into the valley the next afternoon. The sky glows a sickening green, and nothing feels right to Margie. Heat settles thick and humid, the wind holding its breath before the storm pushes in hard. Sally seems oblivious, sorting through the guidebooks, flipping through the pages with an almost manic intensity.

"Whatcha looking for?" Margie asks. She crouches next to her sister but keeps glancing out the window. The air's so saturated it's hard to see much farther than the porch.

"West Virginia." Her voice comes out almost breathless, that kind of sound you get on the edge of panic. "I can't find West Virginia. We haven't finished the route through, and I need to find someplace where we can stay the second night or we'll be trapped outside."

She looks up at her older sister with eyes wide and wet. "We can't be outside, Margie," she whispers harshly. "We have to be inside where it's safe, and I can't find the book of inns and hotels."

"It's okay." Margie lays a hand on her sister's shoulder, but she shrugs it away. "We had it last night. It's here."

"It's not here!" Sally cries, shaking her head. "It's not here," she says again.

"We'll keep looking," Margie reassures her. Beyond the window the storm finally hits, wind hissing and rain bending trees to the ground.

Margie convinces Sally to skip West Virginia for now and figure out where they should stop in Maryland. "I've always heard they have great crab cakes there," Margie says. She finds the Maryland guidebook and sets it on the table.

The picture on the cover shows a faded blue bay and white sails, with a red crab bursting from the text. It makes Margie ache for something she's tried to give up. It makes her feel lonely in a way she hasn't before—an intense desire to share something as simple as a chair by the water with someone who understands.

Sally keeps her head bowed low over the map, stringy tips of her hair brushing the crinkled pages. "After that we'll go to Maine. It'll be safer up north in the winter," she says without looking up. "They don't move as much in the cold."

Margie presses her lips together tight. She remembers planning vacations that didn't revolve around monsters. When snow meant sledding and snowmobiles and fun. The aching part inside her wells deep, spreading fast and hard through her—pounding in her blood.

"Right," she finally says. "That's right."

She leaves Sally sitting at the table and steps out onto the porch, where the rain beats against the ground as if to punish it. In two steps Margie's deluged, letting the heavy drops sting her skin and mix with her tears. She feels helpless under this weight of water. The world's too big for her to survive in, much less for her to keep another being safe.

She knows a day will come when it's too much. When she'll trip up and miss a sign or signal, and that will be the end of that. She feels like a windup clock—and now she's winding down and doesn't know what to do next, how to twist herself back up again to keep on going.

The storm shifts and the wind howls like the dead. They're out there, she knows, climbing the mountain, pushing at the circle of laurel, tripping over strings of tins cans that beat and rattle in the storm.

Eventually this tiny fortress will no longer keep them safe. She'll have to tell Sally to plan the next trip, and they'll move on, and the clock will keep ticking until the gears wind down to nothing.

Margie climbs back onto the porch, every bit of her body soaked and cold with rain. Just as she reaches for the door, the glint of light off water makes her pause.

There's a puddle at the end of the porch with two ovals of mud dissolving in the middle, the edges blurring and washing away. A strip of damp leads up the wall, as if someone in dirty shoes recently stood there, leaning against the cabin.

Margie's throat closes. Her body jerks rigid. Behind her the storm menaces—howling and beating and breaking. It's as if the entire world's turning inside out, the cacophony of the mountain splitting apart.

She turns around. The sky's dark, everything that color of deep dusk, when shapes bleed into each other and your eyes play tricks. Movement hums around her but always out of sight. Her teeth chatter as she forces air into her lungs, willing everything to just shut up a moment so she can figure out what's going on.

She waits for someone to burst out of the rain. To throw her against the wall and attack her in the way of men or monsters or both. A thin thread of light from inside cuts across the porch, dissolving into the storm. Through it she watches individual drops of rain plummet and splatter, running together over and around the cabin.

Every muscle in her body tight and trembling, she slips into the cabin and wraps her hands around the shotgun, its weight a comfort. She carries the lantern from room to room, listening for a sound out of place under the beating of the storm. Everywhere's empty just the way it should be, but she leaves the lantern burning on the table because she can't bear the dark.

Tucking the gun under her arm, she climbs up to the loft and pulls the rope ladder after her. Sally's gone to bed long enough before that she already sleeps deep and even, her breathing a syncopated hiss mixing with the storm. Margie spends the night pressed against the wall, staring out the windows to the clearing around the cabin. Tiny squares of light spill from downstairs, flickering like fire against the darkness.

The storm clears before dawn and, exhausted, Margie sneaks back onto the porch. She's almost convinced herself she dreamed the puddles—of course no one had been there, of course it was just the rain collecting under the eaves. The cabin's old, the gutters unrepaired.

There are a million explanations for what she saw the night

before. Margie's just about convinced herself of all of them as birds wake up around her and start calling to the day.

But then she sees the book. It lies on its spine, flipped open to the middle, pages fluttering in the remnant wind. When she picks it up, the cover curls a bit and wet fingerprints smudge some of the corners.

It's the *Visitor's Guide to West Virginia*.

"Found your book." Margie tosses it onto the table, causing one of the chipped plates to rattle. "You should be more careful with it—if it hadn't been tucked behind one of the planters on the porch, it would have gotten soaked," Margie adds.

Sally looks up at her, lips stained dark with juice. "I didn't take it outside, duh."

Margie stands at the sink and looks out the window. She loves her sister, knows she's probably right. But she has to believe Sally's lying because otherwise someone came into the cabin and took the book. Someone stood leaning against the wall, flipping through pages while Sally and Margie sat inside, oblivious.

Her fingernails scratch against the old dingy grout of the tiled kitchen counter. This cabin's the safest they've found since the change time. They've built a quasi-life here perched on the tip of a steep mountain. Margie's garden is coming in, she has supplies enough to can and pickle, and the well has a hand pump so they don't have to worry about water.

Though she lets Sally plan road trips in the evenings, Margie's indulged herself with the idea of staying for a while. Settling in further. Spending the winter beside the fire quilting. Simple things you don't dare dream about while the dead rumble around you.

Margie's shoulders sag. Whoever's out there hasn't hurt them. Not yet. But if there's anything Margie's learned about the world since it changed, it's that it's only a matter of time.

She's learned that lesson well.

"I'm going to check on the laurel walls." Margie shoves a water bottle into a ragged backpack with extra shells and a plastic yellow flashlight. "It might take me a while. You going to be okay without me here?"

Sally lies on her back on the leather couch, an old paperback romance held above her head.

"I'm not a baby anymore, you know." She says it slow and even. "I can tell there's something going on. You're not as good at hiding it from me as you think."

Margie looks at the baby fat still visible under the smooth planes of her sister's face. "It's nothing," she says.

Sally rolls her eyes. "Whatever."

Margie isn't lying about checking the perimeter, but that only takes an hour and then she finds a thick copse of weeds where she has a clear view of the cabin. Bugs swirl around her, creeping along her neck and tangling in her lashes, but she sits calm and still through dusk and into the late evening.

Through the window she watches her sister fix something to eat and flip through the atlas listlessly before selecting another novel and carrying it up to the loft. The lantern burns inside, beckoning to Margie, but she keeps to the weeds, waiting while stars begin to catch fire overhead.

He comes a few hours after nightfall, just as the moon burns a bright halo on the horizon. He creeps up the steps and eases into the swing, gripping the rusted chain to keep it from creaking. The ax he'd been carrying lies forgotten against the railing as if he's not afraid of anyone or anything out here.

None of her traps signaled his approach, and Margie wonders just how many times he's circumvented their defenses. She watches him a moment; it's been so long since she's seen a living human being other than her sister that she's fascinated, even if this guy's some sort of creeper who's been in their cabin and touched their things. He hunches over himself so that most of him's hidden in shadows, and she can't get a good look at him except to tell that his hair's tattered and his clothes ragged along the edges.

He jumps up as she steps from the weeds, but he doesn't move for his ax. His body's pole-bean thin, but even so she notices coiled muscles twined around his bare arms and knows he's strong. She figures he's her age or a little older.

"Just in case you can't see out here," she says, even and strong,

"I've got a shotgun aimed at your gut. I wouldn't reach for that ax." Margie walks into the clearing, toes hitting the ground before she rocks onto her heels. She listens for movement just in case the boy isn't alone, but she hears nothing but the night bugs screaming.

The boy raises his hands. "I'm not planning on doing anything stupid," he says.

Margie swallows. She feels off balance inside, not really knowing what to do next. "Who are you and what do you want?"

"My name's Calvin. I'm here because . . ." He looks down at his feet. He wears old yellow boots with knots in the laces holding them together. He shrugs. "I saw the light and I just . . ." He twists his face like it hurts him to say it. Then he looks up like he can see her in the darkness.

"I was lonely, okay?" He sounds defensive, his shoulders hitched forward.

The words cut into Margie—she doesn't know what to do with them. "Where'd you come from?" she finally asks.

He shrugs. "Around. Here and there."

Margie watches him, the slow rise and fall of his chest. He doesn't seem as scared as he should with a gun pointed at him. "You know I don't trust you, right? And I'm not going to trust you?"

He nods.

"Kick your ax off the porch," she tells him. "And if you've got any other weapons, toss them too."

Calvin reaches out with his toe and nudges the ax until it slips under the railing into the overgrown bushes. From his pockets he pulls two knives and a bag of bullets but no gun— they've become too scarce in the past years.

Margie keeps the shotgun on him as she climbs the steps. For a while they stare at each other, her trying to put the piece of his existence into the puzzle of her life up here.

"What's it like back down the mountain?" Margie finally asks.

Calvin doesn't hesitate. "Horrible." He slumps into the swing. "There aren't a lot of safe places left, and finding food's impossible." He stares at his hands, his elbows propped on his knees. There's dirt under his nails and filling the cracks of his skin.

They sit like that for a bit, nothing of the world between them that's the same except for the monsters. Margie thinks about what it was like before the big change, when you could talk about things like movies or television or some funny joke from the internet. She grapples for some sort of bridge she could pull between them so that the gap across the porch wouldn't seem so big and wide.

"I can't let you leave," she finally says. "You know that, right? I don't want you sneaking around out here and, even if you left, I can't have you mention to someone out there that we've found a safe place."

He nods his head. "I was hoping maybe if I promised not to

tell anyone . . ." He looks at her and sees that she's not the kind to offer false hopes to strangers. His face falls. "I understand."

"I can tie you up on the porch or inside—I'll give you that option."

He looks through the window at the lantern spilling over the atlas and guidebooks. "Why West Virginia?" he finally asks.

Margie rubs her fingers along the stock of the shotgun, tracing the edge of the trigger. She still has the safety on, but he doesn't know that. "My sister gets to choose where we go and she remembered some show about West Virginia."

"It's a nice place," he says. "Prettier than you'd think."

"You've been?"

"Yeah. Before. My family used to go camping up on the Cacapon in the spring." He no longer looks at his hands but at her. She's tucked into the darkness, but still there's something about the way he sees her that makes her feel a sort of intimacy.

"I'll get the rope," she says, because she doesn't want to talk about families or vacations or the time before.

"There's a guy tied to the porch swing," Sally says when Margie comes down from the loft in the morning. Margie watches as Calvin slowly rocks outside, his wrists still lashed to the chains.

"You know you're terrible at knots, right?" Sally says, flipping through one of the guidebooks spread around her. "He could have gotten out easy if he'd wanted."

She traces an interstate across the mountains on the map, cross-referencing a set of directions in her notebook. "Don't know why he wouldn't just escape if he had the chance," she mumbles without looking up at her older sister.

Margie stares at Calvin. "Me neither."

Margie pats him down to make sure there aren't any more weapons tucked in his clothes, and then all three of them go to pick berries. Sally pesters Calvin about where he's been and what the mountains out West are like compared to those in the East. Calvin's patient and kind and always aware of the fact that Margie has a gun and is willing to blow some part of his body off at the slightest provocation.

Days pass one after the other: gardening and taking care of the cabin in the day, Calvin tied up at night, time rolling after time as the great clock unwinds.

"She knows the trip is a lie," Calvin finally says one night as Margie wraps rope around his arm and the swing.

She hesitates.

"She knows more than you think. About the world. About what your chances of survival are." He pauses. Her face isn't far from his, and she smells the berry sweetness of his breath.

"Our chances of survival," he says softly.

Margie lets the rope trail from her fingers and stumbles to the other end of the porch until the railing bites her hips.

"What do I have to do to prove my loyalty to you, Marg?"

Calvin asks. "How many nights do I have to sit out here tied up when we both know your knots are crap and I could escape anytime? What will it take for you to trust me?"

Margie slumps, sliding down until she sits on the edge of the porch. Fireflies flash in the gardens, bright reminders that for some creatures the world hasn't changed.

"I'm the one who had to kill my mother," Margie confesses. Her chin trembles, her whole body shaking. A breeze trips up the mountain, cool and crisp like fall. "After the change we got out of the city and we found a place and for a while it was safe, but then we were ambushed. My father yelled but no one could hear. They took my mother, and my father resisted, and I didn't know what to do but grab Sally and run into the woods. I watched what they did to my mother, and when my father tried to fight, they killed him and tossed his body aside. I could smell the death and hear the moans and then they just left my mother on the ground while they ransacked inside. I told Sally to stay and I found my mother and there were bite marks all over her and she said nothing when I held the gun against her."

She inhales as if she's never known air before. "We had somewhere safe, and they took it."

Calvin strips the ropes from his arms and pulls her against him. More than anything else in the world Margie wants to sob and grab hold. Just to know that there's someone out there to help her survive so that she doesn't have to carry it all.

He holds her so tight she feels like she might snap, and she pushes against him because she needs to hear his heart and feel every inhalation. "Sally doesn't know," she says against his shoulder. "She doesn't know what it takes to survive."

He presses his lips against the crown of her head and whispers, "Hush," into her ear with his hot breath. Around them night peepers scream to each other, tree frogs wailing for the darkness.

Margie doesn't tie Calvin up but instead lets him help her inside, where they lie on the couch and she thinks that maybe there is such a thing as survival in this world.

When the two men charge into the cabin, Calvin's the first to reach for the gun. Margie falls from the couch to her knees and wants to scream for Sally but presses her lips tight, hoping that maybe the strangers won't know there's someone else inside.

Calvin flips off the safety and raises the gun to his shoulder. The strangers are tall and broad, one of them with a tangled beard and the other with black hair slicked back behind his ears. It's almost too easy to see the family resemblance to Calvin, and Margie goes numb as she notices.

"How quaint," the bearded man says. He strolls inside as if there isn't a shotgun pointed to his chest. He glances around—at the map on the table, at Margie's face that's still rubbed a little raw from Calvin's unshaven cheeks.

He turns to face Calvin while the slick-headed man leans

against the door frame. "Nicely done, little brother," he says. "You checked there's food enough for winter and the other guns are secured?"

Calvin nods, eyes downcast.

Margie chokes. Her body flames a deep burning red as shame churns inside. It feels like the moment her family was ambushed on the road, when time seemed to slow down and she noticed the most pointless details. Now she feels the grit of the hardwood floor biting into her knees and realizes how badly she needs to pee.

Slick Hair moves toward the loft. "Where's the other one?"

Margie tries to block his way and she's shoved to the ground, her head hitting the corner of a chair as she falls. She paws at the man, hooking her fingers in his clothes, but he bats her away, crushing her hand until she feels something pop and give.

"Sally!" she screams, loud and raw and filled with rage. The bearded one grabs her, lifting and twisting until her arm's behind her back, his knife against her throat. She struggles, not caring at the bite of the blade into her skin.

"Margie," Calvin says. It's his voice that stops her. He's still holding the gun. Her gun. She wants to close her eyes, but she doesn't because she deserves this. To see what she's brought down on her sister.

Her lips still vibrate from when Calvin kissed her, and she spits at him, hating the taste of him still in her mouth.

He blanches and sidesteps her attempt at outrage, and his two brothers laugh, Slick Head reaching out and slapping his shoulder hard enough to make him stumble. Calvin's cheeks flare a bright embarrassed pink, and his eyes leap to Margie's and then away again, a shuttered mortification flashing through them.

"Tell her to drop the ladder," Beard says into Margie's ear.

She shakes her head. Already she can feel the sobs coming, and they taste like failure. She swallows and chokes trying to get the words out: "Don't do it, Sally. You stay where you are!"

"Drop the ladder or I start carving your sister!" Beard shouts up toward the loft. He slides the blade along her collarbone and then digs it into Margie's shoulder. Even though she bites her lips, she can't stop the scream. The pain's nothing like she's ever known before, an explosion of fire as her body realizes how deeply the knife has sunk.

Margie's knees give out, her legs limp and useless. As she slides toward the floor she looks to Calvin for help, but he just stands there, his hands tight around her gun and his eyes on the blood curling down from the gash in her shoulder.

He kissed that exact spot the night before. Traced his lips over that stretch of skin as she gasped and pulled him closer with a type of need he'd said he'd never been a part of before. Now the flesh is torn, the edges ragged from the unsharpened knife, and he looks like he can't stop trying to figure out how something once so whole and perfect can become that broken so easily.

Margie braces her uninjured arm against the floor, fingers splayed to hold her weight before she collapses. She's wheezing—loud and gagging from the pain. Beard grabs her hair and drags her out into the middle of the room to make sure Sally can see what he's doing.

He pushes Margie to her knees, yanks her head back until her spine arches. Presses the knife against her throat, sweat glistening along the ridges of her tendons. "I don't like asking twice," he growls up at Sally, who huddles behind the banister, eyes wide and hands pressed over her mouth as her shoulders shake.

"Stop it!" Sally shouts. "Okay, I'm coming down. Just stop hurting her!"

She unfurls the ladder as Margie begs, "No, Sally, stay up there," but Sally ignores her.

She's halfway down, her bare toes wrapping over the wooden rungs, when Slick Head grabs her around the waist with a thick arm. Sally's already anticipated the move because she pushes herself back, twisting the rope of the ladder around his neck and hauling his feet from the ground.

He kicks out, the rope tightening, and his mouth wrenches open—a black, choking maw ringed by yellowed teeth.

"Jeffrey!" Beard shouts as his brother starts to scratch wildly at his throat, his face flaring red.

"The knife!" Slick Head wheezes out, and Beard throws Margie to the ground. He jumps toward his brother, but Margie kicks at his feet, throwing him off balance so that he trips and falls, the knife skittering from his hand as his fists slam against the hardwood floor.

Sally's there in the middle of it, swooping in for the knife as it slides past her. Everything stills as the pieces of the moment reorder and shift back together again: Margie struggling to her knees, Slick Head choking and pawing madly at the noose, Beard pushing himself up with his hands out in front of him as Sally crouches, knife held steady.

Calvin's still in the corner by the door, shotgun clutched in his fingers.

"Shoot her," Beard orders him, never taking his eyes off Sally or her knife.

Calvin jumps toward Margie, lowering the gun. She's kneeling on the floor, one arm useless. She looks up at Calvin standing over her, the shotgun pressed against her temple in the same spot he kissed the night before. She doesn't close her eyes. She won't make it easy.

"You said you understood what it takes to survive," Calvin says to Margie. "How hard it is to find somewhere safe." He's sweating, his lips pale. "You've got Sally to take care of like I have my brothers."

Margie just stares at him. He knows what she's done for her sister. What she would do if their situations were reversed.

Behind them, Slick Head's chokes become high-pitched wheezes.

Margie winces, and Calvin's finger jumps on the trigger before slipping away. "Cut him down," Calvin orders Sally without taking his eyes off Margie.

"You have to understand this." He speaks like he needs Margie's absolution.

She feels the perfect roundness of the barrel of the shotgun pressed hard enough against her skin to leave an indentation. One flick of his finger and she's done worrying. Done planning and patrolling and constantly fighting against the incessant fear.

She's failed Sally. She always knew that she would. In the same way her father failed her and she failed her mother. In the world with the dead, her failure was always inevitable.

Slick Head's gags become desperate—wet, smacking sounds that fill the cabin as streaks of blood tear along his neck from his nails scratching for air.

Sally's breathing hard and fast as she steps toward Slick Head, his face puffy, with busted blood vessels in his eyes turning them red. She draws the hand holding the knife over her shoulder as if preparing to hack at the rope. He claws at her, trying to get his fingers around the blade, but she just swings her arm hard, knuckles cracking against his jaw but the hilt of the knife keeping her fist solid like a brick.

Blood dribbles from his mouth and she pulls back to strike again as the hanging man chokes on broken teeth.

Beard roars and leaps for her, but he's too late. She's already sliced the knife across Slick Hair's throat, a ragged gurgling gash of frothing blood that drips from his neck as his mouth gapes open and closed, open and closed.

Sally spins toward Beard, holding the bloody blade between them, but that doesn't stop him. He crashes into her, dragging her to the ground. His fingers rake at her, claw at her face, and pummel her throat.

She tries to hold him off but she's a young girl and he's a massive man—it's like a fawn beating back a bear, and Beard howls and spits with his rage as blood from his brother's neck twines down his arms and drips to the floor.

Margie's eyes flare and she drags her broken body across the room to her sister's defense, not caring that the barrel of the shotgun traces her movement. "Stop it!" she screams, reaching for her sister's tiny hands, trying to drag her away from the mauling monster.

Beard roars up, rising tall on his knees as he swipes at Margie, hand slapping at her busted shoulder, which causes a surge of pain bright and intense to shatter across her mind, shutting her down.

Sally pulls into a ball, pressing her face against Margie's side, trying to protect them both. Beard huffs, his mouth foaming as he stares at them huddled under his brother's mangled body.

He holds out his hand. "Give me the gun," he demands of Calvin, but Calvin doesn't move. He stares at the two girls. Two broken bodies that moments before had been whole.

He did this. He helped break the world.

Beard spins toward him, his fingers clawed in a fervent fury. "Shoot them, Calvin. Stop acting like any of this means something and just do it!"

Margie's senses clear bit by bit and she watches as something clicks in Calvin's eyes. He aims the shotgun at her, and she takes a deep breath, waiting for him to pull the trigger. She always thought she'd be relieved in that moment but instead she feels the most intense regret.

She's spent too much time scared. She should have gone to West Virginia with Sally. She shouldn't have locked them in a cabin she knew would one day fail to protect them.

She thinks of all the notebooks filled with her sister's handwriting. The trips had always been a lie.

Calvin stares at Margie. "You care about me?"

She doesn't answer, just clenches her jaw as her cheeks burn with her own stupidity for trusting a stranger.

He steps closer to her, urgent. "Would you kill me for her?" He says it like they're the only two people in the room. As if one brother isn't dead and the other asking for her and her sister's murder.

Margie doesn't have to think before answering. "Yes."

Calvin pulls the trigger. Outside a few birds scream and scatter into the trees.

"They wouldn't have," Calvin finally chokes out. "I've never meant enough to them. Ever." Smoke twines around him, pungent and sweet. "Jeremy was wrong. It should mean something. Killing someone—I need it to still mean something. Or else everything in the world falls apart."

Next to Margie, Sally rolls to her hands and knees and beats at Beard's shot-shredded chest, blood splattering her fists and arms, caking her hair. It's not enough she's given up the world because of the dead, but to have been asked to give up this place, and the dreams it held, because of the living is too much.

Margie stares at Calvin. He pushes the gun into her hands, guiding the barrel until it's wedged into the hollow of his collarbone. She doesn't understand how everything's changed again. How one minute she was death and then she was life and now she holds death in her hands again.

"I understand," he says. "I know you'll never trust me now. I understand that, and maybe that's the way it goes. My death can mean something too."

He pushes her finger onto the trigger. Behind her Sally finally sags against the wall, sobbing as her fingers curl on themselves, slick and bright.

Margie climbs to her feet, shoulder screaming as torn muscle protests the movement. Clutching the gun, she walks to the table where the maps are spread out, blood now spattered along the mountains and towns. She tries to wipe it away, but only ends up smearing them red.

She'd wanted to keep her sister safe. She'd wanted to keep a part of the world the way it was, before the change time, for Sally.

But she knows, now, there's no escape from the monsters. They'll always be there; you just choose to live with them or not. Sometimes you have to plan for another day—sometimes that's all you have. "You said you've been to West Virginia," she says. "You'll show it to us?"

RED RUN
by Kami Garcia

No one drove on Red Run at night. People went fifteen miles out of their way to avoid the narrow stretch of dirt that passed for a road, between the single stoplight towns of Black Grove and Julette. Red Run was buried in the Louisiana backwoods, under the gnarled arms of oaks tall enough to scrape the sky. When Edie's granddaddy was young, bootleggers used it to run moonshine down to New Orleans. It was easy to hide in the shadows of the trees, so dense they blocked out even the stars. But there was still a risk. If they were caught, the sheriff would hang them from those oaks, leaving their bodies for the gators, which is how the road earned its name.

The days of bootlegging were long gone, but folks had other reasons for steering clear of Red Run after dark. The road was haunted. A ghost had claimed eight lives in the last twenty years—Edie's brother's just over a year ago. No one wanted to risk a run-in with the blue-eyed boy. No one except Edie.

She was looking for him.

Tonight she was going to kill a ghost.

Edie didn't realize how long she had been driving until her favorite Jane's Addiction song looped for the third time. Edie was beginning to wonder if she was going to find him at all, as she passed the rotted twin pines that marked the halfway point between the two nothing little towns—when she saw him. He was standing in the middle of the road, on the wavering yellow carpet of her headlights. His eyes reflected the light like a frightened animal, but he looked as real as any boy she'd ever seen. Even if he was dead.

She slammed on the brakes instinctively, and dust flew up around the Jeep and into the open windows. When it skidded to a stop, he was standing in front of the bumper, tiny particles of dirt floating in the air around him.

For a second, neither one of them moved. Edie was holding her breath, staring out beyond the headlights at the tall boy whose skin was too pale and eyes too blue.

"I'm okay, if you're worried," he called out, squinting into the light.

Edie clutched the vinyl steering wheel, her hands sweaty and hot. She knew she should back up—throw the car into reverse until he was out of sight—but even with her heart thudding in her ears, she couldn't do it.

He half-smiled awkwardly, brushing the dirt off his jeans.

He had the broad shoulders of a swimmer, and curly dark hair that was too long in places and too short in others, like he had cut it himself. "I'm not from around here."

She already knew that.

He walked toward her dented red Jeep, tentatively. "You aren't hurt, are you?"

It was a question no one ever asked her. In elementary school, Edie was the kid with the tangled blond braids. The one whose overalls were too big and too worn at the knees. Her parents never paid much attention to her. They were busy working double shifts at the refinery. Her brother was the one who wove her hair into those braids, tangled or not.

"I'm fine." Edie shook her head, black bobbed hair swinging back and forth against her jaw.

He put his hand on the hood and bent down next to her open window. "Is there any way I could get a ride into town?"

Edie knew the right answer. Just like she knew she shouldn't be driving on Red Run in the middle of the night. But she hadn't cared about what was right, or anything at all, for a long time. A year and six days exactly—since the night her brother died. People had called it an accident, as if somehow that made it easier to live with. But everyone knew there were no accidents on Red Run.

That was the night Edie cut her hair with her mother's craft scissors, the ones with the orange plastic handles. It was also the night she hung out with Wes and Trip behind the Gas & Go for the first time, drinking Easy Jesus and warm Bud Light until her brother's death felt like a dream she would forget in the morning. The three of them had been in class together since kindergarten, but they didn't run in the same crowd. When Wes and Trip weren't smoking behind the school or hanging out in the cemetery, they were holed up in Wes' garage, building weird junk they never let anyone see. Edie's mom thought they were building pipe bombs.

But they were building something else.

The blue-eyed boy was still leaning into the window. "So can I get a ride?" He was watching her from under his long, straight lashes. They almost touched his cheeks when he blinked.

She leaned back into the sticky seat, trying to create some space between them. "What are you doing out here, anyway?"

Would he admit he was out here to kill her?

"My parents kicked me out, and I'm headed for Baton Rouge. I've got family down there." He watched her, waiting for a reaction.

Was this part of the game?

"Get in," she said, before she could change her mind.

The boy walked around the car and opened the door. The rusty hinges creaked, and it reminded Edie of the first time Wes opened the garage door and invited her inside.

The garage was humid and dark, palmetto bugs scurrying across the concrete floor for the corners. Two crooked pine tables were outfitted with vises and tools Edie didn't recognize. Wire and scrap metal littered the floor, attached to homemade-looking machines that resembled leaky car batteries. There were other salvaged and tricked-out contraptions—dials that looked like speedometers, a portable sonar from a boat, and a long needle resting on a spool of paper that reminded her of those lie detectors you saw on television.

"What is all this stuff?"

Wes and Trip glanced at each other before Wes answered, "Promise you won't tell anyone?"

Edie took another swig of Easy Jesus, the liquid burning its way down her throat. She liked the way it felt going down, knowing it would burn through her memories just as fast.

"Cross my heart and hope I die," she slurred.

"It's hope *to* die," Trip said, kicking an empty beer can out of his way. "You said it wrong."

Edie stared back at him, her dark eyes glassy. "No, I didn't." She tossed the empty bottle at a green plastic trash can in the corner, but she missed and it hit the concrete, shattering. "So are you gonna tell me what you're doing with all this crap?"

Wes picked up a hunk of metal with long yellow wires dangling from the sides like the legs of a mechanical spider. "You won't believe us."

He was right. The only thing she believed in now was Easy Jesus. Remembering every day to forget. "Try me."

Wes looked her straight in the eye, sober and serious. He

flicked a switch on the machine and it whirred to life. "We're hunting ghosts."

Edie didn't have time to think about hanging out with Wes and Trip in the garage. She needed to focus on the things they had taught her.

She was driving slower than usual, her hands glued to the wheel so the blue-eyed boy wouldn't notice how badly they were shaking. "Where are you from?"

"You know, you really shouldn't pick up strangers." His voice was light and teasing, but Edie noticed he didn't answer the question.

"You shouldn't get in the car with strangers either," she countered. "Especially not around here."

He shifted his body toward her, his white ribbed tank sliding over his skin instead of sticking to it the way Edie's clung to hers. The cracked leather seat didn't make a sound. "What do you mean?"

She felt a wave of satisfaction. "You've never heard the stories about Red Run? You must live pretty far away."

"What kind of stories?"

Edie stared out at the wall of trees closing in around them. It wasn't an easy story to tell, especially if you were sitting a foot from the boy who died at the end of it. "About twenty years ago, someone died out here. He was about your age—"

"How do you know how old I am?" His voice was thick and

sweet, all honey and molasses.

"Eighteen?"

He lifted an eyebrow. "Good guess. So what happened to him?"

Edie knew the story by heart. "It was graduation night. There was a party in Black Grove and everyone went, even Tommy Hansen. He was quiet and always kept to himself. My mom says he was good-looking, but none of the girls were interested in him because his family was dirt-poor. His dad ran off and his mother worked at the funeral home, dressing the bodies for viewings."

Edie saw him cringe in the seat beside her, but she kept going. "Tommy worked at the gas station to help out and spent the rest of his time alone, playing a beat-up guitar. He wanted to be a songwriter, and was planning to leave for Nashville that weekend. If the party had been a few days later, he might have made it."

And her brother would still be alive.

Edie remembered the night her brother died, his body stretched out in the middle of the road. She had stepped too close, and a pool of blood had gathered around the toes of her sneakers. She had stared down at the thick liquid, wondering why they called the road Red Run. The blood was as black as ink.

"Are you going to tell me how that kid Tommy died?" The boy was watching her from under those long eyelashes.

Edie's heart started racing. "They had a keg in the woods, and everyone was wasted. Especially Katherine Day, the prettiest girl in school. People who remember say that Katherine drank her weight in cheap beer and wandered into the trees to puke. Tommy saw her stumbling around and followed her. This is the part where folks disagree; in one version of the story, Tommy sat with Katherine while she threw up all over her fancy white sundress. In the other version, Katherine forgot about how poor Tommy was—or noticed how good-looking he was—and kissed him. Either way, the end is the same." Edie paused, measuring his reaction. At this point in the story, people were usually on pins and needles.

But the blue-eyed boy was staring back at her evenly from the passenger seat, as if he already knew the way it ended.

"Don't you want to know what happened next?"

He smiled, but there was something wrong about it. His eyes were vacant and far away. Was he remembering? He sensed Edie watching him, and the faraway look was gone. "Yeah. How did he go from making out with the prettiest girl in school to getting killed?"

"I didn't say he was killed." Edie tried to hide the fear in her voice. She didn't want him to know she was afraid.

"You said he died, right?"

She didn't point out that dying and being killed weren't the same thing. If Edie hadn't known she was in over her head the minute he got in the car, she knew now. But it was too late.

"Katherine was dating a guy on the wrestling team, or maybe it was the football team, I can't remember. But he caught them together—kissing or talking or whatever they were doing—and dragged Tommy out of the woods with a bunch of his friends."

The boy's blue eyes were fixed on her now. "Then what happened?" His voice was so quiet she had trouble hearing him over the crickets calling out in the darkness.

"They beat him to death. Right here on Red Run. Some guy who lived out in the woods saw the whole thing."

The boy nodded, staring out the window as the white bark of the pines blurred alongside the car. "So that's why no one drives on this road at night?"

Edie laughed, but the sound was bitter and cold. About as far away from happy as it could be. "This is the Bayou. If you avoided every road where someone died, there wouldn't be any roads left. Folks don't drive on Red Run at night because Tommy Hansen's ghost has killed six people about our age. They say he kills the boys because they remind him of the guys who beat him to death, and the girls because they remind him of Katherine."

Edie pictured her brother lying in the glow of the police cruiser's spotlight, bathed in red. She had knelt down in the sticky dirt, pressing her face against his chest. Will's heart was beating, the rhythm uneven and faint.

"Edie?" She felt his chest rise as he whispered her name.

She cradled his face in her hands, but he was staring blankly beyond her. "I'm here, Will," she choked. "What happened?"

Will strained to focus on Edie's tear-stained face. "Don't worry. I'm gonna be okay." But his eyes told a different story.

"I should have listened . . ."

Will never finished. But she didn't need to hear the rest.

Edie could feel the blue-eyed boy watching her. She bit the inside of her cheek to keep from crying. She had to hold it together a little while longer.

"You really believe a ghost is out here killing people?" He sounded disappointed. "You look smarter than that."

Edie gripped the steering wheel tighter. He had no idea how smart. "I take it you don't?"

He looked away. "Ghosts are apparitions. They can't actually hurt anyone."

"Sounds like you know a lot about ghosts."

It was the same thing Edie said the second time she hung out with Wes and Trip in the filthy garage. Wes was adjusting some kind of gadget that looked like a giant calculator, with a meter and a needle where the display would normally have been. "We know enough."

"Enough for what?" She imagined the two of them wandering around with their oversized calculators, searching for ghosts the way people troll the beach for loose change and jewelry with metal detectors.

"I told you, we hunt ghosts." Wes tossed the device to Trip, who opened the back with a screwdriver and changed the batteries.

Edie settled into the cushions on the ratty plaid couch. "So you hang out in haunted houses and take pictures, like those guys on TV?"

Trip laughed. "Hardly. Those guys aren't ghost hunters. They're glorified photographers. We don't stand around taking pictures." Trip tossed the screwdriver onto the rotting workbench. "We send the ghosts back where they belong."

Wes and Trip weren't as stupid as Edie had assumed. In fact, if the two of them had ever bothered to enter the science fair, they would've won. They knew more about science, physics mainly—energy, electromagnetism, frequency, and matter— than any of the teachers at school. And they were practically engineers, capable of building almost anything with some wires and scrap metal. Wes explained that the human body was made up of electricity—electrical impulses that keep you alive. When a person died, those impulses changed form, resulting in ghosts.

Edie only understood about half of what he was saying. "How do you know? Maybe it just disappears."

Trip shook his head. "Impossible. Energy can't be destroyed. Physics 101. Those electrical impulses have to go somewhere."

"So they change into ghosts, just like that?"

"I wouldn't say 'just like that.' I gave you the simplified version," Trip said, attaching another wire to his tricked-out calculator.

"What is that thing?" she asked.

"This—" Trip held it up proudly, "is an EMF meter. It picks up electromagnetic fields and frequencies, movement we can't detect. The kind created by ghosts."

"That's how we find them," Wes said, taking a swig from an old can of Mountain Dew. "Then we kill them."

Edie was still thinking about that day in the garage when she smelled something horrible coming from outside. It was suffocating—heavy and chemical, like burning plastic. She rolled up her window, even though the air inside the Jeep immediately became stifling.

"Don't you want to let some air in?" the blue-eyed boy ventured.

"I'm more concerned about letting something out."

He waited for Edie to explain, but she didn't. "Can I ask you a question?"

"Shoot," she said.

"If you believe there's a ghost on this road, why are you driving out here all alone at night?"

Edie took a deep breath and spoke the words she had rehearsed in her mind since the moment he climbed into the car. "The ghost that haunts Red Run killed my brother, and I'm going to destroy it."

Edie watched as the fear swept over him.

The realization.

"What are you talking about? How do you kill a ghost?"

He didn't know.

Edie took her time answering. She had waited a long time for this. "Ghosts are made of energy like everything else. Scatter the energy, you destroy the ghost."

"How do you plan to do that?"

Edie knocked on the black plastic paneling on her door. It was the same paneling that covered every inch of the Jeep's interior. "Ghosts absorb the electrical impulses around them— from power lines, machines, cars—even people. I have these two friends who are pretty smart. They made this stuff. Some compounds conduct electricity." She ran her palm over the paneling. "Others block it."

"So you're going to trap a ghost in the car with you and— what? Wait till it shorts out like a lightbulb?"

"It's not that simple," Edie said, without taking her eyes off the road. "Energy can't be destroyed. You have to disperse it, sort of like blowing up a bomb. My friends know how to do it. I just have to keep the ghost contained until I get to their place. They'll do the rest."

Tommy glanced at the black paneling. "You're crazy, you know that?" His arm wasn't draped casually over the seat anymore, and his hands were balled up in his lap.

"Maybe," she answered. "Maybe not."

He reached for the handle to roll down his window, but it wouldn't turn. "Your window's—" He paused, working it out in his mind. "It isn't broken, is it?"

Edie took her foot off the gas and let the car roll to a stop. "You didn't really think I'd pick up a hitchhiker, on a deserted road in the middle of nowhere?" She turned toward the blue-eyed boy, a boy she knew was a ghost. "Did you, Tommy?"

His eyes widened at the sound of his name.

Edie's heart felt like it was trying to punch its way out of her chest. There was no way to predict how Tommy's ghost was going to react. Wes had warned her that ghosts could psychically attack the living by moving objects or causing hallucinations, even madness. His mom had walked off the second-story balcony of their house when Wes was in fourth grade. It was only a few weeks after she had started hearing strange noises and seeing shadows in the house. Wes' father wanted to move, but his mom said she wasn't going to be driven out of her house by swamp-water superstition. She didn't believe in ghosts. Not until one killed her.

Now Edie was sitting only inches away from a ghost that had already murdered six people.

But he didn't look murderous. There was something else lingering in his blue eyes. Panic. "You can't stop here."

"What?"

"There's something I need to tell you, Edie. But you have to keep driving. It's not safe." He was turning around in his seat, scanning the woods through the windows.

Edie bit the inside of her cheek again. "What are you talking about?"

Before he had time to respond, the light outside flickered as a shadow cut through the path of the car's headlights.

Edie jumped, jerking her eyes back toward the road.

There was a man a few yards away, waving his arms wildly. "Get outta the car now!"

"It's too late," Tommy whispered. "He's already here."

"Who?"

"The man who killed me."

Edie didn't have a chance to ask him to explain. The man in the road was still yelling as he moved closer to the car. "Hurry up! Before that blue-eyed devil skins you alive like the rest a them!"

Tommy's ghost grabbed her arm, but she couldn't feel his touch. "Don't listen to him, Edie. He wants to hurt you, the same way he hurt me. And your brother."

"What did you say?" The words tore at Edie's throat like razor blades.

"I didn't kill any of those kids that died out here. He did." Tommy pointed at the man in the road. "I watch the road. I try to make sure no one stops near his cabin. I tried to warn all of them, but they wouldn't listen."

Edie remembered her brother's last words.

I should have listened . . .

She had assumed he was referring to the stories—the constant warnings to stay off Red Run after dark. What if she was wrong? What if he had been talking about a different warning altogether?

"No." Edie shook her head. "Those guys beat you to death—"

Tommy cut her off before she could finish. "They didn't. That's the story he told the police. And no one believed a bunch of drunk kids when they denied it."

The voice outside was getting louder and more frantic. "Whatever that spirit's telling you is a lie! He's trying to keep you in there with him so he can kill you! Come on out, sweetheart."

It was easier to see the man now that he was just a few feet away. He was about her dad's age, but worse for the wear. His green John Deere cap was pulled low over his eyes, and he was wearing an old hunting jacket over his broad shoulders despite the heat.

He was shifting from side to side nervously, his eyes flitting back and forth between the woods and the car.

"He's lying. I swear," Tommy—it was becoming harder to remember that he was a ghost, not a regular boy—pleaded. "Why do you think I got in the car? I wanted to make sure you didn't stop. He doesn't like it when people get this close to his place. Especially teenagers."

"You expect me to believe some old guy is killing people

because they're coming too close to his house?" Her voice was rising, a dangerous combination of fear and anger burning through her veins.

"He's crazy, Edie. He cooks meth back there at night, and he's convinced people can smell it. He's always been paranoid, but after being cooped up in a tiny cabin with those fumes for years, it's gotten worse."

Edie remembered the nauseating stench of melted plastic. She never would have recognized it. Still. The man was pacing in front of the car, wringing his hands nervously. There was something off about him. But then again, he was facing off against a ghost.

Tommy was still talking. "That's what he was doing the night I got lost in the woods, only back then it was something else. He's been cooking up drugs in his cabin for years, supplying dealers in the city. I was looking for this girl who wandered off, and I got all turned around. I didn't realize how far I'd walked. There was a cabin." He paused, looking out at the man in the green cap. "Let's just say, I knocked on the wrong door."

The man stopped in the path of one of the headlights, a beam of light creating shadows across his face. "You can't trust the dead. No matter what they say, sweetheart."

Edie reached for the door handle.

Tommy—the boy-ghost—grabbed her other hand. For a second, Edie thought she felt the weight of his hand on hers. It was impossible, but it gave her goose bumps all the same. "He beat me to death, Edie. Then he dragged my body all the way back to the party, and left me in the middle of Red Run."

Edie didn't know who to believe. One of them was lying. And if she made the wrong choice, she was going to die tonight.

Tommy's blue eyes were searching hers. "I would never hurt you, Edie. I swear."

She thought about everything Wes and Trip had taught her, which boiled down to one thing: You can't trust a ghost. She thought about her brother lying in the road. *I should have listened*. He could've been talking about the man in the green cap—the one begging her to get out of the car right now.

What was she thinking? She couldn't trust a ghost.

Edie threw the door open before she could change her mind. The smell of burnt plastic flooded into the Jeep.

"Edie, no!" Tommy's eyes were terrified, darting back and forth between Edie and the man in the road. In that moment, she knew he was telling the truth.

She reached for the door to pull it shut again as the man in the green cap rushed toward the driver's side of the car. When he passed through the headlights, Edie saw him grab the buck knife from his waistband.

Edie tried to close the door, but it felt like she was wading through syrup. She wasn't fast enough. But the man in the green cap was, his arm coming around the edge of the door. His knife was in his hand, reddish-brown lines streaking the dull blade.

"Oh, no you don't, you little bitch!" The man grabbed the

metal frame before she could close the door, the blade of the knife waving dangerously close to her face.

Tommy appeared just outside the open car door, only inches from the man wielding the knife. Before the man had a chance to react, Tommy rushed forward and stepped right through him.

Edie saw the man's eyes go wide for a second, and he shivered.

"Back up!" Tommy shouted.

Edie didn't think about anything but Tommy's voice as she turned the key, grinding the ignition. She threw the car into reverse, slamming her foot on the gas.

The man swore, his hand uncurling from the handle of the knife. He tried to hold onto the doorframe, his filthy nails clawing at the metal.

Then his fingers slid away, and Edie saw him hit the ground.

She heard the scream as the Jeep bucked and the front tire rolled over his body. Edie didn't stop until she could see him lying facedown in the dust. She could see the crushed bones, forced into awkward angles. He wasn't moving.

Edie didn't notice Tommy standing next to the car. He pulled the door open, bent metal scraping through the silence, and knelt down next to her. "Are you okay?"

"I think I killed him." Her voice was shaking uncontrollably.

"Edie, look at me." Tommy's was calm. She leaned her head against the seat, turning her face toward his. "You didn't have a choice. He was going to kill you."

She knew Tommy was right. But it didn't change the fact

that she had just killed a man, even if that man was a monster.

Tommy's blue eyes were searching her brown ones, their faces only inches apart. "What made you trust me?"

"Your eyes," Edie answered. "The eyes don't lie."

"Even if you're a ghost?"

Edie smiled weakly. "Especially if you're a ghost."

She looked out at the road. For the first time in forever, it was just a road—dirt and rocks and trees. She tried to imagine what it would be like to spend every night out here, so close to the place where you died.

"You're the first person who ever believed me," Tommy said. "The first person I saved."

"Then why did you stay here for so long?"

Tommy looked away. "I didn't have a choice."

Edie remembered Wes telling her that most ghosts couldn't leave a place where they had died traumatically. They were chained to that spot, trying to find a way to right the wrong.

When he turned back to face her, Edie noticed the sadness lingering in his eyes. And something else. . . .

Tommy was fading, flickering like static on an old TV set. He stared down at his hands, turning them slowly as if seeing them for the first time.

"I think you can move on now," Edie said gently. "You know, to wherever you're supposed to be. Red Run doesn't need protecting anymore."

"I don't know where I'm supposed to be. But wherever it

is, I'm not ready to go." Tommy was still fading. "There are so many things I never had a chance to do."

Edie ran her hand along the black paneling inside the Jeep, and looked at him. "Get in."

Tommy hesitated for a second, smiling. "Just don't take me to meet the friends who made that stuff."

Edie smiled back at him. "You can trust me."

As she drove away, Red Run disappearing into the darkness, Edie felt the weight of this place disappear along with it. "So where do you want to go?"

Tommy was still watching her.

The girl who wasn't afraid to hunt a ghost.

"Maybe I'll hang out with you for a while." Tommy put his hand on top of hers, and she didn't need to feel the weight of it to know it was there. "There are always things that need protecting."

THINGS ABOUT LOVE
by Jackson Pearce

LAWRENCE

The thing about genies is they still act like it's a big deal when they show themselves to me—even though I've been around them for almost three years now. They're still offended when I roll my eyes at them.

"So you're my new guard?" I ask as we pass the science building. I actually had to get a single dorm room, because I was worried a roommate might wonder about me talking to myself constantly. No way would a genie show himself or—in today's case, *herself*—to a roommate just to make my life easier.

"Sort of," she says. I try not to look at her as we enter my dormitory. I should call Viola and tell her there's a new guard here. She'd want to know, as she's the reason I'm mixed up in genies to begin with. She fell in love with one, I got involved, and boom—for "security reasons" the genie police send an officer down to watch me every few months. I don't really know why it matters—what, do they think I'm going to hit the talk show circuit and gossip about invisible genies? Yeah. That sounds like a good idea.

The girl follows me upstairs, sidestepping a few lacrosse players who don't see her. She has golden skin, like all the genies do, and long dark hair. She's beautiful. They're all beautiful, and with the exception of Jinn, the one Viola loves, they all seem heartless. She adjusts the straps of the blue satin tunic she's wearing, straightens out the swirly *I* on the breast. It stands for *ifrit*. Ifrit: genie police. If they'd only show themselves to the cameras, I swear I could create a franchise bigger than *Cops*.

JULIET

Here are the things I know about love:

It involves kissing.

It changes you.

It's never where you expect it.

I learned it all from the animated movies I studied before coming here. I asked the other jinn, the one who loves the mortal girl, to tell me more about love. He tried to describe it. He used words like *beautiful*, *elegant*, and *peaceful*, but I don't really understand how all of those things combine to create an entirely new emotion. I wanted to ask the mortal girl, but he wouldn't let me near her. So I pulled some strings and got myself assigned to this mortal instead, the girl's best friend. He's used to talking to jinn. He's better than no help at all.

And I need his help. See, I'm not usually an ifrit—I'm really a historian, a keeper of records, the youngest one in ages. I know all the jinn lore, all the myths about why we exist. I know all the traditional tales about why our kind live in a perfect world, yet are forced into subservience to mortals. We were too proud, we forgot compassion and caring and love. So we were punished. Exiled to another world, Caliban, and forced to serve mortals.

But we haven't forgotten those things, clearly—or at least, one of us hasn't. Jinn and the mortal girl, they're in love. Everyone knows it. The Ancients don't know what to do about it. I don't know what to do about it. Caliban doesn't know what to do about it—their love has turned everything we know about our kind upside down. If we can love, should we have the choice to? Should we try to? Doing so would mean revealing ourselves to mortals willingly, which has long been forbidden. Will they want us only for our powers? Will they break our hearts, if we have them to begin with?

We don't know what our truths are, not anymore.

So I decided to do what I do best: research. Study. Observe. Record. But I want to do something the other jinn haven't: I want to study love by experiencing it. That's the only way to really understand it, as best I can tell. I only joined the ifrit so I could come here and figure it all out, so I could be the hero that answers Caliban's questions about love.

Based on what I know, I can't exactly go looking for love. I need to be kissed, and something will change afterward—a notion that frightens me, but doesn't destroy the excitement of figuring out what the rest of Caliban can't.

"So here are the rules," the boy—Lawrence, that's his name—says to me as we enter his dorm room. It's somewhat messy, bed unmade and philosophy textbooks piled high. He opens the blinds and daylight pours in. "One, no watching me change. Two, no practical jokes. Three, no talking to me while I'm in class." He says them so sternly that I take a step back. Humans ordering their jinn around, that's one thing. But I'm not his jinn. I'm not here to grant his wishes. Still, I nod.

"Four—most important of all—no magic on me. No magic on my friends. No tricking people into thinking or being however you want. If you've got to spy on me, fine, but that doesn't mean everyone in my life is your magical playground. Understand?"

I feel my face fall—I guess it's only natural he would include that rule. Another ifrit used magic on him once. It was justified, at the time, but still. I imagine it makes him wary. He's staring hard at me, waiting for an answer.

"What if I break the rules?" I ask, both curious and a little embarrassed that he's making me feel guilty over something I didn't do.

"Then I'll remind you every few minutes until the moment you leave just how your hair is starting to look longer since you got here. How long *have* you been here anyway?" he asks, and looks pleased when I cringe. We don't age in Caliban; we only grow older when we're here. It's a horrible feeling—going from immortal to mortal, from endless life to impending death—one all jinn desperately try to ignore while earthbound. I don't exactly want to be reminded of it regularly.

"Fine. I promise," I mumble.

Lawrence sits down and opens up a laptop. He messages someone—Viola, I suspect, because he tells her that I'm here. They have a quick conversation about me, then he starts to work on something, a long paper of sorts.

This won't work. He's got to talk to me. Though really, why should he? I guess he's as interested in jinn and Caliban as I am in mortal sports games.

"What are you working on?" I ask, sitting on the edge of his bed.

"A paper for English," he answers. "I have to finish it before the play tonight."

"Oh."

How do you ask someone to describe love to you, moments after you've met them? I had it all planned out in my head, exactly what I'd say, but it all feels stupid now. Maybe I don't need to ask him, maybe I can just work it out. . . . I look at him, narrow and widen my eyes at once, the way Jinn looks at his mortal girl.

"Why are you looking at me like that?" he asks, raising an eyebrow.

"Never mind," I say dismissively. "I have a name, by the way."

"A name?" Lawrence looks at me, almost amused. I glare at

him again as he turns his desk chair around entirely.

"Yes," I say brusquely. "If he—*Jinn*—if he can have a name, I can have a name."

"Why do you want one, though?"

Because that seems to be the first step to being in love for jinn. A name. The mortal girl called a jinn Jinn, and then they fell in love. I didn't see why I should wait around for a mortal to give me a name, so I chose one myself. I almost tell him that, but it feels like I'm sharing too much, letting him know me too well too fast. Instead, I shrug.

"Well, what is it?" Lawrence asks.

"Juliet," I say, tossing my hair over my shoulder. I picked it out of a book that's supposed to be a great mortal love story. I'm an excellent researcher.

LAWRENCE

Juliet is a lot of things the previous ifrit weren't. She asks questions, for starters, instead of watching me suspiciously in line at the cafeteria like the others did. She lurks in the lighting booth with me and seems to actually watch the stage during all four nights of *The Tempest*. She wants to know things. I've asked her why she cares, but she's always evasive. I've gotten used to answering her constant questions subtly, a skill that comes in handy at the cast party backstage on the last night of *The Tempest*.

"How did it look?" Jeffrey asks, grimacing at me. He still has remnants of stage makeup on his face, and his voice is low.

He doesn't speak a lot, but when he does, I feel like I could talk with him for hours. We've known each other since the semester started, and he's only recently spoken louder than a whisper to me. Onstage he seems to know exactly who his character is; in life he isn't so sure—a trait I apparently find incredibly charming.

"It was great," I answer, opening a can of Coke. "Really. You're better than Jonathan."

"Hey, you've still got a part!"

"Yeah, as a townsperson," Jeffrey answers, smirking. "Townsperson or Jonathan's understudy. Look out, theater world."

"It's only because Jonathan is precious and sexually non-threatening. The girls in the audience eat that up," I joke, nodding toward Jonathan. He has a baby face and ice-blond hair, but he's practically salivating over the lead actress's legs.

"Are they in love?" Juliet asks beside me, pointing to Jonathan and the girl. Jeffrey can't see or hear her, of course—I shake my head slightly, almost imperceptibly.

"Why aren't they?" she asks. "Because they haven't kissed?"

"Do you want to get out of here?" Jeffrey suddenly says to me, staring at the floor. He sets his can of Sprite down on a prop table. I watch him rock back on his heels, watch his eyes run to mine. It's always a mystery to me, trying to figure out what guys want. If they're being nice, or if it's something more. But now I'm positive, absolutely positive that the smile tugging at Jeffrey's mouth isn't simply friendly. I try not to smile too hard, try not to let myself get too eager, too hopeful, and I—

"Why aren't they in love?" Juliet repeats, tapping my shoulder. She glances from me to him, her eyes irritated. She'll follow me to wherever we're going. I'm going to spend all night trying to ignore the prying, dark brown eyes of a genie girl over my shoulder. I close my eyes. It's going to actually be *painful* to say this.

"Actually . . ." I grit my teeth together when I pause. "Maybe another time, Jeffrey?"

"Sure," he says swiftly, easily. So easily that it crushes me. "No problem." He waves at someone across the room, and walks away. I turn to Juliet, and can feel my eyes light up in irritation.

"Come on," I snap. I grab my coat and head for the door.

JULIET

"So, what are you really here for?" he asks as we leave the theater. He slams the door behind him.

"The Ancients sent me," I answer, jogging to keep up with his long strides.

"The Ancients have sent an awful lot of ifrit after me," Lawrence answers, shoving his hands into his pockets, "and not one of them has asked as many questions as you. Or studied me the way you do. Or wrecked a chance for me to hang out with a guy I honestly like. So what are you really trying to do? Single-handedly wreck my love life?"

"You have a love life?" I ask genuinely.

"Oh *come on*," Lawrence says, rolling his eyes. It's cold out, and cloudy puffs of air emerge from his mouth as he turns to face me. "What do the Ancients want to know? I'll tell them. I don't care."

"Okay . . . they don't want anything," I begin slowly. "It's me. I'm . . . researching love."

Lawrence gives me a withering look. "The Ancients didn't send you? You're messing around in my life to *research*? You've got to be kidding." The withering look has transformed to frustrated. I speak before it becomes angry.

"Look, you don't understand. Jinn loving Viola changed things for us, it raised questions. No one understands what it means, if we should be allowed to come here when we aren't summoned, if we shouldn't—no one knows *anything* anymore. I'll make a deal with you: help me fall in love, and I'll report back to the Ancients that you don't need an ifrit guard anymore. You'll be totally free of us."

Lawrence's eyes widen, and he laughs. Loud. He turns his head to the sky and laughs animatedly. I glare at him, fold my arms, and wait till he's done. When he finally turns back to me, his face is red.

"I don't see what's so funny." I really don't—I can't read Lawrence's wishes, his hopes, his desires, the way I can read those of most mortals. Apparently Jinn taught him how to hide them from us.

"That's the thing about you guys," he says, waving a hand at me. "You just don't get it. People here don't work the way people work in your world. You can't analyze and rule and make decisions. And you can't *make* someone fall in love."

"Sure we can. I can make anyone love you, if I want," I remind him. He gives me a dark look, an almost threatening one, and I press my lips together apologetically.

"That's magic," he finally says, and we continue walking toward his dorm. "Not love. And remember—that's rule number four. You promised."

"How am I supposed to know the difference between magic and love if no one will show me?" I complain. "You said you have a love life. Are you in love?"

Lawrence grimaces, but doesn't answer. I repeat the question.

"No," he finally says. "I'm not."

"But you want to be."

"Sure," he says, opening the door to his dorm.

"With . . . Jeffrey? The guy from tonight?"

Lawrence sighs as we walk down the hall. He doesn't answer.

LAWRENCE

Of course I want to be in love. Maybe with Jeffrey, maybe not, but with *someone*. That's the problem when your best friend is in the middle of her own fairy-tale romance. It means you know that sort of love is real. It means you're even more aware of how you've never been in love, how you've never felt sparks or fire or anything other than plain, ordinary lips when you kiss someone.

We walk into my room and Juliet collapses into my desk chair, spins around once with her legs pulled up to her chest. "Could you ever be in love with *me?*"

I snort before I can stop myself. "No. Sorry."

"Why not?"

"I'm not attracted to you. Or to girls in general," I explain.

"That doesn't make sense though. The storybooks say love knows no obstacles."

"That's why they're shelved in 'fiction,' Juliet."

She doesn't seem to understand, but nods anyway. "Do you think someone will love me?"

I had a joke all prepared, but it gets caught in my throat. I turn to look at her, eyebrows knitted together. All the power in the world, and jinn are the most naive creatures I've ever met.

"I'm sure someone could," I answer.

She doesn't seem as certain. Juliet spins around in the chair again, then picks up the ends of her long hair and stares at them. I recognize the look on her face—the one Jinn used to wear when he'd dismay over how he aged while in this world. She scrutinizes how long her hair has grown—a millimeter at most, I imagine—then looks back up at me.

"Some of the Ancients think Jinn was a one-time thing. That

mortals won't love jinn, not normally. That we're not meant to understand love like you do."

"Is that what you think?"

"That's what I'm researching," she says pointedly. "Come on, help me. Please? I'll help you. Tell me who you want."

"No," I say sternly, quickly. I've been under the influence of magic before, been forced to love someone. I'm not at all interested in doing the same to someone else.

"Not like that," she groans. "But I know what they want. I can tell you what they're wishing for."

I stare at my hands. What they want. She can solve the mystery, the thousands of questions that plague me not only about Jeffrey, but about every boy I come across. Are they after me because I'm just the first gay guy they met at college, or because they want what I want?

A love story.

I shouldn't do this. Viola and Jinn would tell me not to do this.

"How am I supposed to help you?" I ask Juliet cautiously.

"I need to kiss someone."

"Kiss someone?"

"That's how it starts. With a kiss. That's what I need to do." She seems a little embarrassed, and looks at the floor.

"And you think that'll help you understand love?"

"You have a better idea?" she asks pointedly, and I shake my head. I suppose I don't.

"You realize you'll have to let them see you? That you'll

have to break all sorts of protocols? Won't the Ancients be furious?"

She nods, looks out the window. "The Ancients don't have all the answers."

JULIET

My kind don't sleep here. Lawrence is curled in bed—he told me not to watch him sleep. I think he knew I was still here, just invisible, but he didn't say it out loud. I don't know why I'm staying here, save for the fact that Lawrence feels safer to me than the outside world. I'm a little afraid to go out there without him. Some researcher I am.

I look at the pictures lining his desk. Him and Viola, him and Jinn. I remember Jinn telling me that his favorite times with Viola are when they lie down in bed together and talk and kiss and whisper. Seeing one of my own kind in a photograph, looking so mortal, so imperfect . . . it confuses me. I don't even understand the *appeal* of love, if it can make you so flawed. Jinn's hair is too long, the skin on his arms dappled with an uneven tan. But his right hand is locked firmly in hers, his left arm slung around Lawrence's shoulder. He was a wish-granter when they met, a servant.

Now he's a lover. I think that's what might really bother the Ancients the most: that Jinn chose this world. Chose a mortal. Over Caliban, over beautiful, perfect, ageless Caliban. Maybe it's like the fairy tales—maybe Jinn kissed Viola, and it broke a spell that made him like the rest of us jinn, a spell that made him not believe in love or fate or romance. It broke the Ancients, broke Caliban itself, broke all the rules.

Maybe it was *just* the kiss, in fact, not the resulting love. Maybe kissing a mortal is what makes us understand, is what changes us. Maybe that's all I need to solve the mysteries of Caliban and what love means for my world, not love itself. It certainly seems a lot more manageable than falling in love, and it *is* one of the things about love I'm certain of. . . .

I glance over at Lawrence in the bed. He doesn't love me, he can't—he's already told me. But someone will kiss me. I think. I hope.

LAWRENCE

Juliet looks even more beautiful than usual. Of course, when you've got magic powers, it's probably easy to look beautiful. Even though I'm not her biggest fan, I'm worried about her— she's been here a week, and she seems as clueless as she was the day she arrived. I don't remember Jinn being so naive, or so curious.

We walk up to the gallery side by side.

"Can they see you?" I murmur.

She pauses, like she's thinking. "Now they can."

"Right." I raise my hand to the gallery door, push it open. The scent of wine and clay swoops over us. I think everyone in the theater department was invited, but the artist, a guy named

Sampson who works in set design, sent me an invite himself. He said he was worried no one would come, and he wanted to see one friendly face in the room. I was surprised—I wouldn't call us friends. We barely know each other. But it was a good opportunity to keep my promise to Juliet.

The art gallery is an old antebellum house on campus. All the walls of the house have been painted black, and in each room are a few tables with sculptures in the center. It's all weird stuff—animals with houses growing out of their backs, their faces twisted into looks of agony. It makes it hard to stare at any one sculpture for too long.

"Lawrence," a warm, quiet voice says, and I see Jeffrey coming toward me. He's smiling, his eyes are flickering.

"Hey," I answer, reach forward, and shake his hands. They're soft but strong, and he smells like dryer sheets. The scent makes me want to step closer to him, makes me wonder if this is what his bedroom smells like.

"Hi, I'm Jeffrey," he says, leaving my hand to reach for Juliet's. She grins widely and takes it, shaking it a little awkwardly.

"I haven't seen you around before, Juliet," Jeffrey says curiously, glancing at me.

"She's a friend," I say. "Visiting from Virginia."

"Right," Jeffrey says, nodding at both of us. "I don't really know anyone here," he admits, looking at the crowd. "I'm glad you showed up."

I try not to smile too big, not to look too ridiculously eager.

The three of us meander around the room, toward the first in the rows of sculptures.

JULIET

Everyone is staring. I think, anyhow—their eyes slide on and off me, but it still *feels* like staring. I cling to Lawrence like he's anchoring me; he gives me a strange look but then touches my forearm gently, leads me along behind Jeffrey. I see wishes filtering around Jeffrey's face, but I'm too distracted by the onslaught of eyes to tell exactly what they are. Even though I can't read Lawrence's mind, it's very clear what he's wishing for. They're obvious in the way he watches Jeffrey's movements. It's like a broken, shattered version of the way Jinn watches Viola.

"I don't get it," Jeffrey says as we arrive at the first piece. He shakes his head. It's a miserable-looking ceramic dog with a two-story cottage growing out of its back. He looks at Lawrence, who is staring at the piece, analyzing it.

"I think," Lawrence says, frowning, "maybe it's about how things that are normal, things that most people want, can be painful?"

I stare at the piece, baffled. But Jeffrey nods at Lawrence, says that maybe that's what they're all about, and that they should ask Sampson later if they can find him. They talk easily, fluidly. I understand why someone might love Lawrence, even why someone might love Jeffrey, with their kind voices and soft smiles. We move on to another piece, this one a rabbit looking even more miserable than the dog. I just don't understand mortal artwork, I guess.

"What do you think, Juliet?" Jeffrey says, glancing toward me as we come to a statue of a bear with an armchair lashed to his back.

"I . . ." I shake my head and glance toward Lawrence. I have no idea what to say. He comes to my rescue.

"*I* think *I* look old enough to scam a glass of wine off the bartender," Lawrence says, nodding to the guy manning the bar—he can barely be twenty-one himself. "Either of you want one?"

"Yes," I say quickly, just so I can get away from the conversation for a moment.

Jeffrey shakes his head. "I don't drink, but thanks."

Lawrence seems surprised, but nods. Together we walk toward the bar.

"Anyone you want to kiss yet?" Lawrence asks as we grow closer.

"I don't know." I shrug. He sighs and introduces me to a few other people from the theater department. We approach the bar. Lawrence was right—the bored bartender doesn't think twice before filling two glasses of red wine.

"Will you . . . um . . . Jeffrey . . ." Lawrence struggles for words as he takes the glasses from the bartender. It's a moment before I understand what he's asking. What he doesn't want to say.

"You want to know what Jeffrey is wishing for?" I ask, forgetting the bartender can hear me. He gives both Lawrence and me strange looks. I respond by sipping my wine, but cringe at the taste. We turn our backs to the bar and look at Jeffrey, who has wandered into the main hallway.

Focus, Juliet. I study him, wait for him to glance this way. It's easiest to tell wishes if you can see their eyes. . . .

"Never mind," Lawrence says loudly, stepping in front of me, breaking my line of sight. "I never should have asked anyway, to be honest."

"Why's that?"

"It just seems . . . wrong. I've had it used on me before. I can't believe I was going to do it to someone else. To use magic and find out about people I . . ."

"Love?" I say eagerly.

"No." Lawrence cuts me off quickly. "Not even close. People I'm *interested* in."

"But it was part of our deal," I say, a little frantic—how am I supposed to get kissed without Lawrence's help?

"Relax, I'll still help you," he says. "Although really, you could introduce yourself to people. You don't need me, you know. Just try it." We stand together for a moment while I think about the possibility of walking around, talking on my own.

What would I talk about? I've been to this world plenty of times, but I can count the number of conversations I've had with humans on one hand.

"Lawrence?" a voice from behind the bar asks. It's a boy I don't recognize, with short hair and blue eyes that seem too bright for his face. Lawrence nods at him.

"Sampson, hey," he says. I turn away from them. I can do this. I walk toward the other side of the room, arms crossed. First person I see wishing to talk to me, I'll introduce myself to. It'll be easy. I turn and look, and a wish seems to grab me. It tugs at me desperately, the longing to talk to me hot behind the boy's eyes.

Behind Jeffrey's eyes.

LAWRENCE
Sampson is confident, certain. While everyone else looks at his sculptures with a slightly bewildered expression, he looks thrilled. He talks me through how he creates them, and by the time I turn around I've lost track of Juliet. This place has so many walls that unless she's standing in the main hallway, I won't be able to see her. I notice Jeffrey has disappeared as well.

"Are you okay?" Sampson asks. "You're not looking for a way to run out of here, are you? Because that's occasionally the reaction to my long explanations about sculpting."

I laugh. "No, not at all. I was just looking for my friend. The girl I came in with?"

"Pretty, dark-haired girl?"

"That's her." I nod. "Let me go make sure she's not getting

into trouble. . . ." Sampson nods and claps me on the back as I walk away, back to the room with the dog sculpture.

JULIET

"Did you lose Lawrence?" Jeffrey says, glancing at his hands like I make him nervous.

"No, he was talking to someone else," I answer. Now that I've seen one wish, it's impossible not to see dozens of them flooding out of Jeffrey. He likes me. He wants to hold my hand. He wants to see what kind of music I listen to and know if I saw the play he was in.

"Oh. Hey—have you been in this room yet?" he asks, pointing toward another gallery room. There are paintings in there, mostly portraits of the sculptures that are to the front, but the room is darkened so that the lights on the paintings shine bright in comparison. I shake my head.

Lawrence wants Jeffrey. I know this.

Jeffrey wants me.

I want to be kissed. I want to break the spell. The spell that makes jinn different than humans, the spell that keeps us from understanding love. I want it gone.

I squeeze my eyes shut for a moment, then follow Jeffrey into the darkened room.

LAWRENCE

Juliet isn't like Jinn. He was cocky, overly sure at first. He always had a plan, till Viola turned it upside down. I'm sure

Juliet can take care of herself—she's a genie, after all. Still, it makes me nervous that I can't find her, knowing people can see her—I'm more protective than I realized, I guess. I set my wine down on the edge of a table and weave through the small crowd. I keep an eye out for Jeffrey as well, wondering if he's looking for me.

I hope he is.

JULIET

"I have to say," Jeffrey muses, "there is no way I would hang these things in my apartment."

"Yeah . . . me either," I answer honestly—we don't really have art in my world. Certainly not art like this.

"Makes me feel sort of mean," Jeffrey says. "Because it's not that it isn't good."

"No. It's really good," I say. I keep watching the doorway for Lawrence, unsure what to do. Jeffrey is looking at me, eyes on mine. His gaze never drops to my body, but his hands do reach out. He grazes my arm with his fingertips. It makes me jump, makes me warm, makes me almost disappear without meaning to.

I could change him. I could change him right now, make him not want me. Make him want Lawrence, even. Maybe I should. It would make Lawrence so happy. He should have someone like Jeffrey, if that's what he wants.

But that doesn't seem like a very nice thing to do to someone you're *interested* in, even if you're only interested in a kiss.

I can't help myself. I lean forward a little.

Jeffrey smiles softly and gently, carefully. I squeeze my hands into fists. I shouldn't do this. Lawrence loves him, or wants to love him or plans to love him. I shouldn't do this.

Jeffrey kisses me.

His lips brush across mine so easily that I barely know we've kissed at all.

Until he pulls away. Until I understand exactly what has just happened.

LAWRENCE

"Hey," I say to Jeffrey, who is standing in the center of the darkened painting room. He looks at me, eyes confused. "Have you seen Juliet?"

"Actually . . . yes and no," Jeffrey says. "She was here, like . . . seconds ago. And now she's gone. I have no idea how she did that. . . ."

Was she called back to Caliban? That's how it happens—I've watched them disappear before. Here one minute, gone the next. Did I somehow get her in trouble? I lick my lips, unsure what to feel—I'm surprised to find I miss her. She's the first ifrit I've ever missed.

"Did she say she had to leave or anything?" I ask, walking toward him—I suppose there's a chance she just left the party, in which case, I should keep looking. Even though I'm worried, the dryer sheet smell coming off his clothes wraps around me; I take the scent in with a deep breath.

"No . . ." Jeffrey shuffles his feet. He sighs. "I'm sorry, Lawrence. But I think I upset her."

"How?"

"Well, she's just . . . she's beautiful, and I guess . . . we were in here looking at art, and everyone says I need to stop being so shy all the time."

"I like that you're shy," I break in with a smile.

Jeffrey gives me a strange look before continuing. "So I . . . well . . ."

I blink, waiting.

"I kissed her," Jeffrey finishes, deflating. "Nothing serious, just really quick, and then she was . . . gone."

I don't move. I can't move. He kissed her.

Her.

And I guess she got what she wanted, and now she's gone. She's no different from the other ifrit after all. Just as selfish. Just as cold. I grit my teeth and try not to look at Jeffrey, try not to think of his lips on hers instead of mine. Her; he wanted her, not me. I feel sick.

"I know, it was stupid. I'm sorry," Jeffrey says, holding up his hands.

"No. It's fine. She's fine, I'm sure."

Jeffrey doesn't seem to know what to say. Neither do I, as I'm way too busy replaying every time he's looked at me. Every time he's invited me somewhere. Every time I clearly interpreted a friendly gesture as a romantic one. I want to smash my forehead against the nearest painting, crush the canvas and tear it to shreds with my fingers.

"Maybe we should look for her," I suggest flatly. I lie to myself: I don't actually care where she is. I don't care where Jeffrey goes looking for her.

"Okay," Jeffrey says, and it's obvious he knows something is wrong. He steps away from me, stealing the scent of his clothes away with him. "I'll take the upstairs?"

"Sure."

Jeffrey nods and walks out to look for Juliet, whom I'm sure is long gone. I look at the paintings and try to pick which one would be best for head smashing. I feel stupid. I feel used—she knew how I felt about him. I told her. I am furious, hurt, angry, stupid. I am . . .

Unloved.

I shake my head, clench my fists, and turn to leave. I'll walk fast, get out the front door, go back to my dorm. I think about calling Viola, but to be honest, I'm not sure I want to talk to someone happily in love at the moment. I take the first angry step toward the door.

"Wait."

Her voice is small and fragile, but it snares me easily. I whirl around and see her, lurking in a shadowy corner. Her arms are folded and her head is down. She steps toward me. I bite my tongue to keep from snapping. Juliet comes closer, and I finally see, to my surprise, that she's crying.

JULIET

My kind don't cry, not really. But when Jeffrey's lips touched mine . . . I thought of Lawrence's eyes, of the way he watched Jeffrey, of the thousands of hidden wishes that must be beneath his calm surface, so many of them the same as mine: to understand love. To be loved.

Maybe the kiss worked. Maybe it broke the spell. But maybe the spell wasn't what I thought it was. I don't understand love, but I understand pain, I understand regret in a way I didn't only a few moments ago. And now I'm here, crying in front of a boy I barely know over the love that neither of us have. Our kinds are more alike than we think.

He should yell at me. I wait for it.

"Don't . . ." Lawrence looks at the ceiling, then his voice softens, defeat still lacing his tone. "Don't cry." A couple enters the room; they can't see me. Lawrence nods his head to the door and mouths, "Let's go." I follow him to a side door, and we slink outside into the night.

We're in a wide brick stairwell, one on the side of the building with an iron railing. Lawrence sighs and sits down on the top step, mouth a firm line. I pause, unsure, then sit down beside him.

"I'm sorry," I say, winding my fingers through my hair. "I didn't see the wishes ahead of time. I'd have warned you he wasn't *interested* in you. Not the way you were interested in him. And the kissing, it just . . . it just happened. . . . I disappeared as soon as I did it, I didn't know it would feel like this. . . . I didn't know kissing was like that." I don't know what to say, don't know how to explain myself to him. Everything feels cheap, like a poor imitation of friendship, and I shut my mouth before any more of it escapes.

"Right," Lawrence says, exhaling. His breath is visible in the chill, fluffy clouds by his lips. "I believe you. I just . . . I don't know how to make you understand."

But I do understand now, in a way: I understand that love is not kissing. Love is not movies or laughter or any of the things I so carefully studied. It is something else, and *that's* what's still a mystery to me. Lawrence gets it, I can tell—even if he hasn't experienced it. He gets it in a way I don't. I wish he would show me, let me into his mind for just a moment.

I look at him meaningfully, desperately, and Lawrence sighs. He closes his eyes, and in one swift movement, his walls collapse.

LAWRENCE

Jinn is the only one who has ever seen my wishes—really seen them. But I give in. I don't want to fight anymore, don't want to hold back. I feel spent, like I'm falling to my knees after a race. I've always held off the ifrit by keeping a single image alive in the back of my mind—a smooth, white snowscape, one that covers all of my desires.

I let it melt.

I hear Juliet gasp, see her eyes scanning me, like she's watching too many fireworks at once. I sit still. I know what she's seeing. I wish for the fairy-tale romance. I wish it involved Jeffrey. I wish it involved anyone, really, that would love me unconditionally, without restraint. I wish for a thousand other things that have nothing to do with love, but I'm sure that at the moment, the wish to be loved is the strongest. I can feel it all around me, like the wish might swallow me whole. I'm not sure if I'm showing her what love is. But at least she can see what wanting it feels like for me. For mortals. I wonder if she's ever felt like this before.

Juliet reaches forward and gingerly places her fingers on my hand. I turn it, and she responds by sliding her hand down, gripping mine tightly.

"Did you get *some* research out of this, at least?" I ask. My words are supposed to be teasing, but they mostly come out defeated. I manage a weak smile at her, and she sniffles and blinks away a few last tears.

"I guess," she says, shrugging. "I still don't understand. But I get the impression no one does."

"Maybe mortals and immortals aren't as different as we thought," I answer. I lift her hand in mine and kiss the back of it. I have to admit, of all the ifrit, she's the only one that I've liked. Even if she kissed Jeffrey. She smiles at me, and for the first time I don't think she's analyzing anything, researching anything. She's just smiling.

The door behind us swings open and, to my surprise, Sampson is there. He looks at me strangely, then takes off his shoe to prop the door and keep it from locking behind him.

"You talking to yourself?" Sampson asks. Juliet jumps up as Sampson sits down beside me on the top step.

"Yeah," I say instantly. "I do it from time to time. Voices in my head, you know."

Sampson laughs, bright and powerful. Heat from inside the gallery trickles out and flattens itself against our backs. Juliet, standing a few steps down so that we're eye level, watches. Her cheeks are chapping in the cold.

"I'm glad you came by. How many of my sculptures are going to give you nightmares?" Sampson asks, grinning. His smile makes me smile back, like I don't even have a choice in the matter.

"A good half," I admit.

"Excellent," Sampson says. "I'll never be the classic poor, starving artist if I start creating stuff everyone wants in their bedroom."

"He wants to sit out here with you. He hasn't stopped thinking about you since you came in," Juliet says suddenly. I see her eyes on Sampson, intent, focused, like she's reading very faraway text. I start to shake my head at her, but her words seem to have thawed me. I lean back a little, exhale.

"I don't know. That's the type of stuff certain rock stars might want in their home. I bet if you added a naked girl in the shower of one of those houses, they'd pay you millions."

"Sculptor of the stars . . ." Sampson nods, thinking it over, then grins again.

"He doesn't know what to say to you. He wishes you'd tell him more about yourself. Or ask him more about himself. Or anything, really . . ." Juliet's voice drifts off and she meets my eyes hopefully, almost desperately.

I mouth "thank you" at her, which makes her beam. She glances from me to Sampson a few times, and then vanishes. Emptiness sweeps over me. I turn back to Sampson, who is trying to figure out what's in the blank space I'm staring at.

"I get distracted easily," I say, turning my body toward his. "So, are you studying creepy-ass sculpture, or is that concentration not officially offered here?"

JULIET
Here are the things I learned about love:

It involves kissing.

It changes you.

It's never where you expect it.

NIEDERWALD
by Rachel Vincent

"Emma, wake up!" I shook her shoulder and she jerked upright, blinking, her normally golden complexion tinted green by the clock numbers blinking in the dashboard.

"Where are we?" she asked, pushing long blond hair from her face as we passed the road sign that answered her question.

NIEDERWALD, TEXAS, POPULATION 542. What the sign didn't say was that only a dozen or so of those were human.

"We're still about three hours from home." After the world's lamest extra-credit road trip to some bullshit cultural fair. I would *not* be writing the corresponding essay.

"Why are we stopping? Where's the highway, Sabine?" Emma twisted to stare out the rear windshield, like I-35 might magically reappear.

"Took a detour. I have to do something." A couple of things, actually. I'd only come with her in the first place because my car wasn't running and Em's trip would take her within shouting distance of where I needed to be. But the downside of my free trip to Neiderwald was an entire day spent with my ex's new girlfriend's best friend. Em and I had nothing in common other than Nash and Kaylee, and calling the two of us friends would have meant redefining the term entirely.

I turned right into the Sac-N-Pac parking lot, the only break in acres of empty farmland, other than the occasional mobile home and a few houses in clusters too small to be called neighborhoods. I parked in front of the building, a couple of spaces down from several other cars. Two sets of eyes watched me from the first vehicle, colorless reflections of light, and I could feel more from the other cars.

I hadn't been to Neiderwald in nearly a year, but nothing had changed.

Emma frowned. "Fine, we'll take a bathroom break. But then I'm driving. No more detours."

I pulled the keys from the ignition and pointedly shoved them into my pocket, letting a small beat of alarm and intimidation pulse through my carefully constructed mental shields—feeding her fear, like fattening up a cow before the slaughter. A reminder that just because I *hadn't* turned her into a quaking mass of terror and tears didn't mean I *couldn't*. Or wouldn't.

There were several upsides to being a Nightmare—a *mara*, to the well-informed—but getting my own way was easily the best of them. "This isn't a pit stop. You'll have to hold it."

"Why?" she demanded, and I let that pulse beat a little stronger, but she just stared back at me like she hadn't even felt it.

"Your ignorance is truly astounding, even for a human." I leaned toward her until she scooted back against her door, finally properly intimidated. "This is *Niederwald*. Do you know of another place name that sounds like Neiderwald?"

She blinked. Then she blinked again, and I could practically see her connecting the dots, though her confusion never quite cleared. "The Netherworld? Is that really what *Niederwald* means?"

I shrugged. "In German, it means 'woodlands,' or something like that. But I think that's just a coincidence, because *they* aren't German." I nodded toward the line of vehicles as their doors started opening. "They aren't human, either."

Em glanced at the people getting out of their cars, openly watching us. "Start the car, Sabine." Her voice was dark and even, but her tense grip on the door handle ruined the calm facade. She knew just enough about my world to know she should be scared.

"Just relax and sit still—this'll only take a few minutes."

"What are we *doing* here? I should never have let you come with me!" she barked through clenched teeth.

"*Now* you're learning. . . ." I reached for the door handle, but her hand closed around my arm.

"What is this place—really?"

I considered not answering, but Emma was stubborn enough that if she thought she was alone and didn't understand the danger, she might actually get out of the car, just to spite me.

"There are a few places where the barrier between our world and the Netherworld is very thin. Thin enough to be an easy pass-through for some things that normally can't cross over on their own." She started to interrupt, but I cut her off. "And before you ask, I don't know why. That's just the way it is."

"Niederwald is one of those places?" Emma crossed her arms over her chest, and I could actually see the goose bumps forming. "So, hellions can . . . ?"

"No," I said. "Hellions can't cross over, barrier or no barrier. But a lot of other things can." I nodded toward the small group now forming in front of the store. "They're here to keep us on this side, and everyone else on the other side."

"Like border patrol," Em said.

"Yeah. I guess." I twisted the small silver hoop in the cartilage of my right ear. "I'll be back in a few minutes. Stay in the car. And in case you're tempted to do something stupid, take a look." I nodded over her shoulder at the locals.

Tall, thin, and angular, they'd probably pass as human at a glance. Or at a distance. But up close, they were disproportionate enough to terrify someone like Emma, whose knowledge of the supernatural world included only the censored bits her *bean sidhe* best friend deemed psychologically safe.

The eyes watching us were too small and round. A woman

sitting on the hood of her car—Nea—tapped fingers that were too long and pointy. Almost like claws. Her shoulders were too broad and her neck too thin. Humanity was a thin disguise on her, and one she wouldn't mind shedding, should the need arise.

"What are they?" Emma whispered, and I had to respect the curiosity that ran almost as thick in her voice as the appetizing tremor of her fear. Some humans freak out when they realize they're not alone in the world, but so far, she'd shown some pretty decent backbone.

"Harpies," I said, but her blank look spoke volumes and added to my frustration. "I'm not going to sugarcoat it for you like Kaylee does, so pay attention. Niederwald is the largest harpy settlement in the western hemisphere. They've been guarding this thin spot in the barrier for a couple hundred years, and for the most part, people leave them alone, 'cause they're creepy as hell even if you don't know they're not human."

"No shit." Emma frowned, openly staring at them now. "What do they . . . do—harpies?" she asked, sneaking another peek at them.

"Not as much as you'd think. They can cross into the Netherworld at will and they have an unfortunate affinity for raw foods." And I wasn't talking almonds and broccoli. "Other than that, they like to snatch things."

Her pale brows rose in what may have been amusement. Or skepticism. "Like, kleptomania?"

"Kinda. Only they don't hit stores. See how they're all wearing jackets, even though it's seventy-five degrees?" I didn't bother trying to watch them subtly. Our stares were both open and mutual. "That's to hide their wings."

She studied the backs of the two girls facing away from us, but with the bulky cut of their jackets, she wouldn't find any noticeable lumps. "Actual wings? Like, angel or butterfly?"

"Like *harpy*," I snapped. "Think giant bats."

"What do they snatch?"

"Whatever catches their interest," I said, pushing back the urge to take just a *taste* of her fear. "Jewelry, coins, clothes, dolls, pewter Lord of the Rings figurines." *Dismembered body parts* . . . "But they don't mess with humans." Usually. "That would draw too much attention. You should stay in the car, just in case, though."

"I'm not staying here alone!"

"I'll be back, and you'll be fine. Just stay put and try not to freak out on me, okay?"

"No promises," she whispered, as I got out of the car. When I closed the door, she leaned over the driver's seat and slapped the lock, then sat with her purse in her lap while I rounded the front of her car toward the flock of harpies watching my approach.

"Sabine Campbell," Nea said, stepping to the front of the group.

"Yeah. My name hasn't changed."

"Neither has anything else. . . ." Nea's brother, Troy, eyed me up and down, like he'd just invented the whole visual invasion thing. Troy hadn't changed either.

"Including my standards." I flipped him off with both hands, then turned back to Nea. "I'm here to see Syrie. I need to ask her something."

"You still looking for that guy? That *bean sidhe*?" Troy said, but his grin was more malicious than amused. "Don't give up easy, do you?"

"I *never* give up. But I already found him."

"Then what's this about?"

"That's none of your business," Nea said, glaring up at her brother, and I was pretty sure that if male harpies weren't rare to the point of mythological obscurity, she and her flock would have eaten the jackass alive years ago.

Desi, the skinnier girl harpy, tossed long brown hair over her shoulder to reveal a wickedly pointed ear, pierced with a tiny bone—she'd once told me it was a human fingertip—near the top of the cartilage. "Can you pay?"

"If not, I know how you could work off your debt," Troy suggested, ever eager to flaunt his utter lack of originality.

"What, they're paying people to neuter harpies now?" I said, both brows raised in challenge, and he hissed, an oddly feline sound coming from someone with wings. "Relax, your balls are safe for the moment." I slid one hand into my hip pocket and pulled out a plastic test tube I'd taken from the school's chemistry lab. I held it up to the light flickering overhead, and the harpies leaned forward for a better look at the dark, greenish liquid.

"What is that?" Nea reached for the tube, and I pulled it away.

"Nothing you wanna touch. At least, not at full strength." I'd kept it in a glass vial at first, until it started eating through the tube. "This is hair from Invidia, a hellion of envy."

"Hair?" Troy frowned. "That's a liquid."

"Congratulations, you've mastered at least one state of matter." I tilted the vial, and the residue it left on the side of the plastic looked even greener and murkier than the bulk sloshing at the bottom. "Invidia's hair *is* liquid. Like her follicles secrete pure liquid envy—toxic, caustic, and a real bitch to scrub out of leather. I've asked around, and everyone says a vial this size is worth way more than a single audience with Syrie. So why don't you scurry back there and tell her I'm here."

Troy stared at me for a minute, then gestured for me to follow him until Nea put one arm up to stop us both. "Where did you get hair from a hellion? How do we know that's not just river water and food coloring?"

"You want a sample?" I gripped the stopper, like I was ready to pull it out. "Fine. But I gotta warn you, this shit sizzles like acid. Plastic is the only thing I've found that'll hold it."

Nea frowned, a sharp look of frustration on her angular features, but the others all seemed interested. I'd just dangled a very fat carrot—an exotic addition to their collection of . . . stuff—in front of several hungry rabbits. Rabbits with claws, and wings, and teeth that could strip flesh to the bone, no matter what they looked like on this side of the world barrier. I'd seen them on the other side, and without that mask of humanity, harpies were a very scary—and ugly—species.

I slid the vial carefully into my pocket and backed toward the corner of the convenience store, shooting a glance at Emma as I passed her car. "Are you going to take me to Syrie, or do I get to wander back there on my own?"

"That wouldn't be very smart," Nea warned.

"Yeah, well, I'm not known for my brains." I stepped past the corner of the building and could see the house behind it, a hulking outline against the darker patch of woods beyond.

"What's this you brought with you?" Troy asked, and I looked up to find him running the long, sharp nails of his left hand over the hood, eyeing Emma through her windshield while she stared boldly back at him. "Food or plaything? Or both?"

"Neither. She's a friend." For lack of a more accurate description. "And she's human." Which meant she was off limits for the harpies. At least, for those playing by the rules. They got to live on our side of the divide on the condition that they only hunt on the other side, to keep from decimating the local population. Or drawing the attention of the human authorities.

"You never let me have any fun," Troy complained, trailing

his fingers over the hood one more time toward the edge of the building.

I shoved him around the corner ahead of me. "And I'm not gonna start now."

"You get twenty minutes, whether she talks or not," Nea said, one hand on the front doorknob of the house behind the Sac-N-Pac. "If you don't come out on your own, I'll let Troy drag you out."

Troy grinned at me from the steps, a joyless note of anticipation stretched over long, harsh features.

"Come near me and I'll rip your wings off and beat you with them."

"I had a feeling you like it rough," he taunted as his sister pulled the door open.

The hinges creaked and the floorboards groaned beneath my feet, but the old house was a lot sturdier than it looked. It predated the gas station by several decades and was the oldest—and at one point had been the only—building in Niederwald.

"Try not to upset her this time," Nea said, crossing the dim, sparsely furnished living room toward a closed door on the right. "Last time she wouldn't eat for days."

I reached for the doorknob, but Nea stuck out one bony hand, palm up. I gave her the test tube, then brushed past her into Syrie's room, where the first part of my business in Niederwald would be conducted.

"Syrie?" I bent to unzip the top left pocket of my cargo pants as Nea closed the door behind me. "It's Sabine. I have something for you."

What most people don't realize when they come to see the oracle is that what you pay Nea only covers access to her. If you want Syrie to talk to you, well . . . she doesn't take payment in the traditional sense of the word, but a little kindness goes a long way.

A floor lamp stood in one corner, its dim, naked bulb shedding just enough light to outline shapes among the shadows. But as my eyes adjusted, I began to pick out more detail, in the room and on the walls.

"I brought you some pencils." I saw no sign of her among the old, scarred furniture—a low twin bed, a dresser, and a three-legged table with two folding chairs. But as far as I knew, she'd rarely left the room, and her years of solitude were documented in the massive mural her walls had become. All of the walls.

Every inch of wall space she could reach was covered, charcoal sketches blending seamlessly into oil paintings so intricately detailed I was half convinced I could step right into them. But most of the images were done in plain old number 2 graphite or black ballpoint ink. Because the harpies were cheap bastards, and they wouldn't spend money if they didn't have to.

Most of the color had come from supplicants—a good deal of it from me. Crayon drawings near the floorboards showed an eye for perspective and proportion before she'd even been out of diapers—long before I'd discovered Syrie and her glimpses into the future. Eerie collages of faces, places, and events marked the maturity of her ability, which had prompted the harpies to start charging for her time. But the occasional sketches of her own face were the most haunting. And the most puzzling.

To my knowledge, Syrie hadn't seen her own face since she was a toddler. Her attached bathroom—also claimed by her art—had no mirrors. Yet there the self-portraits were, sprinkled among the other bits of genius at odd intervals. Some were achingly realistic, while others showed an understanding of cubism and surrealism she'd surely never been exposed to. But all of them—every last one—defined her scars in meticulous detail.

Left eyelid, slashed and left to heal crooked. Skin shrunken and puckered around the pale red tissue inside her empty eye socket. Troy said she'd tried to dig both eyes out of her face when she was little, to make the visions stop. That was her first and only trip to a human doctor, but even the doc couldn't save her left eye. And the visions had only gotten stronger.

Sometimes I wondered what those self-portraits said about her self-awareness. Like maybe she actually had some. More likely, hers was just one of the many faces in her visions. She might not even know who it belonged to.

"Syrie," I tried again, still staring at the art, which stopped about five feet from the floor—as high up as she could reach. "I brought paper too."

The sudden shuffle behind her dresser said I'd made contact, and I headed for the table, careful not to step on the images that had begun to trail across the floor since the last time I'd been here. The footpath was clear—she'd obviously learned that art couldn't survive the traffic—and a second after I set the mini notebook on the table, Syrie slid into her folding chair, without even glancing at me.

I sat across from her and put the twelve-pack of colored pencils next to the notebook. Syrie snatched them, setting the whole box on her lap with one hand while the other flipped the notebook open.

Her long, slim fingers were stained with ink and smudged with charcoal, but they were definitely bigger than the last time I'd seen them. *She* was bigger. Her hair was past her waist now, hanging over her face in hopeless tangles, in some dark color that might once have been auburn, but was now just . . . dirty. She was growing, in spite of the lack of sunlight, questionable diet, and minimalist hygiene philosophy.

"Syrie, I need to ask you something," I said, and a rare pang of guilt clanged around in parts of my mind I seldom found use for. I felt bad using her like everyone else did, but not bad enough to leave without what I'd come for. I would absolve myself later with the understanding that if people stopped paying for Syrie's time, the harpies would have no use for her, and I didn't want to think about what would happen to her then.

She didn't answer. I didn't expect her to. But her plum-colored pencil flew over the inside cover of the notebook—she wasted no surface—sketching something that looked vaguely human in shape.

"Do you remember what you showed me last time?" I asked,

and her hand never paused. "I asked you to show me what I'd lost." The only person I'd ever loved, and the other half of my heart he'd taken with him, when his family moved away while I was in state custody at Holser House.

I had no idea if Syrie understood me, or if she'd understood what she was doing the night she'd drawn Nash, sitting on the end of a pier in a letter jacket with a big green *E* on one side and the number nine on the other. It had taken me weeks to find him, based on only that jacket, and months after that to get myself placed with a foster mom in his school zone. And on my first day at Eastlake, I'd discovered what hadn't been obvious in Syrie's sketch. Nash had stopped looking for me. He'd found Kaylee Cavanaugh instead.

But I knew what neither of them seemed to understand: Kaylee wasn't right for him. She wanted to "fix" him—to drive out every dark impulse that didn't fit into her romantic ideal. She was sterilizing him, bit by bit, excising the pieces she didn't like, as if love were a buffet you could pick and choose from. She didn't understand that those dark bits were an important part of him. Those were the bits of his soul that recognized the darkness in mine. The parts that let him see me as more than a born predator.

"I need to know one more thing, Syrie." I took a deep breath, silently stamping down my own nerves. "I need to know if I'm ever going to get him back."

The only indication that she'd even heard me was the smooth

slide of her pencil from the inside cover of the notebook to the first page, where her fingers moved almost too fast for me to follow. Syrie was talking to me the only way she knew how—by showing me what she saw.

My heart pounded as the drawing took shape, beautifully detailed, yet frustratingly incomplete. Syrie wasn't sketching now, content to fill in the details later. She started on the image and drew her way across the surface so that what she'd finished was unmistakable, but the rest of the page was blank.

The wait was agonizing, but the payoff was . . . unreal.

When she'd finished and moved back to the inside cover, I stared at the image on the first page, rendered all in plum, but expertly shaded, with particular attention to depth and a set of eyes that would be bright blue in life. Kaylee.

I couldn't see the face of the boy holding her—his embrace too intimate to mean friendship or comfort—but I could see his short curls and the outline of his shoulders. It wasn't Nash.

For nearly a minute, I couldn't look away, and I couldn't stop smiling. I'd tried and failed to drive a wedge between Nash and Kaylee, when—if I'd been willing to wait—someone else would have done the work for me.

Sure, Nash would be heartbroken for a while, but then he'd get over her. And I would get a second chance. He would finally truly see me again.

"Thank you, Syrie." I leaned over the table and slowly reached for the notebook, afraid with every second that she'd snatch it away. But her pencil never paused, the exposed tip flattened now, almost flush with the wood around it. She kept sketching as I carefully tore the first page from the notebook and folded it, then slid it into my back pocket, eager to go. I had mere minutes left before the harpies would come back, and I'd only gotten half of what I needed from Neiderwald.

When I stood, Syrie looked up, as if surprised to realize she wasn't alone. Her right eye—her *only* eye—was still bright green and shiny, and she was as alert as I'd ever seen her. But when she blinked, her disfigured left eyelid didn't completely close, and I had the sudden eerie certainty that the empty eye socket still watched me, and that it somehow saw more than her remaining eye ever could.

Uncomfortable, I glanced down at the table—and gasped at what she'd drawn on the inside cover of the notebook. Emma, in perfect detail from the terror in her eyes to the dark freckle high on one cheek. And behind her, holding her, if the suggestion of an arm around her waist was accurate, was Troy, broad, dark wings spread and ready. All around them stood mounds of stuff—junk, mostly—collected by the harpies over a lifetime.

"Oh, shit! When is this? Is this now?" I asked, not really expecting an answer, yet hoping for one anyway. Em could be a pain, but that didn't mean she deserved to be eaten alive. Besides, if I started feeding the harpies, they'd expect a meal *every* time I came. . . . But Syrie just turned to her drawing again and began detailing Troy's arm.

I ran for the door, hardly noticing the art I stepped on, then raced through the living room and into the grimy kitchen, where I threw open the basement door. The stairwell was dark, but a weak glow lit the bottom step and a rare glimpse of the concrete floor. But I heard nothing and sensed no movement from below.

Emma was fine. Troy didn't have her yet. And if I got back into the car and drove off now, I could probably prevent whatever Syrie had seen the start of.

Or . . . I could get what else I'd come for. But could I manage both?

I started down the stairs slowly at first, to make sure I was really alone, but once I was sure, I pounded down the rest of the steps and skidded to a stop in the lone patch of uncluttered floor. For one long moment, I could only gape at the huge basement, lit by one bare bulb dangling from the ceiling. I'd seen it once before, but my memory of the harpies' stash didn't do it justice. Or maybe their collection had grown.

There was stuff *everywhere*. Stacks of it, spilling over and under tables, burying chairs. Drifts of it, piled against the walls. There were clothes, books, toys, dishes, patches of carpet, parts from cars, and even a tower of roof shingles, obviously never used. The harpies had coins, jewelry, polished stones, and glittering hunks of glass in all colors. There were photos, and pillows, and a table piled high with pill bottles, an entire tribute to the pharmaceutical industry, the contents of which they'd probably never even sampled—a tragic waste.

But the worst—or the best, depending on your viewpoint—was a series of human bones displayed on long shelves in descending size order, from femurs all the way past phalanges to bones too small for me to identify, crowned by a macabre display of naked skulls on the top shelf.

The whole thing was overwhelming. It was disgusting. It was . . . a lot to have to sort through. And I only had minutes.

I scanned the basement quickly, and my gaze snagged on a low table covered in boxes full of shiny things, so I picked my way through the ocean of junk toward it.

Normally, I'm not into jewelry—piercings aren't jewelry; they're body art—but I'd worn the necklace Nash gave me every single day. Until the night Nea had demanded it as payment for an opportunity to find him. I'd handed it over, but promised myself that I'd get it back, first chance I got.

But the table held dozens of jewelry boxes, most full of tarnished junk, and I had no way of knowing if there was another stash just like it buried beneath a pile of clothes or a stack of books. So I took the trinkets one at a time, tossing rings, earrings, necklaces, and brooches over my shoulder, then shoving the empty boxes onto the pile. I'd gone through eight of them before I finally found my necklace, buried in a collection of silver-plated rings and charms. Holding it again was like holding it for the first time, the night Nash had given it to me.

The silver horse shone in the light from above, wavy suggestion of a mane blowing back in some unseen wind as she raced toward something I was sure I'd been chasing all my life. Her stylized rider was golden and willowy, riding bareback and naked, long hair trailing behind her. Nash said it reminded him of me. Of the old stories about *maras* riding people in their sleep, feeding from their bad dreams, and the archaic association of the word *nightmare* with a female horse.

I would only have given the necklace up for a chance to find Nash, and now that I'd found him, I wanted it back, so I could hold at least that piece of him, while Kaylee claimed the rest.

I slid the chain over my neck and tucked the horse and rider into my shirt—then froze at the familiar dry whisper of wings folding and unfolding behind me, a habit comparable to fidgeting in humans and a sure sign that the harpy who'd snuck up on me was either excited or pissed off. Or both.

Shit, shit, shit! I turned slowly to find Troy watching me from the bottom step, his leathery black batlike wings half extended behind him. "You broke the rules."

I shrugged. "I'm pretty sure they're going to carve that on my headstone." But not for a while, hopefully.

"That means I get to break one too," he said, and before I could argue, he glanced over his shoulder and shouted. "Nea! Come look what I found!"

A second later, Nea jogged down the steps, followed by Desi and the third female harpy, all missing their jackets. They'd dropped the human disguises in their own home.

"Sabine wants her bauble back, and I think we should let her keep it. But she's gonna have to leave us something else instead."

Troy stalked toward me, and I looked past him to the stairs. But Nea stood at the base of them, and I'd never get past her.

"Hold her," Nea ordered, and the two other girl harpies rushed me.

I punched the first one in the gut, but before she even hit the ground, Desi grabbed my other arm and nearly dislocated my shoulder. I can hold my own in a fair fight, but two on one? While the other two had harpy speed and strength, clawlike nails, and jaws that could bite through a human tibia? I should have brought a weapon.

The downed harpy stood, and Troy grabbed my right hand. "I think this little piggy is a fair trade, don't you?"

"Piggies are toes, dumb-ass," I snapped.

Troy only shrugged. "Want something to squeeze, for the pain?"

I glanced pointedly at his groin, my heart racing so fast my vision was starting to blur. "How 'bout something to break off?"

He shook his head slowly and squeezed my fingers until I had to bend them or let him snap them. Then he pulled my index finger back up, preparing to rip it off. "Should I count to three?"

But before I could answer, a loud thud came from the kitchen. Something heavy crashed down the stairs, tumbling end over end. Nea jumped out of the way in time to avoid the rolling wooden cart, but the microwave hit her leg when it flew off the top. She went down, stunned, but not out.

Emma ran halfway down the stairs holding the rail in one hand and a steak knife in the other, and I blinked, sure I was hallucinating. I would never have expected fight over flight from her. Did she actually give a damn about me, even after I'd driven her straight into hell? Or did she just want the car keys?

Troy dropped my fist and ran to help Nea. I jerked my other hand from Desi and punched the other harpy. Then I stumbled my way through the piles of junk toward the stairs. But Emma was gone.

Pulse racing, I whirled around to find her in the middle of the basement, buried knee-deep in crap, eyes wide with fear, jaw stiff with defiance. Troy stood behind her, one arm tight around her waist, his chin resting on her shoulder. Just like in Syrie's picture.

"Em, you okay?" I asked, as the three others gathered around them, heedless of the mess they stood in. All four sets of harpy eyes watched me, shining in the light from overhead. All four bodies looked tense and eager to lunge at me, finger-claws ready to shred flesh.

"Been better," Emma said, and I was surprised by how steady she sounded. "What the hell is all this?"

"You were supposed to stay in the car."

She shrugged, the gesture limited by Troy's grip on her. "I *told* you I had to pee."

"I think I'd rather have this than your tiny little finger." Troy stuck his nose into Emma's hair and she flinched, but remained resolutely, impressively still while he sniffed her. "She looks good enough to eat."

If I gave her to them, they'd let me go. But though I was a predator, I wasn't a murderer, and crossing that line would make Nash see me like everyone else did—as a monster. Hell, *I'd* see me as a monster if I left her, especially since she'd come down to help me.

But Em saw my moment of indecision, and that's when she truly started to panic. "Sabine . . . ?" She struggled against Troy's grip, but he held her easily.

"Let her go."

Troy's mocking smile widened. "But she's good for several meals, and I swear we'd savor every bite."

"Get the hell off me, you sick fuck," Emma spat. And I realized she was going to try something an instant before she threw her head back.

There was an audible crunch, then a screech as Troy dropped her to grip his ruined nose. Emma ran for the stairs. Nea and the other harpies lunged for her. Pulse racing, I spun in search of a weapon and grabbed the only possibility nearby—a human femur.

I turned as the redheaded harpy tripped over a box on the floor and went down hard, and I was already scrambling after the other two, Nea in the lead.

Emma hit the first step and grabbed the rail.

Stumbling over a cracked mop bucket, I fought for balance

then swung the bone. The ball joint smashed into Desi's skull, and I spared a moment to be thankful she hadn't spread her wings, probably because of the low ceiling.

The redheaded harpy crouched and hissed at me as Nea grabbed a handful of Emma's hair and hauled her down three steps to the floor.

I swung again as the redhead raked pointed almost-claws toward my face. Her nails scored my cheek. My club—someone's bone—slammed into her temple. The old femur broke in half, but she was down for the count.

At the base of the staircase, Nea stood with one hand tangled in Emma's hair, the other around her throat. Emma looked scared, but she was holding it together. I stepped forward, ready to fight bare-handed since I'd lost my club—until something heavy landed on my back.

I stumbled forward, scrambling to regain my balance, and Troy's screechy voice whispered in my ear. "Shoulda just let me have her. . . ." He threw his weight to one side, trying to knock me off balance. If he hadn't been light—necessary physiology for anything that flies—that would have worked. Instead, I braced one hand against the wall and reached back with the other. My fist curled around a leathery handful of wing, edged by a long, thin bone, like the elongated fingers that frame a bat's wings.

I pulled. Hard. Something tore with a satisfying, visceral pop. Troy screamed and when he fell, his wing ripped all the way to the pointed joint at the top. His screech hit notes that would have made a *bean sidhe* wince.

Troy would never fly again.

While he screamed and clutched what he could reach of his ruined wing, I race-shuffled through piles of junk toward the stairs, where Nea had already hauled Emma halfway to the first floor.

I jogged up the steps. Nea heard me and tried to turn, but she was confined by the tight space. I grabbed the base of her left wing and pulled, clinging to the stair rail with one hand. Nea screamed and let go of Emma. I shoved the harpy with both hands. She fell over the rail and crashed into a pile of old-fashioned metal toys.

"Go!" I shouted to Emma, as injured harpies got to their feet below us.

Em bent for something on the next tread, then raced up the last few steps and into the kitchen. On the first floor, I grabbed her arm and hauled her through the house, only pausing for a second when Emma gasped at the sight of Syrie standing in the middle of the living room floor, empty left eye socket aimed right at us, purple pencil clutched in one fist.

Then we were moving again. We ran out of the house, across the yard, and around the side of the store, ducking twice when a harpy lookout dived toward us from the sky. I dug the keys from my pocket and popped the locks remotely as we rounded the corner into the parking lot.

Em pulled open her door while I slid into the driver's seat, and a second later, she slammed one hand down on her lock. I started the car, shifted into drive, and cut across the corner of the sidewalk, then shot toward the dark road.

"Who was that girl?" Em demanded, panting as the speedometer bobbed toward eighty and I finally remembered to turn on the headlights. "The one missing an eye?"

"Syrie." I glanced in the rearview mirror. They couldn't follow us without losing their jobs and forfeiting their lives. But not checking seemed careless. "She's an oracle. I don't know where they found her, but they've been charging for her services for years."

"She gave you this?" Emma plucked Syrie's drawing from the center console, where it had fallen.

"Don't. . . ." I tried to grab the paper, but she unfolded it, holding it out of my reach.

"Uh-oh," she said, staring at the image of her best friend.

I shrugged. "From my perspective, it's more of a 'Woo-hoo!' kind of moment."

"Are you gonna show her?" Emma breathed, and I could feel her staring at me. "Are you gonna show *Nash*?" Then, before I could answer, she gripped my arm. "You can't tell them. You don't know that this is really going to happen, just because some half-blind little girl drew it on a piece of paper."

"She's never been wrong, Em. Syrie is how I found Nash in the first place."

"Fine. But you don't know the context. This could be nothing—unless you make it into something."

And that was just *one* of the options I'd considered. . . .

"Sabine, if you show this to Nash, I'll tell him you nearly got me eaten by a harpy."

"I'm not going to show him." For now.

"Good. Then I guess I won't dump this all over you." She shifted onto one hip to dig in the opposite pocket, then held something out to me. "I found it on the stairs. It's yours, right?"

I glanced at the vial of liquid envy cradled in her open palm and couldn't resist a smile. "Thanks, Em," I said, and she smiled back, like we might actually be friends someday. But we wouldn't, because we lived in different worlds, and mine wasn't as simple as black and white, truth and lie.

My version of the truth was that I *wasn't* going to tell Nash—not yet, anyway. But that had nothing to do with her lame-ass threat and everything to do with not tipping my hand until the time was right.

I didn't want to win the battle. I wanted to win the war.

MERELY MORTAL
by Melissa Marr

"*I* want *this*." Keenan stared out at the expanse of snow that coated the lawn of the Winter Queen's house. *Our house. Our* home. Outside of her domain, it was still autumn, but within her immediate area, it was always winter. For most of his nine hundred years, that would have been debilitating to him. Now—because of Donia—he had rediscovered how perfect snow and ice could be.

The Winter Queen came to stand beside him. Without any of the doubts—*maybe a twinge*—that he'd felt with her for decades, he wrapped an arm around her waist. She was the reason for everything he had that was good in his life. During the past few months with her, he'd known a peace and happiness he hadn't ever experienced. Even if he lived the rest of his life as a human, he was happier than he'd ever been in all of his years as a faery. *All because of Donia*. Unfortunately, the faery who had given him such bliss wasn't as happy as he was.

"We could stay home," Donia offered again.

"No. You asked what I wanted." He turned to face her, studying her expression for some clue as to her mood, as he had been the past few weeks. Her worry over his new humanity had created an unpleasant tension in her, and all Keenan wanted was to erase her worries and fears, and prove to her that they would be happy whether or not he remained merely mortal. "I want to go away with you. Just us."

"But—"

"Don, it'll be fine." He caught her hand and pulled her into his arms. "We've never taken a vacation. *Ever*. We'll go away, spend some time together, talk, relax."

She exhaled softly, her sigh of cold air muffled by his scarf, and then whispered, "It's so near winter starting, though."

"And last month it was too warm. I'm *not* objecting to being here at the house or on the grounds with you, but we have a few days between summer ending and winter beginning. It's a perfect time to steal away. Let's take time for *us*." He leaned back and stared directly into her frost-laden eyes. "The world was nearly frozen for years, and even if things do stay warm a little longer, the mortals won't object."

Donia turned away, staring past him as if doing so would hide her worry.

Carefully, even though he couldn't hurt her with his touch now, Keenan threaded his fingers through her hair until she looked at him again. "Come away with me. Please?"

"Maybe we should take a few guards. Cwenhild says—"

"Cwenhild worries because she saw you when you were . . . when you almost . . ." Keenan's voice faltered at the memory of Donia's recent brush with death. Nothing had ever terrified him as that injury had.

He kissed her with all of the intensity that the thought of *that* day brought to him. He'd almost lost her.

She was his reason for living; everything that he'd ever dreamed of, perfect in ways that he'd long believed made their relationship impossible. All he had to do now was convince her that whether he remained mortal or tried the admittedly risky routes to regain his faery nature, they *would* be happy.

He felt snow fall around them as she relaxed into the kiss. Big fluffy flakes formed in the air; the brush of each flake was a welcome sensation, proof that she was happy.

Then she leaned away.

"You shouldn't do that," he whispered.

"What?"

"Stop kissing me to worry." He trailed his fingertips along her face and down her throat. "We'll be fine, and even if we did need the guards, they are only a blink away. You know she'll send guards trailing after us." He paused and hid his fear under teasing. "Or is it that have I lost your attention already?"

Donia smiled, as he'd hoped she would, and said, "No. I'm just not as . . . ridiculously *optimistic* as you are about everything, but that doesn't mean I'm uninterested."

MELISSA MARR

He widened his eyes and shook his head, hoping that his flashes of insecurity weren't as obvious to her as they were to him. Whenever she pulled away, he had the irrational fear that she'd decide his mortal state was reason to give up on the years they could have, that his loss of faery strength and longevity was grounds for sending him away, that his change was going to lead to her rejection. Lightly, he said, "I don't know. You may have to prove it. There was definite wandering of attention."

"You're incorrigible."

"Yes," he agreed, "very much so."

Smiling, she took his hand and led him to their room.

Two hours later, Donia was smiling to herself. She watched as he tossed their bags into the trunk and opened the door to let her wolf, Sasha, into the backseat of the Thunderbird. She gave Keenan another kiss and then climbed into the car. With the sort of laughter she'd enjoyed more and more since he'd moved into her house, he spun the car in a circle in the icy drive and zipped into traffic.

As they left Huntsdale behind them, her fears of all the things that could go wrong—the enemies that could break the now-mortal boy beside her, the fear that her own Winter would slip out and injure him—seemed more manageable. They were together; they were taking a vacation; and they were very obviously being trailed by the Winter Court guards.

I could tell him that I asked Cwenhild to send guards. I could tell him that his mortal fragility terrifies me . . . but that would lead to talking about his foolish plan to risk taking Winter inside his skin. He hadn't brought it up in the past few days, but he would do so again. He had latched on to the idea that he could lift the Winter Queen's staff, much as she had all of those years ago, and that in doing so, Winter would fill him. He'd even reasoned that it might be painless because he was fey until recently. He discounted the risks: that it would hurt him, kill him. He wasn't any more willing to bow under impossible odds than he had been when he was a bound faery king. *Or when I was dying.*

Donia had tears in her eyes as she looked over at Keenan. He didn't take his attention from the road but still unerringly reached out and twined their fingers together.

If he knew how much becoming fey could hurt, would he still want to try?

If he knew what it felt like to take ice inside a human body, would he want to try?

Would I have decided to risk it if I had known?

"Don?" He squeezed her hand. "It'll be fine. Whatever it is, it'll be fine."

"You're . . ." She let her words drift away with a cloud of frosty air.

"Relax, please." He glanced over at her. "Next week we can deal with whatever you're worried about. Right now, I just want to be together, have a holiday with the faery I love." He smiled before chiding her, "Remember: you already agreed. Faeries don't lie."

"I did agree." She smiled even as the reminder of faery

rules—of the fact that *she* was fey while he was not—made her want to weep. *Faeries* might not lie, but he wasn't a faery now. He'd given that up to save her life.

She angled her body so that she was staring at him. "And I *am* enjoying the scenery."

Keenan laughed, but he kept his gaze on the road as she continued pointedly looking at him. Once she'd thought she took pleasure in looking at him because she couldn't touch him, but now, she realized that it was simply the sight of him that pleased her. His sunlit skin hadn't entirely faded when he'd become mortal. Unlike the mostly snow-pale faeries of her court, Keenan retained the sun-darkened skin he'd had as Summer King. His eyes were an icy blue now, but they were still beautiful enough to remind her why she'd stumbled over her own name when he'd first approached her almost a century ago—back when *she* was the mortal one.

He was relaxed, and even though he'd shed some of the volatility of the Summer Court, he was still impetuous. He'd been born of both Summer and Winter, so even after surrendering his sunlight and his faery nature, his nature was mixed in a way that hers wasn't. Although, as he reminded her regularly, Winter wasn't *only* calm either. Together, they'd found a peace, but it hadn't dampened their passion at all. If anything, their passion had increased because they understood each other more fully.

Even if I'm not able to be impulsive.

Even if I must worry that I'll injure him.

As a queen, not merely a faery burdened with the ice, she had control of herself. It was difficult, though, and she understood why Keenan had never lain with mortals. Every time they touched, she worried that she would lose control too much, but then he smiled at her, and she couldn't say no.

For years, Keenan had made her believe in the impossible; he had made her strong enough to believe she could defeat monsters, to risk everything for his smile, to laugh even when they were facing daunting trials. *Because he is beside me.* She wanted to believe in the impossible now, but it was different when the risk was that she would lose him. Now that he was truly hers, she wasn't sure she was strong enough to risk anything that could take him away. *Is it better to have him for a few years, knowing he will die, or to take the risk that could either give us eternity—or end the years we do have?*

"Are you with me?"

"I am," she whispered. "I love you."

He did glance at her this time. "You too. Always." He paused, looked back at the road, and asked, "Okay, I give. What's up? I know you, Don. You have that faraway look again."

"I was thinking about us and . . . things." She squeezed his hand. "I'm glad you suggested this trip."

"And?"

Donia gave him a reassuring smile. "You make me happy, and I want *you* to be happy. So . . . no more worrying. We're out here on a normal 'human' holiday." She swept her arm out, gesturing at the traffic on the freeway, the roadside advertisements, and the lights of buildings she could see along the exit. "You're *new* to being human, and it's been almost a century since I was human. Back then . . ." She laughed at the sudden memory of her father's scowling face. "Do you remember when you asked Papa to let you walk me home?"

Keenan switched lanes and directed the car onto the freeway exit. "He thought I had impure intentions."

"You did," she teased.

"I wanted your heart more, Don." He said nothing else until he pulled into a parking spot. He turned off the engine and grinned at her before adding, "Of course, I wanted your body too. I still do. I *always* have."

She laughed. "Likewise."

Keenan felt tension he hadn't even realized he was carrying slip away as he opened Donia's door and took her hand. Traveling with Donia was new. In all of the years they'd known each other, they'd never simply traveled for fun. *Or alone.* In truth, vacation itself was a peculiar experience for Keenan. He'd only ever been away from his court for a few short months in his centuries of living, and even then, he hadn't been able to step away from the thoughts of the conflict he'd be returning to confront. Now, however, he was determined to enjoy an utterly peaceful trip with his beloved.

"Rest stops," Keenan said. "I'm not sure about these."

"You wanted a 'human experience.'" Donia smothered a smile. "'Road trips,' you said. 'Perfectly ordinary nonroyal travel,' you said."

Keenan looked at the litter-strewn ground, tables fastened down, and overtired families who all seemed to have dogs in their cars. With Sasha in the backseat, they almost looked like they fit in.

Nonroyal. Just us.

"You're right." He zipped his jacket. "I believe these sorts of trips include nonscheduled diversions too."

The look Donia gave him was more suspicious than he expected. "Keenan . . ."

"Be right back. You can . . . walk our dog." He grinned at Sasha, who bared his teeth in reply. Keenan laughed.

Donia and Sasha both watched him with expressions somewhere between bemused and irritated as he went into the building advertising itself as a "Welcome Center."

Inside, he started gathering pamphlets on everything from wine tasting to caving to antique malls to a "miniature golf extravaganza." He pulled out one for a hiking trail, another for an indoor racetrack, and several for bed-and-breakfasts.

"Can I help you?" an older woman offered.

"I'm on a vacation," he said. "With my . . . girlfriend." He looked over his shoulder as the door to the small building opened and a gust of cold air blew in. *Because Winter herself stepped inside.* He stared at her, his forever love. Quietly, he told the human woman, "I'm going to marry her. She's perfect."

The woman looked at Donia. "Is that a *wolf?*" she asked. "You can't bring animals in here. . . . Actually, you can't bring *wolves* in anywhere. What—"

"Sasha, wait for us at the car." Donia opened the door, and the wolf padded outside and to the car.

As Keenan watched through the window, Sasha leaped onto the roof of the car and stretched out. His gaze didn't waver from Donia.

"Apparently I'm not protection enough in my . . . condition." Keenan looked back at the rack of pamphlets.

Donia walked over to stand beside him. She pulled out a pamphlet and flipped it over. "What's a zip line?"

The pamphlet she held out showed a girl hanging from a wire in a contraption that looked like a cross between a trapeze and a saddle of sorts. The girl wore a helmet and gloves, and she looked like she was mid-laugh as she was suspended over a chasm. Keenan skimmed the pamphlet and read *Evergreen Hills . . . four seasons resort . . . trails . . . zip line . . . ski slopes.* He looked at Donia. "Our destination."

Several hours later, they pulled into the parking lot of a road-side motel. It wasn't their final destination, but Keenan saw no need to drive all day. *Stops to rest and enjoy ourselves.* He walked inside, feeling relaxed and exceedingly pleased with how well their trip was going.

The motel was everything that their home wasn't: it was plain and impersonal and somehow oddly charming.

"Do you need me to do this?" Donia asked in a deceptively innocent voice.

"I can do it." Keenan stepped up to the counter. "We need a room."

The woman at the counter looked at him from the tips of his boots to the jeans to gray leather jacket to the loosely wound scarf around his neck. "I'll need ID."

"ID?" he echoed.

"You need to be old enough to rent a room, pay up front, and—"

"Why?" He didn't know if he'd ever rented a room. As he stood there at the faux wood front desk, he realized that his guards or advisors had handled this sort of thing. He glanced over his shoulder at Donia. She turned her back, but not quickly enough that he missed her smothered laugh.

The receptionist said, "You need ID and a deposit in order to rent a room here."

"Identification cards and deposits in case we"—he forced himself to look away from Donia and turned to the receptionist again—"do what?"

"Break things. Steal them." She rolled her eyes.

"What do you think?" he asked Donia as she walked up behind him.

She wrapped her arms around his waist, and whispered,

"I think you are used to having someone else do this."

"True." He read the name badge of the woman at the desk—Cinnamon—smiled at her, and asked, "Cinnamon, do you suppose—"

"No." She scowled. "No ID, no deposit, no *room*. Your sort all think that works. Smile pretty, and we'll roll over. Not going to happen."

Donia was laughing out loud. Between giggles, she said, "Just like old times, isn't it? You think turning on your charm will work, and I get to watch you fail."

Shocked, Keenan turned to look at his beloved, and for a moment he was speechless. Donia was *laughing* over the curse, the competitions they'd waged over the mortal girls he'd tried to convince to take the test to be his queen.

As he turned, Donia kept her arms around him. She looked up at him. "If the girls who weren't charmed had known what I know, they'd have been a lot easier to convince."

"What's that?"

She released him from her embrace and put her hands flat on his chest. "The . . . person behind the smile." She stretched up and kissed him, twining her arms around his neck as she did so.

Without stopping kissing her, he swept her up into his arms. They stood in the motel lobby kissing until someone called, "Get a room."

Donia pulled back and laughed. "That was the plan. They said no."

At that, Keenan smiled. *This* was what he wanted: Donia

happy. That was what he wanted every day now. The Winter Court mattered to him as much as the Summer Court had, but there was no struggle, no worrying over *how* to take care of the court. Donia's court was healthy and, quite simply, the strongest of the courts. Whether Donia agreed to let him test his theory to become fey again or not, Keenan's primary responsibility would still be one he undertook gladly: making sure Donia was happy. The difference, unfortunately, was that unless Donia agreed to let him try to become fey again, he'd only be able to do so for a blink. Mortal life spans were so brief as to be a heartbeat in the eternity that they *could* have if he became fey again.

He carried her out of the lobby and to the car, where Sasha waited. Beside the car, he lowered her feet to the ground. "So, navigating this human world seems a bit more complicated than I thought."

Donia slid a hand into his inside jacket pocket and pulled out his wallet. She opened it, and extracted two cards. "Not really. Hand her these." She held one up. "Identification." Then she held up the other one. "Credit card."

"Oh." He frowned. "Are those new?"

"No. Cwenhild had them procured for you last month." Donia slipped them back into the wallet, returned it to his pocket, and kissed him again. A few moments later she pulled back and opened her car door. "Come on."

"But if I had them . . ."

She shrugged. "I figured if you couldn't charm her, she has

bad taste. Why stay in a motel where they have bad taste?"

"You're a peculiar faery, Donia." He walked around the side of the car and got in.

"We'll find a nicer place. There's a bed-and-breakfast I saw that looked pretty," she suggested as she sorted through the pamphlets they'd collected.

And Keenan figured it didn't much matter why she wanted to stay elsewhere. He'd walk in and out of every hotel and motel along the road if it made her smile and relax.

A short while later, they were settled into an admittedly nicer hotel. Sasha was out wandering now that they were stopped for the night, and Keenan and Donia were alone in their "honeymoon suite." He had opened the doors to the balcony, and snowflakes were fluttering into the room. Donia still marveled at seeing her once-sunlit faery not flinch from the snow. *From me.* She'd thought she was done being surprised when she became Winter Queen. She hadn't expected that—or becoming a faery or that the boy she'd fallen in love with so many years ago was anything other than human.

Or that he'd ever become a human.

He'd sacrificed immortality and strength for her. In part, he'd sacrificed his court for her. Now, he wanted to risk the brief human life he still had. *For me.* She knew there were plenty of dangers if he remained human: he was vulnerable to threats from any faery that crossed their path—and Keenan had nine centuries of living during which he had made enemies; he was susceptible to human diseases, aging, and any number of threats; and he was in danger from her. The Winter that she carried in her skin could easily kill him if she lost her temper or lost control in a moment of joy.

But he's alive.

Trying to become fey could take away the few human years he had.

Or give us eternity.

"You're awfully far away," he said.

She realized she'd been staring, but she wasn't embarrassed as she had been for most of the years she'd known him: he was *hers* now. She could stare all she wanted, so she did. "I was thinking about how beautiful you are."

He smiled. "Can you think that *nearer* to me?"

"Not if I want to have dinner." She walked toward him even as she said it.

"Do you?"

"Not now," she murmured as she slipped into his arms.

Later, when Keenan came out of the shower, he was greeted by the sight of the Winter Queen standing on the balcony looking out over the not-yet-snowy mountainside. She could've been carved of the ice that was her domain.

Beautiful.

He walked over to stand beside her. Unlike her, he was

not as comfortable with the chill. To the Winter Queen, it was *more* comfortable to be cold, but he was mortal now. He shivered.

Silently, Donia drew the cold into herself, pulling the bite from the air with only a moment's effort.

"No." He went to the bed and pulled the heavy quilt from it. After wrapping it snugly around himself, he returned to her side. "I'm fine."

When she didn't release the cold back into the air, he repeated, "I'm *fine*, Donia. In fact . . ." He bent to the floor, opened his bag, pulled out thick socks, boots, several warming layers, a heavy coat, mittens, a scarf, and a hat. As she watched, he dressed, and once he was completely bundled up, he caught her gaze. "I'm going for a walk."

"But . . . I don't have all of that." She pointed at his winter-weather clothing. "I didn't know *you* had all of that."

"You're a faery," he said gently. "Unless you choose other-wise, the only one here who will see you walking with me is *me*. You don't need all of these layers."

He held out his hand.

She looked down at the thin nightdress she wore.

His hand stayed outstretched to her. "Walk with me. The cold is pressuring you, so we'll walk a little ways."

"We're in higher elevations, and I didn't think about the temperature here and—"

"Walk with me," he interrupted. "I'm already dressed, so

you might as well give in before I overheat."

She winced at his words; her reaction to his loss of Summer and his loss of immortality was still as sharp as it had been the day he woke up human. Keenan stepped closer to her and took her hand.

"Donia?" He waited until she met his gaze. "I'm happy. If I'm human or if we find a way to return me to being fey, I'm happier *now* than I've ever been in nine centuries. The only sadness in my life is that you worry over things you don't need to . . . so stop."

Donia half hid a small sob. "I thought about going out later while you slept, but I didn't want you to worry so I thought about telling you I was going but—"

He kissed her, swallowing her frosty breath, pulling her ice-cold body against his heavily clothed one, and silently cursing those layers. He'd happily freeze to death rather than be separated from her skin.

Which is exactly why she worries.

With that sobering thought, he pulled back. "I can be careful." He cupped her face in his hands and stared into her eyes. "I grew up in a home of ice with Summer inside of me. That's not so different from living with Winter as a human. I've been trained for this. I can *do* this."

Then he stepped back, held his hand out, and asked in an even voice, "Would you like to take a walk with me?"

❧ ◦ ❧

Donia could feel the weight of Winter inside her skin; the bliss-ful pressure tangled with worry over the now-very-human love of her life.

"Trust yourself. Trust me. Trust *us*." He spoke quietly as they walked through the lobby, and she realized with a smile that there was something oddly freeing in being invisible to the humans they passed, but not to Keenan.

She'd never shared the joy of the first snow with anyone. It was a heady feeling, this first. She leaned in and whispered in his ear, "No one but you can see me, but they can *all* see you."

He couldn't answer just then, as they were passing the front desk.

The Winter Queen flashed him a wicked smile before nip-ping his earlobe.

Keenan startled visibly enough that the desk attendant gave him a puzzled look.

"They can't hear me either," she said in a level voice, and then she told him how she wanted to celebrate the first snowfall.

Keenan laughed and said, "There are days I feel like the luckiest person alive."

"That's nice," the desk clerk said tiredly. "Have a nice night."

"I will," Keenan answered with a look at Donia, who under-stood now the sort of joy that made Summer faeries dance and spin.

She blew him a kiss and raced outside.

By the time Keenan caught up with her, she was standing at the edge of the parking lot. He took her hand and led her farther from the light. Once they were hidden from any passing humans, he kissed her soundly.

When he pulled away to catch his breath, snowflakes were falling like a thick curtain all around them.

"Where to?"

She pointed at the ski slopes in the far distance. "There."

"That's miles away. Let me get the keys," he started.

"No." Donia shook her head. "No cars. I am the Winter Queen, Keenan. I'm not going to start my season with a *car*. We go on foot. Anyhow, the slopes aren't open yet, so we'd attract attention." She paused and frowned. "You'd attract attention with the whole *visibility* problem."

Keenan thought yet again that he'd be too much of an encumbrance to her if he didn't shake his mortality. He didn't bring it up, not tonight. He wasn't going to risk the change back to fey without her agreement. They'd spent too many years at odds for him to want to start his second stretch of eternity with discord between them.

"If you hold my hand, I can be invisible with you."

"Exactly . . . and we can still *run* as if you were fey. Hold on to me," she invited him.

"Always."

Without another word, they ran.

❦ ⋅❖⋅ ❦

It felt but a few moments until they reached the very top of the mountain, despite their having gone miles. Donia closed her eyes and exhaled. Keenan stayed beside her, but he released her hand—becoming visible as he did so.

Reflexively, Donia became visible as well. He had faery sight, but they were alone on the mountain. She wanted to be as he was; she wanted him to watch her with his mortal eyes. Never had she scattered snow on the earth when she was visible to any other than faeries. Here, in front of her newly mortal beloved, she would be truly visible. She knew that faeries had seen her create snowfalls, but she'd never noticed their presence. With Keenan, she was as aware of him as she was of the snow and ice.

Neither spoke as she cloaked the world in white. It could have been moments or hours as she walked through the night and covered the earth; all that Donia knew was that everything in her world was perfect.

With Keenan.

In the cold.

Where we both belong.

Finally, she stopped walking and turned to look at him. He lowered himself to the ground as they stared at each other. She stood barefoot and barely clad in the snowy air; he sat in his bulky layers of warm clothing, a mortal in the midst of a thick fall of snow. Her eyes were frost filled, and her skin glistened with the same icy rime that coated the trees. His eyes were damp from the sting of wind, and his exposed skin was red from the cold.

He couldn't have been here when he was the Summer King.

I couldn't be here if he hadn't surrendered his immortality to save me.

He is mortal, but he is here with me.

"If you're never fey again, I'll still be happy because we are together now." She walked toward him, her bare feet leaving the first marks on the freshly fallen snow.

"Let me try to be fey," Keenan pleaded. "Let me be a *true* part of Winter. Let us have forever."

The wind swirled faster and whiter all around them as Donia lowered herself to the snowy ground in front of him. "What if I lose you?"

"If I stay mortal, you *will* lose me. Mortality means I'll die." He came to his knees so that they were kneeling, facing each other. "We *can* have eternity, Don."

"You don't know how it hurts, Keenan. How do I agree, knowing what that pain feels like? How do I agree, knowing it could *kill you?*"

"I won't do it if you say no, but I believe it'll work." He leaned his forehead against hers. "I don't want you to have to hold yourself back from me. I don't want to be a weakness, but someone who can be fully in your life. I want you, all of you, forever."

Instead of answering, she drew a wall of snow toward them and shaped it into an igloo. Outside, she let the storm rage.

She felt it: snow spiraling wildly in the air, the icy wind she'd released continuing to shriek, and ice coating the trees. Inside the snowy shelter she'd built, she had no need to release any more cold. She'd let it loose outside, and now she was able to free Keenan of those layers of clothes and celebrate their first winter together.

Late that night, Sasha crept inside the igloo, plopped down beside them, and nudged them with his head. The wolf didn't speak—as far as Keenan knew, he'd never spoken—but the nudge was message enough.

Donia stood and stretched. "Time to go back."

After Keenan dressed, Donia exhaled and scattered their shelter; the snow that had only a breath ago been a building now joined the rest of the snow spread over the ground. She smiled as she looked around them. The moon was high in the sky, and the perfect snowfall all around them gleamed in the clear white light.

"Beautiful."

"It is," she agreed.

Keenan laughed. "I meant *you*, but the snow is lovely too."

Beside them, Sasha butted Donia with his head again, and a prickle of alarm went through Keenan. He looked to the open expanse of the snow-covered ski slope, but no tracks marred the white ground. He attempted to see farther into the woods, but his human vision revealed nothing.

She is the Winter Queen. In her element. At her strength.

The mental reminders didn't allay his fears. Sasha wouldn't hurry them on without reason.

Absently, Keenan lowered one hand to the wolf's head—and was rewarded with a gentle nip. He looked down as Sasha tugged on his hand.

"Don?"

"I don't see any threat." Donia answered the question without his needing to voice it. She understood Sasha more than anyone else ever had. He'd been her companion for years, and he'd chosen to stay with her when she became Winter Queen.

Sasha growled.

"We're coming," Donia assured him as she took Keenan's hand in hers and they began to run back to the hotel.

Nothing pursued them, and no danger greeted them when they arrived. Keenan told himself that he was simply too used to there being threats, that he was worrying about his mortal strength being insufficient to protect her, that he was being foolish. None of that eased his mind, but he had no way to ask the wolf what had prompted his behavior.

The following morning, they checked out and were walking across the hotel parking lot when they were stopped by Cwenhild.

The head of the Winter Guard bowed her head to Donia. "My Queen." Then, she frowned at him. "Keenan."

He nodded in reply, but said nothing yet. The cadaverous Scrimshaw Sister still reminded him of other Scrimshaw Sisters who'd drifted through his long-ago childhood home protecting him from the world even as their mien terrified him. An angry Scrimshaw Sister was a gorgeous terror, and like the rest of the Scrimshaw Sisters in the Winter Court, Cwenhild was one of Donia's guards. Seeing her waiting was not comforting. However, she looked irritated rather than alarmed. After a lifetime of needing to assess situations quickly, he relegated this to the "not life threatening" category—which meant the interruption was unwelcome. Moreover, the stern look on her face pricked Keenan's temper. He might not be a king, or even a faery, anymore, but centuries of ruling didn't predispose him to responding well to censure.

"Is anyone dead?" Donia asked.

"No," Cwenhild said.

Keenan put an arm around Donia. "Then why are you here interrupting our *first ever holiday?*"

"Because there were witnesses to your . . . to . . . Human video exists of you looking very inhuman." The way Cwenhild glared at him made Keenan want to either apologize or send her away. His having had Scrimshaw Sisters as nursemaids in his childhood had the unsettling effect of his now feeling guilt when any one of them scowled at him.

"You've certainly left me a mess to fix," she said. "This business of your being *human* is not ideal for our queen. If you were fey, none of this—"

"Excuse me?" Keenan snarled at her. He was grateful then

that his temper was easier to restrain than it had been when he was a faery regent, but even so, he had to remind himself that Scrimshaw Sisters rarely wasted time with politeness. He forced himself to say almost calmly, "I am human because our queen was—"

"Explain what happened," Donia interrupted.

"There was a *camera* on the ski slope last night," Cwenhild announced. "You, my Queen, were recorded creating a building in an instant after standing barefoot in a nightdress in a snowstorm a moment prior. The same video shows that building vanishing. It shows you with him"—Cwenhild nodded at Keenan—"embracing in the snow as an igloo *forms around you.*"

"Oh," Donia murmured.

Cwenhild continued, "We had to hire *mortals* with technical skills. There is some sort of video page on the computer-net."

"The internet," Keenan corrected. "There are *numerous* video sites."

Cwenhild waved her hand. "The technician said there were many 'hits.' This is troubling. I propose killing the video maker, but as it's a human, I require your consent."

"You can't kill someone for sharing a video," Donia said resolutely. Her cheeks were tinged pink. "I apologize for causing you trouble. It's the first of Winter and—"

"My Queen!" Cwenhild interrupted. "*You* don't need to apologize. I'm sure you had good reason to be visible." She glanced at Keenan and, after a moment, sighed and said grudgingly,

"And I suppose you aren't *truly* at fault. You are human because you saved my queen's life, and she loves you, and . . . I'll find a solution to this exposure before any of the other courts learn of it."

"Without killing any humans," Donia reminded her guard.

"As you wish." Cwenhild paused and shot a hopeful look at them. "I don't suppose we could destroy this internet thing?"

The laugh that slipped from Keenan's lips was quickly turned into a cough as Donia elbowed him sharply.

"No," Donia said.

Cwenhild sighed. "You might want to return home. Many, *many* people are seeing this video."

Behind Donia, a small group of humans were clustered. One of them pointed at Donia, and a boy who looked of an age with Keenan's mortal appearance stepped away from the group and began to walk their way. Keenan started to move so that he was between Donia and the approaching boy, but Cwenhild snagged his arm. "No."

"No?"

"You are *finite*, and you are valuable to my queen." Cwenhild bodily moved him behind her, and Keenan cursed the scant human strength that made it so easy for her to do so.

She'd do so if I were fey too, he reminded himself. As an average faery, he'd be weaker than the Winter Court's strongest fighters. He *knew* that, but logic did little to assuage his pride.

"Get in your car," Cwenhild instructed. "Sasha!"

The wolf bounded toward her. He looked every bit the feral creature he could be, and Cwenhild—despite her human glamour—didn't look much more civilized. She towered over the humans, a fierce young woman with corded muscles and an unwelcoming expression.

At the sight of her, the human boy faltered. He looked over his shoulder, and his friends came to join him.

Keenan opened Donia's door as if there was no alarm, and in reality, there wasn't *true* danger. Humans—like him—were no match for either of the faery women. The true danger was in gaining too much human attention. He'd lived among them for most of his life and had only the barest brushes of exposure. Now that he himself was human, he'd unwittingly contributed to the largest exposure he'd ever known of. *Video of us.* The wrongness of it all made him feel helpless.

Silently, he slid into the driver's seat and turned the key. Without any further attention to the words Cwenhild was exchanging with the group of humans, he eased the car around them and onto the road.

"Turn left."

"Left?"

"Left," Donia repeated. "I am not going home because of one stupid video."

"Don—"

"I am on vacation." She gave him a look, daring him to quarrel, but he wasn't going to refuse the opportunity to enjoy at least one more day with her.

He turned left.

As they drove, Donia sat quietly at his side. They were almost at the resort when she reached out and took his hand. "I'm sorry."

"Me too," he said tentatively. After a moment, he added, "What are we sorry for this time?"

She laughed, and a small cloud of frosty air brushed his cheek. "For letting my fear keep us from trying to change what you are. I don't want to make your choices any more than I'd want you to make mine. If I were mortal, I'd risk anything to be with you. I *did*." She took a deep breath. "I can tell myself that I might not have done so if I'd known how it hurt or knew that it could kill me, but I walked into what I thought was certain death twice out of love for you. I shouldn't try to stop you, and I shouldn't expect that you'll be happy being mortal. I can't pretend to be mortal. You can't tell me it's enough for you . . . and I don't want to try to keep my Winter leashed. Last night . . . I wanted you to be breathing the snow into the world *with me*. At the very least, I want you to be able to be safe from it."

He steered the car into the resort and waited until he pulled into a parking spot before asking, "Does this mean we can try to make me fey again?"

No stillness in the world could compete with the still of Winter, but he had learned centuries ago that sometimes patience was the best choice. He waited as the car filled with frosty air. He waited as Donia exited the car. He waited as they registered and checked into their room.

Then, she turned to him. "We can look at all of the possibilities before we decide *what* to try, but between the centuries you've lived and the centuries some of our friends have lived . . . I am willing to believe that there is an answer. We can find a way."

Several icy tears slipped down her cheeks, but when he tried to embrace her, she held up a hand. "Your word that we will only try it if we are reasonably certain you won't . . . die."

"You have my word." He knew that the things she wasn't saying were as important as the one she did say: the compromise he'd sought was what she'd accepted. Her other objections—to his servitude, to his pain—were no longer given voice. It was only his death that she was unable to accept.

He stepped forward until the hand she'd held up in a halting gesture was resting against his chest. "Now, what do we do about this video? And more importantly"—he caught her gaze—"can we watch it before it's gone?"

For a moment, she didn't say anything, but then her serious expression gave way to a mock chastising one and then to laughter. "Did I mention that you are incorrigible?"

"Not for hours."

TWO WEEKS LATER . . .

Donia and Keenan watched the "making of the new ad for Evergreen Hills Resort." In it, they were joined by various faeries pretending to film them, apply makeup, discuss costume difficulties, and one particularly entertaining segment when Cwenhild talked about the fact that their "technical team" and "effects team" refused to be seen on film because of their paranoia that they would be pressured to take on more work than they could handle.

"We thought it was all going to be ruined when someone uploaded the raw footage," Cwenhild said on the screen. "Luckily, the client thought the viral video was an asset, so it all worked out."

The video cut to a resort representative who smilingly added, "Everyone who's been to Evergreen Hills knows it's an escape from the busy lives we all lead, so we thought we'd use a campaign to show that a visit to our resort is filled with magic."

Off camera, Cwenhild snorted. "Magic."

The resort representative sighed. "If you've been on the slopes for one of our moonlight specials, it's easy to believe in magic." Pointedly, he glanced at Cwenhild. The camera followed his gaze as he challenged her. "Come see us. We can enchant even the skeptical."

As the video ended, Keenan laughed. "Your plan was genius."

"I decided what to do with the money from the ad," Donia said in a casual way. She stepped between Keenan and the monitor. "I bought several houses for the court's use."

"With *one check?*"

"Well, no," she admitted. "I added a bit more. . . . I thought maybe if we wanted another vacation, I could send *them* away for the week, and we'll stay home alone this time."

Keenan laughed again.

"And then, we could go back there on our own. . . ." The Winter Queen nestled closer to him.

He wrapped his arms around her. "Oh?"

"Since everyone keeps assuring me your plan will work, I figure we ought to start planning regular vacations." She looked up at him. "And you promised me a honeymoon too."

The joy that filled Keenan was larger than he thought he could contain. "I think we ought to have two of them, one before I become fey again and one after. Everything I—"

But the rest of the words he would say were lost as Donia pulled him to her.

Everything I could want in eternity is possible because of you, he thought, and then he stopped thinking and simply enjoyed being in the arms of the one person in all of forever who made his life complete.

FACING FACTS
by Kelley Armstrong

As I lay on my back, gasping for breath, I began to suspect that Tori enjoyed our self-defense lessons a little too much.

"Come on, Chloe, get up," she said, dancing around me.

"Actually, I think I'll stay down here. It's safer."

Simon walked over. As he helped me up, he whispered, "Watch her face. She telegraphs her moves."

He was right. By keeping an eye on her expression instead of her hands, I managed to evade her twice and bring her to her knees once. Then she flicked her fingers, and I went flying into a tree.

Simon sighed. "No powers, Tori. You know the rules."

"I don't like the rules."

"Surprise, surprise."

"Seriously. We're training for real-world confrontations, right? In the real world, if we're attacked by some Cabal goon, we're going to use our fighting powers."

"But Chloe doesn't have fighting powers."

"Sure she does. She has a poltergeist. Well, when Liz is around. And when she's not, Chloe has the awesome power of zombies at her fingertips." Tori waved at the woods behind our rented house. "Raise a dead bunny. It can nip my ankles while I'm throwing you down."

"And infect you with the bite of a rotting corpse?" I said.

"That would be bad." Simon turned to me. "Go for it."

As Tori flashed him the finger, I grabbed her arm and flipped her, then danced back before she could retaliate.

"Are you blind, ref?" she said to Simon. "Call that."

"Nope. Distraction is a valid—" He glanced behind me. "Hey, Dad."

I turned as his father—Kit—walked over.

"Sorry to interrupt your lessons, guys, but I need to speak to Tori."

As he led Tori into the house, I stared after them. I had a good idea what Kit was about to do—drop the bomb that would explode what remained of Tori's old life. She already knew her mother was dead. Now she was about to discover that her dad wasn't her real father. Kit was.

It had been a month since the four of us—Tori, Simon, Derek, and I—had been reunited with the guys' dad and my aunt Lauren. A month since I'd seen Kit look at Tori for the first time, and known, from his expression, that he'd heard the same rumor I had. But he'd said nothing. Not to her or to Simon.

I'd begun to think maybe he wasn't going to tell them. Maybe he didn't believe it. Or maybe he'd wanted to confirm with DNA first, and now he had the answer.

When they'd left, Simon walked over. "We'd better cut the lesson short. Somehow I don't think Derek would appreciate me wrestling with his girlfriend on the back lawn. As much as I hate to suggest homework, your aunt's going to expect us to have that biology project done by tomorrow."

We headed to the old farmhouse. Two weeks ago, Kit and my aunt Lauren had decided that, if the Cabal was coming after us, they weren't hurrying. Kit wasn't surprised. While the scientists who'd genetically modified us had been eager to get us back, the massive supernatural corporation that funded them—the St. Cloud Cabal—knew Kit would keep our powers in check. So, they could bide their time, which meant we could rent a place and try living like normal people for a while.

As we reached the house, I heard a vehicle and glanced over, hoping to see our van. When a truck drove past, I felt a pang of disappointment, but I told myself I could better support Tori post-bombshell if Derek wasn't around.

Derek is Simon's adopted brother and the guy I'm dating, though we have yet to go on what you'd call a real date. That's not Derek's fault. While we're on the road, we're pretending to be a blended family, with Kit and Aunt Lauren as our parents.

That means I can't be seen at the movies holding hands with my supposed stepbrother.

Derek grumbles that it's not like we'd be blood relatives, but Kit says it would still call attention to us. We can't take that risk. So while Derek and I can go out together, we have to keep a foot apart, like at those old-fashioned dances where teachers would walk around with rulers. On the plus side, because Derek's a werewolf, we always stay in places near a forest. Derek and I spend time alone "walking" in the woods. A lot of time, actually.

When Derek did come back, he'd want to go for a walk, to relax after grocery shopping with my aunt. It'd been her idea. She'd joked that since he ate most of the food, he should help her get it. Derek had resisted. His dad had taken him aside and said he should go, get to know Aunt Lauren better and show her that this "werewolf dating her niece" thing wasn't as scary as she thought.

Right now, though, I could have used Derek's superhearing. While Simon hunted for his notes upstairs, I eavesdropped on Kit's conversation with Tori, trying to hear if he was dropping the bombshell. But I couldn't pick up more than the murmur of his voice.

Then, "No!"

"I'm sorry, Tori. I know this isn't—"

"No, okay? You're wrong. You're just . . . wrong."

The door flew open. Tori barreled out, not even noticing

me as she ran for the back of the house. Kit came after her, then stopped short when he noticed me.

"You told her?" I asked.

He nodded. As his gaze flitted in her direction, hurt glimmered in his eyes.

"I'll talk to her," I said.

He hesitated, like he wanted to be the one to do that, and he should be, except he didn't know her well enough yet, and right now, he was the last person she'd want to speak to. After a moment, he nodded and said, "Bring her back to talk to me, if you can."

Simon was thumping down the steps as I hurried past.

"Tori's upset," I said. "I'll catch up with you later."

"Simon?" his dad called. "I need to talk to you too."

As Simon turned to follow his dad, I paused. Simon was about to get a shock of his own, finding out Tori was his half sister. Should I stick around for him? No. Simon wouldn't be thrilled by the news, but it was Tori who'd need me.

I found Tori hidden behind a huge, old oak. She brushed her arm across her eyes and snapped, "What?" then took it down a notch and said, "Sorry, I'm not good company right now. Better go hang with Simon for a while."

"He's talking to his dad."

She hesitated, then realized he'd be getting the same news she had. Her shoulders slumped and she leaned forward, clutching her knees, face resting on them, hiding her expression.

I lowered myself beside her. "I know what Kit said."

"He told you?" She looked up, then scowled. "He shouldn't have. It's a mistake, and if he goes around telling everyone . . ." She swiped her damp cheeks. "It *is* a mistake."

"Okay."

"What? You think it's true? Duh. *Obviously*, Kit is not my real father. Do I look Asian to you?"

She was right. Kit was Korean, and you could see that with Simon, even with the dark blond hair he'd inherited from his mother. With Tori, it wasn't so apparent. Her coloring was right—skin tone, dark hair, and dark eyes—but all fit for Caucasian, too, and she *looked* Caucasian. That was why I'd dismissed the rumor when I first heard it. But that was before I met Kit. When I saw him, I knew it was true, because there's more to "looking like" someone than race.

Should I play along and let her think it was a mistake? While I was tempted to, I knew what she'd want. The truth.

"The demi-demon in the lab saw what your mom did," I said. "She didn't have an affair with Kit, though. It was in vitro fertilization."

"Oh, well, that makes it so much better. She didn't cheat on my dad. She just had another man's baby and passed it off as his."

"She was . . . ambitious. You know that."

"So it wasn't enough to genetically modify her witch daughter. She had to double the dose, give me a sorcerer for a father.

Not like that was liable to blow up in her face. Wait, sorry, blow up in *my* face, because whatever's wrong with me, as far as she was concerned, it was my fault, and now she's not even around to blame, because she's dead."

I thought of that. Of Diane Enright's death. Of what happened next.

When I flinched the look she turned on me was so fierce I almost flinched again. "Don't think of that, Chloe."

"I wasn't—"

"Yes, you were. Dr. Davidoff was holding a gun to your aunt's head, and you raised my mother's zombie, which killed him. She killed him. Not you."

Yes, but she had been under my command. I gave the order.

Not only that, but I had to take some responsibility for the death of Tori's mother, too. She'd been killed when part of the ceiling collapsed on her. That collapse began because I'd freed the demi-demon, and I hadn't asked her about the possible consequences first. So Diane Enright died. Dr. Davidoff died. Others died. And maybe they all deserved it, but that didn't seem my call to make.

After it happened, I'd started staying up late every night, reading or writing until I was so tired I fell straight to sleep, too exhausted to lie there worrying. That didn't stop the dreams, though. Dreams endlessly replaying that day, showing me all the ways it could have gone differently. All the ways I could have avoided killing Dr. Davidoff. Avoided feeling as if I'd been responsible for the death of Tori's mother.

Derek makes me talk about the dreams, pointing out the logical flaws in my alternate scenarios, insisting I'd done what I had to. It should help. It doesn't, because I'm still convinced there had to be another way.

"So, apparently, my mother is dead and my dad isn't my dad," Tori continued. "And the guy I was crushing on? My half brother." She blinked. "Oh God. Simon." She looked like she was going to be sick. "That's just . . . That's just . . ."

"It's not that bad," I hurried on. "Derek says it'd be kind of natural, because you guys share the same genetics, so what you were attracted to wasn't really Simon but, well . . ."

"Myself? Oh, yeah. That's better." She paused. "Derek? When did you discuss this with—? Wait, you said the demi-demon mentioned it? Back at the lab? How long have you known, Chloe?"

"I, uh . . . heard rumors, but it wasn't until the demi-demon said it was true—"

"And you didn't tell me?"

"I, uh . . . I didn't think it was my place."

"It's your place if you're my friend, which is what I thought." She glowered at me, and in that glower I saw genuine pain. "My mistake, huh?"

She got up and started to storm off. When I ran after her, she hit me with a knockback that sent me flying into the tree, hard enough that I slid to the ground and sat there, dazed, for a moment before looking up to see her a quarter mile down the road.

I glanced back at the house, checked my pocket for my cell phone, then ran after her.

I really needed to start getting more exercise. Long walks and self-defense lessons weren't compensating for a lifetime spent opting out of sports because I was always the smallest kid on the team. I could point out that, before embarking on my current career path to Zombie Master General, I'd planned to become a screenwriter-director, which didn't require an active lifestyle. But then I look around at my comrades-in-genetic-modification: Derek the science whiz, Simon the artist, and Tori the computer geek, all of them disgustingly athletic, meaning I have no excuse. Also meaning that when Tori wanted to leave me in the dust, she did.

Predictably, Tori headed for town, most likely the mall on the outskirts. I was close enough to see the parking lot when my phone barked. Derek's ringtone. Not my idea—Tori set it up. I figured it wasn't like Derek would ever hear it, and it is fitting. If he ever finds out, I'll just pretend I didn't know how to change it.

Speaking of barking . . .

"Where the hell are you?" he snapped when I answered.

"You're back? Good. So how was—?"

"You're not here."

"Because I'm supposed to be waiting by the gate?"

"You know what I mean. Simon said you went to talk to Tori, but you're not on the property, so I'm really hoping you're *with* her."

I glanced at Tori's back, a half mile away. "Kind of."

"She took off, didn't she? And you went after her, knowing you aren't supposed to leave the property unaccompanied."

"Tori needs—"

"Tori can look after herself."

"And I can't?"

A growl. He knew better than to answer. Despite my lack of defensive superpowers, I'd gotten myself—and Tori—out of plenty of scrapes. Sometimes, knowing you don't have the skills to fight can be a bonus. With Tori, overconfidence equals lack of caution and, yes, as Derek would say, common sense.

"I'm just going to talk to her," I said. "I'll bring her home—"

"No, you'll come back. Right now. That's an order."

"Well, in that case . . . no."

A louder growl.

"Seriously?" I said. "An order? Has that ever worked?"

He grumbled something I couldn't hear and probably didn't want to.

"I'm not kidding, Chloe. Stop running, turn around, and—"

"I'll be back as soon as I catch her. 'Kay? Bye."

I hung up and turned my phone on vibrate.

I used to think that once we started going out, Derek would change. When I admitted that to Tori, she nearly laughed herself into an aneurysm and gave me a lecture on the stupidity of expecting to change a guy. Maybe I didn't have her dating experience, but I knew you didn't go out with someone because you thought you'd change him. That wasn't what I'd meant. I liked

Derek the way he was. I'd just hoped getting closer would mean landing on the sharp side of his tongue less often.

I should have known better. He did the same to Simon, who was not only his brother but his best friend. Derek had spent the first five years of his life in a lab. No mother; no father; nothing even remotely like a family. That does stuff to you. Stuff that's hard to overcome.

I had to understand, like Simon did, that Derek lashed out when he was worried about us. We're like the weaker members of his pack, and he's always trying to herd us back behind him, where it's safe, growling and snapping if we wander off. That doesn't mean I need to let him get away with it. Just follow Simon's lead—understand he doesn't mean anything by it, but don't let him push me around either, and push back when he steps over the line. Like now.

Right before the turnoff into the mall parking lot, there's an abandoned house. Once when we went to the restaurant across the road, Kit asked about it, and the server told a story about how the dead owner's son didn't want to move back, but didn't want his family home razed for parking spaces either. After she left, Kit said the guy was probably holding out for more money and locked in legal battles with the developers.

When I saw Tori running through the yard of the abandoned house, my heart did a double thump. For necromancers, that's exactly the kind of place to avoid, in case there are ghosts in residence. For a genetically modified necromancer, who can accidentally raise dead rats and bats and other beasties, it's trouble, guaranteed.

I rounded the house to see a broken window and no sign of Tori.

Please tell me you didn't climb through that window.

I called her on my cell. Voice mail picked up right away, meaning she'd turned off her phone. Great.

I made my way through the waist-high weeds.

"Tori?" I called. "You know I can't go in there."

Which is why she is in there.

"Tori?" I stepped toward the window. "Can we talk about what happened?"

A flicker of movement. I glanced over to see Tori vaulting the back fence and running into the mall parking lot. Whew.

I tore off after her.

Finding one teenage girl in a shopping mall on a Saturday was like finding the proverbial needle in a haystack. That day, I swore half of the teen girls had short dark hair, white T-shirts, and jean shorts. I was hurrying over to a promising one, when a deep voice behind me rumbled, "If you're looking for Tori, I think she's a girl."

My target turned. "She" had a scruffy beard. I stopped short and sighed as Derek stepped up behind me, arms sliding around my waist. I leaned back against him and relaxed.

"Thought I told you to come home," he said, bending to my ear. There was no trace of anger in his voice now.

"Did you really expect me to listen?"

Now it was his turn to sigh. "Always worth a shot."

As people passed, they glanced over, and I remembered the rules and reluctantly stepped out of Derek's arms. He grumbled that his dad worried too much, and it wasn't like we knew people in this town anyway. It didn't matter. People were looking over because we caught their attention, and for us, that's bad.

We caught their attention because, well, we kind of stand out. Derek's a foot taller than me and twice my size. I'm hoping for a growth spurt, but I figure he's just as likely to get one, so it won't make much difference. I'm tiny, and makeup makes my skin break out, so I look young for fifteen.

Derek's size means people think he's older than sixteen. He doesn't really appear older, though. His skin has cleared up a lot in the last month, since his first Change, but it's not perfect. His lank, black hair usually seems in need of a wash, even if he showers twice a day. All this means he's learned not to tug me into back alleys for some private time, because someone's liable to call the cops.

"Dad said he told Tori that he's her father," he said as we started walking. "He saw you guys talking by the oak tree. Then when I got home, you were gone."

"She's upset."

"Why? Her dad turned her over to her mother when Tori called him for help. I say good riddance. Now she has a real father."

That was his way of looking at it. The best I could do was try to get him to see things from her point of view, even if he didn't agree with it. Now wasn't the time for that, though.

"I screwed up," I said. "I let it slip that I'd known for a while."

"Yeah, you shouldn't have told her that."

I gave him a look. "I mean I should have told her *sooner*. She considers me a friend."

"Does she? Huh. Never thought friendship started with one girl locking the other—bound and gagged—in a crawl space."

"That was in Lyle House. Tori—"

"—has changed? Right. Like when she left you behind to fight a gang of girls with knives, while she escaped."

"We've come a long way since then."

"Sure. Now she only throws you around in self-defense practice. She really enjoys that quality time with you too. Won't practice on anyone else."

I glowered up at him. "Yes, she's never going to be my BFF. But what do you want me to do? Hang out with only you and Simon? Ignore her?"

"Um, yeah, because that's exactly what she'd do to you."

"Which doesn't mean I should do it back. She's been trying to fit in. You know she has. And if she doesn't have at least one person she can talk to, she's liable to just take off. Get captured or killed. She might not be your favorite person, but you don't want that."

He hesitated a second too long.

"That's cold, Derek. Even for you, that's cold."

"I didn't mean—"

"Just go back to the house, okay? You obviously aren't interested in helping Tori. Or helping me."

"I—"

"Just go."

When he didn't, I did.

Evading Derek in a crowded place isn't hard. I can slip through gaps. He can't, and no one moves for him . . . until he starts scowling, then they move fast, but by then, I'm long gone. Even his werewolf nose isn't very helpful in crowds. He can follow my trail, but it takes a while to tease it out.

Derek and I don't fight a lot. Okay, we do, but it's usually spirited disagreement, not real anger. The subject of Tori is the exception. He's frustrated by how quickly I've gotten over her past mistreatment. I'm frustrated by his inability to get over it. Even Simon sees she's trying and treats her like a part of the group.

Who's right? I don't know. I just know that Tori has lost more than any of us. First, her mother. Now her father. And although she tries to hide it, a big chunk of her self-confidence is gone, too. She went from being the popular girl to the one nobody wants around.

As I concentrated on dodging Derek, I found Tori. Typical. Stop looking for something, and there it is. She was walking straight toward me, so there was no mistake. Then she saw me, and swung the other way, moving as fast as she could without breaking into a run.

I *did* run. I'm not as worried as I once was about what people think. Blame Derek. Or thank him, I guess. Being less self-conscious is a good thing. As Aunt Lauren pointed out the other day, I hardly ever stammer anymore.

When Tori ducked into a back hall, I knew I finally had her. It was a dead end leading to the restrooms.

She hesitated near a service door. A group of girls came out of the bathroom and took up the whole hall. When they'd passed, Tori was gone. I reached the door, and quickly looked around to make sure no one was watching. Then I opened it and peered inside.

The room was empty.

I was about to back out when I heard Tori curse. I followed her voice to a big metal grate on the wall. No way. How would she even get up—?

Well, there *was* a table under the grate. But still, crawling into a vent? Wasn't that a little dramatic? Even for Tori?

Depended on how badly she wanted to get rid of me.

Or was it a test? See how far I'd go to help her?

When I climbed onto the table and peered through, I could make out a distant light. It shifted, and I saw Tori's face, illuminated by the light-ball spell Kit had taught her.

I lifted the cover and crawled in. I could still see Tori ahead, stopped, glancing around as if trying to figure out where to go next.

I felt my way along. When Tori started crawling again, I instinctively picked up speed, then stopped myself. I didn't have a light ball, so it was almost completely dark. I had to take it slow and steady.

My fingers inched along the metal bottom. Then they touched down on empty air, and I pitched forward, but caught myself.

"Chloe?" Tori's voice sounded oddly weak as it echoed down the vent. "Is that you?"

She waved the light ball around and squinted.

"Yes, it's me," I said. "Just hold on."

"I . . . I smell something. It's . . . it's making me dizzy. I need— Oh, God, I feel sick. It's some kind of gas."

"Hold on." I reached out gingerly. I couldn't feel the floor. "There's some kind of gap."

"It dips a little. Just climb over. I . . . I really feel sick."

"I know. Just wait until I—"

Fingers grasped my ankle. I jumped, and if it wasn't for that iron grip, I'd have tumbled right into the gap.

"Careful!" Derek yanked so hard I fell flat on my face. "It drops off right in front of you."

I kicked free and glared over my shoulder at him. "I know. That's why I stopped. But thanks for almost *scaring* me over the edge."

"You're too jumpy."

"Huh. Shocking, really. Between ghosts popping out and my werewolf boyfriend sneaking up, you'd think I'd have nerves of steel." I turned back to Tori. "Sorry! We're coming. Just hold on."

"Who're you talking to?" Derek asked.

"Tori."

"What? Did she fall down that hole?"

"No, she's right there." I pointed.

He squinted into the tunnel. "Well, if she was, she's gone."

The light ball had gone out, but he should have seen her earlier. He had a wolf's night vision, which was how he'd noticed the gap.

"But you heard her, right?" I said. "We were talking."

"I—" He lowered his voice. "I only heard you, Chloe."

I started scrabbling forward. "Tori!"

Derek caught my ankles and pulled me back along the shaft. Next thing I knew, I was standing on the floor, struggling, with his arms around me.

"I need to go back," I said. "I'll be careful. I need to—"

His arms tightened. "She's okay. There must be a logical explanation."

A logical explanation for why I could see and hear Tori, and he couldn't? Of course there was. She was dead.

"And it's not that," he said, as if reading my thoughts.

He lifted me onto the table and leaned down until his face was right in front of mine. "Nothing could have happened to her. Not that fast."

"No?" I looked up at him. "She couldn't have been grabbed by someone following us? Dragged into a hall and shot?"

The flash of terror on his face made me regret the words. He knew it could happen—to any of us, at any time, and there was nothing he could do about it, no matter how hard he tried to protect us.

We tell ourselves we're too valuable to kill. Then Liz pops around, and we're all reminded that she'd been one of us. Another Lyle House resident. Another genetically modified supernatural. Our friend. Now a ghost. Murdered by the Edison Group.

"I'm sorry," I said. "I'm just—" My heart thumped so hard I couldn't breathe. "If anything happened to—"

"It didn't. I . . ." I could tell he wanted to say, "I know it." But he couldn't. The fear flickered again. Then he straightened. "This isn't going to help. Where did you see her last?"

"I—I'm not sure. I mean, there's no way of knowing when it was her and when it was . . ."—I couldn't say *her ghost*—"not her."

"Did you see her open the door to get in here?"

Right. That's how I could narrow it down—when was the last

time I'd seen Tori move something or be noticed by someone?

"I didn't see her open the door," I said. "Kids were blocking the way. The grate was closed, too. And when she was walking through the mall, she was dodging people, but no one looked at her."

"Okay. What else?"

"On the road, a car crossed over to give her room, but it was clearly her then, because she was in my sights all the way from the house to—"

I glanced up sharply. "The abandoned house. I thought she went inside. Then I saw her running across the backyard." I slid off the table. "We have to get to that house."

Outside the service room, there was a second door just past the bathrooms, an exit clearly marked EMERGENCY ONLY. Derek ushered me through it. Someone shouted behind us, but we took off running.

As we jogged, Derek kept his fingers wrapped around my upper arm. At one time, I'd have thought he was pushing me along, telling me to hurry up. I knew better now. It was part protection and part reassurance. Every time I stumbled, he'd keep me upright. Every time my breath hitched, as I thought of what might lie ahead, he'd murmur, "It's okay, it's okay," and stroke my arm with his thumb.

Had I seen Tori's ghost? I knew if I asked Derek, he'd give me a bunch of other possibilities. We were supernaturals; there were always other possibilities. But I was a necromancer. When I saw and heard someone that no one else did, it was never anything *but* a ghost.

And there was no question of *who* I'd seen. She'd looked straight at me in that shaft. Looked at me and pretended she needed help, so I'd fall into some kind of hole. I wanted to say that meant it obviously wasn't Tori, but who was I kidding? If she somehow died in that house and blamed me for chasing her into it, might she try to hurt me back? Absolutely.

We reached the house, and I ran to the open window. Derek caught my hands and pointed at the jagged bits of glass along the sill. There was dried blood on one.

"I-is that—?"

"It's old." He said it quickly, but not convincingly.

He led me to the back door. There, hidden by the shadows of a sagging porch roof, he snapped the lock. When I tried to push past, he grabbed my shoulder and started stepping in front of me. Then he stopped and moved aside.

"I'll be careful," I whispered.

He may have let me go first—a huge act of trust for Derek—but that only meant he settled for walking so close I could feel his breath on my hair.

I picked my way through the kitchen. There was debris everywhere, everything from broken dishes to ripped-off cupboard doors. There were empty boxes too, cereal and cookies that mice and rats had devoured, leaving their droppings dotting the floor.

"About what I said earlier," Derek began as I headed for the hall door. "About Tori. It did sound cold. I didn't mean it like that."

"I know."

"I don't want anything bad to happen to her. I just wish she'd treat you better. Sometimes she does, and other times, I want to shake her and tell her to smarten up. I don't like seeing her mouthing off to you when you've been nothing but nice to her."

I walked down the hall.

Derek exhaled behind me. "Okay, yeah, Simon would say that's kind of ironic, me not liking someone else snapping at you."

"I didn't say a word." I let him squirm for a second, before glancing back. "It's different. I know that. And I know you're trying to tone it down. Occasionally even succeeding."

I moved into the living room. "I should have told Tori about your dad. It would have been easier if it came from me. I knew that. I just . . . I chickened out. We're getting along so much better, and I didn't want to screw that up."

I stopped in front of the window. "Can you get her trail from here?"

"Yeah." He knelt, then glanced up at me. "Whatever happened, it's not your—"

"Let's just find her, okay?"

We could deal with my guilt later. I'd certainly had enough practice dealing with it, after killing Dr. Davidoff.

I didn't say that, but he knew I was thinking it, and the look on his face—that mix of pain and anger and helplessness—reminded me why I was crazy about him. He wasn't always the nicest guy. He wasn't always the most romantic boyfriend. He wasn't about to write me poetry or bring me flowers anytime soon. But that look said more about his feelings for me than all the poems and flowers in the world.

I crouched and kissed him, whispering, "I'll be okay. But thanks."

He mumbled something, gruff and unintelligible. I started to stand. He squeezed my knee, then bent to pick up Tori's trail.

She'd come in that window, as I thought. There wasn't any blood on the floor, though, so no sign she'd hurt herself badly crawling through. Derek followed her scent into the front room. As soon as I walked through the doorway, I saw the hole. Not a big one. Barely two feet wide, the rotted floor freshly cracked, bits of sawdust still scattered around. Fresh blood glistened on a jagged piece of broken wood.

I raced to it. Derek grabbed the back of my shirt when I leaned over the hole. Below, I saw a pale figure, arms and legs askew. Tori.

I ripped from Derek's grasp and ran toward the kitchen, where I'd seen a basement door.

He caught me before I reached the doorway. Didn't stop me.

Just grabbed a handful of my shirt again, slowing me down.

"Be careful," he said. "The floor's rotted. The stairs—"

"—will be rotted too. I know."

Taking my time going down those basement stairs was one of the hardest things I've ever done. I kept leaning and bending and straining, trying to see Tori. Finally, Derek scooped me up and lowered me over the side, then let me jump to the floor.

"Go," he said. "Just be—"

"Careful. I know."

I ran across the room, my gaze on the floor so that I wouldn't trip over anything. There wasn't much down here—vandals had stuck to the upper floors. I was almost to the section under the hole when someone stepped in front of me.

I let out a yelp and stopped short. There stood an old woman with long, matted white hair. She was dressed in a frilly nightgown better suited to a five-year-old.

"What are you doing here?" she said, advancing on me, forefinger extended, yellowing nail headed for my eye. "Get out of my house."

I stumbled back—right into Derek.

"It's a ghost, Chloe." He recognized my reaction, even if I no longer shrieked every time I saw one. "That means you can go"—he put his hands around my waist, lifted me, and walked forward—"right through it."

The old woman let out a screech and a string of curses.

"This is my house," she screeched. "Rebecca Walker. My

name is on the deed. I still own it."

I ignored her and raced over to where Tori lay sprawled on the floor.

"Serves her right!" Rebecca shrieked. "Kids, breaking into my house, stealing my things. Almost as bad as those developers. The floorboards didn't rot so fast on their own, you know. Those people wanted to cause an accident. Force my poor Timmy to sell."

I dropped beside Tori and touched the side of her neck. I thought I could feel a pulse, but my fingers were trembling so much I wasn't sure. I glanced at Derek. He was already kneeling on her other side and checking for a heartbeat.

"Oh, she's fine," Rebecca said. "Well, as long as she didn't snap her neck. But if she did, it would serve her right, breaking into other people's property. Probably meeting some boy here. That's what they all do. Boys and girls. In my house. Upstairs, in my—"

"Would you shut up?" I said, so loud I startled Derek. I turned to him. "Is she—?"

"I said she's alive," the old woman said. "I'd know, wouldn't I? I'd have seen her ghost, and the only one I've seen is that woman who followed you here."

I turned sharply. "Woman?"

"Oh, *now* you want to listen to me, do you? Is this how you treat ghosts, girl? Ignore them until it suits your fancy? Well, let me tell you, I don't—"

She kept ranting. I turned back to Derek, who was on his

phone, calling his dad. I shook Tori's shoulder. Her eyelids fluttered and she groaned.

"She's going to be okay," Derek said. "Your aunt's coming." Aunt Lauren was a doctor. "Did you say something about a woman?"

"She says one followed me here. Another ghost."

I turned back to Rebecca Walker. A month ago, I'd have been tripping over myself to apologize for ignoring her. I credit Derek for that too—teaching me I don't need to be so polite all the time. I still believe in being nice, but with ghosts, if they're nasty to me, I have to give them attitude right back, or they'll take advantage.

"Do you want us to call the police too?" I asked. "Report this accident? Or would you rather we kept it quiet so your son doesn't get in trouble?"

She stopped ranting.

"We'll make you a deal," I said. "We won't tell anyone what happened here. In fact, we'll alert your son to what the developers did. In return, you'll tell me everything you know about this woman."

Now she started squawking that she didn't know much, that it was just some lady who must have been following me because of my necromancer's glow. She'd come in here, seen Tori fall, and taken off.

"I can't tell you more than I saw, girl, so you'd better not hold out on me."

There was genuine panic in her voice. That's another thing

Derek made me realize—I often feel that I'm at the mercy of ghosts, but it's the other way around. They're stuck, and I'm their only chance for contact with the living world.

"We had a deal," I said. "I'll do my part, if you tell me what this ghost looked like."

Rebecca jabbed a finger in Tori's direction. "Like her. Same height. Same hair. Skinny. Blue eyes, though. And older. Maybe forty. Dressed all fancy, too, like she thought she was something special."

"Diane Enright," I whispered. "She's describing Tori's mom."

He swore under his breath. "She used a glamour spell."

"A what?"

"Glamour spell. It makes a witch look like someone else. It only works if you're *expecting* to see the other person."

"Like when that other person disappears from sight, then returns. Or seems to."

I marched from the room. Derek came after me.

"Stay with Tori," I said. "Please. I don't want her to wake up and hear this."

He hesitated, but agreed, and watched me head up the stairs. I went out the back door. As I gazed around the empty yard, I swallowed. I might have marched up those stairs, but my knees were trembling. This was Diane Enright. Tori's mother. The woman I'd raised to kill Dr. Davidoff. To murder Dr. Davidoff.

Oh God. I couldn't do this. Couldn't face her. Couldn't—

I had to.

"Mrs.—" I took a deep breath to steady my voice, then

channeled Derek, putting a snap into my voice as I shouted, "Diane! I know you're out there."

She popped up in front of me, so fast I blanched. I crossed my arms, willed my feet to stay still, and reminded myself she was just a ghost.

"Little Chloe Saunders, looking so fierce," she said. "I suppose that's what happens after you kill someone?"

I tried not to flinch, but I must have, because she laughed again. "Or not so fierce after all."

"What do you want?"

She looked down at me, and she was still smiling, but it gave me goose bumps. "I think you know."

I just stood there, staring up at her.

"You killed Dr. Davidoff, Chloe. You used me to do it. I'm sure you're telling yourself you didn't, that I fired the gun and you had nothing to do with that. A terrible misunderstanding."

No, I'd told her to do it. I knew that. I accepted responsibility. But did I completely believe it? Or was there part of me that wanted to pretend it was a misunderstanding? It wasn't. Seeing Diane Enright again, I knew that. I remembered everything she'd done to us. Everything Davidoff did to us. In that moment, seeing her corpse, seeing Davidoff holding the gun to Aunt Lauren's head, and I was back in the laboratory and I felt what I had then. Clarity. Resolution.

"It wasn't a misunderstanding," I said. "I told you to shoot him. You were a zombie. You had to obey me."

The look she gave me then was even more chilling, because

there was no anger in it. She was studying me, appraisingly, as if murdering someone was a sign of character.

"You blame me for everything that happened, don't you?" I said. "I freed the demi-demon, which brought down the building, which killed you. Then I forced you to kill Dr. Davidoff. You want revenge. You were following me on the other side of the veil, so I couldn't see you. When Tori fell, you lured me away. You left your daughter to die. Then you tried to kill me."

"Please, Chloe, I know you love movies, but drama doesn't suit you. Victoria wasn't in mortal danger, and neither were you. It was simply"—she pursed her lips—"a lesson. A small show of what I can do, if I wish."

"Again, what do you want?"

"Nothing. Yet." She stepped forward, and I resisted the urge to back up. "I merely wish you to remain open to the possibility that we can help each other. I find you interesting, Chloe. You know that."

"No, you find me useful, especially now, when your options are so limited that you're willing to work with the person you blame for your death." I looked up at her. "You told me before that we could help each other. That I was stronger than your daughter."

"You are."

"No, I'm not. It was never about who was smarter or stronger. It was about who you could control. You couldn't control Tori. You thought you could control me. You still think you can. That's what this was about. To show me what you can do—leave Tori alone and hurt, lead me into another hole, where I can lie, alone and hurt too, until I'm rescued. Then I'll do whatever you say." I met her gaze. "Only I won't."

I imagined giving her a mental shove. She staggered back.

"Don't you dare, Chloe Saunders. If you banish me—"

"You'll come back. I'm sure you will. But you won't trick me again, and by then, I'll have learned a way to get rid of you for good." I stepped forward, right under her nose. "I'm not sorry you're dead. I'm not sorry Dr. Davidoff is dead. I just feel sorry for myself because I had to kill him. But if I didn't, someone else would have had to, and that would only have put the guilt on them. So I'm going to stop thinking of all the other ways we could have stopped you, because there weren't any. And when I find a way to banish you for good, I won't worry about where you might go. I'm just going to stop you."

I closed my eyes and gave her a huge mental slam. She let out a howl of rage, cut short as she was knocked into another dimension. When I opened my eyes, she was gone.

I let out a shuddering sigh. Then arms went around me, solid and warm, and I leaned back against Derek.

"She's gone," I whispered. "For a little while."

"I know." He kissed the top of my head.

I let myself enjoy the embrace for a moment, then remembered and pulled away. "Tori."

"Your aunt and my dad are here. They came in the front.

Tori might have a broken ankle and a concussion, but she's okay." He reached down, hand going under my chin. "I know how hard that was for you, confronting Tori's mom."

He bent, lips coming to mine and—

"Derek? Chloe?" It was Kit, opening the back door.

Derek let out a low growl.

"Never fails." I turned to Kit. "How is she?"

"We're going to take her back to the house now. She's unconscious again."

"Then we'll walk back," Derek said. "Give you room in the van to lay her down."

His dad agreed and went back inside. As we walked toward the steps, I looked down at Derek's hand, holding mine.

"No one's around," he said. "And we can take the back way."

"Good," I said, and entwined my fingers with his.

LET'S GET THIS UNDEAD SHOW
ON THE ROAD
by Sarah Rees Brennan

"A vampire craze has taken the world by storm. It seems as if everyone is developing a taste for blood.

"Riding this crimson wave is the English boy band 4 the One, who rocketed to the top of the charts a couple of months ago and stuck.

"And as we all know, two months at the top is eternal life in showbiz. We at *Sizzling Hot News* were lucky enough to score an exclusive interview with the four hot young things and their manager, Faye Fanshawe."

The flickering screen was the only light in the tour bus, but unfortunately Christian was a vampire and could see in the dark. He was trying to concentrate on the television, because he was afraid to look at anyone in the room.

The camera panned down along Faye's body; her mulberry-colored suit; her chestnut-colored coif, highlights gleaming with copper and evil; and her literally killer shoes, with wooden heels that she was always threatening to use to stake Christian if he avoided the wind machine at concerts.

Faye's face was suddenly in close-up beside the reporter's. They smiled at each other with all the warmth and sincerity of two skulls placed side by side.

"Why do you think that 4 the One has struck such a chord with their audience?" Christie (no last name) of *Sizzling Hot News* inquired, and as Faye opened her mouth, Christie went smoothly on, "With so many competitors, do you worry that 4 the One will get lost in a forest of fangs? Take Night Is Falling for You, a band of Canadian vampires who combine menace with folksy charm—"

Faye's lip curled. "I'd rather not. I like my boys." She sent a smile at the camera that combined menace with ferocious intent. "I don't believe, Chrissy—may I call you Chrissy?"

"Christie."

"Thanks," Faye cooed. "I don't believe the glut of vampires on the market will affect us at all. For one thing, I think part of what draws people to the group is that we have three humans and only one vampire. Chris is a bit of a special case. He isn't part of a group of vampires, and I think people respond to his essential loneliness—"

The bus behind them rocked gently but visibly. Christie started. Faye remained absolutely calm.

Christian's eyes flicked to Faye's face offscreen. She had a fixed, murderous look about her, and even though it was dark and she couldn't possibly have known he was looking at her, he saw her lip curl back from her teeth.

He cringed and returned his gaze to the TV screen.

"He's the only vampire in a sea of humans," Faye on the television continued serenely. "He yearns to be human, but he can never truly be one of us. He's the alluring other who makes us feel good about ourselves. Emo bangs to fangs, he's the whole package."

Behind her, the door of the bus slammed open, and out staggered Christian. He was moving with all the vampiric grace of a cat. A cat with its head stuck in a tin.

"And here's that package now," Faye said, sending him a glittering smile. "Practically almost on time. And his lovely bandmates."

Bradley, lead singer of 4 the One, came out stretching like a stripper, wearing only skintight silver trousers and a look of innocent surprise.

"Are the reporters here already?" he asked, stretching some more. "I'm so sorry," he added, artfully rumpling his already artfully rumpled blond hair. "What must you think of me?"

"I can't tell you what I think of you," Christian muttered. "There are ladies present."

Offscreen, Christian winced. He hadn't realized he'd said that loud enough for the cameras to catch.

Even with his vampire eyesight, Christian could only make out the dark shape on the screen, slinking behind Bradley, that was Josh. Someone as shy as Josh should probably not be in an internationally famous boy band.

Like Christian was one to talk about being temperamentally suited to the job.

The fourth member of the band, Pez the drummer, came outside and beamed beatifically upon all of them. He looked as if he was not entirely certain who any of them were.

Christie clapped her hands together in a way Christian thought was meant to display enthusiasm. It actually reminded him of a teacher calling her class to order. "Boys! Are you excited to be on your first tour?"

"Oh, we're on tour," Pez said, regarding the tour bus with an enlightened air. "I was wondering why our new house had wheels."

Bradley, Christian, Josh, and Faye all shared a moment of embarrassed silence.

"I'm really excited to be on tour!" Bradley announced finally, saving the day and flashing his trademark boyish grin.

Christian had to briefly stop watching the screen in order to roll his eyes.

"As you can see," Bradley said, dimming the smile expertly from dazzling to bashful, "I've been working out."

Christie frowned. "Do you always work out covered in glitter?"

"Actually," Christian said, "it pains me to admit this. But he really does."

Christie's nose almost twitched as it turned toward him, like a hound on a scent.

"Chris," she said.

"Christian," said Christian.

"Chris, darling," Christie said firmly. "How do you feel about this?"

Christian blinked. "Well, he does get a lot of glitter in the carpets, but in the end I guess it's his business."

On the screen, Faye's face was perfectly serene. In the darkness of the tour bus as they watched the interview, Faye's snort rang out like a gunshot. Christian flinched.

"I meant about the tour," the interviewer said patiently.

"Oh, well," said Christian. "I am obviously excited to meet the fans and thrilled about this opportunity—"

"Where do they put your coffin?" Christie inquired brightly. "Do they store it in the luggage hold?"

Bradley's shining blond head turned. "In the luggage hold?" he demanded. "Like an animal? No way."

He leaned over and hooked an arm around Christian's neck. Christian leaned away.

"Chris is one of the band," Bradley announced. "His coffin rides in the tour bus with us. Anyway, you know, he's cooped up in the coffin all day long, he needs to be amused. I play knock-knock jokes on the coffin lid for him. We have a blast together."

Now that Bradley had moved to snag Christian, Josh's face was clear, thin and pale behind his wire glasses. It expressed exactly how thrilled he wasn't about having a coffin in the tour bus with him.

Just as clear was Christian's murmur of "Put me in the luggage hold. I beg you."

"One of the stops is in Birmingham, near the area where you grew up," Christie continued. "The word is that you haven't been back there for almost two years, since your mother threw you out of your home."

Christian's mouth tightened. "My mother didn't throw me out."

Christian's mother had not thrown him out. But they had all been uneasy around him after the change, and his fifteen-year-old brother Rory had stopped hero-worshipping him and become afraid of him instead. He'd had nightmares every night Christian stayed in the house, and Mum had said, well, you're eighteen, after all . . .

Eighteen forever. Rory was the one with the future.

Christian had left. They hadn't thrown him out, it hadn't been like that, but he'd had to leave, and he'd liked playing guitar in his garage band, and there had been auditions for a boy band.

He had never thought it would spiral out of control like this, but as soon as he had signed the contracts, Faye had been in control. He'd been a very new vampire, not sure who or what he was.

Faye had been sure, and had shaped them all according to

her vision. Now, with success, her vision had expanded, become as huge and glittering as one of the onscreen projections of their concerts. It was hard to know what lay behind that vision.

But that wasn't this interviewer's business, and things were better now with his family. Rory owned the band's CD, and the new single. They were proud of him, Mum said when she called him. She'd started calling him more and more often after their first single had hit the charts. Everything was fixed between them, and he'd see them soon.

"Really?" asked Christie, sweet as candied arsenic. "I understood that after you, ahem, transitioned into an alternative state—is that the term you prefer?"

"I prefer 'became a vampire.'"

"Well, since you . . . did that, I understood that your brother was afraid to have you in the house, and your mother threw you out?"

"I said she didn't throw me out!" Christian shouted.

There was a blur of movement on the television screen, away from Bradley and toward Christie. Then all movement ceased.

It took Christian a second to realize this was because Faye had pressed pause.

She flicked the light on.

"Well, one could call that a very successful interview. If one also wanted to call the voyage of the *Titanic* a lovely pleasure cruise. Can anyone tell me what Christian did wrong?"

Pez put up his hand. "Can I go to the bathroom?"

"Thank you for that valuable contribution," Faye told him. "And no, you may not. Just because I feel like being unkind. Anybody else? Josh."

"He menaced that poor woman with his vampire powers," Josh said in a low voice.

"Exactly," Faye said. "Exactly! He moved too fast and loomed over her, and she was scared and stumbled back, and he did it all on camera! Can you all tell me what he looked like?"

"A vampire," Christian remarked drily.

"Exactly!" Faye said again. "That's exactly my point."

If Christian had still been human, he would've bitten his lip, but he'd learned the hard way that that was extremely painful as a vampire.

"Faye, I am a vampire."

"That's absolutely no excuse," Faye said sharply.

Christian stared.

"You see, Christian, being a vampire in the context of a boy band is a lot like knocking boots."

"What?"

Bradley, who had been lounging across three seats at once, leaned over and whispered helpfully, "She means making love, Chris."

Christian transferred his horrified stare to Bradley.

"You guys are a boy band," Faye said. "Your job is to make girls think about sex, dream about sex. Your clothes and attitudes are meant to suggest sex. Under no circumstances are you to be caught actually having sex with one of these deeply under-age fans. If possible, I would like no indication to appear that you ever really have sex at all."

"By caught, do you mean there should be no visual evidence?" Bradley inquired. "Like photos or say, hypothetically speaking, videos released online involving whipped cream?"

Faye looked appalled.

"Whoops," said Bradley. "Oh well."

Faye visibly made the decision to ignore this. "Or the way Pez, who is doing an excellent job portraying the perfect stoner drummer, is not permitted to take real drugs. And he very seldom actually does so!"

They all turned and looked at Pez, sleepy-eyed under his crown of dreadlocks. He gave them all a double thumbs-up.

"I really don't think resorting to snorting baking powder is helping him," Christian said eventually.

Faye ignored that too. "And vampirism is like sex."

"How?" Christian demanded. "How is it like . . . that . . . at all?"

"Little hints of vampirism are very alluring," Faye said. "Subtle touches. But we don't want them thinking of real vampirism, any more than we want them thinking of real sex. That stuff is scary. What we need is for the danger to seem perfectly safe."

"That's impossible," Christian told her flatly.

Faye gave him a brilliant smile. "That's showbiz."

She pressed play again, so that on the screen Christian was looming, the reporter was shrinking back, and Bradley was interposing himself between them, talking lightly and easily, speaking lines that Faye had approved.

In the brightly lit tour bus, Faye uncrossed her legs and rose from her perch on the table, and began giving instructions.

Christian wasn't sure which he found most depressing, Faye's list of commands or Bradley's earnest platitudes on the screen.

"This tour is going to be a journey. Journeys are all about discovery: we'll learn things about each other, about the fans. About ourselves." Bradley flashed his safely dangerous grin for the ladies. "We'll be bonding closer than ever as a band. And who knows who we'll meet along the way. . . ."

"You do realize what this interview means," Faye said. "It means that I want the rest of the tour to be perfect. See to it, boys. Don't let me down."

Their first tour stop was in Liverpool, which was always an intimidating venue for any band, as the shadow of the Beatles hung over the city. But it went off pretty well: the acoustics of the hall were good, and there was standing room only, nine hundred people chanting their names and snatches of their songs.

Sometimes Bradley just sang while Christian took lead guitar, but mostly Christian and Bradley ended up taking lead guitar and bass while Josh and Pez backed them up on the keyboard and the drums.

Bradley was always at the forefront, but he was a pleasure to follow. Onstage it wasn't annoying that he was their golden leader: onstage it worked, and onstage Josh wasn't afraid to be with Christian. They all played very differently, but somehow when they were performing, it ended up in harmony. Somehow they were able to sweep everybody else along with them.

These were the only times Christian had ever felt like he belonged to something, like he belonged to some people, since he had become a vampire.

They came off the stage with most of their makeup sweated off, except for Christian, as vampires didn't sweat, and beaming, except for Christian, as Faye had forbidden him to look anything but vampirically brooding when there might be cameras around.

But he was possibly smiling a bit, face turned toward the inside of the high collar of his deeply embarrassing cape, as Bradley swept them all into their dressing room.

"How about that, then, boys?" Bradley asked. "The Beatles have nothing on us. Well, none of the Beatles were vampires, were they?"

He ruffled Christian's hair. Christian was in a good enough mood to let him.

"There were some rumors about John Lennon," he said.

He recounted the whole thing to his mum on the phone that night, and she seemed really impressed. She thanked him again for the front-row tickets for the show in Birmingham. He told her again how much he was looking forward to seeing her.

Christian hung up the phone and drew the lid of his coffin shut, and was content for a brief moment in the dark.

Then the lid of his coffin was pulled away with a wrench, leaving him blinking at his white hotel-room ceiling.

Until his ceiling was obscured by the face of a woman, leaning over his coffin with her black hair hanging into his eyes and her fangs glittering. Before he could speak, before he could even move, her cold hand was fastened at his throat.

"Hello, Chris," the vampire whispered.

Christian had never met a girl vampire before.

She was so quiet. There was no heartbeat, no breath or crackle of living cells. Christian found he did not want to meet her eyes and see how far from human he looked to everyone around him.

She said her name was Lucille.

She'd let him rise from his coffin. Now she was perched gracefully on a sofa in Christian's hotel suite and she'd refused his nervous offer of a glass of blood.

"Sometimes I enjoy a chilled glass of white wine, with a dash of blood warm from the wrist," Lucille remarked. "I call it the true rosé. Have you ever tried it?"

"Uh," Christian said. "No."

"I highly recommend it."

She was one of the vampires he'd read about, the ones who drank from human beings.

"So, Chris," Lucille said. "Are you going to share information with me willingly?"

She did not describe how she might persuade him if he was reluctant. She did not have to.

He could almost manage to look at her now, stealing glances and every time coming up with a new way in which she did not look human. Even the position in which she leaned back against the sofa, the precise arch of her spine, did not look right, as if she had forgotten entirely the limits her body used to have and the way her body used to work.

"Let's not play games, Chris," Lucille said softly. "What nest do you belong to?"

"Uh," Christian said. "Nest?"

"The other vampires you are associated with," Lucille explained. "Your eternal family." The expression on Christian's face must have remained pretty blank. Lucille's lip curled. "Who sent you here? What's your agenda?"

"I really don't understand."

"Come now, Christian," Lucille said, her voice more like an actual jungle cat purring than a noise an attractive woman should be able to make. "I'm entirely in sympathy with you. Making vampires more popular, making them part of the mainstream. Starting this whole revolution in how vampires are seen. It's quite brilliant. My nest is interested in forming an alliance with the vampires behind this scheme. So tell me, who made you?"

Christian looked away from her. "I was attacked," he said quietly. "They never caught the man who turned me. He never even meant to turn me. I cut him when I was trying to fight him off and swallowed the blood."

"Oh," said Lucille, her voice as hushed as if she were in a library.

Christian glanced back at her. She was looking at him as if she was seeing a human being for the first time.

No, wait; of course she wasn't: she was looking at him as if he was a person. And to her, the real people were vampires.

"Not a lot of vampires come into this alone, I take it," said Christian.

"Not a lot of vampires survive this alone," Lucille corrected. "So you have no nest?"

"There's no nest. There's no scheme," Christian said, and added quickly, "Sorry."

Lucille's alabaster brow wrinkled. "Seriously?"

"You're the second vampire I've ever met," Christian said. "Seriously."

Lucille regarded Christian with cool, suspicious eyes. Christian hoped she found his total fear and confusion convincing. They certainly convinced him.

"Why are you doing this, then?" Lucille asked at last. "If there's no plan, why?"

Christian thought of being up onstage tonight, facing the

Beatles' legacy and smiling at it, listening to the surge and roar of the crowd, and being companionable in the dressing room afterward.

Lucille had come here because of some gathering of vampires she'd called her nest. She might understand the urge simply to not be alone, to belong.

But Christian didn't want to have anything in common with her.

"I enjoy it," he said.

Lucille stared at him with cold, cold eyes, as if trying to judge his sincerity, as if measuring whether it would be worth her time to kill him.

"Well," she responded eventually. "I suppose there's nothing more to be said."

She got up, the movement a sliding, gliding thing more like an eel's than a woman's, and left.

She did not go far. Christian was just up himself the next evening, going through the blood bags in the big kitchen he shared with the rest of the band, adjoining onto all their suites. He was trying to find some O positive.

He was very surprised when Lucille staggered in.

She was still not moving like a human. She was moving a little bit like a giraffe on stilts. She was also wearing a green T-shirt with LOVE IS THE DRUG on it in purple letters, and her hair was all sticking up on one side of her head.

"Good evening, Christian," she said, and sat herself with

great, solemn care at the kitchen table.

Then she toppled forward, her face smacking against the wood.

In a slightly muffled voice, she said, "I feel most peculiar."

"Would you, er, like some bagged blood?" Christian offered, trying to be a good undead host. "It's A positive."

Lucille, her face still planted on the kitchen table, gave a full-body shudder. "Drink from a bag? I could never."

"Right," Christian said. "Because you shouldn't pop down to the shops and buy yourself a steak. You should go find a field and take a big bite out of a cow."

"All I had to do was knock on the door directly beside yours," Lucille said. "It was very simple. Much simpler than cows. Cows never have hotel rooms. Well, I suppose some cows might. Cows with credit cards."

"You knocked on Pez's door," Christian said. "Didn't you?"

"Sweet boy," Lucille told him. "Very amenable. But now I really do feel most peculiar. Have I said that already?"

At that point Bradley wandered in, wearing a headband and a muscle shirt. He looked at Lucille on the table and gave Christian a thumbs-up.

"She's a vampire," Christian said.

"I see that," said Bradley.

"She knocked on Pez's door last night," Christian continued, just to make things clear. "And now she feels most peculiar."

"Oh," said Bradley. "I realize this is a personal question, and

I have no wish to pry into a lovely lady's intimate affairs, but is Pez, er, alive?"

"Of course," Lucille told him in an offended voice. "I haven't lost control and killed a human in years."

"Awesome," Bradley said.

"Well, one year," Lucille conceded.

Christian and Bradley exchanged worried looks over Lucille's head.

"The O positive's in the back of the second shelf," Bradley told Christian. "Give her the A negative, you're always chugging that stuff trying to ignore the taste. Can you snag me a rhubarb-crumble yogurt?"

"Almost a year," Lucille murmured. "Ten months."

Christian passed Bradley the yogurt. Lucille propped herself up on one elbow. The elbow did keep slipping and getting away from her, but after a few tries she managed it.

Bradley regarded her with some concern. It had taken Christian a while to realize that Bradley, who was ridiculous and terrible in so many ways, was also naturally very kind.

"How many fingers am I holding up?" he inquired.

Lucille regarded him blearily and said, "Avocado," before her elbow got away from her again. "What was in that boy's blood?" she demanded, sounding feebly outraged.

"Hard to say," Christian told her. "I saw him eating dishwasher powder once."

Lucille twisted about in her chair, horribly graceful again

for a second, and focused on Bradley.

"Is your blood clean?" she asked.

Bradley hesitated. "My body is my temple," he said eventually. "Glowing and gorgeous inside and out."

Lucille tensed. Bradley was already a bit tense. Christian wondered what the hell he should do, and as he wondered he moved between them, shielding Bradley.

Josh came in through the door, saw the hungry look Lucille had fixed on Bradley, and backpedaled so fast he hit the door with a bang.

"No," he almost shouted, his breath coming too quickly. Christian opened the cupboard and started rummaging around for Josh's emergency inhaler, but Josh took a few more fast breaths and repeated, "No. Having one of you things around is bad enough—"

"Hey, don't talk about Chris that way!" Bradley snapped.

"Having a wild one that bites people—"

"I'm not a tame dog," Christian snarled. He saw the flicker of fear on Josh's face, and stepped back, the inhaler pressed hard against his palm.

Lucille stood, still a little shaky. "And we don't think of you as people."

Christian put the inhaler on the counter and seized her arm. The way Lucille stiffened and looked at him, her lip curled back from her razor-sharp teeth, he knew it would have been suicide any other time.

Fortunately, right now she was debilitated enough that

turning around rendered her so disoriented she swayed and had to hold on to Christian's arm.

She dug her pointed nails into his arm as she did so, and he swept her out of the room, safely away from Bradley and Josh, then faced a dilemma: she was a vampire preying on his bandmates and had to be eliminated, and yet she was also a lady in distress.

He called her a cab.

When he got back, Pez was sitting at a table being lectured by Josh and Bradley both at once.

"You've got to be safe, dude," Bradley told him. "Next time you sleep with a vampire, you've got to make her wear a gum shield."

"Or you could not consort with vampires!" Josh screeched.

"Josh, I swear to God," Bradley began.

"I didn't mean Chris," Josh said, somewhat to Christian's surprise. But then he assumed Josh meant "consorting" in a certain way, and despite the allegations of certain tabloids, Christian was not in the habit of consorting with his bandmates all night long.

"Wait," Pez said slowly. "That girl was a vampire?"

Christian had only been out of the coffin for half an hour, and he already had a migraine.

"What did you think was going on?" Bradley asked after a while.

He'd stopped looking frustrated, and now looked a little bit like he wanted to laugh. On the whole, Christian was glad: if the stress had given Bradley worry lines, Faye would have made them all suffer for it.

"I just thought she was a little rough-and-tumble," Pez said dreamily. "I went with it. I mean, whatever you're into, am I right? Don't be a hater."

Bradley really did laugh then, collapsing backward into a chair with his yogurt in one hand and his other hand held palm up.

"All right, then," he said. "Liverpool down, and the band scored a vampire groupie. High five."

"I don't think she counts as a—," Christian began.

"Hey," said Bradley. "She came, she saw, she sampled. She counts. High five."

Christian gave him the high five, and not too long after that they were in a tour bus trundling along the Mersey River, leaving Liverpool, city of the Beatles and their vampire groupie, far behind.

Birmingham was their third stop, and time for Christian's surprise. He had been surreptitiously collecting supplies behind Faye's back for weeks.

He still felt scared and sure that she was watching him, even though he'd used vampire vision and speed to take out the spy cameras on the tour bus and every hotel they'd stopped in. He found himself looking wildly around the hotel room as he slipped what he needed out from behind the lining of his coffin.

First came the orange T-shirt, with the picture of a giant turnip sitting on a sofa. The big green letters read BECAUSE COUCH POTATOES HAVE TOO MUCH AMBITION.

Then came the flip-flops, the sunglasses, and the baseball cap.

Christian could have tried for the lift, but that meant walking the halls of the hotel, where Faye could be prowling.

He was too much of a coward. So he decided to jump out the window.

The rush of the night air through his hair and the glitter of city lights too far below made a dozen remembered human survival instincts get together and carol, Oh my God, oh my God, we are going to dieeeee—

Then he landed, on one knee with his hand placed out in front of him, like a runner who was about to sprint.

He was barely on his feet when one of the hotel staff came outside for a cigarette. The guy gave him a critical look, and Christian fiercely resisted the urge to zoom away at vampire speed. Faye would know then, and she would find him. He knew she would find him.

Instead he tilted his head at the guy and tried to think of the least vampiric possible thing to say.

He settled for "'Sup?"

He could practically see the wheels turning in the man's mind—*That looks like* and *He is staying in*—a dozen thoughts, all being steadily turned away by the insistent, prevailing conviction that a vampire would not be caught undead in flip-flops.

"Hey," he said eventually, his voice creaking with unease.

"Nice night," Christian dared to offer, and then he walked at a steady, human pace, in his flip-flops, around the corner to freedom.

The house looked just like he remembered it. He would've thought it might seem smaller; that was what they said about coming back home and how you never really could. But it was the same size, the crazy paving forming the same pattern as it had when he had wound his way up it every day. All you had to do was follow it home.

It was when he was home, when he knocked on the door and it was thrown wide, that everything went wrong.

Rory answered the door. He was much taller than he had been: he was taller than Christian was, now.

Christian had been expecting a hug—the kind they used to give each other when Rory's football team won, thumping each other on the back hard and holding on.

Rory moved awkwardly, clumsily, backward. As if he still wasn't used to his new height, or he was scared.

Christian panicked, and tried out his new not-really-a-vampire mantra. "'Sup?"

"Mum!" Rory shouted, his voice cracking as he did so. "Mum! Christian's here!"

And maybe Christian wouldn't keep insisting that was his name to Faye and the band. Not when he had to hear it spoken like this.

They let him in, of course. Home was the place where when you came there, they had to let you in.

That didn't mean they wanted him there.

"Sorry," Mum said as soon as she gave Christian the cup of tea. She'd made it in jerky, slapping movements, like a tea-making robot, and she only seemed to think about what she had done once she had to be still.

Christian curled his cold fingers around the hot mug anyway. "That's okay, Mum. Thanks."

She hadn't hugged him either.

"We thought we'd see you at the concert tomorrow," Mum told him abruptly. "Rory's really been looking forward to it."

"Right."

"Not that it's not lovely to see you now, Christian!" Mum told him hastily.

He didn't like the way his mother said his name any more than he liked the way his brother had said it.

"Tell me," his mother continued, fumbling. "Tell me about the boys in your band. I always like to hear stories about your friend Bradley. He's a caution!" Her cheeks went pink. "Quite a good-looking boy too."

"Mum!" Christian exclaimed, scandalized.

Just the same, he told her about the time girls had literally hacked through the walls of Bradley's trailer with an ax, and as Mum refilled their cups of tea, she moved jerkily again and put her hot human hand against the angles of Christian's cheek.

It felt like she was sorry, then.

He still didn't belong there anymore. Rory still did not come down from his room. Nothing was the way it had been before, and it never would be again.

The next day the band played to a packed house, and Mum and Rory and a bunch of Rory's friends were in the front row, watching them with shining eyes, glitter and smoke in the air.

Christian was far enough away then, something to admire and be proud of, but not to take home.

This might be what Faye had meant. Nobody wanted the vampire for real.

Someone had invented the myth that vampires had to be invited in, because people wanted vampires to stay out.

Christian went into his dressing room, and thought, I could just go, now. They were just humans, they didn't have to be people to him, like Lucille had said.

He might as well go, because soon enough they would all be dead, but he was going to live forever.

He went. He went outside, and Faye's assistants ushered Mum, Rory, and his friends backstage, and he introduced them around. He was careful not to touch Rory, and Rory sent him a grin, shy and pleased and still a little nervous, before resuming his intense conversation with Josh about lighting and acoustics.

"Chris never told me he had such a—and I use this term advisedly—hot mama," said Bradley, leering and kissing her hand.

Christian's mum looked absolutely delighted. Christian smacked Bradley in the head.

Later Mum and Rory went home. Christian did not suggest accompanying them. He went back to the hotel with his bandmates, and Josh was a little more friendly to him than usual, as if it was a revelation to him that Christian had a family and might love them—that Christian could still be that much of a person.

Not enough of a person for his family.

Just before dawn, there was a knock on his door. Bradley stood on the threshold looking as subdued as he ever was, which for Bradley meant he was wearing very subtle glitter.

"I wanted to check if you were all right," he said, and Christian wondered how much Bradley had seen and understood about his mother and Rory.

He'd never heard Bradley talk about a family of his own.

"I'm getting by," Christian told him.

When Christian's coffin lurched and hit something, he assumed Bradley had got bored of playing knock-knock jokes and had decided to use Christian's coffin as an indoor surfboard in some sort of misguided band-bonding exercise.

He snapped awake and yelled, "Cut it out!"

Christian eased the coffin lid up with care, in case one of the band was actually stupid enough to be on top of it and, when nobody was, he tossed it aside and sat up.

Then he looked around at the dim, gray cell. Josh and Bradley were sitting close together, obviously having a heated discussion. Pez was sitting up by the coffin and rubbing his head.

"Are you hurt?" Christian asked him.

"Not really," Pez answered, with a grimace. "Our coffee was drugged. It knocked the other two out, but the guy who came inside the tour bus once they were down had to knock me out."

"You didn't drink the coffee?"

"No, I drank it," Pez said. "Found it quite soothing."

"You found the knockout drops quite soothing," Christian repeated.

"Sort of a mellow buzz," Pez told him earnestly.

At that point Bradley turned around and said, "Oh good, Chris, you're awake. We've been kidnapped."

"You sound extremely calm about this!" Christian exclaimed. He was not feeling terribly calm about it himself.

"That's right. I want everyone to stay calm," Bradley said. "It's fine. Someone will just want us to play a song just for them, or hold us for ransom, or want to marry one of us. Or all of us. I don't know and I don't judge; it takes all sorts in this beautiful world. Nobody panic."

So soothing was Bradley's voice, despite the completely

lunatic content of what he was actually saying, that nobody did panic until several hours later when they all noticed that Josh had scuttled, crablike, while still sitting down, through the gray dust on the floor and into the farthest corner of the room. He sat there, tense and trembling as a child being punished, until the combined weight of all their questioning stares pressed a cry from him.

"Have you noticed there's food for us?"

"Excellent, Josh, look on the bright side," Bradley said, with a beam of approval. For once Josh did not smile back.

"No," he said, his voice shaky. "Have you noticed there's food for us, but there's no food for him?"

Everyone looked at Christian, and it was as simple as that: the divide between "us" and "him," so neatly made.

"We're trapped in here with a vampire," Josh said slowly, as if this needed spelling out. "Exactly how long do you think it will take for him to start seeing us as juice boxes?"

There was a silence. Pez was glancing cagily, back and forth, between Bradley and Christian.

Eventually, Pez said, "Look, I'm really sorry, but I've forgotten: which of you is the vampire again?"

Josh looked despairing, but it made Bradley laugh, and once Bradley had laughed, apparently he thought he was in control of the universe again.

"This isn't a problem," he declared. "It won't be long before Faye comes to save us, right? And we all trust Chris."

He fixed both Pez and Josh with an imperious stare. Pez

looked blank, and Josh's mouth was a hard line. Christian remembered how Josh and Rory had got along, heads bent together in perfect understanding.

Josh was never going to trust Christian, or forgive him for being what he was.

"I wouldn't," Christian said quietly. "I would never—"

"And I'm totally happy to donate a little blood to keep him going," Bradley said.

Everyone else in the small cell went still, and that actually made Christian feel a little more kinship with the others. Now the line was not between the humans and the vampire, but between the sane and the crazed.

Bradley the lunatic rose from his lotus position with all the easy grace of someone who could do seventeen pop-and-locks in a row.

Christian shot backward with vampire speed, and hit the wall. "No!"

"Aw, Chris," Bradley said, and sounded very disappointed in him.

"I am not going to feed from a human being."

"Chris, this is really no time to be a fussy eater," Bradley told him, and advanced, holding up one arm. But not to protect himself from the vampire, no, that would be too sane for Bradley. "Here comes the vein train," Bradley coaxed. "Choo-choo!"

"Bradley, stop it."

"I see the problem," Bradley told him, and nodded. "You've

never done this before. You have performance anxiety."

Christian covered his face and said, "Oh my God, I hate you so much."

"But that's okay, I can help! There's something you guys don't know about me," Bradley said. "After I got bored with my modeling career, and before I joined the band, I dabbled in a little bit of acting."

Bradley struck a dramatic pose, sniffing the air, and then drew his own wrist close to his mouth.

"Ah," he murmured passionately. To his own wrist. "The blood is the life! The blood is the life!"

Even Pez was starting to look a little embarrassed by Bradley at this point.

Christian stood up, not like a dancer who could pop and lock, but like a vampire, like a storm coming in fast and relentless and inescapable. He seized Bradley's wrist, and slammed it up against the wall.

"I know you're trying to help," he said, fangs bared. "But don't."

He retreated then, back over the invisible line drawn between him and humanity. He sat against the wall and stared, knowing what they saw when they looked back at him: the vampire, alone and hungry, and no way to keep him out.

He couldn't continue to watch them. He didn't want to see their fear, not when he could already hear the pulsing, beckoning beat of their hearts.

Not when he was too hungry already.

For the humans, the days and nights bled into one another in that gray cell.

It was different for him.

There were no windows there, but Christian could feel the time changing, his body responding to the sun's coming and going. For the first two days, he put himself in the coffin and closed the lid over his face.

As the third night drew to a close, he realized he really didn't have the strength to get back into his coffin. He lay in his corner, in the gray dust, and felt the rise of the sun he could not see affect every molecule of his body. It felt like he was drying out, becoming something so dry that a single spark would set him on fire, turn him into a blaze of hungry, lunging flame, with no purpose but to be quenched or destroy everything in his path.

He could hear the others talking about him, their voices soft and worried and soothing. Even Josh sounded concerned for him rather than about him, so he knew he must look terrible.

A fuzzy halo of dreadlocks obscured his vision at one point. He mentally searched for a name, and found it: Pez.

"Hey," Pez murmured. "Hey. Look. I've already been bitten by one vampire, right? And it wasn't so bad. Besides, you're my pal."

Christian felt his dry lips split as he spoke. "Get away."

He had never been able to imagine it before, biting another person. It had been as alien to him as the thing he'd compared it to as a human, going down into a field and sinking his blunt human teeth into a cow.

Starvation made even humans wild.

Real vampires are scary, said Faye's voice, soft and imaginary in his ear. *We don't want that.*

He could picture doing it now, doing what had always repelled him before. He saw why vampires back in the old days had been thought of as savage beasts, before it was possible to keep the beast fed and trained, make the dangerous stay safe.

He could almost feel the slide of his teeth against a neck, the breaking skin and the warm sweet flow of blood in his mouth, penetrating every parched cell of him.

They were just two idiots and a coward who had always hated him.

Bradley was the stupidest man in the world. He spent all his time learning to pop and lock and bestowing his radiant handsomeness on the world, and he'd taken an actual vampire under his wing despite all of Christian's efforts not to be so taken. Nobody that stupid deserved to live.

And Pez let every passing vampire snack on him and forgot sometimes what their job was, but remembered to thank Christian for buying the groceries.

Then there was Josh, Christian thought. Josh had never liked him, had always feared him. Josh would not even be surprised if Christian attacked him. He had been expecting Christian to act like a monster from the moment they met. Christian had never been able to prove him wrong.

Maybe it was time to prove him right.

As if Christian's thoughts had summoned him, there was Josh, hovering over him. The wire-rimmed glasses Faye had assured him were the height of geek chic gleamed.

"Chris," he whispered. "Chris. I can see you're really trying, and I know—I know drinking from Pez made that girl act awfully weird, and I know you don't like Bradley. I know you're the one who keeps spare inhalers for me in the tour bus. If you really have to, if you have to . . . you can."

Christian's ears were filled with the anxious, alluring beat of Josh's heart.

He turned his face away, the gray dust bitter between his lips, and waited for Josh to go away.

But Josh didn't go away.

He reached out, as Rory hadn't, at the door of the place that had once been Christian's home. Christian felt the inside of Josh's wrist, skin stretched thin over the vein, brush his mouth.

Christian reared up, sent Josh flying backward, and was on him before Josh hit the ground.

He could hear the hiss of breath from everyone in their little cell who could breathe. He could hear the thump of Josh's heart, clearer than ever, as he drew the collar of Josh's button-down shirt away from his throat and saw the darker thread of a vein against his pale skin.

Christian bowed his head to that tracing, like a line on a map leading Christian to life, and bit.

Blood filled his mouth and then was gone. He gulped again, heat running down his throat, lacing its way through and through his body. His skin was tingling, waking back up, and all he wanted was more.

Then he felt Bradley's hands on his arm, on the back of his neck, tugging gently. Bradley was so warm it burned.

"Chris," he whispered. "Oh, Christian. Come on, please. Let go."

That vampire Lucille drank from humans. She couldn't go a year without killing one.

Christian swallowed one last hot, sweet mouthful of blood—not enough—and let Bradley pull him back.

"Get your hands off me," Christian whispered, "or I'll kill you."

It was strange to say something like that, to be something like this, and to mean every word.

He retreated from them all, watching them, drawing the line between him and them for their own protection. Bradley looked ready to advance and comfort him at any time. Pez was frowning worriedly. Even Josh was sitting up, glasses askew, and squinting at him in what looked like concern. There were two small holes on his throat, but they were barely bleeding; Christian listened to his heartbeat, and it was strong.

He'd bitten one of them, and it almost seemed as if they understood.

But he knew he would need blood again, and he had to protect them from that.

"Thank you," he said, and shut his eyes.

"Maybe they left us down here with Chris on purpose," Josh

whispered, some time later. "Maybe they're some sort of anti-vampire hate group, and they want us all dead and for Chris to get the blame."

"Well, Chris hasn't hurt us," Bradley said sharply.

"I know," Josh whispered back, to Christian's faint surprise. "But what will they do to us, when they see he hasn't?"

Pez spoke, in an unexpectedly clear voice. "I calculate that our chances of dying are approximately ninety-eight percent," he said, and then, "What? Sometimes I like to do mathematics in my head for fun. I find statistics fascinating."

"No you don't, you eat dishwasher powder," Josh said.

Pez asked, "I can't have depths?"

Everyone was lying flat on their backs in the dust, telling secrets. Christian thought vaguely that it was supposed to be a show of solidarity for him.

"I've never loved another woman like I love Faye," Bradley said dreamily, and that was when the door swung inward.

And Christian could move after all, move using all the strength given to him by Josh's blood, a promise of death launched at the throat of their enemy, and he snarled, "Leave my nest alone!"

His survival instinct stopped him with his fangs an inch from her throat, because he caught the scent of chrysanthemum perfume and evil. It was Faye.

It was Faye, as if Bradley had conjured her like a genie by speaking her name, and as she applied her sharp wooden heel to his kneecap in an almost affectionate way, Christian collapsed onto the floor with a sense of overwhelming relief.

It wasn't an antivampire hate group. It wasn't a crazed fan who wanted to marry one or all of them. It was just some guy—a rumpled, ordinary-looking guy—who blinked at them as if he didn't recognize them and managed to drawl out, "I wanted to be on TV."

When the colonel—because somehow Faye had managed to come to their rescue with the army at her back—asked him why he had left a vampire in a room with three humans and no other sustenance, he said, "Oh," in a dismayed voice. "I just forgot that one was a vampire. Gee, I'm real glad nothing bad happened." He paused for a moment, and then added, "If something bad had happened . . . would there be more cameras?"

And there it was, as banal and ridiculous as that, some guy who did not care about them at all but only about the insubstantial and strange notion of fame, which had barged in on Christian like an uninvited and confusing guest, leaving glitter in the air and his eyes half blinded by the snapping glare of those cameras.

A lot of what seemed to be about them was about the fame, really.

Christian had drunk three bags full of blood—and sweeter than the cold, viscous liquid was the crackle of plastic under his fingers, the knowledge this was not a human being—and then they had put him in his coffin.

He could hear them still talking as he lay in the cool, clean silk, rescued, not having hurt a soul.

"How did you get soldiers to turn out, Faye?" asked Bradley, admiring and flirtatious at once.

"The man came from an enemy nation," Faye told him.

Bradley hesitated. "Canada?"

"They're a rebellious people. All that ice hockey, it fires the blood. I required soldiers to bring them down." Faye paused. "Besides, my father is in the army. He's a general, actually. Do you know, he taught his little girl how to kill a man in twenty-seven different ways with my bare hands?" She paused again, this time possibly in dreamy reminiscence. "But the army wasn't cutthroat enough for me," she concluded. "It had to be showbiz. Or being an assassin for hire, of course."

"Of course," said Bradley.

"I'm scared, and I want to go back to the kidnapper," Josh announced, his voice closer to the coffin than Josh usually allowed himself to be.

"And who are you again?" Pez inquired benevolently. There was a rustling noise, and Christian hoped he'd hidden all the actually poisonous stuff where Pez couldn't find it this time.

"That was a lovely shot of Chris leaping to defend you guys," Faye told them all. "What did he call you? His nest?"

"I heard 'best,'" Bradley said. "As in . . . best mates."

"That's what I heard too," said Josh, who turned out to be the worst liar in the world. He giggled nervously as he said it.

"What's that on your neck, Josh?" Faye asked.

"It was a very, very enthusiastic groupie," Bradley said with conviction. "Don't worry, though, Josh didn't encourage her. She wasn't his type."

There was a long silence. Josh giggled again, this time sounding a little hysterical.

"Oh, all right, I'll let it go," Faye conceded. "But I'm hiring your next kidnapper myself so I can set the stage properly."

The tour bus was rocking as they moved toward their next stop, so gently that it was almost like being rocked to sleep in the darkness of his coffin. Oddly enough, Christian thought of the nonsensical rote lines Bradley had spouted about a tour being a journey of discovery. He didn't mind where the journey was going, he thought, and his eyes slid shut.

Then, directly above his head, there was a rapping of knuckles on wood.

"Knock, knock," Bradley caroled joyfully.

"Who's there?" Christian asked.

There was a long enough pause to let Christian know that Bradley was actually startled. Christian had never replied before.

We'll learn things about each other, about the fans. About ourselves.

"Me," said Bradley, on a laugh.

"Me who?"

"Meow," Bradley responded, with great satisfaction. As he proceeded to tell an enormously stupid joke about a cat,

Christian let his mind drift away again, into thoughts of vampires who were scary and not safe but who just might manage to be safe enough, enjoying his job, having humans around who he could not stop remembering were people before they were food, humans who might be something like a nest.

Bradley had said the tour meant they would be bonding closer than ever as a band.

It was possible, even though it was a genuinely terrifying thought, that Bradley was a genius.

BRIDGE
by Jeri Smith-Ready

Everyone knows
Elvis died in the bathroom.
Thanks to the internet,
everyone knows
that I did too.
But at least I was wearing pants.

My favorite Quiksilver cargo shorts,
which I'll wear every moment
that I stay in this world.
No laundry needed,
because ghosts never sweat
or piss
or anything.
I'm as dry as the bones
crumbling in my casket.

"Must be nice,"
Aura mumbles into her pillow
when I tell her
I'm going to meet George Clooney.
That's our code
for "the beach,"
because when lifelong Baltimoreans
say "down to the ocean,"
it sounds like
"Danny Ocean."

When we were kids,
our gang of friends
pretended we were in *Ocean's Eleven*.
My big brother, Mickey, was Clooney
and I was Brad Pitt.

We'd stroll down the Ocean City boardwalk,
not nearly as slick as we imagined.
Our illusion of cool would crumble
whenever Aura or anyone younger
had to dodge the dead.

"Post-Shifters," they call themselves,
the generation who sees ghosts.
I'd be one

if I'd been born two months later.
I'm glad I wasn't,
since ghosts can't see each other,
not even the ghosts of post-Shifters.
It was bad enough to lose the living
without losing the dead too.

"Senior Week trip,"
I remind Aura.

She opens her
espresso-drop eyes.
And though the morning light
washes out my violet glow,
making me invisible,
those eyes find mine.

Aura never looks through me.

She whispers, "Good luck,"
and reaches out her hand.
I cover it with my own,
wishing I could hold it.
I'd pull it to my lips,
against my cheek,
around my waist,
down my back.

Both hands,
squeezing,
sliding,
stroking.

It never ends,
this desire.
Not for me.

But Aura dreams of other hands.
In her sleep,
she whispers his name.
I wonder how much is hope
and how much is memory.
I don't want to know.
Because whether she sighs for the past
or sighs for the future,
she sighs for him.

"It's sooooo hot."
My sister, Siobhan, winds her hair
into a purple-streaked black knot,
then cranks up the car's air-conditioning.

I can't feel the breeze,

but the rattle and hum of the compressor
sound comfortingly normal
to this paranormal dude.
We're stuck bumper to bumper on the
Chesapeake Bay Bridge,
just like old times.

In the driver's seat,
Mickey turns the AC knob back down.
"It spits out hot air
when you put it on max."

Siobhan scuffs her Skechers
against the Corolla's frayed blue floor mat.
"*When* are you getting rid of
this old piece of shit?"

"When I can afford
a new piece of shit."

She stretches her neck—
a fiddler's habit,
but she does it when she's stressed.
Her mouth opens, ready to shout,
"You *can* afford it!"

But Mickey won't spend a penny

of what he calls my "blood money."
The millions our folks won
from the record company,
who sold me a dream
and gave me the bullet
that took my life.

In the backseat beside me,
Siobhan's boyfriend, Connor,
sleeps,
lips pale and slack.

"We deserved that money," she tells Mickey,
"for what they put us through."

"We deserve nothing."
Mickey's voice is as flat as the farmland
beyond the bridge.
"We were supposed to take care of him."

(They won't say my name.)

"Stop punishing yourself."
Siobhan sounds too scared
to be mad,
which is saying a lot.

"Please."
"Spend the money," Mickey says,
"if it makes you feel better."

Our sister's eyes fill with tears,
and I want to kill him.

"I hate you," she whispers to her twin.

"I hate you too," her twin whispers back.

I want to wake Connor,
tell him to make peace.
That's what bass players are for, right?
But he hasn't been
our bass player
since the night I died
and killed the Keeley Brothers
forever.

As the car creeps,
and Connor sleeps,
and Siobhan weeps,
Mickey . . .

Mickey exists.

Siobhan has to pee.
But the truck stop is new,
so I can't follow them.
Ghosts can only go in death
to the places they went in life,
like a hamster in a Habitrail.

Mickey puts on his blinker.

"Don't leave me."
I lunge forward,
grab for the steering wheel,
hoping
this time I'll touch something,
this time they'll hear me.

This time is like all the rest.

The car turns,
and I'm left standing in the highway.
A red Jeep,
the top down,
full of blondes
already sunburned,
drives through me.

I'll never get used to that.
Screw this traffic.
I can go anywhere in an instant.
I can be Danny Ocean in three . . . two . . .

A seagull shits right through me.

I wander the beach,
the sun blaring my form
into nothingness.
Invisible, I can stare all I want.

A girl with Aura's dark wavy hair
and bronze skin
sips an iced tea,
then sets the open cup on her belly.
As she swallows,
her throat bobs,
then her tongue peeks through her lips,
gathering the moisture she missed.
Water beads on the cup,
plummets fearlessly,
like a skater on a half-pipe.
When it reaches her skin,

it joins her sweat
and travels on,
over her waist
and under the string of her
candy-striped bikini.

I could write an entire song
about the journey
of that one drop of sweat.

But I turn away.
It feels wrong to watch.
These girls are here to be seen,
but not by someone they can't see.
So guilt keeps me from lingering.
I may be dead,
but I'm still Catholic.

I head for the boardwalk
to find someone
who can speak my words to Mickey.
I can't use Aura
or my little brother, Dylan,
or anyone else I care about.

Only a stranger

won't judge
me
or Mickey
for letting this keep us apart.

Only a stranger
can hold up the wall
we need between us.

Until we're ready to tear it down.

Occasionally,
sometimes
—okay, usually—
people ignore me.
Post-Shifters pretend they can't see
the ghosts around them.
It's cool, I get it.
They have lives that can't stop
every time a ghost needs help.
(And we all need help.)
They have lives.

But after 233 days of death,

I can tell the difference
between being ignored
and being invisible.

The arcade is full of shadows.
I'm standing in one now,
next to the Skee-Ball court.
But no one sees me.

I step in front of a scrawny guy
who looks fifteen or sixteen
in his oversize D.C. United jersey.

"Dude, help me out. I just need—"

He walks through me,
counting his tickets
out loud to himself.

A girl with blond pigtails
sucking a green lollipop
bends over to slip tokens into a driving game.
Her jean shorts ride up,
giving a glimpse of pink underwear.

I step up next to the game.
"Sorry to interrupt,

but I need a huge favor."
She plops her teeny ass
into the driver's seat
without so much as a twitch
at my voice
or my semifamous face.

As she starts to play,
I wave my hand between her and the screen.
She holds the wheel steady,
pressing the accelerator,
sucking the lollipop,
which twists her muttered curses
into drunk-sounding slurs.

I step back.
Survey the crowd.
Try not to panic.

Above us,
a banner stretches the length of the arcade,
The BEST WEEK EVER logo
frames the words
Congratulations, Class of—

"Damn it."
Senior Week.

No one here is young enough to see me.
I fly through the arcade,
turning somersaults,
flailing my arms like a clown,
hoping someone brought
their little brother
or sister
or niece or nephew
or cousin.

But who would bring a kid to Senior Week?
Parents know better.
They hear the stories.

I am so screwed.

The boardwalk never seemed so loud,
so bright,
so *complete*
as it does tonight.

I'm here
but not.

They stagger through me,

"the way you held him the night he died."
The statue shatters on the floor.
Jesus's head pops off,
shoots through my feet,
rolls under the shelf across the aisle.

Mickey brushes past Krista,
making another escape.

She grabs his wrist,
her fingers a handcuff.
"Look! I don't have time to chase you
while you pretend you don't want to talk to him.
So let's just do this, okay?"

He scowls down at her.
"Who are you?"

"I'm no one."
She lets go of his wrist.
"I think that's the point."

The ocean's rhythm
isn't.
I count the seconds between waves

and realize that
they crash when they crash,
with no regular timing,
like our ex-drummer
when he was drunk.

Like my heart's final beats,
1,000
in three minutes.

The waves' arrhythmia
is all I hear in my brother's silence.

We sit side by side on the pier,
our legs dangling over the edge.
He and Krista pass a cigarette
back and forth
through me.
Mickey has quit smoking
six times in two months.

I splay my fingers,
admiring how the smoke curls
around and within
their violet glow,
like dry ice at a rock concert.

Mickey drops the cigarette butt
into his can of Pepsi.
It sizzles as the fire dies.

"He was so heavy."

He presses the back of his hand
against his mouth,
as if those four words
are the first drops in a flood
that will drown us all.

"Heavy, like a sandbag,
in my arms.
And behind that door.
It took both of us,
me and our sister, Siobhan,
to push it open.
I thought, What idiot got so wasted
they passed out on our bathroom floor?
And probably puked all over
Mom's favorite guest towels,
and we'll have to clean it up,
and I swear to God,
this is the last party
we'll ever have."

He shakes the Pepsi can,
the cigarette butt rattling
staccato.

"So the door finally opens,
and there's no puke,
no blood,
no nothing.
Just him.
Clean and dead."

I remember watching Mickey
drag my body into the hall,
start CPR with Siobhan.
No matter how much they pressed
and breathed
and cried
and cursed
and screeeeeeeeeamed,
I couldn't come back.

"I'm sorry."

Krista repeats my words.

"Who's sorry?" Mickey asks her.
"You or him?"

"When I speak for myself,
I'll hold up my hand."
She makes a Boy-Scouty gesture,
then lowers her hand.
"Logan is sorry."

He flinches at the sound of my name.
"What the hell's he sorry about?"

"I don't know," I tell him.
"But you were really pissed off that night,
so I figured I should apologize."

Mickey puts his head in his hands
when he hears my answer.
"I didn't mean to yell at him."

"You always yelled at me."
I pause to let Krista translate.
"Why would you stop when I died?"

"I did not always yell at him!"

Krista raises her hand.
"You're yelling at him right now."

"Well—he—"

Mickey chokes out six
or seven
incoherent syllables
before lurching to his feet.
He stomps away,
down the boardwalk.
Fast enough for drama
but slow enough to follow.

"Sorry."
I hunch my shoulders
as Krista stands, sighing.

"Stop saying 'sorry.'
Mickey should be saying that."

"He won't."
I get up to join her.
"He's a douche."

❧ ·❀· ❧

"Your turn to talk,"
Krista tells me
as we catch up to Mickey
down the boardwalk.

The first question is easy.
"Ask him why he hates me."

She rolls her eyes,
but does as I ask.

"I don't hate him," he says,
but too quick,
like a reflex,
like someone,
maybe a therapist,
has asked that question before.

"You think I'm a sellout," I tell him.
"You think I don't care about the music."

This he doesn't deny,
just shoves his hands deeper
into his pockets,
slows his pace,
glares harder at the wooden slats
in front of his feet.

"So if I'm a sellout,"
I continue, slowly enough
that Krista can translate,

"then why did we play
all those songs I wrote?
Why were they good enough,
when I wasn't?"

Mickey glares at her.
"I never said he wasn't good enough."

"Don't talk to me," Krista tells Mickey.
"Talk to Logan."

He stops short and turns to her.
"Okay, L—"
My name catches on his tongue.
"You were good.
You were amazing.
You took my fucking breath away."
His eyes skewer hers.
"But it wasn't enough, was it?
No, you had to be famous.
You had to be famous *yesterday*.
You couldn't wait until we were older,
when you could handle it.
You were just a kid,
a stupid kid."

Mickey's face crumples,
red with rage
and something else.
He clutches his hands
in his thick brown hair,
like he could tear it out.

"And now you'll never be older.
You'll never be
anything,
ever,
but a stupid kid."

As I stare at Mickey,
feeling twelve years old again,
a whimper comes from my right.

I turn,
and Mickey turns,
to see Krista,
her eyes wide and wet,
lower lip trembling—
classic
girl
pre-cry
symptoms.

Mickey's hands come up,
as if to grasp her shoulders.
"Oh God, I'm sorry.
I was looking at you,
but I swear I was talking to him.
You were just—"

She slaps him,
hard enough
to knock the self-righteous mask
clean off his face.

"Logan's right," she hisses.
"You are a douche."

❧ ❧ ❧

Jim Morrison died in the bathtub.
They buried him in Paris,
but some people think he's still alive,
just like Elvis.
That he'd had enough
of this bogus life
and decided to get
a brand-new one.

My brother and I

catch up to Krista
near the entrance to the
Jolly Roger Amusement Park.
She's wiping away the tears
with her fists,
as if she can pummel her sadness
into submission.

"I'm sorry," Mickey says
(to her).
"Can we start over?"

"No."
Sniffle.
"But we can keep going."

"Your turn," I say to Krista.
"Tell us why you freaked.
But first, make Mickey buy you
a funnel cake."

On a bench
by the Ferris wheel
they eat.
I crouch a few feet in front of them,

in the middle of the foot traffic.
Apparently I never sat on that bench
in my whole life.

"My brother died when I was ten."
Krista tugs off a long string of fried dough
and dangles it into her mouth.
Powdered sugar
showers over the edge of her lips
down to her chin.
I wonder if Mickey wants to lick it off.
I would
if I could smell
and taste,
or think of anyone but Aura.

"What happened?" Mickey asks.

"OD'd."
A strong breeze
sweeps her hair into her mouth
as she speaks and eats.
She tucks it behind her ear.
"Officially an accident."

"Officially?"

"I think he killed himself.
Otherwise he probably would've haunted me."

Right.
To become a ghost,
your death has to be a surprise.
(Boo.)
People who thought it'd be easier
to be a ghost
than to be alive
found that out the hard way.

"How old was he?" Mickey asks Krista.

"Eighteen.
Like you."
Another bite,
another struggle
against the blowing hair.
"You're thinking of doing it, aren't you?"

If I had breath,
I would hold it now,
waiting for Mickey's answer.

"I don't think of dying," he says,

"so much as I think of not living."

It starts to rain,
suddenly,
strenuously,
as if heaven itself
is bawling,
spitting,
pissing
on my brother
and his death wish.

You go, God.
If he doesn't want his life,
can I have it?
I'd be a miserable,
pretentious
son of a bitch
if it meant living again.
I'd be him.

"Keep most of the lights off,"
Krista tells Mickey
as we enter our cousins'

beachfront condo,
where our family has stayed
since I was fourteen.
"That way I can still see Logan."

"I'll get you a towel.
And do you want a dry—"
He looks away
from her sodden T-shirt.
He has a girlfriend,
after all,
a girlfriend he's barely touched
in 233 days.

He heads down the hall,
but she lingers by the front door,
checks that it's unlocked.

"He won't hurt you," I tell her.

"I know," she whispers.
"But after that Cindy girl died
at spring break,
my parents gave me the Talk.
They said,
'Just because you graduated a year early

doesn't mean you can't be stupid.'"

We go to join Mickey,
passing the open door
of Siobhan's room
and the closed door
where my younger brother Dylan and I
used to stay.
I've been there a hundred times
since I died.

Mickey stands before his bed,
his suitcase open.
"My sister'll kill me if I steal one of her shirts,
so take this.
Keep it."

She unfolds the army-green T-shirt,
and the light spilling from the hall
reveals the skull-and-shamrock logo
of the Keeley Brothers.

I blink hard,
memories bathing my brain
like acid.
"He never wears that," I tell her.
"Why does he have it with him now?"

She asks him.

Mickey slaps shut the suitcase,
but not before I see
the hint of
dull
black
metal
tucked into the corner.

"Don't leave him alone," I tell Krista.
"He's got a gun."

She steps back,
fear in her eyes.
"Is it loaded?" she asks him.

He stares at her,
making the connection.
"Not yet."

She snatches the dry towel splayed across the bed.
"Turn around. Both of you."

I watch him instead of her,
count the ribs showing
through his skin

when he changes his own shirt.

"Now what?"
Krista's stuffing her wet bra
into the front pocket of her jeans.
Mickey's shirt is huge on her
but not huge enough
to hide her curves.

I spy the guitar case in the corner.
"Ask him to play."
We have to get something
into his hands
besides that gun.

Music was always my savior.
Maybe it'll be his too.

He tries a few tunes
by candlelight
on the living room sofa,
but his fingers seem numb,
his voice, starved.

Krista looks dubious.

"Mickey's much better than this," I tell her.
"He got accepted to a conservatory,
but don't bring that up.
He's not going."
I answer her quizzical look with,
"Because of the money."

Mickey stops
at the start
of the third verse.
"I forget the rest.
You should go."

He looks through her,
toward the hallway,
toward the bedroom,
toward the gun.

"Wait!"
I jump out of my seat.
"Ask him to play my song,
the one he's writing for me."

"Play Logan's song," she tells him.

He glances in my general direction,
then focuses on her.
"Dylan told him?"

She nods when I nod.

"Brat can't keep a secret."
Mickey sets the guitar in his lap again,
tunes.
Tunes some more.
And then some more.
Tunes
tunes
tunes,
But never plays.

Krista shifts in her chair,
stretches her bare feet,
which are probably
falling asleep.

Her movement stops Mickey,
fingers on the guitar's pegs.
He lowers the head
and lets the instrument
roll forward,

strings facing down
in his lap.

"I haven't written it yet," he says.
"Not one note, in all these months."

Krista holds up her hand,
speaking for herself.
"Why not?"

He traces the curve of the guitar's body
with his palm,
and I want more than ever to be him
for one moment,
touching the smooth wood.
I would make it sing.

Finally he says,
"Writing his song
would be too much like saying good-bye."

I can't believe I'm hearing this.
"That's bullshit, and you know it!"

Before she can finish translating,
I point straight at his heart.

"You've been saying nothing
but good-bye
since the night I died.
All you care about
is me passing on,
getting out of your life."

Krista speaks my words,
inflecting them just like me,
and I wonder how much anger
is mine
and how much is hers.

Mickey says,
"I just want him to be at peace."

"No!" I hurl back.
"You want *you* to be at peace.
And you think dying—
or at least not living—
is the best way to find it.
And I totally don't get that."

Krista says what I said,
then turns to me.

"I get that," she chokes out.
"He thinks he could've stopped you.
He thinks he could've saved you."

"I could have."
Mickey grips the neck of the guitar.
"I could've kept the drugs
out of his hands."

I shake my head.
"You saw me turn it down,
just like you and Siobhan—"

"I should've known,"
Mickey says over me.
"I should've known
that record company rep
would push him harder
when I wasn't looking.
He was always so eager to please.
I should've asked later.
One question:
'Did you keep the cocaine?'
But I was too busy
and too annoyed,
thinking, He's a such a big shot now

he can take care of himself,
and if he can't,
that's his fault."
Mickey closes his eyes.
"One question.
It could've saved his life."

I turn my head
from the sight of the pain
that's twisted Mickey's memory
and broken his soul.
I did this to him.

"He knows that's not true," I tell Krista.
"He knows I would've lied.
I always lied
to keep from pissing him off."

He gives a bitter laugh.
"Yeah, or to keep from pissing off
Dad."

Then Mickey freezes,
his eyes creasing harder than ever.
"Oh God."
He clutches his elbows,

bends forward like he'll be sick.
"He was afraid of me."

Krista raises her hand.
"He still is."

"Why? When?
I thought . . .
I thought we were friends."

I try to remember
when Mickey and I were friends.
Before we were
the Keeley Brothers
with a capital B?
Maybe when he was George Clooney
and I was Brad Pitt.

"So what do you want?"

I realize Krista's talking to me.

"Huh?"

"What do you want?" she repeats.
"You brought us together

so you could talk to him.
What do you want him to know?"

Mickey braces himself,
hands squeezing his knees,
eyelids squeezing each other,
like he's about to be sprayed
with poison.

After 233 days,
I have no eloquent speech,
no moving lyrics.

"Besides being alive again,
I want . . . more than anything . . ."

I wait while she translates,
then continue,
so she won't have to stop
through this next part.

"I want you to know
that I love you, dude.
And no matter what you think,
it wasn't your fault.
It was mine.

But I forgive you
for not saving me
from myself."

I wait for him to explode with,
"*You* forgive *me?*
That's a good one.
You should beg *me*
to forgive *you*
for ruining my life,
for hurting
Mom
and Dad
and Dylan
and Siobhan
and everyone else
stupid enough to love you."

But instead,
Mickey's shoulders rise
and fall
in the longest,
fiercest
breath
I've seen him take in months.

He closes his eyes
and pulls the head of the guitar
toward his own,
presses the pegs
against his forehead,
so hard,
that when he turns
to look straight at me,
not through me,
there's a dent
in his skin.

"Thank you."

And then.

(Uh-oh.)

He starts to cry.

I haven't seen this
since the night I died.
I don't know what to do.

But Krista does.

She kneels before him
and takes the guitar from his lap.
He sinks forward
into her arms,
adding his tears
to the water from her hair
speckling her new shirt.

They cry together
for their
loved,
lost,
dumb
brothers.

❧ ❧ ❧

Kurt Cobain
didn't die in the bathroom,
because he died on purpose.
Anyone with a plan
wouldn't choose the bathroom,
unless they're super considerate
and thinking of the mess.

I don't know

if Mickey was thinking of Cobain
when he decided
Ocean City would be the last stop
on the road trip of his life.
I don't know
what he was thinking
when he packed
that gun
and that shirt.

But the important thing is,
Krista now has both.

When the rain ends,
we take Mickey's guitar
to the beach,
find a spot where I sat
when I was alive.
He plays
with trembling fingers
and a voice
rough from weeping
but stronger than before.

Others gather around,
in twos and threes.
Mickey takes requests,

but mostly he plays
our old favorites.
For once, I carry the harmony
instead of the melody,
since Krista's are the only ears
that hear me.

Siobhan and Connor appear,
fiddle and guitar in hand,
summoned by a text from Mickey.
And now it's like
a Keeley Brothers
acoustic reunion gig.
Perfect.

But after a while,
I fall silent
and just watch
my brother and sister
sing without me
smile without me
live without me.
They'll be okay.
Without me.

I give Krista a soft "Thanks"
and brush her shoulder

with a hand she can't feel.
She watches
as I stand and turn away.

I'm pretty sure
what she's done tonight
wouldn't count as
an official Senior Week
"Play It Safe" activity.
But Mickey was long past
being saved by safety.

I walk to the edge of the water
where I can still hear their voices
mixed with the ocean.
The lifeguard stand beside me
is empty and bare
except for one thing:

a long black ribbon
faded to gray,
the name *Cindy*
printed in gold-turned-yellow.

The girl who drowned at spring break.
That's how she'll be remembered—

for her death,
not her life,
as people our age always are.

Did she become a ghost?
Is she standing next to me
right this second?
Has she already passed on?

My own trip to peace,
too long and too strange,
is nearing the end.
Mickey was my last,
biggest,
scariest
detour.

Behind me I hear Krista say,
Something-something "lifeguard stand,"
and I want to run
or swim
or just disappear.
But I stay.

As the next song starts, it's missing
one voice.

Soft feet thump the sand behind me,
one pair.

I don't turn,
don't hope,
don't dare.

My brother stands beside me,
alone.
He takes a deep, soft breath,
and speaks my name.

SKIN CONTACT
by Kimberly Derting

Rafe stopped where he was in the middle of the blacktop and stared out ahead of him, straining to see through the darkness. He tried to gauge how far the road stretched before him, tried to calculate how much farther he had to walk.

He really didn't need to see, though. He knew, even without ever having been there before. He was close now.

He started walking again, counting his paces as the chain that hung from his wallet slapped against his hip in a steady rhythm. Trees rose up from both sides of the narrow stretch of deserted highway, and the sound of gravel crunching beneath his heavy black boots was the only noise he could hear. It seemed too loud, and it reminded him of how alone he was out there, in the dead of the night. He felt like a target, walking down the middle of the road like that.

It had been easy enough to ignore the strange look from the trucker he'd hitched a ride with, when he told the old guy he'd be walking the rest of the way. Rafe knew what he'd been thinking when the rig shuddered to a stop in front of the insignificant mile marker—not even a real exit—with no restaurant or gas station in sight: Walking to where? Where the hell was this kid going, out here in the middle of nowhere?

But it didn't matter what that grizzled old fart thought; Rafe *needed* to be here. He had to find out if this was real or not.

From somewhere behind him, he heard a bird—an owl, probably. He'd never actually heard one in real life before, he'd only seen them in cartoons as a kid, but that was exactly what they'd sounded like on TV.

He continued counting his steps and doing the math in his head. Fifty-six down. A hundred and sixteen to go.

A hundred and fifteen . . . fourteen . . .

How do I know that? How can I possibly know how many more steps I have to take till I get there?

He shrugged, feeling the weight of his backpack, heavy on his shoulder. He just did, that's all. He used to doubt them—his dreams, the ones that came to him like memories—but he was starting to realize that they were rarely wrong. Even when he wanted them to be, like this time. He wanted so badly for this one to be wrong . . . just a plain old stupid fucking dream.

He reached into his coat pocket and pulled out the cell phone he'd bought at the truck stop where he'd hitched his last ride. It was one of those prepaid deals, so no one could track him down, so no one could figure out where he'd gone.

He flipped it open to make sure he still had service—way the hell out here. There were three bars left; he shouldn't have a problem placing the call when the time came.

When he tucked the phone away again, his fingers brushed over the doll Sophie had given him before she'd disappeared, and his chest ached as he rubbed his thumb and forefinger over the woolly hair sticking up from its head. He missed Sophie. He missed holding her, kissing her, arguing with her.

The doll was one of those ugly little trolls with a scrunched-up face and a naked stocky body and shocking neon-pink hair. Only this one had been altered. Sophie had used a Sharpie to streak its pink hair, and to paint its fingers and toes her favorite color: black. She'd even given it a piercing, shoving a tiny silver stud through its wide, flat nose. She called it her lucky doll.

"Here, keep him," she'd said, pressing the doll into Rafe's hand and forcing him to close his fingers around it.

"I'm not keeping Goober."

"His name is *Goob*, and I want you to have him. This way you won't forget me while I'm gone."

Rafe had tossed the doll onto the bed behind him as he reached for Sophie, pulling her down onto his lap and squeezing her, crushing her against his chest as he inhaled the scent of her cheap strawberry shampoo. He didn't want to think about letting her leave. "Damn it, Soph, don't go. I don't want to have to remember you with some fucked-up doll."

Sophie gazed up at him, her eyes glittering. She'd cried so

many times since she'd told him she was leaving that he wondered how she could possibly be doing it again. He, on the other hand, hadn't shed a single tear, and he knew that made him some kind of prick or something, but he didn't care, he was too pissed to cry. "I mean it, Sophie. Stay with me; I'll keep you safe. If that bastard tries to come anywhere near you—"

She shook her head, wisps of her dirty-blond hair tickling his chin. "My mom needs me, Rafe." She pushed away from him, wiping her nose with the back of her hand. "She can't take care of Jacob by herself. She can't get a job if she can't afford a babysitter, and she can't get a babysitter without a job."

"So you're supposed to . . . what? Just quit school so you can babysit your little brother? *Connie's* supposed to be the mom, not you." Same goddamn argument, different goddamn day. One he'd already lost, even before it had started.

And Sophie knew it. She bit the ring in her lower lip, the sparkle in her impish pale-gray eyes telling him she was no longer interested in fighting. She shoved him backward until he fell onto his twin bed—the one that was almost too cramped for the two of them. Almost. She wrapped her arms around his neck, and he felt the familiar jolt, the charge of electricity he always felt whenever their skin touched. She pressed her chest—*her breasts*—against him. Sophie was great at distractions. "C'mon, it won't be forever. I'll only stay until she can get settled somewhere, get a job, and get Jakey into day care or something. Then I'll come back." She nuzzled his neck, her lips and her tongue promising all of the things her words didn't.

He sighed, surrendering to everything she offered. But if he was going to let her go, he needed her to have a keepsake too. He tugged at the ring on his finger, a black stone surrounded by carved stainless steel that he'd picked up when they'd gone to get her lip pierced. He'd bought it because of its cool biker vibe, but it had never meant anything to him. Until now.

"I want you to have this." He inched back just far enough so he could hold the ring between them.

Sophie's eyes filled with tears again. He loved that about her: she was an emotional wreck.

He grinned. "Does that mean you'll take it with you?"

She sniffed, her fingers shaking as she took the ring. "Does that mean you'll keep Goob?"

Rafe grimaced. He reached behind him, his hand searching for the ugly-ass doll. When he found it, he held it up by the tips of its hair. "I'll keep him safe till you come home, but then you have to take him back."

Sophie slipped the chunky steel onto her finger. It was way too big and it spun in loose circles, even when she tried it on her thumb. "I'll get you a chain," Rafe promised. "You can wear it around your neck."

She'd left just three days later. That was less than two weeks ago.

Rafe hated her for leaving that doll with him. If he'd never had it in the first place, he might not be here now.

He jerked his hand out of his pocket as he tried to remember what number he was on. He didn't want to lose track of how many steps he had left . . . not now, not when he was so close.

Twenty-seven.

A part of him wondered what would happen if he just turned around, if he stopped counting and went back to the interstate. If he went home. Ignored the dream.

He laughed under his breath, an ugly sound. *Like I could do that*, he thought bitterly. *Especially not this time.*

Even with no light to show him the way, he knew he was close. And he knew it was time to make the call.

Thirteen.

Still walking, he reached for the cell phone again, but he hesitated before dialing. He wasn't sure he was ready to ask for help yet; he didn't know if he was ready to trust anyone with his secret.

But what if he was right? What if it had been more than a simple dream?

Five.

He stopped. He could see the ghostly shadow of a tiny house now; it was quiet and dark. There were no lights on—inside or out. His skin tightened painfully as he stared at its inky cutout against the backdrop of trees. It was a carbon copy of the house from his dream. He hit *Enter* on the phone and waited.

"Agent Sara Priest speaking." Her voice was familiar, even

behind the crisp, clipped facade she used for the FBI.

He paused. And then: "Sara?"

"Rafe? Where the hell are you? Jen's freaking out. She's been calling me every half hour to see if I've heard anything." Hearing Sara say his aunt's name made him feel guilty all over again; he knew she'd be worried sick when he just . . . *vanished* like that. Still, there was no way he could have told her what he was planning. Or why.

But now he felt backed into a corner, he needed help. And Sara was the only person he could think of who might believe him.

"I had a dream."

"What kind of dream? What does that mean, *you had a dream?*"

"It means sometimes my dreams are more than just dreams, Sara. Sometimes my dreams are real. It's like I can see things before they happen." He paused, wondering what his confession sounded like from her end. But he didn't have time to worry about that. Not now.

There was a long silence, and Rafe wondered what she was thinking . . . or more likely, what she'd already done. He wondered if she was tracing this call yet. "Can you tell me about your dreams? About this one in particular?" she finally asked.

Rafe shook his head against the handset. "I will, but I need to see if I'm right about it first."

"Can you at least tell me if someone might be hurt? Did you dream that someone was in trouble?"

Rafe pulled up the images from his dream, the ones that would be forever etched into his memory, branded into his mind's eye. He flipped through them like photographs— quickly, only wanting to see the ones he needed for the moment, ignoring the ones that were too difficult to look at. He felt sick all over again. "I . . . I don't know yet."

"Rafe . . . please . . . don't do anything stupid. Wait for the authorities to get there. Or at least wait for me; I'm on my way." On the other end, he could hear her car's engine, and he realized she must have been waiting for him to call, she must have had the trace already in place. That was the rub about knowing an FBI agent, but this time he needed her.

"Call Jenny and tell her I'm okay," Rafe responded, and then he hung up the phone.

He stood there for a moment longer, at the end of the road where the small driveway began, staring at the dark outline of the house. He wanted to yell her name: *Sophie!* But he was too afraid she wouldn't answer. *Couldn't* answer.

Sophie used to say that they were connected, that they shared something stronger than just love, something that transcended this world. He'd told her that all that cosmic stuff was bullshit and he'd laughed at her for romanticizing everything.

But she hadn't been wrong. Even when he'd turned it into a joke, he knew she wasn't wrong. She *was* different—special—and they'd belonged together from the moment he first laid eyes on her, when she stopped in the hallway on her first day of school and boldly announced that they were going out on Friday night.

She'd already been hiding from her father then.

He closed his eyes, trying to *find* her, but there was nothing. He was afraid that whatever connection he'd once felt had been severed. And he was terrified of what that meant.

He started walking again, slowly, trying to remember how this was all going to play out.

The back door, he realized. If his dream was right, the back door would be open.

He prayed he was wrong.

He felt safe moving through the darkness, sheltered by the shadows that masked him, shielded by the night. He passed Connie's car in the driveway, and felt a burst of panic when he realized it was the only one there. *That doesn't mean I'm too late*, he reminded himself. *Maybe I got here in time to change things.*

But when he reached the back of the house, he knew otherwise. He moved up the steps, to where the rear door stood slightly ajar. Just as he'd known it would be. Just as he'd hoped it wouldn't be.

Exactly like in his dream.

He didn't stop to think about what this meant. He pushed the door and it opened silently as he slipped inside, setting his backpack on the floor. The air was still—stale—and once again, Rafe sifted through the mental images that had come to him in his sleep, flashing like unwelcome memories that didn't belong to him.

Sophie's dad showing up without warning.

Connie screaming at him to leave them alone as she positioned herself between him and the kids, Sophie and Jacob, yelling for them to run. To hide.

His fists. Relentless. Beating Connie until her face was bloodied and unrecognizable.

Sophie dragging her little brother out the back door. But to where? Rafe couldn't be certain; they were no longer a part of the pictures in his head.

And then: *the knife.* Rafe hadn't seen where it had come from. Had Sophie's father found it in the kitchen, or had it been with him all along? But its appearance, even in his dream, had made Rafe shiver with icy warning and had given him a purpose: *Get to Sophie. Save her!*

That was all he had; that was where his dream had ended, when he awoke drenched in sweat and foreboding. He'd gathered a few items into his backpack, along with some cash and that fugly doll, and he'd left without telling his aunt where he was going. Or when he might be back. He hadn't known the answer to either question.

Now, standing inside the darkened kitchen with the lights still off, he no longer measured his steps by distance but by weight, each one pulling him down, drawing him deeper into despair.

One. On the other side of the couch, he could see a limp hand on the floor, white even in the shadows of the stark room.

Two. Three. It was Connie, her face pale and her eyes wide as a crimson puddle of her own blood crusted around her.

Four, five, six. More blood. Everywhere, blood.

Now was the time Rafe should call out for her—for Sophie—but his voice felt thick, his airway too tight to find enough space for it to pass. Nausea gripped him, making him suddenly dizzy. He wasn't ready to know if Sophie could answer.

But it didn't matter what he wanted.

Twelve. He slipped past Sophie's mother, lying in the small living area, as he scanned the house, looking inside the tiny bathroom with a dirty tub and chipped porcelain sink, a linen closet housing an ancient hot water heater and only a handful of towels. Until he came to a closed door.

Blood rushed past his ears, and his heart hammered against the walls of his chest.

He squeezed his eyes shut as he pushed open the door. He didn't know if he could do this, if he could handle what might be inside.

As he opened them again, he released a heavy breath. The sparsely furnished bedroom was empty.

Outside, he thought in a rush. *They must still be outside.*

He told himself not to look as he passed the dead woman in the living room, but it was impossible not to. He might not even have realized it was Connie, save for the bleached blond hair that was now matted with clumps of her own flesh and bones and blood.

At the back door, he hesitated again, listening to the night, hoping for a clue but picking up nothing. He strained against the godforsaken blackness, even darker back here than out at the road, where there was at least a break in the trees to allow the light from the moon overhead. But after a moment, once his eyes adjusted, he could see a break here too. Ahead, a small clearing had been carved out for a rickety-looking shed that stood beneath the towering trees, clutched in the grasp of barbed blackberry vines that threatened to consume it.

Rafe froze, suddenly unable to take another forward step. He was still unsure where Sophie's father might be, and he'd already witnessed what the man was capable of. His lungs felt brittle, like they were made from crisp parchment and were no longer capable of true function. He waited there, trying to decide which need would cause him to move first: his need to breathe or this new, all-consuming fear that gripped him.

He had known death, and understood it; the dreams had helped with that. When his mother had gotten sick, when the cancer had metastasized, spreading violently throughout her body—unstoppable—he had known. He had seen what it had done to her, even when she'd tried her best to hide it . . . tried to keep it a secret from him.

He'd watched her while he slept—in his dreams—seeing what the drugs were doing to her as she cried and vomited, whimpered and pulled clumps of her own hair from her head.

He'd watched night after night, seeing her lose the battle to the disease, along with her will to fight.

All the while, her brave front never faltered. She smiled and squeezed his hand whenever he came into the room, and he pretended not to notice when her fingers no longer had the strength to curl around his. Instead, he squeezed hard enough for the both of them.

And when he knew she couldn't do it for herself, he gave her permission, whispering softly against the sharp bones of her too-thin cheek, "It's okay, Mom. I'll be all right, I promise. Aunt Jenny will take good care of me."

He had been there when she'd taken her last shuddering breath, releasing it on a ghastly sigh.

But he had never considered the possibility of his own death before this very moment, standing here beneath the dark Montana sky. He had never entertained the notion that he wasn't indestructible. Until now. Now he felt differently. Now, after seeing the bloodied body of Sophie's mother, he *knew* differently.

His dreams could be dangerous. *He* could be in danger.

He gasped for air, no longer able to sustain himself on sheer will alone.

That moment freed him and he found his stride again as his desire to find her—to find Sophie—was renewed.

His boots dug into the earth beneath his feet as he searched everywhere.

"Sophie!" He finally yelled, no longer able to stop himself.

Desperation was clear as his voice cracked. "Sophie! Answer me, Sophie!"

He almost didn't notice the soft scrape beneath his boot, the metallic scuff that he felt more than heard. It could easily have been a coin, dropped carelessly in the soil, but Rafe didn't think so, and as he bent down to get a better look, his stomach revolted.

It was hers. The necklace. The ring he'd put on a chain for her to wear.

His hand hovered just above it. He was afraid to touch it, afraid to let his fingers close around it.

If he touched it, if his skin made contact with it, he would know for sure.

But time was running out, and behind him the far-off drone of sirens wailed, setting an eerie mood for what he was about to do.

He glanced up, to make certain he was still alone, and, closing his eyes, curled his hand around the ring, lifting it to his heart and clutching it there.

Electrical impulses caused him to convulse, like tremors coursing along every muscle fiber in his body. His eyes opened, rolling back in his head as the images began flashing inside his mind.

Flash. *Sophie and Jacob, hiding in the shed. Cowering. Trying not to cry.*

Flash. *Their father splintering the door to get to them. The gun in his hand.*

Flash. *Sophie—the same way her mother had done—standing*

bravely between her little brother and her father.

Flash. *Jacob running away, searching for cover beneath the canopy of the trees.*

Then: *the gunshot.*

Rafe's body jerked, as the sound from the borrowed memory exploded within him. He tried to loosen his fingers, to pry them apart, away from the ring, but it was too late, the images had come too fast, and he'd already seen them.

The siren screamed, louder now, almost upon him. He was suddenly grateful for an overprotective aunt like Jenny. And grateful that he'd already called Sara. He'd known, of course, that she would trace the call, and he'd expected her to send backup. It was what she did.

He knew, too, that when the police arrived, they would arrest him; they would have to when they witnessed the gruesome scene inside the house. He was the only one here, after all, and they had to blame someone.

Rafe would let them, staying silent, explaining nothing.

It wouldn't be until Sara got there that things would get straightened out, that he'd tell her everything, about his dreams and what he saw in them. She was the only one who would understand.

Rafe clutched the ring, the images still assaulting him.

And he would tell Sara exactly where she could find Sophie's father: hiding out at a cheap motel just off the interstate, less than twenty miles from this very spot.

But even without Rafe to tell them where the bodies were,

the local police would have already found Sophie. And Jacob.

They'd never stood a chance against their father.

He tried to keep the images from flashing, again and again, but they kept coming, faster and faster now.

Flash. *Sophie hiding the necklace in her hand, squeezing it and rubbing the steel furiously with her thumb, her eyes wide as she faced her father.*

Flash. *Sophie turning to run, stumbling. Trying to get away as her father raised his gun. Coldly. Unemotionally.*

Flash. *Sophie, her body going stiff. The necklace falling from her hands as she reached up to touch the wound that had opened up on her chest, where the bullet had ripped right through her. The disbelief on her face as she stared down at the blood glistening on her fingertips.*

Flash. *Sophie falling forward. Her eyes glazed and empty.*

Rafe dropped to his knees as he heard car doors slamming and saw the flash of lights split the dark sky behind him. He hadn't cried when his mother died or when Sophie had left, and he couldn't seem to do it now either. But something in him was forever changed, he knew. Something in him had died along with the both of them.

He felt cold and bare. Exposed and abandoned.

He uncurled his fingers and looked down at the steel ring in his hand, not sure why he wanted to keep it. He half thought he should just chuck it into the woods and forget it—*forget her*—forever.

Instead, he slipped the chain around his neck. And as he heard the voices shouting, screaming at him to *get down on the ground*, he tucked it inside his shirt, against the hollow space where his heart should be.

LEAVING
by Ally Condie

*B*efore my father left for good, he put the small glass sphere down on the table in the three-room apartment where we lived. The sphere rolled a little and I had to catch it before it fell. "It's a globe," he told me, not exactly meeting my eyes. He looked at me, in my direction, but his gaze stopped somewhere just short of mine. "A full globe," he added.

He meant unlike the Globe we live in, which is a curved half sphere above the earth. The Globe protects us and encases us, our apartment buildings, our grid of transports. Our cities. There are other shapes—Cubes, Pyramids—that enclose other people and other places. "We live in half a world," my father said sometimes. He said it then, before he left.

I'm walking down the hall at school when this memory comes back to me, brought to my mind by the light glancing off the perfect circle of a girl's earring as she stands next to a window. Once, I would have pushed away any memory of my father's leaving. I used to try not to think about when and how he left, but now that I'm planning to follow I think about it all the time.

I picked up the globe and looked to see what was inside. Something swirling, white but clear, lit from within.

"I'll leave it behind for you," he said. "If anything goes wrong, use it if you can. If you can't use it, break it." I looked at him, at his graying hair and his eyes that seemed to be graying too. The expression on his face wasn't quite an expression of happiness or satisfaction, but maybe a little of the hope of those things. But most of what I saw on his face could be summarized in a single word: purpose.

Someone bumps up against me and then pulls away as if I've burned them. I look up. It's a girl I don't know, younger than me. "Sorry," she says. She seems embarrassed and I don't know if she's apologizing for bumping into me or for pulling away.

No one should have to pull away anymore.

But they all do. It started because of my father, and it continues now because of me.

I turn away from the girl and keep walking, listening. The people around me only discuss one thing. The Heavens Dance. Tonight.

I won't be there.

Everyone in the school knows it and I know it and I move around Mia Turner in the hall, around her long silver-blond hair and her bright silver clothes and her voice and her laughter and her group and her big blue eyes staring right at me.

"Sora," she says behind me, just as I've passed.

What does she want? I turn to look at her. She was a friend, last year, as they all were. Before my father left. Before I became Untouchable for those two weeks that changed everything. Them. Me.

"The assembly is this way," she says, pointing toward the doors of the auditorium. The stage floats a few feet above the ground, and the chairs have been arranged in rows for us. She smiles. She's standing right next to me. And then she reaches out to me.

For a moment, my heart almost stops. Not in fear, though I've seen what Mia Turner can do. But because with her hand outstretched and her eyes wide open like that, she looks like one of them. One of the Beautiful People from the Beautiful Time. The time we always try to recapture, here in the Globe, with our hair, our clothes, our music, the way we talk. We all wish we could have lived then, just before the Burn and the making of the Shapes. We've tried to recreate the era, but we're missing the most important element of all: the Beautiful People themselves.

Bad things happened even in the Beautiful Time, but Beautiful People always came to the rescue. I've seen video footage of a giant wave, of an earthquake. All those devastated citizens, all that ruined land, and then a Beautiful Person came in and made everything fine. You could see it by the way the people smiled and reached out to touch the hands of the visitor.

I don't say anything. But then Mia moves, impatient, and pulls back her hand. She's not a Beautiful Person, not that kind anyway. She can't heal anyone.

Fifteenth century, I think to myself, standing in the doorway, feeling perversely amused by the fact that people have to move around me so carefully in this tiny space. They're moving around Mia as well, afraid to touch her too, but not for the same reasons. *Maybe that's the right century. Maybe that's the time for me. They worked and went to church and ate and slept. They wouldn't have had time for school like this.* I imagine I can feel all the heavy weight of woolen skirts and long hair piled on my head or braided down my back. *That's a time when people like Mia would be called witches.*

Which she is. A witch, and worse.

But wouldn't I get hanged myself the minute I appeared there? In most eras, my clothes might get me stared at, laughed at, noticed, but I'd rather not get killed.

Not the fifteenth century, then.

"Go," Mia says, shoving me a little, and I stumble forward toward the auditorium. I can feel exactly where she pushed me. Someone else behind her laughs nervously at her bravery at touching me. I don't look back but I stand up straight. I won't be here forever. They don't know that, but I do.

I might even leave tonight.

I walk right through the auditorium and back out the door on the other side. I don't know if Mia sees me leave. I don't know why she tried to get me to go to the assembly, but I'm not going to do it. I'm going home. The crowning of the sun and moon and stars for the Heavens Dance happens every year. I've seen it before. Last year, before my father left, when things were still bad but he wasn't gone, I sat there with friends and watched the students a year older than me get chosen. The most handsome boy: the sun. The prettiest girl: the moon. A handful of oth-ers—three boys, three girls—as the stars.

My father said you could only go backward, not forward. I wonder if he was right? Maybe I could go a hundred years from now. Maybe by then the Outside would be clean again and the trees would be growing and we could live beyond the Shapes. But maybe the air would be gone, even though the president says that we have plenty of everything if we just stay inside. Maybe the Globes would be empty of life and full of dead people.

There are plenty of little transports lined up in front of the school. The assembly isn't mandatory, and it doesn't matter if I don't go. I climb inside a transport and punch in the coordi-nates of my apartment. The transport slides up along the metal gridwork that webs through our city. Other transports, more solid and secure than these intracity ones, go outside our Globe to the other Shapes. But only politicians, transport workers, and other approved citizens are permitted to leave, and even they are never truly Outside.

I lean my head against the plastic windowpane and look out at our tiny, tight world.

My father also said this: It's probably best not to go back in your own life.

But if I could, I would go back in my own life to three years ago, before my father was really gone. I would go back to the day when Elio Morrow and I were with the rest of the class at the weather center for a field trip, and they chose the two of us to stay inside and make it rain. The weather center director showed us which buttons to push. We sat side by side with our arms brushing each other as we took turns. Elio didn't flinch away. This was before I was Untouchable, of course, but I still noticed.

"What color should we make it rain?" the director asked, and Elio and I answered at the same time. We both said, "Orange," and we looked at each other in surprise, and the director was surprised too. "We don't do that often," he said. "Everyone likes clear, or blue."

Elio and I stood inside. We watched our classmates looking up to see what we would do. When the drops started to fall, everyone started to laugh, including Mia Turner. And Elio and I ran out together to join them, and everyone acted like we were kids, not thirteen and mostly grown, and it was one of the last times and one of the first times and certainly one of the best times.

But. Even if I could go back in my own life, I would still arrive, eventually, back at today.

In my apartment—a two-room—now that I live alone, I take off my shoes and sit down on the rug from the old apartment, right in the spot where my father vanished.

I know I'm leaving tonight, but it's not time now. Instead, I place the glass sphere on the patterned rug. Its reds and oranges and browns are as familiar to me as the backs of my own hands. Soon, one of the other single females who live in this block of apartments will come to make sure I'm all right. I have to wait until after that visit before I start to leave.

My father vanished so completely that they think he must have left the Globe and died out there in the Middle. That's why I was an Untouchable: I vowed that I'd seen him go, that we'd stolen a transport and gone out of the Globe, where he climbed out and died. It took two weeks before all the tests were finished and they were sure I was clean. Two weeks of being an Untouchable. It wasn't long, in some ways.

But it was long enough.

When I think of their version of how he left, I picture him stepping out of the transport and into the black, dead landscape and then sizzling up, just like that.

When really he left so much more carefully. When really it took so long.

"I'm going to go find one of the Beautiful People," he said. He pointed to a picture of a woman with huge eyes and red lips and long, luscious hair. In the picture, she reached down to a child of another color. The child reached up, smiling. "That one, if I can. It might be a long time, but I'm going to try to bring her back."

I nodded.

"We can't keep living like this," he said.

What he meant was, "I can't keep living like this." Without my mother, he meant. She died when I was born. I don't remember her at all.

But my father did.

I think he stayed as long as he could.

"Don't touch me when I leave," he warned me. "I don't know what could happen."

So I didn't.

He sat down and I watched him go.

He got darker, and darker, and more solid, more real. He didn't fade; he condensed. Smaller, smaller, sharper, sharper, until I realized with surprise that he was tiny, that I'd been watching him for hours. My vision had narrowed until all I saw was him. There he was, and then he wasn't. And he was gone and his glass sphere sat alone in the center of the rug.

I knew right away that if I could focus as long and as well as he did, that I might be able to do it too. But for those first shocked days and weeks, I didn't want to think about leaving.

And then, after I realized that I would forever be Untouchable, it became the only thing I wanted to think about.

There's a knock on the door.

Laura from upstairs stands there, smiling, an excited look on her face. "How are you doing today?" she asks, stepping inside. She's much older than I am, probably thirty. She lives alone.

"I'm doing well," I say. Laura is kind. She stays at arm's length, always, but I hear genuine warmth in her voice.

Laura beams at me, and for a moment, I think she's going to hug me. But of course she doesn't. I'm imagining things. "I got a message from your school," she says.

"You did?" My heart races a little. Since I don't have parents, Laura is the one who gets any news from the school about me, but usually there is no news to receive because I don't cause any trouble.

"About the dance," she says, waiting for me to say something.

"I didn't go to the assembly," I admit, worried. Could that really matter? Suddenly I feel nervous. *No. No complications. I have to leave tonight.* "But it's not mandatory."

"They voted you as one of the stars!" Laura says, beaming.

"That can't be right," I say.

"It is," she tells me. "You have to go to the dance. They're saving your crown for you."

A joke. It has to be. The opening line is perfect: *What happens when an Untouchable comes to a dance?*

I can see myself now, standing in the middle of the room, burning too hot to touch, a star with nothing in orbit and black empty space around her.

"Come on," Laura says excitedly. "We have to find you something to wear."

It's all right, I tell myself. *Just go through with this. Don't cause trouble. Do what's expected. Go to the dance and let them laugh at you and then come home right away. There will still be time to leave.*

I find a dress in my closet and put it on but I can't zip it up.

I go back outside to the front room. "Can you help me?" I ask Laura.

She doesn't hesitate. "Of course," she says, and she zips it right up, but her hands never touch me at all.

The transport drops me off in front of the gymnasium built above our classrooms. The doors stand open wide, and inside I can see figures moving.

I don't want to admit it to myself, but I am curious. Last year, I didn't come because I wasn't asked to the dance, but I didn't know that I never would be. Even with my father getting more and more quiet, I didn't realize how much his absence would change things. How it would change me.

I pause in the empty doorway to watch.

People dance in couples, so close, so tight against each other. The air smells like flowers and tastes like strawberry. A spring flavor. If it were fall, we'd smell spices and taste apples.

Traditions from long ago. There's a wedding scene in the films from the Beautiful Time. In the scene, the woman wears white. The man wears a dark suit. In front of the couple is a lovely cake, flowers, a pile of sumptuous gifts. But it's what is behind them that makes you breathless.

It's the sunset.

And it is bigger than our whole world.

"*There* you are," says a girl whose name I don't know. "Everyone's waiting. Come on." I look where she's pointing and see the sun and moon and the other stars standing together at the front of the gymnasium. I'm supposed to join them. I follow the girl along the side of the room.

Twentieth century, only two hundred and fifty years ago, but different in so many ways. Slow, sluggish cars instead of light-fast transports. Girls with skirts with silly little dogs on them and boys with slick black jackets.

This could happen then. They had dances and they crowned kings and queens too.

No. That's not the right time.

Mia is the moon, of course. I can tell by the crown on her head, made of large silver circles. The other girls who are stars have smaller crowns, and the girl ahead of me turns and hands me one, the silver points of each star sharp and precise in my hand. "Put it on," she whispers. "It's time for the star dance." Something like pity flashes across her face. "You can leave after this song. The next dance is for the sun and the moon."

I'm lifting it to my head when I see him.

Elio.

He's the sun.

I know it even though the boys don't wear crowns like the girls do.

And I don't know if my crown caught some of the light from some part of the room and reflected it at him, or if he heard the girl talking to me, or if he just happened to move at that moment, but he looks at me just as I settle the stars in my hair.

I drop my hands down and look back.

If anyone were to tie me here, it would be him.
But I have to go. And now I know where and when.
There's never really been any question.
The Time of the Beautiful People.
Two hundred years ago. The early two thousands.
The best years.
The kind years.
The years where my father has gone.

When the music starts for the star dance, two of the boys reach out their hands to two of the girls. The other boy, the last star, doesn't even glance my way. He asks Mia to dance.

She turns toward me, her face a pale flash in the pretend starlight filtering down from the ceiling. I don't wait to see her smile. I turn back out to look at the watching crowd. Some people laugh. Some people just look. Some turn away. I don't know who is more cruel: those who watch, or those who pretend they see nothing.

I lift my chin. *After this dance, I can leave. It won't be long.*

I feel their breath in this crowded place and smell their sweat. I'm in the middle of them and I can't get away.

I don't want them to matter. They haven't, for so long. But I don't know if I can do this.

Someone else laughs, and I close my eyes, trying to block it out, for practice. I think of my father and I remember him making animals for me out of bits of folded paper. Small.

Smaller, until the paper became a tiny frog, or a little winged bird. But then he stopped making things. He started bending inward, and I was left with nothing to hold.

Someone says my name, and my eyes fly open.

Elio. He walks toward me. In the artificial starlight, his hair is no color at all, but I know his face.

He stops in front of me.

He puts his hand out for mine. "Will you dance with me?"

"Look," someone behind me whispers. Across the floor, Mia dances on, oblivious for now. The circles in her crown flash in and out of the lights.

I look back at Elio but I don't take his hand.

"Sora," he says. He runs his other hand through his hair, an impatient gesture I remember. "This isn't right. You're supposed to be dancing."

The music behind us from the musicians sounds like everything does here. Like everything looks here. Bright, shiny, hard, with no place for anything deep.

I look down and so I see the moment when his fingers close around mine. I'm glad I'm not looking at him because I gasp, just barely, when our fingers touch.

I didn't remember this. I didn't expect this.

He is so warm. It feels so good.

I look back up. People still watch us, and I watch him. He smiles at me, the way he did when we made it rain, and then he pulls me close.

People behind us gasp in surprise. "What?" Elio says, over

my head. "She hasn't been Untouchable for months. It doesn't matter."

But it does.

The music suddenly seems so full and beautiful. I look up at Elio. He reaches for the crown. "Do you want this?" he asks, and I shake my head. He pulls back long enough to give it to me and I take it and drop it behind me. I don't look to see where it falls. He pulls me back where I was, and this time he rests his cheek on my head. I feel the warmth through my hair, all the way down to my toes.

Maybe all the Beautiful People aren't gone. Maybe Elio is one of them. And I never knew. All I had to do was show the pain.

Could it be that easy?

I wish they'd do a weather pattern; that they'd let it rain or snow above us to explain the drops on my cheeks and those I must be leaving on his shirt. But no—because this is the stars' dance, the weather in the room is black sky and showery silver light. When it's Mia's turn, the room will be bright and white. Everyone will see her dance and everyone will want to look, but for a completely different reason than they wanted to look and laugh at me.

He runs his hand down my back just as the music ends and the silver lights dim.

And suddenly I think he might kiss me. He whispers, "Sora. Are you all right?"

"Yes," I say, and I think he holds me a little tighter.

Please kiss me, a voice in my head whispers, and though I'm hearing my own thoughts, I almost don't recognize them. *There has to be a reason to stay here.*

He leans just a little closer; I feel it in his breath on my cheek and in every piece of me that's touching any part of him.

The lights begin to come back on, slowly. I'm still holding on, holding on, my face tipped back, looking up at Elio.

"Sora," he says, gently, and then when I don't let go, he looks around. People are watching again. And starting to laugh. He lets go and I step back.

Mercifully, the room plunges back into darkness. Someone yells at someone else to fix the lights. It's common, the power shorting out inside the Globe.

I have to leave.

I didn't think one touch would undo me.

I think I might hear Elio behind me but I don't stop. I hurt too much. I feel too much. This is dangerous. My father succeeded because he shut himself off before he left. I have to do that too. Though he doesn't know it, Elio has put everything at risk.

The auxiliary power has come back on by the time I reach the transports, so I can get home. The night sky of the Globe throbs dull gray. We've never seen a real sky. I slam the door of the transport shut and it begins to move.

And I let myself look at other truths as I slide along in the dark.

My father lied to me. He never intended to come back to

me. He never went back to the time of the Beautiful People. He didn't believe in them. He had no faith. He went back to when he first met her. My mother. Just to be with her, even if it was for only a handful of moments.

Someone might say that was beautiful.

I don't think so at all.

I don't know what he planned to do. To stop her from having me, perhaps. I wondered for a long time if I would someday vanish, if he could change the future when he walked back into the past. But I didn't go anywhere.

I'm here, but I've forgotten how to take up space. How to think about anything except going away.

I couldn't change his mind. So I didn't try to change anyone else's mind, either. I let them think I'd been Outside too, and when they looked at me, I gave them the hard, flat stare of someone who has seen too much. When Elio or any of the others tried to talk to me, I didn't answer back, or I said words that meant nothing at all.

What has happened to me is my fault too.

I can't stand to be touched anymore. It breaks me.

I have to be healed. I have to be loved.

And the Beautiful People can do it.

The transport stops.

It's dark inside my apartment, but that doesn't matter. I walk to the little table, open the drawer, unlock the box with the key I wear around my neck. I don't need light to do any of it.

The sphere rolls perfectly into the hollow of my hand.

I know I can leave. It's all I know how to do.

I think of the year: 2011. That will be the one. I look at an image from that time. Not the one of the wedding; I'm worried that if I choose that one, I'll fly straight past the cake and the people and into that sky full of sunset and burn up before I've seen anything. Instead, I look at a picture of one of the Beautiful People. She walks across a red carpet and everyone stands near her, stretching out their hands, screaming, calling to her, while she turns a beatific smile upon them.

I pick up the little glass world that my father gave me before he took what was left of my own.

This is how you leave.

You sit. You are quiet. You close your eyes. You think. You put the stone in your hand and hold it. There is no short way to this, no magical spell. Rushing will do you no good at all.

And not many people can do this. There is always something that holds them back and ties them down.

Not me.

I'm gone.

I didn't expect to like it so much in here, in the in-between. So dark, so quiet. Maybe there is no sense in trying to find any time. Any place. Just leaving might be enough.

If you stay here, you become lost. And no one can find you.

I like lost.

Wherever I am, in the corners of my mind, in the edges of space, wherever it is, I lie down to rest.

There is no time.

There is no me.

And then something happens. A light here, another there.

Is it them? Are the Beautiful People coming to find me?

No.

I'm alone.

I'm standing in the stars. I'm standing on top of the Globe, I think, and then I look down and see it's the moon under my feet. Or maybe the sphere. I can't tell if I am tiny or enormous, and it doesn't matter because I'm really *outside*, under the stars.

I stand there for a long time, trying to find the right words for what I see. Spending minutes, hours, years perhaps, choosing each one.

Infinite.

Bright.

Beautiful.

And I remember: I should think of the Beautiful People, if I want to find their time and escape my own.

Their time. My time.

The real gift is to have any time at all.

And suddenly, in the clarity of the starlight, I can see how things really are. The Beautiful People are real and they are not real. They lived, but they are not who we have made them out to be. The Beautiful People were not beautiful. Not any more or less than any other people throughout time and space. They reached out their hands sometimes and not others. They were kind like Laura and Elio and cruel like Mia. We made them beautiful because we needed to believe in them. And we wanted to believe they would heal us. We—I—wanted to believe they would *love* us.

And I see that my father chased a memory when there was someone real who loved him right there in his imperfect world. Me. He shut down and folded in, and his body became small because he had let his mind become even smaller. As I have done.

It will hurt, I see, to try to open up again.

I am stronger than he was.

I take one last look at the stars.

For a long time I feel only the pain. Then other things nudge at the edges of my mind. The feeling of my face pressed deep into the rug. My fingers clasped tightly around a glass sphere.

The sound of a voice at the door.

"Are you there?" he asks.

Elio.

His voice is rough but soft, as though he's been calling for hours. And in all the distances traveled tonight, the one I think of now is the one when Elio reached out his hand and touched me.

The room is dark and quiet and still. I stand up and walk to the door. I let go of the sphere. It doesn't make a sound as it falls onto the thick rug at my feet. But there is a sharp snap when I crush it under my heel.

"I've been Outside," I say through the door.

There is no sound on the other side for a moment. Is he still there?

And then, he speaks.

"So have I."

AT THE LATE NIGHT, DOUBLE FEATURE, PICTURE SHOW
by Jessica Verday

The worst thing about cannibal Girl Scouts are the badges.

You would think it's the fact that they want to chase you down and strip the flesh from your bones. I mean, what's worse than *that*? But you'd be wrong.

It's the badges.

The badges tell you exactly *how* those little green devils will turn your skin into bite-size Fruit Roll-Up pieces. Trust me, I've seen it happen before.

The one that was tracking me now had four badges: knot tying, tree climbing, fire building, and archery. Basically, that meant she could shoot me with an arrow, hang me from a tree (with a proper knot, of course), and then roast me over a big ol' campfire.

Girl Scouts. They're doing it wrong.

A twig snapped behind the bush on my right and I honed in on it, focusing again on the task at hand. Waiting for the little girl to come out and just show herself already, so that I could do my job and *prove* to everyone at home that I was part of *their* team.

Well, a bigger part than I already was.

My phone vibrated, the special one-two-three vibration that told me it was Andy. I ignored it and tried not to think about how much my back was killing me.

"Come *on*," I whispered. "Nice, juicy piece of meat sitting right here." I was pretending that my shoelace was tangled and I'd been fidgeting with it for the last twenty minutes.

Something crunched in the woods. There was a flash of dark green, and she catapulted herself at me from the trees.

"Hrrrruuunnngggghhhh!"

She made the unintelligible sound midlunge.

I sidestepped and whirled out of the way. Little brown shoes and carefully styled blond curls went flying as she crashed into the tree on my left. She couldn't have been more than ten. Hands raised into dainty claws, she turned around and came at me again.

Fishing for the pouch on my utility belt, I counted the seconds as she came closer and closer. *One Mississippi . . . Two . . .*

And then she was on me.

Sixty-five pounds of squirming, snapping, biting child that wanted to tear off my nose, ears, fingers, *anything* she could get her little chompers on. She opened her mouth wide, using both hands to hold me down. Tiny bits of fragmented flesh were caught between an ingrown baby tooth and a new adult tooth.

"Damn it!" I yelled, fingers finally grabbing hold of my saving grace. The one thing that would hopefully distract her long enough to stop her from turning any of my digits into her next Happy Meal. "Stop! Here!"

I withdrew a piece of turkey giblets. It's the closest thing to human flesh that I've found without it actually *being* human flesh, and I thrust it up under her nose. Her face turned frantic, nostrils flared as she greedily grabbed onto it with both hands and shoved it into her gaping jaws.

She ripped and tore her way through the entire thing. I pulled up my watch and timed her.

Eight seconds. *Not bad.*

Her eyes glazed over and she looked down at me, a tiny smear of blood staining the corner of her mouth.

"That's it," I said. "You're not getting any more."

She cast a glance at my arm. The one that I was still holding up to look at my watch.

My fingers groped at my belt again, but the pouch was empty. *I'm out of meat.* "You were supposed to restock me, Andy. You little shit!" I said between gritted teeth.

The girl didn't care. Her eyes were glazing over even more, but there was still enough wildness there that made me uneasy. Her mouth opened . . . teeth bared . . .

And then she fell over.

I shoved her off and rolled, using the ground to push myself up to a standing position. "Didn't see that one coming, did you? When's the last time your food fought back?"

Nudging her with the toe of my boot, I saw a small bit of plastic resting next to her hand. It was a piece of capsule that still had some allergy medicine in it.

Benadryl. Fastest, easiest, cheapest way to take 'em down.

My phone vibrated again. "Andy, what do you want?" I hissed into it. "I'm in a movie theater." No one at home knew what I was *really* up to.

"Dad needs you to get some birchwood. From the farm. He wants to carve some more stakes tonight."

"I can't," I said hastily. "I have to—"

"Just do it, Jane. Dad needs it. How's the movie?"

"Boring part. They just had a chase scene through the woods. Some guy with a chainsaw. Now the blond bimbo is suggesting they split up."

"I thought you went to go see a chick flick? *The Notebook* or something."

Andy, Andy, Andy. Always trying to trip me up. *Too bad little sister is better at this game than you are.* "Why would I go see that piece of crap?" I snorted. "I told you I was going to see *The Texas Chainsaw Massacre* and *The Crazies*. It's a double feature."

"Oh, yeah. That's right. I must have gotten the titles mixed up."

"*You* got a chick flick and a horror movie mixed up? I might expect that from Dad, since he doesn't watch horror movies, but come on, big brother. What chick flick has the word *chainsaw* or *massacre* in it?"

"What, you've never heard of *My Heart's Massacre* or *Chainsaw Beauty*?"

He laughed and I did too, but then I saw something that made me stop laughing. Glancing at Polly Prissy Pants, I told myself that it wasn't true. I didn't see what I *thought* I'd seen. "He's back with the chainsaw. I have to go."

Her foot twitched. She was waking up.

"Have fun at your movie, little sister!" Andy's voice was sickeningly sweet.

"Oh, bait me," I said.

Andy laughed so hard it made my ear hurt, and I hung up on him. *Bait me* was our replacement for *bite me* . . . in more ways than one.

Bait is what I was. Literally.

My family were hunters. Supernatural hunters. Everyone gifted in their own way with some unique power or skill. Everyone but me. And so I became the bait. It was my job to be the helpless girl in a dark alley. The clueless teenager with a flat tire. The lost hiker with a broken shoelace. You'd be surprised at how many demons, vampires, and vengeful spirits there are out there.

Normally, each hunt we went on had to be carefully vetted and approved by every family member. But this time, I'd wanted to do something on my own. To bring in a catch without them, and *prove* that I was ready to be more than just bait.

Bait me, my ass.

I had just enough time to turn, when the trees parted. Green berets and sashes came crashing through the branches as a swarm of hungry Girl Scouts caught sight of me. According to their badges, it was the rest of Troop 409.

And I was all out of meat.

"Shit."

All those years of obstacle course training and nighttime avoidance maneuvers that Mom and Dad had *insisted* upon when I turned nine suddenly came in handy. I hooked left and started sprinting, jumping over roots and ducking under tree limbs as I went.

The Girl Scouts had a surprising amount of endurance for being so young. Either that, or I was getting soft.

But I still had a few tricks up my sleeve. I took out my knife and sliced my hand. Crisscrossing my path, I left traces of blood on each tree that I passed in order to confuse them. They were only capable of focusing on one thing right now: food.

Suddenly, the trees came to an end and I found myself back on the road. Where my car *should* have been.

My car that was now gone.

Stolen. Or towed. Who knew which one?

"This is *so* not what I need right now." I turned around in a circle, but my car didn't magically appear. I quickly clicked my heels together three times, but that didn't do it either. "Damn Dorothy bullshit. That stuff from the movies never works."

My phone was in my pocket. All I had to do was make one

call, and Dad or Andy would come pick me up. But that would lead to several problems. First, I'd have to explain the whole "I'm not really at a movie" thing, but more importantly, I'd have to explain why I'd driven to woods that were two hours away from home to try and track cannibal Girl Scouts on my own.

That, I definitely did *not* want to do.

"Please, won't you come play with us?" a voice said, from the trees on the right.

"We want to play with you," said another, on the left.

Close. Too close.

I couldn't let them see me panic. That was Dad's number-one rule. So, I yelled back, "Don't you know you're not supposed to play with your food?"

One of them giggled.

The giggle was what set me off. It made the hairs on the back of my neck stand up, and I started running down the road.

When I finally saw headlights, I knew it had to be divine intervention.

I waved my arms wildly to flag down the driver of the black SUV. Stealing a glance at the woods behind me, I was sure that I could still hear them giggling and grunting.

"Hurry, hurry, hurry," I chanted, as the driver rolled to a stop and opened his window.

"Everything okay?" he asked.

"My car broke down. Can you give me a lift?" Already, I was opening the back door.

"Okay, sure."

I climbed in, surprised to see that there were three other people seated inside. "Go, go," I urged the driver. "Just get out of here." I tried to look out the back window, but it was tinted. So darkly tinted that I couldn't see anything.

"Is something chasing you?" the driver asked, shifting gears. "Was it a bear?"

"Something like that."

The doors were all safely shut now, but I wouldn't feel better until we were moving again. "If you can just take me to the interstate, that would be great. There's a movie theater at the second exit. I can get a ride home from there."

"Headed that way ourselves."

He hit the gas pedal and we moved away from the woods. Not fast enough for my liking, but at least it was in the right direction. *Away from them.*

The inside of the car was dark, but my eyes were adjusting and it was then I started noticing what my traveling companions were wearing. Feather boas. And . . . corsets. With high heels and fishnet stockings.

Then I noticed something else. The smell.

It's a very unique scent, and hard to describe what it is exactly. Dad has this theory that it's the chemicals given off by a body when it's slowly starting to decay. It takes years to be able to hone your sense of smell to even be able to recognize it.

But I knew what it was.

That smell, plus the tinted windows and the boas could only mean one thing: I was catching a ride from a car full of vampires in drag.

"So," I said casually, putting a hand down by the top of my boot. I always carried an extra stake in there. "Where are you guys going?"

"Denton," the vamp next to me replied. "We're on a road trip."

"We can call a mechanic for you," the driver offered. "When we get there."

"A satanic mechanic!" the rest of my traveling companions sang out.

And that was when I acted.

Grabbing hold of the stake, I slid it free and slammed it under the chin of the guy in the seat next to me. "If I were you, I'd start praying to whatever god you believe in *right now*." With emphasis on the last two words, I dug the tip of the stake into his skin and heard a gasp of pain.

"Whoa, whoa, whoa!" he cried.

Suddenly, the tires locked and we swerved wildly as the driver slammed on the brakes. We came to a stop in the opposite lane.

I kept my grip firm. Little hiccups of sound filled the car and I realized that the big, bad vampire was crying.

"Please," he said. "I swear, we won't hurt you. We're just going to a—"

"Oh, stop it. Like I'm going to believe a vampire?"

Light from the overhead console flooded the interior, and I blinked at the sudden brightness.

"How do you know what we are?" the driver asked.

I glanced at him and saw that his face was covered in white makeup. A black circle had been drawn around the edges as an outline, with exaggerated blue eye shadow and heavy red lipstick completing the look.

"This has got to be the weirdest capture ever," I said, shaking my head. "Vampires in drag . . ."

"We're not in *drag*," Front-seat Guy said. "We're in *costume*."

"Costume? It's not Halloween."

My stake-to-the-neck companion spoke in a whisper. "It's for a convention."

"That's why we're going to Denton," the driver said. "You know, like in *The Rocky Horror Picture Show*? They hold a convention there every year. Besides, not every vampire wants to hurt people. Some of us just want to have fun. We've been defanged."

"Open your mouth," I instructed my captive, pinning him with a steely glare. He complied. There were four identical holes where the enlarged canine teeth should have been, two on the upper level and two on the lower level.

"Now you." I pointed to the driver, and he showed me his holes. Front-seat Guy was next, and then a girl on the opposite side of my companion. All were clean. Just like they said, they'd been defanged. "Okay then." I pulled my stake back and put it away. "So what exactly are you supposed to *be?*"

"Dr. Frank-N-Furter."

"Dr. who?"

"Haven't you ever *seen The Rocky Horror Picture Show?*"

"No."

Every single one of them gasped.

"Why don't you tell me?" I suggested. "While we *get back on the road.*"

The overhead lights dimmed and everyone talked at once as we started driving again.

"It's a story about Brad and Janet—"

"They get stuck out in a storm and have to go stay at Dr. Frank-N-Furter's castle—"

"But he's an alien from the planet Transylvania—"

"A sweet transvestite—"

"And he's creating a man, Rocky. But then Rocky gets loose because Magenta—"

"—a maid—"

"And Riff Raff, a handyman, want to go back to their home planet. . . ."

"In the end Dr. Frank-N-Furter and Rocky die—"

"And the Transylvanians go back home!"

"Uh-huh," I said. "And there's dressing up? Like this?"

"Oh, yeah! And choreographed musical numbers."

The vampires started singing a song about a sweet

transvestite from Transsexual, Transylvania, and I considered asking them to drive me back to the cannibals. At least *they* didn't sing.

The exit is coming soon, I told myself over and over again.

"Hey, I'm thirsty," Front-seat Guy said suddenly, when the never-ending song was finally done.

The vamp next to me reached behind us and pulled out a big blue cooler. Flipping open the top, he revealed a row of beer cans. "Want something?" he asked me.

"No," I said. "Thanks." Andy let me try his beer once, and I'd thrown up for two days straight.

"All the good stuff is at the bottom anyway," he replied, removing the top tray to reveal a fake bottom. He lifted that up and showed me plastic bags filled with red liquid and packages of raw hamburger meat.

"*Nice*," I said, impressed. "Regular human stuff on top in case you get pulled over?"

"Yup. The cops don't give you a hard time if they see a cooler full of beer. A cooler full of blood, though, is harder to explain." He reached in for a Baggie and tossed it up front. Then he pulled out a package of hamburger.

Ripping open the plastic, he pushed the meat aside and started slurping at blood left behind on the white Styrofoam tray.

"Dude, gross," I said, trying to ignore the queasy feeling in my stomach caused by the slurping sounds. "That's nasty."

He paused and looked up at me. "How do you think we get our blood?"

"I thought you guys had access to blood banks or something like that."

He snorted. "TV and movies get vampires all wrong. We don't have inheritances or multimillion dollar fortunes to pay off the people who work at places like that. If you're just a regular Joe like me, which is my name, coincidentally, you can't get into a blood bank. They put your name on a list and do a bunch of background checks on you. Do you know what I was in my regular life?"

I shook my head.

"A *dental assistant*. Seriously, why the hell would a dental assistant need to get into a blood bank? I made twelve twenty-three an hour. Not enough to start a savings account for my eternal afterlife. Hamburger meat is easier. And cheaper. No one puts your name on a list if you buy fifty pounds of it."

"I never thought about it like that."

"This Vampire Public Service Announcement has been brought to you by The More You Know," Joe said. Then he went back to licking his Styrofoam. "Vampires on TV give us all an unhealthy body image stereotype too. Do you know how hard you have to work out to get a body like those actors on *True Blood*, or *The Vampire Diaries*? Try doing it when your blood vessels don't work anymore and your muscles are slowly starting to waste away."

Like I want to talk about all the problems a vampire *has.* "Can someone turn on the radio?" I asked.

"I've got a better idea!" the girl vamp said. "'Ninety-nine Bottles of Blood on the Wall'!"

"Ninety-nine bottles of blood on the wall," Joe sang. "Ninety-nine bottles of blood . . ."

"Oh, God," I muttered, "I'm stuck in a car full of vampires singing road trip songs. Somebody stake me now."

"Take one down, pass it around . . ."

" . . . ninety-eight bottles of blood on the waaaaaaaall!"

"Enough!" I grabbed my stake again and whipped it into the air. "The next person to sing another verse of that stupid song is going to get staked, so help me God. I don't care if you *are* defanged, I'm going to—"

A loud pop came from outside the car, followed by a steady thumping.

The girl vampire screamed, and Joe yelled, "What was that?" as we kept bumping along. Then the driver slowed to a crawl and our thumps slowed with him. Every time the tire rotated, we heard a dull, slapping noise.

The sound of a flat tire.

"I think it's a flat," the driver and I both said at the same time.

"Just like Brad and Janet," the girl vamp whispered.

The driver pulled the car onto the shoulder. I followed him outside and came around to his side. "Definitely a flat," he said, kicking the deflated piece of rubber.

"Do you have a spare?" I asked.

"Yes, but I've never . . ."

I sighed, rolling up my sleeves. "Get it for me. I'll do it."

He went to the trunk and came back a moment later with the tire and a jack in hand. The other vampires got out of the car too.

Kneeling down, I started to jack up the car. In the background, I could hear Joe instructing the others, "No, no, you have to be in sync when you jump to the left and then step to the right. Kelly! It's a pelvis *thrust*, not a pelvic wiggle. Like this!"

"Call me *Magenta*," I heard her whine. "You know that."

I couldn't help myself. I stopped to watch.

Three vampires in fishnets and feather boas were lined up, knees pushed together, doing a dance that looked like something straight out of a bad Ke$ha video.

It was the strangest thing I'd ever seen.

So I did what any normal person would have done in the same situation. I hauled out my phone and started filming it. This baby was going viral.

When I turned back to the spare and picked it up, I knew immediately that we had a bigger problem. "Damn it."

"Janet! I love youuuu!" came the reply.

"We have a problem," I called to the driver. He was too busy trying to get in on the "jump to the left and step to the right" action to pay any attention to me. He didn't respond, and I yelled, "Hey, *you*. Driver. What's your name?"

He turned. "Me?"

This night was only getting better. "Yes, you. Name?"

"I'm David. That's Dickson, you already know Joe, and she's Kelly." He pointed at each one.

"Magenta," Kelly hissed.

"Great. Thanks for that. I'm Jane. We have a problem, David. This spare tire won't work. It needs air." I looked at my phone. *No service.* "Seriously?" I shook it, but nothing changed. "I can get reception in the middle of the woods, but not on a main road?"

I turned back to David. "Do any of you have a phone? I'm not getting service."

He looked sheepish. "We really don't like cell phones. Can't we just use the tire until we get to the next exit? There's bound to be a gas station there. Someone can help us."

"The next exit is twenty miles down the road. The tire won't take us that far; we'll bend the rim."

"Oh."

"Yeah, oh." I stood up and rolled my sleeves back down. "We're going to have to walk to the nearest house, or at least until we have reception."

Joe, Kelly/Magenta, and Dickson were still lined up, only now they were doing high kicks and throwing their boas around. "Guys, hey, guys!" I called. "*Guys!*" I shouted louder.

"Would you stop doing those stupid dances and come join the conversation? We have a problem here."

"But we have to *practice*," Dickson whined. "How do you expect us to win the talent show? There's going to be a lot of stiff competition."

"There isn't going to *be* any talent show or any *Ricky Hopper Show* convention if we don't find someone with a phone, or a car. We are stuck out here. S-T-U-C-K. Do you understand?"

"It's *Rocky Horror*," Dickson said, sulking.

I pulled out my stake. Just a little bit, but enough for him to get the message.

"So," he said, quickly coming over to join the powwow David and I had going on. "Which way should we go for help?"

I scanned the woods. There was a light in the distance. "Over there." I pointed. "There's a light."

"Over at the Frankenstein place?" Joe said.

"Huh?" I looked at him.

"Burning in the fireplace?" Kelly replied.

"There's a liiiight," they all sang.

I put up one finger and they all stopped. "New rule: no more singing. Agreed?"

Silence greeted me, but there were nods all around.

"Okay. We go that way."

I led the way to the house and we traipsed through the dark woods. Of course, *of course*, the house was a giant monstrosity of a thing that looked like something from a horror movie. The grass in the front yard was up to our knees, with rusted vehicles littering the lawn. Vehicles that had busted-out windshields and cracked driver's side windows.

"Nothing says 'Hey, I'm normal' like a car graveyard in front of your house," I muttered. I pulled out my phone. *Still* no service.

"Should we knock?" Dickson asked. "It's kind of . . . creepy."

"Let's go to the next house," Kelly urged. "I don't think they're doing the Time Warp in there."

"Seriously? A vampire is freaked out by a *house?*" I gave a disgusted shake of my head and pushed on the doorbell.

The door swung open.

No one was there, but instantly all of the vampires took a step back. Joe actually nudged me forward a bit.

"Go on," he said. "Ask if they've got a phone. And while you're at it, go see what's on the slab."

They all snickered, and I glared at them. "Why me? You're the fiends from hell."

"I resent that," Joe replied. He pointed back at himself with both hands. "Dental assistant."

"Fine," I muttered. But I took a step forward. "Stay *here*." The last thing I needed was for some overly zealous fanatic with a strict belief system to take offense at a vampire in a feather boa. "I'll be right back."

The door slammed shut behind me as soon as I was across the threshold, but at this point? I was expecting that. Spooky slamming doors went hand in hand with spooky houses. Besides, I've trained for years to learn not to jump at loud noises.

"Hello?" I called, adopting the tone of a lost and scared teenage girl. "Is anyone home?" It was always to my advantage to let people think I'm something I'm not. "I need to use your phone. My car broke down and I—"

It was a soft noise that stopped me. A noise coming from the heat vent in the floor.

I moved closer, being careful to keep my back to the wall. The sound came again. A scream. Muffled, like it was being held back by something. *A gag? A piece of cloth?*

"Shit, shit, shit." I opened my phone again, holding it at a higher angle to see if the reception was any better.

It wasn't. I was on my own.

"Remember, this doesn't have to be supernatural," I reminded myself. "You could have just stumbled onto a normal serial killer's house. Or backwoods mutants. Hillbilly Bob and the Freakshow gang."

I looked down into the hallway. The coast was clear. Moving stealthily, I rounded the stairs and came upon the living room. An old wooden door with telltale red stains at the bottom of it was there. *Blood*. The door probably led to the basement.

Right on cue, the muffled scream came again. Followed by a scraping sound that made my blood run cold. Someone was sharpening a tool. Maybe an ax?

I debated between the stake and my silver dagger. Sure, a wooden stake could cause massive amounts of damage, even to a human body, when thrown properly, but the dagger was my favorite. Gripping the plain hilt (no jewels, they made it too slippery), I crossed the floor and slowly opened the door.

As I did that, the front door behind me blew open and I could hear the vampires screaming. I tried to turn back, but the basement door was slippery underneath my hands. Wet with blood on the other side. I could barely hang on, it was threatening to close on me, but I jammed my boot inside and wedged myself into the stairwell.

It was poorly lit, and I stepped carefully as I made my way down. The basement smelled moldy, with the scent of rotten meat hanging heavy on the air. Dirty kerosene lamps were strung up in a row around the ceiling, and some of them were still smoking. Hastily blown out in an attempt to conceal whatever was down here. Luckily, whoever had done it had missed one.

A whimper came from the corner.

With my free hand I dug out my mini flashlight and directed it to where I'd heard the sound. The lamp wasn't strong enough to cast its weak glow all the way over there.

Steeling myself for what I'd find, I was sure that it was going to be something hideous. Something monstrous. It would be deformed. Missing arms and legs. Maybe the head would be gone, or tossed in a corner. And it . . .

It . . . was a boy.

A shirtless boy, with a fresh cut across his bare chest.

So, I did what any normal person would have done in the same situation. I just stared at him. I mean, what are the odds of finding a cute, shirtless boy strapped to a table and waiting for me? I thought about taking out my phone to video him, but figured that was probably too much.

His arms and legs were held in place with heavy leather straps that looked like they belonged in a psych ward. But his eyes were wild and pleading. He made a sound again and strained against his bonds.

That shook me out of my lust-induced stupor, and I went right to work. Wedging the flashlight under my chin, I freed his left leg, and then the right. "I'm going to get you out of here," I said calmly, switching to his arms. "It won't take much longer."

His head thrashed, and I realized that the gag was still in place. I reached up for it, and he spat it out as soon as it was loose. "Hurry up," he said in a harsh whisper. "A crazy guy lives here and he cut me. I think he wants my heart."

That was bad news.

"He's hideous," the boy said. "Scarred. And his parts . . . I don't think they're all his."

His arms were almost free, but I stopped working for a minute. "His *parts?* What do you mean?"

"His arms and, I think, his legs. They don't match. One is longer than the other. And they're different colors. Sort of blue or purple."

Really bad news.

I knew where this was going and I didn't like the sound of it. "Does he have scars around his neck?"

"Yeah. I think so. Although I wasn't really checking out the guy's neck when he started to rip me open."

"Any scars on his wrists? I need you to think. This is really important."

"Think? All I want to do is get the fuck out of here. Who *are* you?"

"Someone who got lost in the woods," I said absentmindedly, mentally running through the list of supplies that I knew I had with me.

The guy sat up. "Look, I don't know who you are, or if you know who that crazy dude is, but I'm just a guy with a flat. Let me out of here and I swear you'll never see me again."

"You had a flat tire?" I asked.

He nodded.

Great. So our flat wasn't an accident.

Sliding the dagger back into my pocket, I put the flashlight between my teeth and spoke around it as I pulled out what I would need from my utility belt. "I'm not the one keeping you here. Feel free to leave. But if you want to actually, you know, stay alive? You'd better stick with me."

A scream came from the floors above us. An unmistakable woman's scream, and I looked up.

"What does he want?" the boy asked.

"He wants a piece of you. Arm, leg, thumb, heart . . . any of it. All of it. He's a resurrectionist. Sort of a mad scientist."

"Oh, shit. Like Dr. Frankenstein?"

"No. Dr. Frankenstein made a monster. This guy *is* the monster." Resurrectionists were possessed by demons that drove them mad with their constant desire for the perfect body. They would find human hosts who disassembled and reassembled themselves hundreds and hundreds of times just to get the right "match."

Leaving a wave of body parts in their wake.

"How do you know he's a . . . what did you call him again?" the boy asked.

"Resurrect—" I sighed. "Never mind." It would take way too long to explain to him about my family and the fact that we'd already come across one of these guys before in Utah. "I just like to watch a lot of TV, and there's a serial killer who's loose. They gave him a nickname."

Holding up a quarter-sized piece of quartz crystal, I looked it over and then quickly palmed it again.

"What's that?" he asked.

"Protection. A girl's always gotta carry some. But we need to leave. *Now.* Follow me."

He nodded and, thankfully, didn't ask any more questions.

Creeping toward the stairs, he stayed close behind me as we went up. The door was jammed, but my favorite silver dagger easily proved once again why it was my favorite as I jimmied the lock.

I stuck my head out slowly, surveying the scene in front of me. The living room had a dark red streak running across it that hadn't been there before, and humming sounds were coming from the kitchen.

But the path to the front door was otherwise clear.

"Ready?" I whispered. "On the count of three, we run to the door. No matter what, do *not* stop. Do *not* look around. Just hit the door, get outside, and go through the woods. The main road is about eighty feet south of here. Got it?"

"Got it."

"Okay, one . . . two . . ."

Loud sobs filled the air, and I knew, just *knew*, that it was Kelly.

"It sounds like he's got someone else," he said. "Are we going to help them?"

"No."

"No?"

"*No*. They're . . ." *Vampires*. But I couldn't leave them. They were defanged, for God's sake. "Shit!"

Cannibal Girl Scouts were one thing. I'd known I'd be able to find them because the moon was full and that's when their feeding frenzies were always at their worst. But vampires *and* a resurrectionist now too? I could seriously use some backup.

I took a deep breath. "Okay, new plan: on the count of three, you go."

"But what about—?"

"I'll take care of it. You just get free and clear, okay?" I didn't leave room for any hesitation. "One . . . two . . . three . . . go!"

We burst out from behind the door and I focused on finding the vampires. The boy was on his own. Hopefully, he would listen to me.

The living room branched off into a sitting room, where I found Kelly huddled in the corner, with Dickson tied to a chair. His head was down, eyes closed. I ran to Kelly and grabbed her arm.

One shoe was gone and her makeup was running, but she looked up at me and struggled to her feet. "I thought you were dead," she hiccupped. "He has Joe and David. David's leg . . . his leg is . . . gone. . . ." She started crying again, and I forced her to follow behind me as I went to Dickson.

He was harder to wake up. It took a couple of slaps, but then he bolted upright. Straining at the ropes, he loosened them a bit as he thrashed from side to side, and then I was able to get him free. "We gotta get out of here," he kept saying. "We gotta get out of here."

"You two, go," I insisted, pushing them to the door as soon as the last rope fell away.

"But what about Joe and David?" Kelly asked. "It's horrible."

"I'll find them. Just *go*. I don't need the two of you to worry about."

Dickson grabbed Kelly's hand and they took off. One minute they were right there, standing next to me, and the next, their boas were flapping behind them as they scrambled out the front door. I turned to the kitchen. Two down, two to go.

Or so I thought.

The boy, it turned out, had not listened to me.

As soon as I entered the kitchen, I came face-to-face with the resurrectionist sitting on top of him, holding him down. David was in the corner, minus a leg. Just like Kelly had said.

The resurrectionist looked *awful*. Bloated skin and mismatched arms. Even though he was crouching, I could tell that one limb was drastically shorter than the other. It didn't reach the ground. In fact, it almost looked like a woman's leg.

"So, I have a question," I said, holding the crystal behind my back and clutching it with all my strength. If it was torn out of my grip, it could be the end of me. "Are you technically a man, or a woman? I mean, you've pretty much replaced all the important parts, right?"

As I spoke, I felt the crystal growing warmer in my hand. It was absorbing my energy, and I'd need that to help me take this big boy down. "In the Name of God, the God of Israel," I chanted quietly, "may Michael be at my right hand, Gabriel at my left—"

"Why do you do that?" the resurrectionist said, looking over at me. "That does not stop me."

The demon inside him had taken on the voice of a young boy.

"What is *with* the demented children's voices?" I asked, stopping my chant. "Do you creatures *want* to scare me off from ever having kids of my own one day?"

The resurrectionist turned his head to one side with an unearthly calm.

Almost time. "Uriel before me, Raphael behind me, and above my head, the presence of God!" I said.

He just looked confused.

"The protection spell is for me, dumb-ass. It might not be able to stop you, but *this can*." Holding the crystal out in the flat of my hand, I said, "Return to the center of the circle, from whence you came. No man shall come upon you, until the end of time. So mote it be!"

I waited just long enough for the demon to start separating from the man he'd possessed. The room filled with an angry swirl of black haze, and I couldn't see. I had to time it just right, or he wouldn't be captured in the crystal. And I wouldn't be going home at all tonight.

"So mote it be!" I screamed, as the black smoke was sucked into the center of the stone. I smashed the crystal down onto the wooden floor as hard as I could.

It shattered to pieces.

The empty shell of the man that the resurrectionist had been possessing fell over, long dead generations ago. His skin was molting off of him in little flakes, and his eyes were a filmy blue. The boy on the floor just lay there, quivering under the hulk of rotten flesh.

"It's all fun and games," David said suddenly, hysterically. "It's all fun and games until someone loses a leg. He took it! He took my leg!"

I glanced over at the crude chop job that had severed his right limb just below the knee. Luckily, one of the side effects of being a vampire was that they bled very slowly. What should have been a torrential stream from opened veins and arteries was only a slow trickle. The leg in question, however, was nowhere to be seen. And I wasn't going to stick around to find it. Resurrectionists usually traveled in pairs.

"You'll be fine," I told him. "Now you'll have a story to tell all the other vamps at the convention." I leaned over to give the boy on the floor a hand up. "Since *you* didn't take my advice and get out while you could, you're going to help me carry this whiny bloodsucker all the way back to the car."

The boy didn't say anything, but moved when I pushed the body of the former resurrectionist off of him. I rigged David in between us, and a loud whimper came from the cabinets to my left.

"What . . . ?" I turned to glance at it.

The door swung open slowly and Joe came crawling out, his fishnets torn and holey. "I hid when he went after David," he admitted sheepishly. "Sorry, buddy," he said, casting David a baleful look.

David groaned loudly.

"Where's Dickson and Kelly?" Joe asked.

"Already out. You want to go find them?"

He nodded, and David groaned again. Joe led the way to the front door. "Well, *this* has been the best night of my life," I said, as we limped toward it. "I think I'm in the mood to watch *The Rocky Horror Picture Show* now. Maybe I'll even go to next year's convention. You guys want to go with me?"

Joe started to say something, but as he opened the door, we were greeted by a new sight. And a new sound.

Ten little Girl Scouts in perfect green sashes and perfect green bows with bared teeth and raised hands lunged at us, growling in unison.

Troop 409.

I looked back and forth between Joe and the boy, calculating my chances of getting out of here with the least number of flesh wounds. Wondering who was going to get the worst of it.

It was David who surprised me.

"You little bitches," he said, almost growling.

"Ready to do this thing?" I asked Joe. "We're going to have to make a run for it and if you're going to leave us behind, tell me now."

Joe stood taller and straightened his shoulders, eyes turning completely black. Another neat vampire side effect. *Impressive.* Apparently, he'd decided to atone for his act of cowardly cupboardness.

"It's only fair. You didn't leave us behind, so we can't leave you."

The Girl Scouts snarled, moving closer, and I knew my night was far from over. "Okay," I said, preparing to head into battle.

I knew my role. The one I played perfectly. And this time, I had backup.

"Bait me."

IV LEAGUE
by Margaret Stohl

I.

"The thing I mostly care about," I repeat, "is the food."

Hopper ignores the slick pamphlet in my hand. Instead, he pulls his hoodie closer around his face, digging his ratty sneakers into the ratty back of the green upholstered seat in front of him. "Yeah? You checkin' out the eats up North? Thinkin' of knockin' back a six-pack of blue bloods, Wrennie?"

"Maybe," I say, looking out the window. The sign says MASSACHUSETTS AVENUE, which, if you think about it, is not the most original street name in the world, especially for a town that's supposed to be so smart and all. "But I hear you eat like crap up here." Our bus inches down the road, and a dirty city square comes into view. Long-haired street guitarists pull the crowd into distinct encampments. The lone juggler doesn't stand a chance.

Miranda Cooper giggles in front of us. Natalie Anne Rutledge, one seat over, shoots Hop and me the same old look she's been shooting us since the day we met, except now all you can see is eyeliner. She sighs because she's the expert at pretty much everything, which I guess understandably calls for a whole lot of sighing.

"Don't you know, Maynard Hopper Wilson? That's Harvard Yard over there, behind that gate. *Har-vard Yard.*" She says it like it's a hot guy or a hot car or something, which it isn't. Still. *Gyll-en-haal. Fer-arr-i.* As far as I can tell, it's just a gate, and not even as nice a gate as they have over in Charleston, where the iron's all twisted up like pearls and ribbons around every window and every door.

"So?" Hopper shrugs under his hood.

"So, dumbucket, old money just tastes better." First her tongue, then her teeth slide out over her Dr Pepper-Lip-Smackered lips, and I can tell the kill is coming. "But I guess y'all wouldn't know much about that, would you?"

"You still talking to us, Natalie Anne? 'Cause you know we stopped listening about two hundred miles back." I look past her, out the window, and she sighs. Again.

Hopper grunts, pulling the strings of his sweatshirt even tighter. Only in this conversation is Hopper suddenly Maynard Hopper Wilson, and me Wren Lola Lafayette. Natalie Anne Rutledge never calls a person by just one name. She's called us plenty of other names, Hopper and me, but none of them are worth repeating. Hopper because he's Hopper, poor as church dirt and dumb enough not to care. Me because all I got is a name, and that's the most part of what you need to know about my no-good Breather parents, according to my Grandma Hoban. She's not one for what she calls "reachin'." Especially not when it comes to a stray like me, left behind on her door-step seventeen years ago. Might as well be an empty bottle of O-Pos, from way back when the bloodmobile still came around.

She didn't want me to go visiting colleges in the first place, not up North. "Bloom where you're planted. That's what my momma used to say." Her momma also used to say things like "A woman's work is not to work" and "Get U.S. out of the U.N.," but I didn't think pointing that out was going to change my Grandma Hoban's mind anytime soon. So I did what any college-bound, twelfth-grade Drinker would do. Lied to the teacher. Forged my grandma's name on my papers. Went out the back screen door while she was watching her shows and got on the bus with the rest of my class from *Just Keep On Drivin', There Ain't Nothin' to Look At 'Round Here* High School. That's what our sign says—at least, the graffiti on our sign by the free-way exit to our craphole little town. The one at the other end of town says NO TRESSPASSIN WILL SHOOT. Tresspassin's the closest thing we have to a name anymore, now that there aren't any Breathers left in town to do things like clean graffiti off the road signs. Nobody comes, nobody goes. We got nothing.

Which means, nothing to eat. Nothing like they got around here.

We did it to ourselves. We wanted Tresspassin to fall off the map; at least, the folks before us did. No matter what kind of Drinker you were—whether you were a Dirt or a Viral—you agreed to that. Breathers barely even knew we existed, except in the movies. They had no idea we weren't all the same, not that it mattered. The less Breathers knew, the better. Soon as we figured out about the Blackouts, that Breathers couldn't recall a thing we'd done to them after we'd done it—well, we just kept doing it. Things were better that way, at first. Better for them, better for us. Now, it's just how things are, and that's powerfully hard to change. *Mainstreaming.* I hear my Grandma Hoban snort every time Mr. Skrumbett, Tresspassin's principal and mayor and owner of the gas station and, in a way, my college counselor says the word.

Not me. I think of Mainstreaming as living in a supermarket. The answer to my problems, all wrapped up nice in a college sweatshirt, like plastic wrap in the freezer section. *Dinner on aisle seventeen, come back tomorrow now, y'all . . .*

My stomach rumbles. Hopper answers back, digging his elbow into my side. "Shut up."

But I know he's as hungry as I am, and I guess that's why the school approved this trip in the first place. It's time. Mr. Skrumbett himself let us use the computer center, showed us how to fill out the online Common App, which Hopper calls the Common Slap, since the whole process makes you feel about that low. It's not as easy for us as it is for the Breathers. There isn't much to do in the way of extracurricular activities in Tresspassin, unless you count cow-tipping or maybe cow-sipping. I probably could have learned how to play a sport or something, but there's no other school for us to play against, not within about two hundred miles. Hopper and I looked around on the Breathernet for something you could do with just two people, until we found an actual sport called woodcutting once. They have it at Dartmouth or somewhere. It's where you cut wood with a big saw, one person on each end, like something you'd see in an old cartoon. We may not have woodcutting in Trespassin, but at least we have cartoons.

The SAT, that's a whole other problem. It's made for rich white Breathers, who live in cities and talk right and don't worry about things like Drinker extinction. Some of the kids in my class, Dirts from old families who'd been alive for like, centuries, they did all right. Natalie Anne Rutledge says she was actually *in* the French Revolution, so she completely nailed that passage in the Reading Comprehension section. I didn't think it was fair, but Hopper pointed out that she'd also had to live with herself for going on two hundred and fifty years, so things had a way of evening out in the wash. The rest of us Virals who hadn't dug our way up out of the grave like the Dirts had, those of us who still had things like growing up to do, we weren't so lucky. At least when it came to standardized testing.

The rest of us were going to have to rely on our grades. I have great grades; Hopper and I worked really hard on our transcripts. We had to make them up based on Wikipedia, which is helpful like that. Once we figured out what an AP was, I put that I'd taken a million of them. My favorite class was AP Human Geography. I still don't know what that means, but the words are really beautiful together. Hopper says it's a map of the human body. I think it means all the human bodies on the map. Either way, as soon as I get into a real school, I'm going to take it just to find out.

The Common Slap hurts. It's like they speak a whole different language, the Admissions Breathers. Normally, I'm okay with Breathers, but I feel sick to my stomach when I think or talk about the Admissions kind. Sort of like how my Grandma Hoban used to sound when she talked about the people who came around collecting taxes. I did the best I could. Mr. Skrumbett says my teacher recommendations are really strong. I couldn't find any good ones on the Breathernet, so I pretended to myself that Atticus Finch was writing it. He's a character from a movie in the old Breather library and everything he says sounds pretty smart, especially when he's talking to his daughter. Sometimes I like to imagine I'm her. I stole my second letter from this other messed-up Breather movie, where an old guy named George Clooney plays some kind of big jerk who flies around the world firing people until he feels so bad he writes a letter to help some other super-annoying girl get a job. I keep a copy of both letters in my backpack, single-spaced, folded up all small inside my wallet where the money's supposed to go. I don't know why, but I sort of like knowing Atticus Clooney and

George Finch have my back. That was Hopper's idea, to switch the last names in case anyone besides me had seen the movies. Then he signed them.

I signed Hopper's. All he wrote was *M. Hopper Wilson is the smartist kid in the hole school. Respectibly, Lola Lafayette.* The way I signed, you couldn't read the signature. Just in case. Seeing as he's not all that smart and I'm not all that respectable.

The essays were harder. Mr. Skrumbett passed around a book that was supposed to help you write them. It wasn't that helpful, though, because the book mostly told you what you weren't supposed to do. Like, you're not supposed to write about the time you scored the winning touchdown in the big game, but I never did that anyway. I didn't even know what kind of game we were talking about, to tell you the truth. I also never had a dog that died, took a trip that changed me, fed the homeless, or built a latrine. Which was sort of sad, because the bad essay examples were still better than anything that ever happened to me. Eventually I gave up and wrote about being the first person in my family to go to college. I didn't tell the truth.

I didn't say it was because most of my family was dead or gone, or at least my Grandma Hoban talked about them same as if they were. That I fell asleep hungry and woke up that way in the morning. That if I didn't get out of Tresspassin soon, folks were going to find Natalie Anne Rutledge lying in her bed with an ax handle whittled to a point and sticking straight up out of her chest. That Hopper and me, we'd been making plans to leave since we were old enough to walk as far as the highway.

This trip, it's the last thing.

Four days.

Four days and twelve universities, and I'm starting to think Grandma Hoban was right. If I can't manage four days, how will I spend four whole years around here? I haven't had a decent night of sleep, or what passes for sleep. Haven't had myself a decent meal. Haven't even talked to one. Mr. Skrumbett says we can't draw attention to ourselves, but I don't know how much longer I can hold out.

In fact, I'm starving.

Now the engine sighs louder than Natalie Anne Rutledge, and the whole bus jerks forward and back. My backpack falls off the seat, and a week's worth of college brochures go sliding and skidding across the floor. UNC and SC State. Tufts and Georgetown and Penn and Penn State—blue skies and fall leaves and a fat-faced, warm-blooded freshman on the front of each one. The bus is still shuddering, bad as if it has some kind of whooping cough, and I don't try to pick them up. Probably going to stall out again, like it has only about three times a day since we left Tresspassin. I look down through the high window I cracked open somewhere between BC and BU—I forget which is which.

Breather schools. They all look the same.

A tour group of chubby children tumbles past, an uneven

line centipeding down the brick pavement beneath me. I can smell them baking in the late fall afternoon, sort of like a pie resting and sweating in my Grandma Hoban's kitchen window. My stomach turns over, and now all I can think about is a plate piled high with pudgy-sweet little arms, arms like spaghetti, arms laced with salty veins. My grandma always says my eyes are ten times bigger than my stomach, which makes no sense at all. Right about now I feel like my stomach is ten times bigger than this bus.

"Don't do it. You'll be sorry." Hopper barely angles his head toward me. I can see the spread of blue veins underneath his Hopper-white skin. His voice is a pin in a balloon; it always is. Soon as he starts talking, the spaghetti-arms disappear and the kids become kids again.

"What I won't be is hungry."

"You talk big, but you know you got a bigger heart for Breathers than the rest of us." His voice is quiet, for only me to hear, so I don't punch him. It's an insult, but he doesn't mean it that way.

"You're one to talk, *Maynard*." He hasn't said anything, but we all know Hop has a problem. He's soft as a boiled egg, which is one reason I keep him around all the time. Somebody has to. I wonder how skinny he actually is these days, under that hood of his. He never takes it off, not even for me.

"Get your eatin' disorder under control, Wrennie. Skrumbett'll kill you himself if you step outta line up here."

"Just thinking about some Tater Tots." I keep my eyes on the youngest stragglers, the strays at the end of the class. *Safety in numbers*, I think. *Catch up. Or don't. I'm hungry.*

We lurch to a stop, and I hear Mr. Skrumbett's voice up front. "We're here. Off the bus. Try not to make a scene. You know, blend."

Right.

II.

So there's this statue of a guy sitting in some kind of chair in front of a building where the grass is. He's got a shoe, well two, actually, but only one is shiny and brass-colored. You're supposed to rub it; it gives you some kind of luck. It smells like pee.

"Where do they come up with this garbage? Every school has some old dead Breather statue to rub."

"Shut it, Hopper. Just rub the stupid shoe already."

"I'm not rubbing it. I don't want Breather luck. Good Breather luck is bad Drinker luck. They've been lucky enough already."

He's got a point.

III.

I'm late. I'm lost. I can't read the small print on the campus map. And here's the funny thing—I'm afraid to talk to any of them. Me, Wren Lola Lafayette. Afraid of Breathers.

I'd kill them before I'd talk to them.

That's what I think, anyway. I wonder if Hop would say it was true.

So I walk in the nearest brick building, which looks like Independence Hall from my old history book. I guess I'm in some kind of dorm, which is not where I want to be, but I could be wrong. It's hard to tell. It could be the head janitor's office, for all I know. All the buildings here look equally strange to me.

I knock on the first door inside the hallway. No answer.

I push the handle, and it opens.

The Chinese Breather at the desk doesn't look up from his computer.

"Excuse me, but I'm looking for the Admissions office." No answer. I try again, holding up my campus map.

"Uh, hello? You know someone named . . ."

"No."

I'm not surprised.

My stomach growls and I let the door close in my face.

IV.

"His name is Sherlock. Like the detective."

It takes me a second but I put it together. She's talking about the enormous dog curled on the soft carpet between us. It's the first time the admissions officer has spoken to me, now that her office door has closed behind me. After all this time—the Common Slap and the Wiki transcripts and the Breathernet recommendations—I feel like I have stepped into a boxing ring and the match has begun. Then I try to remember if stepping into the boxing ring was on the list of bad college essay topics, the one Mr. Skrumbett gave us. Banned essay metaphors. *Stepping into the ring. Running the race. Going the distance. Leaving the nest.* I can't remember.

I give up.

I can't think of anything, not a single thing, to say.

The woman is speaking but I'm not listening. Her lipstick is so red it makes me uncomfortable. I pat the dog's head. He growls. It's not my fault, or his. Breather dogs like Breathers, and this is a Breather dog. Though when he growls, I can't help but notice he'd make a great Drinker dog. His teeth are even bigger than mine.

"Ms. *La-fay-ette?*"

I look up. Seems like we're not talking about the dog anymore.

"Ma'am?"

"I read your application. You're the first applicant we've ever had from . . ." She squints, looks more closely at the screen in front of her. "Tresspassaunt." She gives the word an extra little twirl, like it was French or something. *Tress-pass-aunt. Har-vard Yard. Gyll-en-haal. Fer-arr-i.*

"You're a first generation college applicant?"

"Ma'am?" I'm still trying to figure out the right answer to that question when she says it again.

"You're the first person in your family to attend a university?"

She speaks more slowly, as if I am deaf, smoothing out the hard words so that I will understand. I understand even less than she realizes.

"Yes, ma'am. Well, my Grandma Hoban says my mom went to beauty school, but I didn't put it down, I wasn't sure that counted." Her look tells me it didn't. "My Bre—my parents left when I was . . . little."

I can't believe I almost said it. *My Breather parents left me behind, a baby with a blood-bruise.* One little purplish spot inside my elbow and they were good as gone.

"I see." I guess it was the right answer, because now her red lips stretch across her yellow teeth. "What a wonderful opportunity you're giving yourself." She sighs, and I can't help but flash on the face of Natalie Anne Rutledge. I grab the carved mahogany fists of my chair arms to keep from punching her. My hands are shaking, but I don't know if it's from hunger or fear.

What are you doing, Wren Lola Lafayette?

You have to be more careful.

Your whole future—four years of fat-faced undergraduates—depends on this Breather woman.

You could be one of them.

More meals than you can count. More anonymity. More opportunity.

They'll never track you here, and if they do, they'll never be able to do anything. Not at the oldest school in the country. You're right in the heart of Breather territory now. Breathers take care of their own.

"You haven't had any trouble in your area, have you? We've been hearing some of the schools around you have fallen on . . . harder times." She sounded hesitant.

"No, ma'am. Just stories, I guess. I've heard them too." I don't look at her.

"Well. It's the South, right? We'll have to thank Anne Rice for that." She laughs, and I laugh, but I have no idea what we're laughing about or what she's talking about.

I mean, not about the Anne person. The trouble, that I'm pretty clear on.

She seems relieved, and gives the mouse on her computer a few extra clicks. "All right, then. I'll be honest with you." I wish she wouldn't. In my experience, when folks are honest, it's never a good thing. But I nod anyway.

"Like many of our first-generation applicants, your scores aren't the strongest." I hold my breath.

"Though your transcript is amazing." I breathe.

"And your teachers truly seem to care about you, which is a good thing."

"Yes they do, ma'am." I think of Hop's face as he signs the letters. "Thank you, ma'am."

I start to feel better. I let my eyes drift over to the picture of the Charles River behind her desk. Mr. Skrumbett pointed it out when our bus drove over the bridge. I read the caption.

I am wondering what a regatta is and what it has to do with all those little boats in the photograph when I hear the break in her voice.

"But . . ."

She pauses, like a cobra about to strike. My heart thumps and almost as if on cue, the boats and the river and her red smile fade away.

"But, I have to say, from your application, I didn't get a good sense of who you are as a person. I felt like you were being less than forthcoming with me."

Who I am is a Drinker. I want to bite your head off at your neck, right above the pearls. . . .

I force my eyes back up to her face. "I don't understand." My voice sounds strange in this dark little room, and I am startled to realize that I am actually here. I must be, because I've imagined this one room so many times, and this isn't at all how I imagined it.

She is still talking, as if I haven't said a word. "You know, who are you? What's your hook?"

"My what?"

"Your hook. The one thing that sets you apart from the thirty thousand other applicants. Musical instrument? Scientific research? Internships? You're not letting us see who you are. What have you been doing all this time, Ms. *La-fay-ette*, aside from studying? What can you bring to our school community?"

I close my eyes, but it's too late. I know my hook. The memories come, a thousand flashing squares of Breather skin stretch in front of me, a checkerboard of pale, naked necks and wrists and ankles. It is as if I am looking down from the window of a plane, taking in a vast expanse of some kind of sea-to-shining-sea farmland. The sun reflects, glinting from rivers that turn to streams that turn to tiny creeks, though I know they aren't rivers at all, but a web of spreading veins. . . .

"I keep busy."

"Yes. I imagine you do." She clears her throat. "Ms. *La-fay-ette*, let me be perfectly clear. On a scale from one to five, which is how we score these interviews, I would have to give you a one. And that would be generous."

I'm not feeling her generosity. I'm too busy feeling like a one. I swallow. "So you're saying . . . ?"

"I'm saying I think you should be prepared to look elsewhere." She stands up, keeping the desk between us. "You, and *your kind*." She lets her eyes rest on my mouth.

I freeze. *My kind?*

She knows.

Still, I say nothing, nothing I am thinking. I feel my hands curl up around nothing. "What's that supposed to mean?"

"It means we don't want you here. That's why we have these interviews. I can spot you a mile away. Spot you, screen you. Stop you. People like you." She smiles but there's nothing friendly about it. I don't smile back.

"Like me?"

" . . . It's fallen to us to keep out the wrong sort for hundreds of years before you came along. We've got the general safety of the entire student body to consider. . . ."

That's not the body I'm thinking of at the moment.

". . . standards to ensure. A population to build. After all, this isn't just the Ivy League. This is Harvard. We're wealthier than a small country, smarter than a large one."

She swallows a smile down her throat. I watch it go.

"I see."

She holds out her hand. "Good-bye, Ms. *La-fay-ette*."

"It's La-*fay*-ette. Ma'am."

"Is it?"

I tighten my grip on her hand, and feel my finger slide down to her wrist. Her pulse flutters like a bird, like a thousand throbbing little birds, flying away as fast as they can.

Turns out, the birds know best.

V.

In the darkness, we move between the trees, crisscrossing the pathways on Harvard Yard. The moon is bright and round, but there is little light, except for the pale glow of our skin, Hopper's and mine.

"Slow down, Hop. I ate too much, too fast. Feels like I'm going to burst."

Hopper slows, and I fall into step next to him. "You know what they call that?" He looks at me in the moonlight. "The Freshman Fifteen." He smiles and I smile back, unbuttoning the top button on my jeans.

"Hope it's a lot more than fifteen."

"Hope so, Wrennie."

I take Hopper's hand and I hear the gravel beneath our feet, beneath the cold bite of the November night. I pull on the strap of my backpack, which holds a full thermos for the road. I'm going to give it to Hopper. Even now I can hear his stomach grumbling, louder than mine ever did. Anyway, we have a long drive ahead of us tonight. South, as far as we can get before the light. Tomorrow I will be happy our town has no name. Sort of slows down any hope of Breather law enforcement, not that I'm worried.

Hopper squeezes my hand. I might let him make out with me on the bus.

My pack feels light. It's nearly empty, I had forgotten. I left behind a trash can full of college brochures and course catalogues back beneath the desk in the Admissions office.

Just after the body hit the carpet.

Just before I'd clicked "ACCEPT."

Twice.

Once for Maynard Hopper Wilson, the smartist kid in the hole school, and once for me.

I almost wished, just this once, the Admissions Breather would know what had happened back there. Almost. As it was, she was going to wake up with a killer hangover, but that was about it. A hangover, and what looked like a nasty purple blood-bruise inside her left arm. It almost didn't seem like enough.

I smile, my teeth sliding into place at the thought of my dinner. I tell myself, for the first time, I am going to fit in here just fine.

"Come on, Sherlock." The dog barks, looking up at me. His teeth appear at the sight of mine. "I think our luck is changing."

John Harvard's toe gleams in the moonlight. It still smells like pee.

I rub it.

GARGOUILLE
by Mary E. Pearson

*B*lood still seeped from the wound in her thigh. The stub of the arrow protruded, catching on the bars every time the cart hit a rut, tearing her flesh a bit more. She tried not to call out because that only made Frans cackle at his fine catch, smug at the riches he surely thought awaited him at the end of the road. A lifetime of wages for his ilk. But the folly was his. Though her thigh would bear the scars of his arrow for the rest of her life, her back was already healing. She could feel the flesh beneath her cape knitting itself back together, erasing the evidence.

She held her face close to the bars, looking to the horizon, knowing they wouldn't come, knowing they shouldn't, but still she searched and hoped for a black cloud in the distance. For two days they had been on the road traveling north, pas~~t~~ and cottage, past thicket, field, and forest. Th~~ey~~ couldn't be much farther. She had never travel~~ed~~

before, and now it was sinking in: by foot or by cart was the only way she would ever travel again—that is, if she lived.

I love you, Giselle. I love you. . . . I choose you.

It was those words that had caused her to be so careless. For that moment she was stronger than the world. Stronger than knife and net. Stronger than fear. After he left, she couldn't contain her joy. She danced for the flowers in the meadow. She sang. She spread her wings without an eye to the world.

"*Gargouille! Gargouille!*" A dozen children rushed across the square, forgetting their game of stones at the sight of the approaching cart and the enormous wings strapped to the top, unmistakable even from a distance.

"Back!" Frans shouted, pulling on the reins. "She bites!"

"I don't bite!" Giselle called out, reaching through the bars. "But come closer and I will ring your tender little necks like capons—and then stew you for supper!"

The children ran away squealing, and Giselle heaved a momentary sigh of relief. The villages were the worst. Frans used their fear to keep them at a distance, but their intense curiosity still prodded them to poke long sticks through the bars and throw rotten food and dung to watch her flinch. Frans didn't mind these antics, but when curious hands drew too close to the precious cargo strapped to the top of the cart, he shouted warnings about her special powers to kill and maim. For this much she was grateful, that their fears and imaginations gave her some distance from their cruelty.

A cautious crowd milled forward. He let them have a good look while he took a long swig of ale and recounted the tale of her capture. The story had changed with each village as Frans learned what held their attention. He also learned when to cough from his dry, dusty throat so that story-hungry villagers would refill his flask, eager to hear of his bravery and his long, harrowing journey.

She looked out at the curious faces staring back at her, their eyes sweeping over her face and arms, scrutinizing her filth, the sweat and dirt streaks, her long black hair now matted with blood and tangles, the dark circles she must surely have under her own eyes by now. She probably did look like a wild beast.

She turned away, gazing to the south at the dim, smoky horizon, no sign of wing or rescue. Soon it wouldn't matter, and that was why they didn't come. Soon she would begin to forget. One day? Two? She wasn't sure. It was so rare that *gargouilles* were captured. It hadn't happened in years—at least to none of her clan. Now she had shamed them and put them all at risk. Anyone associated with her would have to make a hasty departure and begin a new life elsewhere. Giselle would cease to exist. But the worst part was Étienne. She would forget him, and he would be obliged to forget her too. This new reality made her suddenly roar with pain, an unearthly sound that chilled every darkening corner of the town. Shivers ran through teeth. Villagers screamed and crossed themselves. Frans hit the bars with his whip to quiet her. "Étienne!" she cried again, and slumped in a heap at the bottom of the cart. *Étienne.*

Frans bellowed warnings at her to show his bravery to the crowd, but Giselle only looked at the ground surrounding the cart and not at him. Feet edged closer.

"It looks almost human."

"Can I touch it, Mama?"

"Are you daft? Those things are crawling with vermin!"

"And their bite is poisonous—especially the females."

"Poke her with the stick and see what she does."

Giselle felt another jab in her ribs and pulled away to the other side of the caged cart, still casting her face downward to avoid the stares of the crowd. That was when she saw him. Among the many feet crowding the ground around the cart, she saw his shoe. She would know it anywhere. She didn't look up right away. Slowly she lifted her head and deliberately looked at Frans first, trying to brace herself before she turned to scan the crowd. The slightest slip or gasp could bring his doom. She had been careless with herself—she couldn't be careless with his safety too. But then shame overtook her and she cast her eyes downward again. She couldn't bring herself to meet his gaze. How could she have done this to him? To them? Tears formed in her eyes, and trickled down her cheeks. Villagers laughed and jeered at the crying animal who had frightened them just minutes earlier.

Go away, Étienne. Forget me. Soon I will forget you. Her throat squeezed back a sob and she looked up.

His eyes were locked on hers, bright against the darkening sky. His lips pulled tight and his jaw twitched. He was as still as stone except for the breeze lifting the black hair at his shoulders. Her eyes traveled down to his fists clenched at his sides. It took what was left of her strength not to reach out to him, not to reach through the bars and touch the cheek that had caressed her own just days ago. The ache of need ripped through her. If she could speak, she would. Instead she shook her head, trying to tell him to go. It would be more than she could bear if he were found out too. He eyed the padlock on the bars. *No, Étienne, no. It will do no good.*

He shook his head in return and then sneered, spitting on her. His action drew a smile from Frans, who allowed him to take a step closer, so close he could have reached out and wiped the spittle from her face. Giselle feared he would. "A miserable little wretch, isn't she?" he called to Frans.

"She's a *gargouille*, boy, what would you expect? But you should have seen her a few days ago. A beauty she was. Won't be long before the duke has her cleaned up and shining again. She'll be a prize, this one will."

"How much for the wings?" Étienne asked.

"Are you mad? *Gargouille* wings will heal anything and bring a king's ransom. Even the duke will have to scrape his coins together for this one. Too rich for *paysan* blood like you."

"What about the girl?"

"You mean the *gargouille*? Worth just as much. They grow

back their wings, you know?"

Étienne nodded understanding. "A never-ending supply. You're a wise and lucky man, sir, to have made such a catch." Her wings would not grow back, and Étienne knew it. Nor did they hold magical healing powers for the landwalkers. Their powers ebbed as soon as they were cut away. They were worthless decaying flesh now. She knew Étienne only played along, pretending to intently listen to Frans spout the myths that had followed them, and then Frans embellished even those as he went, soaking in the rapt attention of the crowd that closed in around him.

His lies were nothing she hadn't heard before. There had always been stories about their kind, fearful stories, none of them true. The *gargouilles* were as human as anyone else. They lived among the landwalkers and always had, only different in their own way as a redhead is from a blonde, as odd as a six-toed baby, as rare as an albino. The rarity was what grieved her and where she had let her clan down. Their numbers were dwindling. They had been hunted for their wings for centuries, becoming like anyone else once their wings were cut.

The irony was that *gargouille* blood ran through the landwalkers too—only a trace from some long-ago mutual ancestor, but enough to make them take flight in their dreams, to remember the lift, the wind, the freedom and exhilaration of not being bound to this world, to remember the fluttering of hair on currents, the taut stretch of wing and chest, the longing to soar again once their feet touched land, the bitterness when their eyes opened and their flight was nothing more than a trick of sleep. The landwalkers looked at the *gargouilles* and saw their dreams and unfulfilled desires. They looked at them and saw what they secretly wanted to be, and then despised them for it.

"How *long* before the wings grow back?" Étienne asked Frans, his voice laced with doubt as he deliberately surveyed her back, which showed no signs of emerging wings.

Frans rubbed his bristled cheek. "Not sure exactly. A week, maybe two."

"Perhaps with nourishment they might grow faster?" Étienne suggested.

Frans weighed this thought and turned to Giselle. "What do you eat, beast?"

Giselle lifted her gaze to meet Frans. She surveyed his protruding belly and his rotten teeth. "I drink the tears of angels and share the bread of saints."

There were gasps and mumblings in the crowd at the sacrilege. Frans stood silently, perplexed. It was the first question he had asked her and he didn't understand her answer. He finally laughed it off and threw her a piece of hard barley bread, and shoved a stein of water into the cart through the bars, before going back to telling his stories.

Giselle gulped the water, the overflow dribbling down her cheeks. She wiped the drips away with the back of her hand. *The tears of angels give me flight*, she thought. The *gargouilles* had their own legends too. Her grandmother had passed them on to her as all *gargouilles* were bound to do, stories that explained how they came to be who they were, where their kind diverged from those married to foot and ground, stories that elevated them and gave them a reason to hold their heads high. Her grandmother told her that they once flew with the angels; they were the guardians of the sky; they were the watchers who knew and made right. They were blessed with their velvet wings because they were better. They were chosen. When the angels retreated to the heavens, the *gargouilles* became the angels of the night. Those were the stories Giselle wanted to believe.

One thing she knew for certain: they had to preserve their heritage and their kind because they were precious few. There were of course, a few scattered rogue *gargouilles* who lived alone among the landwalkers, assuming their way of life, but even their identities were unknown to the clans. "As useless as a harp with no strings," her mother said of them. Only the clans still preserved the work of the angels. They were all that mattered, and there were only fourteen left in Giselle's clan. Étienne, he came from the north. He was to be a match for Bridet, but the minute his eyes met Giselle's, they both knew. Bridet knew.

He came to visit Giselle often. Her mother was always spare of words, so Étienne would retell Giselle the stories of old, and he told them like no one else she had ever heard, captivating her with every sentence. They flew in the night, circling with stars and moon, diving through treetop and forest, too dark and too fast to be seen as more than a passing shadow, a whoosh of air, a flicker of starlight, and they were gone. And then one night by a sliver of orange moon, they walked. Giselle unfolded her wings, felt the paper-thin but steely strength of their flesh, Étienne's fingers running along the velvet crest of her wings, his lips sliding down her throat. His wings snapped outward, wrapped her in their warmth. His kisses were gentle and tender, always waiting for her answer. And her answer was always yes. Yes.

The next day she knew it before he said it. She knew what was coming as they walked together in the meadow, their wings carefully hidden away in the daylight. She knew the words on the edge of his lips because some things are just known—they don't have to be said, but he said them anyway. "I love you, Giselle. I love you. I choose you."

"And I choose you back, Étienne."

The match was made. It was complete except for the celebrations with their families. He left to tell his parents in the north. And Giselle danced by daylight in the meadow. Danced, and sang. And she spread her wings without a care for the world or who might be watching.

I choose you back.

"She only looks like a simple peasant girl. Are you sure she's a *gargouille?*"

"Look at the wings, boy! I cut them from her myself—and she put up a hellish struggle!"

Étienne's jaw clenched. His shoulders lurched. Giselle gasped, terrified that Étienne would reveal himself and suffer her same fate. "There are too many!" she cried. "Too many! Leave! Go!"

Étienne pulled his shoulders back, his face softening at her distress, and Giselle sobbed in relief.

"Quiet, beast!" Frans yelled. "These good people want to look, and look they will!"

The crowd rumbled approval. A few patted him on the back, eager to show their own bravery by stepping closer to the beast. Still others offered to buy him a meal and brew at the tavern. Frans rubbed his chin wistfully. It had been a long ride. His barley bread was brick-hard and dry, and his small wedge of cheese was nearly gone. A hot meal would be welcome, maybe even a bit of meat or smoked eel with some porridge, and then he could feed the beast the remainder of his barley bread. A few moments ago was the first time he had fed her since he caught her, and she was looking weak, with no sign of new wings yet. A dead, wingless *gargouille* would not be worth nearly as much to the duke as a live, healthy one. But he eyed his treasure on top of the cart. Going into the tavern was too big a risk to take. "I'll have my meal out here."

Several villagers rushed to the tavern to bring their honored guest some food, and the rest of the crowd dwindled, eager to get home to their own suppers and their twilight chores, possibly more mindful than usual of the darkening sky and the creatures that might inhabit it.

Frans turned to Étienne, who was brave enough to step close

to the cart and was broad-shouldered and a head taller than most in the crowd. Frans flipped him a coin, which Étienne easily caught. "I'm going over there to rest and eat. Two more of those coins for you if you wait here and see that no one touches the cart—or beast." In this village three coins was easily a day's wages. Étienne properly smiled and nodded. "And mind you," Frans added, wagging his finger, "I'll still be watching! I expect diligence for those coins!"

"Of course," Étienne answered.

Frans walked some distance away and settled against the stone wall of the tavern to view the cart from a more comfortable position and await the meal the villagers were bringing him. A half dozen lingered with him, eager to hear more stories about distant lands, since by now Frans had expanded how far he had traveled and the adventures he had seen.

Étienne stood guard, periodically circling the wagon so that he could speak to Giselle without his lips being seen by the watchful Frans.

"When he sleeps and the others go, I'll slit his throat and get the key to the lock."

"No!" Giselle cried through clenched teeth. "It's wrong to take a life!"

"But look what he's done to you!"

Giselle hung her head, ashamed for being so careless. Her clan had often retold the story of a long-ago uncle who had flaunted his wings and brought on not only his own death but also those of three more of the clan. His carelessness had been unforgivable. Tears fell from her eyes to the splintered floor of the cart. "What has been done to me can't be undone," she whispered.

"There must be something—"

Giselle jerked her head up. "There is nothing, Étienne! You must face it. In a matter of hours I will barely be a *gargouille*. I will be as one of them. I will forget our clans and their stories. I will forget who I am. . . . *I will forget you.*"

Étienne shook his head, his eyes glistening. "You won't forget me, Giselle!" he whispered. "I won't let you. And if you do, I'll find a way to make you remember. We will be together again. Do you hear me? *I'll find a way.* Say my name so you won't forget. *Étienne.* Say it! Now!"

"Étienne," Giselle sobbed.

"Again!"

"Étienne." Her voice was barely a whisper, weak with sorrow.

"You love me, Giselle. You always will. A *gargouille* match is forever. Remember that. *Forever.* Look into my eyes. Memorize them. You'll see them again and you'll remember. You'll remember *me.*"

Giselle stared into his eyes, memorizing his pale gray irises surrounded by a rich ring of black, the eyes of the north, but still uniquely Étienne's. He deserved more than she could give him now. More than a landwalker's life. He was still a watcher of the night. Soon she would be fearful of the dark like most landwalkers were. She would cross herself at shadows flitting past the moon. She would recoil at the hideous creatures that adorned the corners of the cathedral and mocked the *gargouilles*. She would wonder at a stonemaster who could carve such monsters. "Forget me. Bridet was your intended anyway."

Étienne shook away her comment. "When you reach the duke's—"

"He's coming!" Giselle whispered, and looked down at her lap.

Étienne continued his walk around the cart until he was facing Frans, who was reaching into his purse. He flipped two coins to Étienne. "Was the beast a trouble? I saw her talking."

"She muttered the sounds of an animal. Nothing I could understand."

Giselle looked up at the voices and for the briefest moment wondered who these two were who imprisoned her in a cage. In the next instant Étienne's name came to her lips, and it made her gasp. It was happening already—she was forgetting. She moaned, unable to bear for him to see her that way, only a shell of who she once was.

She spat at the ground. "This one, he torments me. Send him away!" She glared at Étienne, trying to convince him she wanted nothing to do with him. She saw the wounded squint of his eyes. She forced another sneer. "Leave!"

"You heard the beast," Frans said. "Be on your way now. You've been paid. We have a long journey ahead, and I don't want to listen to her howls the whole way."

Étienne stared for a long while at Giselle, waiting for something, any hint of tenderness, but she only returned his gaze with a steady glare. He finally nodded and walked away.

Giselle followed him with her eyes as Frans readied the horse. She watched Étienne's back as he walked down the road, his figure growing fainter with each step. *Étienne*, Giselle said over and over again in her head. *Étienne. Étienne.* "I won't forget you," she whispered. But by the time he reached the forest, she already had.

The journey took another two days. When they reached the duke's château, Giselle was weak, her lips cracked with thirst and the wound on her leg festering with ooze. She curled in the corner of the cart, too listless to care anymore about the cruel man who imprisoned her, too frail to wonder why she could remember her name and nothing more.

Frans only got a pittance for the wings.

"Imbecile!" the duke shouted at him for believing such tales. "They're probably nothing more than the plucked wings of water fowl! Only good for soup stock!"

Frans sputtered. "I cut them from her myself—"

The duke drew up close. "I'll give you a fair price for the girl. If she lives, she may make a decent servant."

Frans began to argue but then saw the servants of the duke's estate closing in. Two field-workers gripped their hoes and stepped closer. Frans unlocked the padlock on the cart, and the duke's servants lifted Giselle out and whisked her away. The duke counted out payment into Frans's greasy palm. "Never pass this way again."

Frans clutched his money in his fist and looked into the icy gray eyes of the duke. "She's only a beast. You'll find out."

The duke's shoulders lurched forward as if he might strike Frans, but then he carefully pulled them back. It was all that was needed, though, to send Frans scrambling onto his cart and whipping his mare into a frenzy down the road.

By the next day Pauline, the housemaid who helped bathe Giselle and tended the wound on her leg, reported there was no sign on the girl's back of where wings had been cut away. "Her back is completely healed," she told the duke.

"Of course it is," the duke said, rising from his chair. "There never were any wings. She was only the victim of a greedy peddler. Do you *understand*, Pauline? That will be the story if there is to be one."

Pauline nodded and curtsied. "Of course, sir."

Under Pauline's care, Giselle recovered quickly. When she was well enough, the duke gave her duties in the vegetable garden since there was no life that Giselle could remember to go back to. She settled into life at the château, thankful for the kindness of the many servants who watched over her, and grateful to the duke, who gave her a warm, comfortable room off the kitchen. But every day as she worked, she searched for memories, something from her past life, a trigger that would bring it all back. *I'll find a way*, but even that thought seemed to have no root within her, just words rattling in her head like they belonged to someone else. An overwhelming longing grew inside her, and she tried to will a familiar face into her mind's eye. But there was none. The garden became her solace.

She found that she loved her work, the sweet peas and the soil, the squash and the sun, and wished for the days to last longer than they did. At the end of the day she would stare out at the horizon long after the sun was gone, searching for something that never materialized, searching for something that had no name even in her own mind, but she watched with a bewildering anticipation until the last ray of light had vanished. She dreaded the nights the most because of the dreams that accompanied them. When she closed her eyes she saw twinkling stars, felt the rush of crisp air across her cheeks, felt the exhilaration of speed as she glided over the world, the tickle of forest tops on her fingertips, a soaring freedom that filled every breath with indescribable joy, but with the joy of the dreams came the inconsolable loss she felt on waking. Too many times she woke to tears already on her cheeks. And sometimes mixed with the tears was a name on the edge of her lips, and she would suck in a breath, trying to take hold of it again, but it always evaded her no matter how hard she tried to get it back.

At the end of one day, only a fortnight after she arrived, she paused to look down the road that had brought her here, longing to know what came before, when the duke walked up behind her, catching her by surprise.

"Waiting for someone?" he asked.

Giselle whirled around. "Of course not," she answered quickly, wiping her hands on her apron. "I'm not waiting for anyone. I'm just on my way to help Pauline with dinner."

It was only the next day, standing in the same spot, that Giselle spotted a cart coming down the road. Children ran to meet it, shouting their excitement. Giselle hurried to the shadows of the stable to watch as it approached, fearful of the cart, which resembled the one she had arrived in. She could already hear the peddler boasting about his catch. "This one was easy. It practically fell right into my hands. The *gargouilles* may fly like the wind, but they are as dull as lead. I didn't even have to unfurl my net. It only took two easy slashes to part this one from its wings."

The creature thrashed in the cart. *Like a beast*, Giselle thought. Pauline came and stood beside Giselle, shaking her head. "What poor soul has been stolen away now?"

"But there *are* wings strapped to the cart," Giselle replied.

"As there were when you came. Who knows where he really got them? The duke will not be pleased. He'll send that poor excuse of a peddler on his way with the back of his hand."

"No!" Giselle cried. "What would become of the one he's imprisoned?"

Giselle's tender heart endeared her to Pauline. "I'll speak with the duke before he comes out to deal with the peddler. I don't think you need to worry," she told Giselle, and walked back to the house to find the duke.

It was as Pauline said. The duke was angry and sent the peddler on his way, but not before he forced him to unlock the cart and leave his victim behind. The peddler warily unlocked the cart and fled as soon as his prisoner jumped from it. The boy was stained with blood, as Giselle had been, but was stronger and had no arrow wound. He thrashed wildly at those who encircled him. The duke's gardeners raised their hoes, ready to strike, but Giselle could see the fear and anger on the boy's face. "Stop!" she yelled, and ran from the shadows to within feet of where he stood, in spite of Pauline and the duke shouting for her to stay back. The boy saw her and froze.

"No one's going to harm you," Giselle told him. "You're safe now." His gaze locked on to hers and his breathing calmed while Giselle's heart raced faster. "My name is Giselle," she said, and held her hand out to him. "Come with me. Please."

His shoulders relaxed from their hunched position and he hesitantly took her hand. She walked him to the fountain, while all the servants and the duke followed, holding their breath at her boldness, but not wanting to break the spell she had cast over the boy. She held a pitcher under one of the streams of water and gave it to him. He greedily drank from it and then handed it back to her.

"Why am I here?" the boy asked.

It was the same question that had passed through her own mind in her first days at the château. She still had no answer. "I'm not sure why," Giselle answered, "but you don't have to fear anyone here. You're among friends. Where are you from?"

The boy thought for a moment. "I—" He touched his hand to his temple, and his brows pulled together in worry. He looked back into Giselle's eyes. "I'm not sure. I can't—" His head shook in distress.

Giselle felt her heart aching for the boy. She couldn't recall where she was from either and wondered at the dark magic the peddlers must have cast over them both. She heard a murmur flutter through the servants surrounding them and knew they noticed the similarity too. "Don't worry about it now. Maybe after you've rested and eaten something—"

The duke stepped forward and the boy jumped at the sudden movement, ready to defend himself. Giselle noticed how agile and fit the boy was and, from the look of him, quite strong, and wondered how a bow-kneed peddler had managed to overpower him in the first place.

"It's all right, boy," the duke assured him, stepping back to give him more space. "It's as Giselle told you. No one here means you harm. This is my estate. My valet can show you where to bathe and tend to your wounds. He'll bring you food too. And then you may stay on if you like. I can use some help in the stables."

The boy nodded slowly, as if he was still wary. He looked down at his filthy, bloodstained clothes. "Maybe I'll stay for one day." He glanced back to Giselle. "Or maybe two would be better."

"As you wish," the duke answered.

The duke's valet led him away to bathe and to take care of the cuts on his hands and a gash on his head where the peddler had beaten him. She watched as he walked away and wondered at his past and who was waiting for him to return. Who was missing him already? What had he left behind? What made him wander from home in the first place?

That evening at supper she discovered that, just like her, the only thing he could remember from his past was his name. As soon as she heard the name, she repeated it quietly to herself. It was odd how easily it rolled off her tongue. After supper she went to the garden to gather some lemon balm and then took it to him in the stable.

"It will help your wounds heal more quickly," she explained.

He took the leaves from her hand and she didn't realize she was staring into his eyes until she blushed and looked away, but even as she rattled on about the lemon balm, she couldn't get his eyes out of her mind. There was something unusual about them. Their light gray was the color of a pale moon, surrounded by a circle of black sky. The kind of sky you could get lost in, and she already had. She dared not look into his eyes again.

She turned abruptly and left, but when she was about half-way to the château, he ran out of the barn. "You're an angel of the night, Giselle," he called to her.

She turned and stared at him, the moonlight sprinkling silver on his dark hair. It was an odd way for him to say thank you for her kindness, but she liked the sound of it anyway. *An angel of the night.* She smiled.

"Tomorrow then?" he called.

Did she say they would meet tomorrow? He waited for an answer.

"Yes, tomorrow, Étienne."

THE THIRD KIND
by Jennifer Lynn Barnes

"We have to go to San Antonio."

My sister Kissy said those words with all the aplomb of someone announcing that they were fixing to drive down to the Sonic for a cherry limeade. Like she hadn't just woken me up at four o'clock in the morning to deliver the statement in question. Like going to San Antonio was no big deal. Like I'd already passed my driver's test and she hadn't been forbidden to climb behind the wheel of a truck ever again, or at least until she turned thirty.

Forget the fact that San Antonio was a nine-hour drive from our slice of just-outside-of Grove, Oklahoma—big sis wanted to pick up and go, just like that.

"Kissy," I said sternly. "We're not going to San Antonio."

I was the reasonable sister. That was my job. I figured I owed it to Kissy to keep us out of trouble, since it was my two-year-old self's creative pronunciation of her name that had kept her from being a run-of-the-mill Kristy for all these years.

I deeply suspected that *Kristy* Carlton wouldn't have needed nearly so much looking after.

"No, Jess. We *have* to go."

I froze, suddenly aware of the fact that despite the aura of calm about her, my sister's eyes were a pale sea-foam green, colored like stained glass with a light shining straight through.

"Well, crap," I said.

Kissy and I both had mud-brown eyes—depressingly average—except when Kissy got the 'pulse, and then her eyes went stained-glass green, eerie and pale and borderline incandescent, depending on how long she'd been feeling it and how urgent the directive was.

"Do we have to go to San Antonio *now?*" I asked.

Kissy gave me a look that resembled the expression on a dog's face when it proudly dumps a dead bird onto your feet. "Yup."

This was highly unfortunate.

It'd been years since Kissy's last 'pulse, when I was twelve and she was fourteen. Three whole years since she'd woken me up in this very bed and told me, eyes shining, that we had to get out. Three years since someone had broken into our old farmhouse and killed our parents in their sleep.

"It's not like last time," Kissy said, following my thoughts with the ease of someone who'd shared my secrets and my room for fifteen years. "Nobody's going to hurt us or Nana or Grandpa Jake. We just have to borrow the truck and drive to San Antonio, is all."

Somehow, I didn't think our grandparents, who'd moved in

with us after Mom and Dad died, would consider this venture the teensy little thing that Kissy was trying to pass it off as. Which meant, of course, that we couldn't tell them. And wasn't that just fine and dandy?

"Don't be mad."

If I'd been the big sister, Kissy might have sounded vulnerable right then, but since she was older, the words came out bossy by habit.

"I'm not mad," I replied, and I wasn't, truly. Kissy couldn't help getting 'pulses any more than I could help having twice as much hair and half as much chest as the other girls my age. I was flat as a board and had an unruly mass of gargantuan curls, and my sister occasionally woke up *knowing* that something had to be done, without having the least little clue as to why. I could hardly complain (about my sister's quirk, not about the hair or boobs, which I complained about just fine), given that whoever or whatever sent my sister these strange compulsions—be it a misfiring in her brain or God Almighty—had already saved my life at least once.

"Fine," I said, looking out the window and gauging how little time we had until Grandpa Jake rose with the sun. "I'll get dressed, you throw us each a change of clothes into a bag. There should be some cash in my sock drawer."

Just enough for gas, if we were lucky.

But as I stripped off my pajama top and eyed my sister and the irises I hadn't seen looking back from her face in three long years, I couldn't help but wonder if our luck had run out before we'd even hit the road.

San Antonio, here we come.

The two of us made it as far as Muskogee before the truck broke down, which wasn't bad, considering Grandpa Jake's Chevy was older than Kissy and me combined—and temperamental to boot.

"Think she just needs to cool off?" Kissy asked me.

I considered the question. "Did you go over forty miles an hour?"

My sister smiled serenely. "I think I hit eighty back on sixty-nine."

"Then the truck needs to cool off."

I leaned forward to get a glimpse of Kissy's eyes, but she popped on a pair of plastic sunglasses before I could assess just how intense the situation had gotten.

I didn't want to think about what would happen if the two of us weren't quick enough—if the truck wouldn't start back up, or we got lost, or the cops pulled us over for playing hooky.

I didn't want to think about it, but I did.

I imagined Kissy seizing, her limbs twitching, the light in her eyes blinding her to anything else. Up until that night three years ago, Kissy's 'pulses had been a regular thing, and I'd seen her with shining green eyes often enough to know that the more she resisted, the worse it got. *Impulse* didn't even begin to cover the strength of this thing that took over my sister, telling her that she had to do this, that, or the other. Sometimes the *this* in question was a little something—walking to school instead of taking the bus, leaving a bottle of water at the end of a long dirt road, whispering nonsense words to a man she'd never met—and sometimes, it was big.

By the time Kissy was five, my parents had learned not to ask, let alone argue, because if Kissy couldn't or wouldn't do what the 'pulse wanted her to, things got ugly. In the three years she'd been 'pulse-free, I'd almost forgotten what it was like to know that my sister's body might turn on her at any second. Fever, seizures, hallucinations—

We have to go to San Antonio.

Good Lord Almighty, I hoped we'd get there in time.

"You think you'd be okay grabbing breakfast while the truck cools down?" I asked Kissy, trying not to make her sound like some kind of invalid, because I was no fool when it came to my sister's temper.

She took a deep breath and then nodded. "We can't go anywhere until the truck cools down anyway."

I got the feeling that it wasn't me she was talking to.

"If we grab something to eat now," Kissy continued, "we won't have to stop later." Having pled her case to the universe, she opened the driver's side door, and I waited to see if she'd be able to do it.

First one foot out of the truck, then another.

"I'm good," she called back.

I opened my door and joined her on the pavement. We'd broken down in full view of a McDonald's, which was either lucky or not, depending on just how fond (or not) you were of Egg McMuffins. I came down on the *not* side, but Kissy had a long-standing love affair with grease, and far be it from me to stand in their way.

After giving the truck an encouraging pat on the hood, the two of us hightailed it across the highway, Kissy in the front and me on her heels, same as always. A few minutes later, I was drinking orange juice out of a little plastic container that felt about a million different kinds of wrong, and Kissy was chatting up the boy behind the counter, who had probably never seen something like her in his whole entire life.

Kissy was the kind of girl who could make sweatpants, mismatched flip-flops, and gaudy red sunglasses look fashionable. The shades hid her glowing eyes, but there was no masking the giddy energy vibrating through her entire body. Kissy always said the 'pulse felt like someone had hooked her up to jumper cables and given her a real good charge, and even just standing there, watching the boy watching her, I knew he could feel it too.

My sister was *electric*.

"You two related?"

I turned to see a new boy—one who hadn't yet fallen under Kissy's thrall—looking thoughtfully at me.

"You two," he said again, jerking his head toward Kissy. "Are you related?" He had an accent, and not a Southern one, either. I tried to place it, but couldn't, and I realized that thinking about his accent probably wasn't good manners, when I could be answering his question instead.

"Sisters," I told him.

The boy nodded. He was older than me, maybe even older than Kissy, like he was already in college or working full-time at his daddy's garage. Taking a closer look, I thought that maybe he'd been out boozing the night before, because he looked real tired, and he was wearing a baseball cap pulled down over the top third of his face. His eyes—what I could see of them, anyway—were shadowed and bloodshot.

"Sisters," he said thoughtfully. "At the McDonald's at six twenty-seven."

I wasn't sure how one was supposed to respond to such a blatant statement of fact, so I went back to thinking about his accent and how his words sounded like they were coming from the back of his throat instead of the front.

That was when I saw the knife.

He held it loosely in his left hand. I was fairly certain this was a recent development, on account of the fact that I wasn't that oblivious, and the knife wasn't exactly what you would call *subtle*—the blade was nearly as long as my forearm and slightly curved. Its edge gleamed in the fluorescent fast-food lighting.

The boy flexed his wrist.

"I have to hurt you," he said.

I tried to take a step back, but couldn't seem to get my legs to move. "I'd really rather you didn't."

"I *have* to hurt you," he said again.

He stroked the thumb of his right hand over the blade in his left, allowing the metal to slice lightly into his flesh. As blood welled up on his skin, he tilted his head to the side and took a step straight toward me.

Not good. Not good. So not good.

A dam burst somewhere inside of me, and miracle of miracles, I was finally able to move. The first thing I did was start shrieking like a banshee in a yodeling contest. The second thing I did was toss the remainder of my McDonald's orange juice right in his face.

The third thing I did was *run.*

"Jess!" I heard Kissy yell my name, and then there was a flash of gray and yellow and plastic-sunglasses red, and the next thing I knew, my sister tackled the guy with the knife. His baseball cap went flying, and for the first time, I saw his eyes, really saw them: black-blue and glowing, like lake water at midnight, like onyx.

Like Kissy's unnaturally green eyes, only darker.

"I have to hurt you. I have to hurt you both."

Now that I could see the boy's eyes, his words took on new meaning, but he didn't exactly sound torn up about whatever compulsions he was feeling. He sounded meditative. He sounded inhuman. He sounded *hungry*.

Kissy got him pinned down, her hands holding his to the ground, her knees digging into his thighs. Her hair fell into his face, and like a wild thing, she growled.

She was so small and he was so big that I didn't know how she was holding him there. He fought her grip and angled the knife upward, closer and closer to her abdomen.

"I have to hurt you. I have to kill her. I have to stop this before it starts."

With each word, the boy's accent grew thicker, and the dark-light shining from his eyes spread outward from his irises until the whites of his eyes were pitch-black, reptilian and fathomless, like someone had drilled two holes straight through his head.

Kissy slammed the knife sideways, slashing her own hand in the process. Her sunglasses fell off her face, and the color in her eyes began to bleed outward the same way my assailant's had, shining brighter and brighter until I had to look away.

"I can't let you hurt her." The voice didn't sound like my sister. It didn't sound like her at all. "I *have* to stop you."

There was a flash of light and a sound like the snapping of twigs, the popping of knuckles. And then there was silence. I glanced at the boy behind the counter, who was now cowering against the far wall, and then turned slowly back toward my sister.

Toward the stranger who wanted me dead.

Kissy was standing. Below her, my attacker's body lay still, his head twisted at an unnatural angle to his body.

She snapped his neck.

This just did not compute. Kissy couldn't even swat flies. She couldn't play chess, because knights looked like horses and she couldn't bare the idea of sacrificing even a one.

She snapped his neck.

Her right hand was bleeding. Her hair was disheveled. She bent over, picked up her sunglasses, and put them back on. She brought her hand to her lips and licked the blood from the wound, then glanced at the boy behind the counter.

"Forget this ever happened," she told him. "You hear?"

He nodded dumbly, and Kissy turned back to me. "C'mon," she said, sounding just the way she always had, since we were little. "We have to go to San Antonio."

After the hullabaloo in the McDonald's, the truck starting up again seemed like such a tiny thing, I didn't even remember to be grateful. I was too busy trying not to chuck my biscuits all over the dashboard. My hands shook as Kissy pulled back onto the highway and put the pedal to the floor.

"Hey, Kissy?" I said finally.

"Yeah-huh?" my sister replied.

I wasn't sure how to phrase this next part diplomatically, so I just spat it right out there. "You killed that guy."

"Seems like," Kissy agreed, amiable to the core.

"Doesn't that strike you as a little, I don't know"—I searched for the right word. Terrifying? Life-altering? Insane?—"weird?"

"It is what it is, Jess." Kissy had never been one to dwell on the downside of things. "One second I was there, talking to the boy behind the counter, and the next, you were screaming, and that thing had a knife, and I just—I *had* to."

As she spoke, the images flashed in front of my eyes again: my attacker's dark, reptilian eyes, Kissy's shining like a pale green spotlight, the curve of the knife, the blood. . . .

I have to kill her. I have to stop this before it starts.

That was what the boy had said, and good money was on the *her* in question being me.

"He was going to kill me," I said, trying out the words to see how they'd sound out loud.

"I wasn't going to let him." Kissy didn't waste a second in issuing her reply, the same way she'd never hesitated to chase off playground bullies when I was in the first grade and she was in the third. "It's you and me, Jess. Always has been. Always will be."

I nodded, but my breath caught in my throat. She was my sister, and I loved her, but I couldn't shake the feeling that she was something else, too, that whatever the 'pulse was, it wasn't some genetic quirk so much as . . .

Possession. The word snaked its way through my mind, all sneakylike, and as much as I wanted to quell the thought, I couldn't quite get a handle on it, couldn't shut it down.

"His eyes were black," I said, sticking to the facts. "They were black the way yours go green."

"Yup." Kissy paused, and for the first time, the expression on her face, determined and sure, faltered. "It's kind of funny," she said, in a voice that just about broke my heart. "I always wondered if there was anyone else out there like me, and now I know."

"That thing was *nothing* like you." Until I said the words out loud, I wasn't sure I believed them, but they came out so fierce and so certain that it settled the matter, right then and there. Whatever Kissy was, whatever had happened to her to make her fight like that, she wasn't a monster.

She was my sister.

"Love you, Jess."

"Yeah, yeah," I said, unable to keep my eyes from her sunglasses. "I love you too."

When it came to stopping for gas, Kissy was of the Russian roulette school of thought, walking on the wild side and daring the universe to do her wrong. By the time she finally gave in and pulled into a filling station outside of Dallas, the tank had been on empty for half an hour, and I was half convinced that we were going to end up stuck on the side of the road.

There was a part of me that was hoping, just a little bit, that maybe we would. Kissy's 'pulses—even the weird ones— had always seemed so benign, but with the sound of snapping bones crackling through my memory, I couldn't help wondering *why* we had to go to San Antonio and what Kissy would be compelled to do once we were there.

She killed that boy. She killed him dead.

"I'm going inside to prepay," Kissy said, her voice cutting into my thoughts. "You want a Coke?"

I nodded.

"What kind?"

I couldn't help but feel like every decision I made, even the tiny ones, would bring us closer and closer to disaster. "I'll come with you," I said, postponing at least this one decision that much longer.

"You're coming with?" Kissy gave me a look. Even though I couldn't actually see her eyeballs, I translated her stare to mean, *You better not be coming with me because you think I can't take care of myself.*

I shrugged. It wasn't like I was actually scared that Kissy was going to go snapping necks left and right. I was just being . . . cautious.

"Maybe I should go alone," I said, knowing that I might as well be poking at an angry bear. "Your picture could be all over the news by now."

"It's not," Kissy said simply. "Nobody's going to find the body. Nobody's ever going to know."

That didn't exactly seem what I would call *likely*, but Kissy sounded so certain that I couldn't help wondering what she knew that I didn't, what the instinct inside of her was whispering that I couldn't hear.

"Fine," I said. "We'll both go in."

"Fine," Kissy replied, and she snapped her mouth shut and didn't say another word until the two of us were inside.

The girl behind the counter wasn't nearly so easily charmed as her counterpart at the McDonald's that morning, and she just gave Kissy and me a once-over before a bored, glassy look settled over her eyes.

"Hi, Molly," Kissy said, lifting the girl's name from the trainee tag on her shirt. "We need to prepay, thirty dollars on pump two."

Molly was not impressed with Kissy's personable nature—or her ensemble. "It's your money," she said, like the two of us were stupid for spending it on something as mundane as fuel. "Anything else?"

"A couple of thirty-two-ounce drinks," I said, since Kissy tended to take other people's boredom as a personal challenge. "And that's all."

Molly rang us up and tapped her fingernails impatiently on the counter as Kissy dug around her pockets for two twenty-dollar bills. She shoved the money across the counter, and Molly moved to take it, but aborted the action halfway through and instead caught Kissy by the wrist, her fake nails digging into my sister's skin.

Oh no. Not again.

I took an instinctive step backward, but Kissy wasn't perturbed. I looked to Molly's eyes, but they were still an everyday brown, a few shades lighter than mine. Molly tilted her head to the side, and Kissy did the same. Then Molly spoke—or at least, her lips moved and words came out, which wasn't exactly the same thing.

"They're close." The voice that spoke those words was androgynous and toneless, vibrating with so much power, it almost hurt to hear it. "Very close, and this time, there's more than one."

The bland expression on Molly's face never changed, but the words coming out of her mouth were everywhere—inside my head and out of it—until I couldn't think or hear or even remember anything else.

"You need to trust us, Jessica Carlton. Trust your sister." Even though Molly was holding Kissy's arm, she was looking straight at me, and her words came out like an order. "It starts with you, Jess. *Run.*"

Molly dropped Kissy's arm, and if she had any recollection of the words she'd just said, she did a real good job hiding it under a healthy amount of disdain. "What're you staring at?" she asked me.

Trust your sister. The words echoed in my head. *Run.*

"We have to go," Kissy said. "Now."

She turned and started walking toward the back exit. My heart beating viciously against the inside of my rib cage, I turned to follow, but not before glancing back over my shoulder at the pumps. A single second stretched itself out into eternity, and then the glass on the store's windows exploded inward, and our grandfather's truck burst—*red and blue and orange and yellow*—into flames.

One second we were in the store, and the next we were out back, and all I could think was, *They're close, and this time, there's more than one.* Kissy's hand latched on to my shoulder, and she dragged me behind her, running faster than she should have been able to run.

"We have to go to San Antonio."

I normally didn't have much of a temper, but these were extenuating circumstances. Someone had already tried to kill me once today, Kissy had snapped a boy's neck, gas station attendants were dishing out prophecies, and now, someone had *blown up our grandpa's truck.*

"What's so bloody important about San Antonio?" I asked, taking solace in the British curse word, which was a lot more satisfying than anything my Oklahoma upbringing had to offer.

"I don't know," Kissy replied, her voice breaking. "I don't know, but we have to get there, we *have* to, and now we don't have a truck." She dropped my arm, and her entire body stiffened, her eyes rolling back in her head.

Not a seizure, I thought. *Not now.*

Behind us, the door to the filling station slammed open, and men and women of all shapes and sizes began pouring out. I shouldn't have been able to see their eyes from this distance, but there was no mistaking the darkness, the light.

"We're going," I said, holding my sister as tight as I could and hoping the words penetrated her trance. "We're going to

San Antonio. C'mon, Kissy. You're okay. You can do this."

With great effort, she straightened, and the two of us began stumbling toward the road—toward San Antonio, because the 'pulse wouldn't let Kissy turn around.

Please, God, I thought. *Please don't let this be happening. Please don't let this be how everything ends.*

We made it to the road, maybe twenty yards ahead of our pursuers. A car slammed its brakes and swerved to avoid hitting us. To my surprise, the owner recovered quickly, leaned over, and threw open the passenger side door.

"Going to San Antonio?" he asked.

Kissy and I were in that car faster than you can say *'pulse.* We didn't question how the man had known or why he was helping us.

His eyes, shining sea-foam green, said it all.

The man's name was Walter, and he was a perfectly nice sort, a few years older than Mom and Dad would have been if they'd lived. Unfortunately, Walter didn't seem to know any more about what we'd gotten ourselves into than Kissy did.

"I just got a feelin'," he said, rubbing one hand over his chin. "And this feelin', it said, 'Get in your car, drive your car, pick up them girls.' So that's what I did."

Like Kissy, Walter was no stranger to "feelings," but he wasn't particularly given to philosophical pondering, so all he'd say about them was that some itches needed scratching and if you

had the sense God gave a goose, you'd scratch them.

Not exactly illuminating, if you asked me.

Still, we made it from Dallas to San Antonio in record time—no stops, no explosions, no black-eyed people gunning for my throat. Walter pulled up next to the River Walk, and as he put the car into park and let us out, the unnatural sheen faded from his eyes, until they were hazel, as ordinary and down-home as the rest of the man.

"You girls take care of yourselves," he said.

Kissy smiled. "We will."

I wasn't feeling quite so optimistic, because even though we were in San Antonio, even though we'd done exactly what the 'pulse had told Kissy to do, her eyes were still shining, so bright that the sunglasses weren't really doing the job anymore.

"C'mon, Jess!" Kissy sounded giddy and free and, if I'm being honest, just a little bit drunk. "We have to go this way!"

She ran down a stone staircase. I followed, and the closer we got to the River Walk below, the more adrenaline flooded into my system, my heart skipping like a stone across water. My breaths were shallow and hot in my chest, and I prepared myself for what might come.

What I wasn't prepared for was Kissy sidestepping the second we got to the bottom and me running right smack into something that felt like an anvil and looked like a guy. He caught me by the elbows and steadied me on my feet. For a moment, I stopped breathing altogether.

His hair was the color of desert sand, his features symmetrical and sharp. He wasn't particularly big or small, and I couldn't pinpoint his age, but there was something unspeakably perfect about his body, his face, the way he stood—so perfect it sent a chill creeping down my spine.

It hurt to look at him. It hurt not to.

This is it.

I wasn't sure if it was good or bad, the beginning or the end, but every bone in my body was certain that this was something, that *he* was something. Beside me, Kissy pulled her sunglasses up onto the top of her head and blinked.

Her eyes were brown.

"I'm starving," she said. "There any place good to eat around here?"

"Kissy." I hissed her name. "All of this, everything we've gone through to get here, and you're thinking about *food?*"

Kissy had the decency to look a tiny bit ashamed of herself. "I never got to eat my Egg McMuffin," she mumbled.

Given the whole people-with-black-eyes-keep-trying-to-kill-us thing, I really didn't think that should be her primary concern, but what did I know?

"You're safe here, Jess." Those were the first words our companion had said to me, and his voice washed over my body, leaving goose bumps in its wake. He didn't sound as alien as the girl at the gas station had, but there was a heaviness to his words, like he'd been waiting to say them for longer than I'd been alive.

I looked into his eyes. They were blue: light and crystalline

and inhuman in ways I couldn't begin to explain. For a split second, those eyes looked away from mine and spared a glance for Kissy.

"You've done well," he told her.

She preened. I rolled my eyes and waited for the flirting to start up, but the next second, the boy with the light-blue eyes was looking back at me.

"My name," he said, "is Ariel."

A dozen offhand comments about *The Little Mermaid* sprang to mind, but I figured it would be in poor taste to say any of them out loud.

"I'm Jess."

"You have questions," he said.

I opened my mouth to start asking them, but he placed two fingers over my lips, and the words stilled on my tongue.

"There are three kinds," he said.

Three kinds of what? I wondered. *Three kinds of questions?* But his fingers were still on my lips, his touch electric enough that I couldn't bring myself to break away.

"There are Guardians. There are Heralds." He dropped his hand to his side. "There is the third kind."

"The third kind," I repeated dumbly. Ariel inclined his head, but he didn't blink—he never blinked.

"The third kind," he said again. "By their sword, darkness bleeds. They are the arm and the fire. They are the beginning of the End."

That should have sounded insane—or at the very least,

eccentric—but I couldn't shake the niggling sensation that these were words that I'd heard before.

Guardians. Heralds. Third kind.

The End.

Each phrase that left Ariel's mouth felt like it had been carved in stone, etched into the surface of the earth a thousand years before I'd ever drawn a breath. There was an element of ritual to his speech, as though each gesture, each word, each second was sacred.

I didn't understand it, any of it, but my mouth wouldn't open. Questions wouldn't come. So I just stood there, frozen in silence—like that was my role to play while Ariel was playing his.

"Guardians protect. Heralds deliver messages. The third kind is the third kind." Ariel stopped talking, as if he knew that my puny little brain needed time to process.

I could still feel the touch of his fingers on my lips.

"Heralds deliver messages," I repeated, feeling like I had to say something. "Like the girl at the gas station?"

Ariel did not nod. He did not reply. He didn't even blink.

"And Guardians, like Walter . . ." I trailed off and finished the thought silently. *Like Kissy.*

"She protects you," Ariel said, lifting the thought from my brain with an ease that made me feel like every thought I'd ever had or ever would have was laid out for his inspection. "When it's called for, there are others she protects as well."

I thought of everything Kissy had ever done because of

a 'pulse: the random acts of kindness, the senseless errands, the night she'd gotten the two of us out of our parents' house. Most of the time, it had all seemed so random, but now I had to wonder if she'd inadvertently saved other people, the way she'd saved me—if there was some big plan, and she'd played the role of the butterfly, flapping her wings in one hemisphere and causing a hurricane in another.

"How do Guardians know what to do?" I asked, my mind spinning with the implications. "Their . . . *orders* . . ." That seemed more official than calling them 'pulses. "Who sends them?"

"They come from where they come from," Ariel replied. "They are what they are."

I got the sense that Ariel wasn't beating around the bush, that to him, that really was the answer.

"What about the other people?" I said slowly. "The ones with the blue-black eyes?"

"Their orders," Ariel said, the muscles in his jaw tensing, "come from elsewhere."

"They're trying to kill me."

Ariel shrugged, as if this was no more significant than the fact that my favorite color was red.

"That's it?" I said tersely. "All of this—getting us up in the middle of the night, running us ragged, *blowing up our truck*—and that's what you have to say for yourself? *Nothing?*"

"You needed to be here," Ariel said. "This is where it must

begin. It starts with you."

"What starts with me?" I felt desperate, but sounded POed and chalked it up as one of those things that you just can't help. *"What starts with me, Ariel?"*

He moved like lightning, closing the space between us and then some. His blue eyes stared at and into mine, and for a moment, I was certain he was going to snap my neck, the way Kissy had snapped that boy's.

Instead, he brought his lips slowly down to mine and kissed me.

Blades. Blood. Light. Burning.

I saw the whole world in an instant, everything that was, everything that would ever be, and something flickered to life on the surface of my skin: a power, a knowing.

Ariel pulled back, and based on the expression on his face, I concluded that it hadn't exactly been as earth-shattering for him as it had been for me.

"It is done," he said, which isn't exactly the kind of thing a girl wants to hear about her first kiss.

"What's done?" I asked, trying not to feel too put out. I could sense the change he'd wrought, feel it rising up inside of me and washing away everything I'd been until now. "Ariel, *what did you do?*"

Ariel was not impressed by my desperation or my ire.

"There are three kinds," he said. "You are the third kind."

And then he was gone.

"What just happened? I mean, seriously, Kissy, who was he? *What* was he? How could he just say all of that stuff and then kiss me and then *leave?*"

I was indignant. Kissy, on the other hand, was in hog heaven.

"This is the best chimichanga I have ever had," she said.

"Kissy," I snapped. "Focus."

"I am focusing," Kissy replied calmly. "I am focusing on my chimichanga."

After Ariel had disappeared, she'd dragged me across the River Walk to the closest Mexican restaurant, and the two of us had been sitting there ever since, Kissy shoveling chips and salsa like she was preparing to hibernate for the winter, and me trying my best to make sense out of chaos.

Growing up, I'd never thought much about Kissy's 'pulses. They were the kind of thing you got used to, and I'd never wondered why I didn't get them too, because you could tell just by looking at Kissy or talking to her for five seconds that she was something special.

Someone special.

But me?

I wasn't anything. I could almost believe Ariel when he said that Kissy was some kind of cosmic Guardian, chosen to protect the innocent, one 'pulse at a time—but after all of these years, I couldn't wrap my mind around the idea that I might be the special one, that whatever made Kissy different from normal folks—maybe I had a version of it too.

Kissy was a Guardian.

The girl at the gas station had been a Herald.

And I was the third kind.

"The third kind of what?" I asked, for what was probably the millionth time.

"I dunno, Jess," Kissy said, her voice real soft, like she was talking a stray dog out from underneath a car. "Sometimes, there aren't easy answers. Sometimes, things are just right. The things I do when I get the 'pulse? They feel right. And this—you, me, here, Ariel—it feels right too."

I didn't want *feelings*. I wanted answers. I wanted to know who Ariel was—*what* he was. I wanted to know why, from the second my lips had touched his, there'd been a burning inside of me, white-hot, liquid, steady.

I wanted to know why it felt familiar.

Why it didn't hurt.

"Sometimes," Kissy told me, waving her chimichanga for emphasis, "you just have to have faith that everything's going to work out the way it's supposed to."

Have faith?

Somewhere out there, someone or something wanted me dead, and we had no guarantee that the black-eyed guardians would back off now that we'd completed Kissy's mission. I had no idea what Ariel had done to me, or what he expected me to do now that it was done. I could feel the change, feel it spreading like wildfire through my body, inch by inch and bit by bit.

I felt older, stronger, connected.

I felt like this was just the beginning.

The beginning of the end.

"Seriously, Jess. Just relax. *Que sera, sera.* Have some guacamole."

I closed my eyes and started counting silently to ten, so as to decrease the chances that I'd leap across the table and beat my sister to death with a chimichanga.

One, two, three . . .

The images I'd seen when Ariel kissed me flashed through my mind, and this time, they felt like memories. I saw a flaming sword, a desert, an army.

Four, five, six . . .

I saw people as cold and inhumanly beautiful as Ariel. I saw their faces twist into something pretty-cruel.

Seven, eight, nine . . .

I saw black eyes and shadows and rivers running with blood.

"Ten." I finished counting and opened my eyes. I tried to remember everything Ariel had said about the third kind, everything the black-eyed boy in the McDonald's had said about why I had to die.

It starts with you.

The third kind—by their sword, darkness bleeds.

"Feel better?" Kissy asked me.

"Just peachy," I told her.

But all I could think, over and over again was: *this is the beginning of the End.*

You'd think that after something like that, nothing would ever be the same, but mostly, life kept right on going, same as it had for as long as I could remember—with a few notable, should-have-been-impossible exceptions.

Probably the biggest—not to mention most impossible—of those exceptions was that after we made it back from our little road trip, every morning from there on out, I woke up with my fingers curled around the hilt of a sword. It didn't matter what I did or how many times I tried to get rid of that darn thing, the blade always showed up again, golden and gleaming and whispering to me in a language I didn't understand.

And for a second, a single second when I first woke up, I would remember—*the sword, the battle, the fire inside.* Then, just as quickly as the memories had come, they would fade, leaving me with a whole lot of questions—and weaponry I shouldn't have known how to use.

The next biggest change in our post-road-trip life—far less remarkable, but life-altering nonetheless—was that Kissy and I were grounded for life. Nana and Grandpa Jake were old-fashioned, and they didn't hold with any of this newfangled nonsense about "destiny" or "powers."

They also didn't hold with blowing up trucks.

Being grounded gave Kissy and me a lot of time to sit around and try and make some form of sense out of the things Ariel had told us, but we didn't come up with a serviceable theory about it all until a month after we got back, when the Walmart started playing Christmas carols nonstop, even though it was just past Halloween. Listening to "Hark! The Herald Angels Sing" on repeat has a way of making you hear one word and think about the other, and that got us to connecting the dots.

Herald. Angel.

Guardian. Angel.

I half expected Ariel to show up—to tell us we were wrong, to explain how it was possible if we were even a little bit right—but he never came. Kissy and I were on our own, her with her 'pulses, me with my sword, so full of questions I thought I might burst.

I wondered and I prayed and I Googled. I read everything there was to read about angels: seraphim, nephilim, watchers, beings—there were about a million different words, different mythologies, different stories.

I read about messenger angels.

Guardian angels.

Warriors.

And every night, I dreamed—about fighting and flying and rivers running red with blood.

Then, one morning, about a month after Kissy and I had come up with our little theory, she woke me up in the middle of the night, saying my name with all the aplomb of someone announcing she was fixing to drive down to the Sonic for a cherry limeade. "Hey, Jess?" she said, her eyes glowing incandescent green.

"Yeah?" I said, my fingers closing involuntarily around the hilt of my sword and my palm singing with the contact.

Kissy smiled. "We have to go to the Mojave Desert."

I saw a flash—of a legion of dark-eyed women, dark-eyed men. Heaven and earth and innocents caught in between.

"Seriously, Jess," Kissy repeated, giddy. "We have to go to the Mojave Desert."

I sat up in bed, sword at the ready and the fire in my belly spreading out to each and every one of my limbs. A tiny voice inside of me whispered that this was it—the thing I'd been made for, the thing that Kissy and I had always been meant to do, but I didn't say a word about that out loud. I didn't say that this was the beginning of the End.

Instead, I fixed Kissy with a look. "Do we have to go to the Mojave Desert *now?*"

AUTOMATIC
by Rachel Caine

There was a new vending machine at the Morganville Blood Bank. In the withdrawal area, not the deposit area. It looked like a Coke machine, only instead of handy ice-cold aluminum cans, there were warm cans labeled O NEG and A and B POS—something for everybody. The cans even had nice graphic logos on them.

My girlfriend, Eve, and I were standing in front of the vending machine, marveling at the weirdness, and wondering a lot of things: first, what the hell did they tell the can manufacturers about what was going into those containers? And second, would the blood taste like aluminum? It already had a coppery tone to it, like licking pennies, but . . . would it be any *good*?

There were twelve vampires in the place, including me, and nobody was making a move to get anything out of the shiny new machine. The withdrawal room itself was clean, efficiently laid out, and not very friendly. Big long counter at one end, with staff in white lab coats. You took a number, you got called to the counter, they gave you your blood bag. You could order it to go, or drink it here; there were some small café-style tables and chairs at the other end, but nobody really liked to linger here. It felt like a doctor's office, someplace you left in a hurry as soon as you could.

So it was odd how all the tables and chairs were full, and the sofas, and the armchairs. And how there were vamps standing around, watching the machine as if they expected it to actually *do* something. Or, well, expected me to do something.

"Michael?" Eve said, because I'd been a long time, staring at the glossy plastic of the machine in front of me. "Uh, are we doing this or not?"

"Sure," I said, resigned. "I guess we have to." I had actually been *asked*—well, ordered, really—to lead the way on this particular new Morganville, Texas, initiative. Morganville is—to say the least—unusual, even for someplace as diverse and weird as our great state: a small, desert-locked town in the middle of nowhere, populated by both humans and vampires. A social experiment, although the vampires really controlled the experiment. As far as I knew, we were the only place in the world vampires lived openly . . . or lived at all.

I was on the side of the vamps, now . . . not through any plan of my own. I was nineteen years old, and looking at eternity, and it was starting to look pretty lonely because the people I cared about, that I loved . . . they weren't going to be there with me.

Somehow, the machine summed up how impersonal all this eternal life was going to get, and that made it so much more than just another Coke machine full of plasma.

I was still amazed that twelve other vamps had shown up today for the demonstration; I'd expected nobody, really, but in the end, we weren't so different from humans: novelties attracted us, and the blood dispenser was definitely a novelty. Nobody quite knew what to make of it, but they were fascinated, and repelled.

And they were waiting.

Eve nudged me and looked up into my face, concerned. She wasn't too much shorter than I was, but enough that even the stacked heels on her big, Goth boots didn't put us at eye level. She'd gone with subdued paint-up today: white makeup, black lipstick, not a lot of other accessories. We were so different, in so many ways; I wasn't Goth, for starters. I wasn't much of anything, fashionwise, except comfortable. And she seemed okay with that, thankfully.

"Swipe?" she said, and tapped my right hand, which held a shiny new plastic card. I looked down at it, frowning. White plastic, with a red stripe, and my name computer-printed at the bottom. GLASS, MICHAEL J. My dates of birth and death (or, as it was called on the vamp side, "transformation"). The cards were new, just like the vending machine—issued about two weeks ago. A lot of the older vampires refused to carry them. I couldn't really see why, but then I'd grown up modern, where you had to have licenses and ID cards, and accepted that you were going to get photographed and tracked and monitored.

Or maybe it was only the humans who accepted that, and I'd carried it over with me.

It was just a damn glorified Coke machine. Why did it feel so weird?

"So," Eve said, turning away from me to the not-very-welcoming audience of waiting vampires, "it's really easy. You've all got the cards, right? They're your ID cards, and they're loaded up with a certain number of credits for the month. You can come in here any time, swipe the card, and get your, uh, product. And now, *Michael Glass is going to demonstrate.*"

Oh, that was my cue, accompanied by a not-too-light punch on the arm.

I reached over, slid the card through the swipe bar, and buttons glowed. A cheerful little tone sounded, and a scrolling red banner said MAKE YOUR SELECTION NOW. I pushed the button—O negative, my favorite—and watched the can ride down in a miniature elevator to the bottom, where it was pushed out for me to take.

I took the can, and was a little surprised to find it was warm, warm as Eve's skin. Well, of course it was; the signs on the machine said TEMPERATURE CONTROLLED, but that just meant it was kept *blood* temperature, not *Coke* temperature. Huh. It felt weird, but attractive, in a way.

They were all still watching me, with nearly identical expressions of disgust and distaste. Some of them looked older than me, some even younger, but they'd all been around for centuries, whereas I was the brand-new model . . . the first in decades.

Hence, the guinea pig—but mainly because I'd grown up in the modern age, with swipe cards and internet and food from machines. I trusted all that stuff, at least in theory.

They hated it.

I rolled the can indecisively in my hand for a few seconds, staring at the splashy graphics—the vampire fangs framed the blood type nicely. "How do you think they got away with getting these made?" I asked Eve. "I mean, wouldn't somebody think it was a little strange?"

She rolled her eyes. "Honestly, Michael, don't you pay attention? Out there"—meaning, anywhere except Morganville—"it's just a big joke. Maybe they thought it was for a movie or a TV show or a new energy drink. But they don't think about it like we do."

I knew that, even though, like Eve, I'd been born and raised in Morganville. We'd both been out of town exactly once in our lives, and we'd done it together. Still, it was really tough to realize that for the rest of the world, our biggest problems were just . . . stories.

As hard as Morganville was, as full of weirdness and danger, Out There hadn't been a walk in the park, either. Though I wished I'd been able to go to a really big concert. That would have been cool.

I was still turning the can around, stalling. Eve grabbed it from me, popped the top, and handed it back. "Bottoms up," she said. "Oh, come on, just give it a try. Once."

I owed her that much, because the black choker around her neck was covering up a healing bite mark. Vampire bites closed quickly, and usually without scarring, but for an awkward three-day period, she'd be wearing scarves and high necks.

It was typically Eve that she was also wearing a tight black T-shirt that said, in black-on-black Gothic-style lettering, GOOD GIRLS DON'T. AWESOME GIRLS DO.

She saw me looking at her, and our eyes locked and held. Hers were very dark, almost black, though if you really got close and looked, you could see flecks of lighter brown and gold and green. And I liked getting close to her, drawn into her warmth, her laughter, the smooth hot stretch of her skin. . . .

She winked. She knew what I was thinking, at moments like these, but then as she'd once told me, smugly, most guys really aren't that complicated.

I smiled back, and saw her pupils widen. She liked it when I smiled. I liked that she liked it.

Without even thinking about it, I raised the can to my lips and took a big gulp.

Not bad. I could taste the aluminum, but the blood tasted fresh, with a bitter streak that was probably from the preservatives. Once I started drinking, instincts kicked in, and I felt the fangs snap down in my mouth. It felt a little like popping your knuckles. I swallowed, and swallowed, and all of a sudden the can was light and empty, and I felt shaky. I don't usually drink that much blood at one time, and I'm more of a sipper.

I crushed the can into a ball—vampire strength—and tossed it across the room into a trash can, basketball style. It sailed neatly through the narrow circle.

"Show-off," Eve said.

I felt great. I mean, *great*. My fangs were still down, and when I smiled, they were visible, gleaming and very sharp.

Eve's smile faltered, just a little. "Really. Showing off now."

I closed my eyes, got control, and felt the fangs slowly fold up against the roof of my mouth.

"Better," she said, and linked arms with me. "Now that you're all plasmaed up, can we go?"

"Yeah," I said, and we got two steps toward the door before I turned back, got the card out of my pocket, and slid it through the machine's reader again. Eve stared, blinking in confusion. I chose another O negative ("This Blood's for You!") and slipped the warm can into the pocket of my jacket. "For later," I said.

"Okay." Eve sounded doubtful, but she got over it. She turned back to the crowd of vamps watching us. "Next?"

Nobody was rushing to swipe their cards, although one or two had them out and were contemplating it. One guy scowled and said, "Whatever happened to organic food," and went to the counter to get a fresh-drawn bag.

Well, I'd done what Amelie had asked me to do, so if it didn't work, she couldn't blame it on me.

But I did feel great. Surprisingly, the canned stuff was better than the bagged stuff. Almost better than when Eve had let me have a taste straight from the tap, if that's not too sick.

I felt them watching us. Eve and I weren't the most popular team-up in town . . . humans and vampires didn't mix, not like that. We were predator and prey, and the lines were pretty strictly drawn. In vampire circles, I was looked at as either pitiful or perverted. I could imagine what it was like on Eve's side. Morganville's not full of vampire wannabes—more a town full of Buffys-in-the-making.

Our relationship wasn't easy, but it was real, and I was going to hang on to it for as long as I possibly could.

"What do you want to do?" Eve asked, as we stepped outside into the cool Morganville early evening.

"Walk," I said. "For starters." I let her fill in what might come after, and she smiled in a way that told me it wasn't a tough guess at all.

Later, it occurred to me that I felt jittery, and it was getting worse.

We were strolling out in Founder's Square, which is vampire territory; Eve could come and go from here with or without me, because she had a Founder's Pin and was pretty much as untouchable as a human got, in terms of being hunted—by vampires who obeyed the rules, anyway. But it was nice to walk with her. At night, Morganville is kind of magical—bright clouds of stars overhead in a pitch-black sky, cool breezes, and at least in this part of town, everybody is on their best behavior.

Vampires liked to walk, and jog, along the dark paths. We were regularly passed by others. Most nodded. A few stopped to say hello. Some—the most progressive—even said hello to Eve, as if she was a real person to them.

I had a wild impulse to jog, to *run*, but Eve couldn't keep up if I did, even in her practical boots. Holding that urge back was taking all my concentration, so while she talked, I just mostly pretended to listen. She was telling some story about Shane and Claire, I guessed; our two human housemates had gotten themselves into trouble again, but this time it was minor, and funny. I was glad. I didn't feel much like charging to anybody's rescue right now.

Up ahead, I saw another couple approaching us on the path. The woman was unmistakably the Founder of Morganville, Amelie; only Amelie could dress that way and get away with it. She was wearing a white jacket and skirt, and high heels. If she'd stood still, she'd have looked like a marble statue; her skin was only a few shades off from the clothes, and her hair was the same pale color. Beautiful, but icy and eerie.

Walking next to her, hands clasped behind his back, was Oliver. He looked much older than her, but I didn't think he was; she'd died young, he'd died at late middle age, but they were both ancient. He had his long, graying hair tied back, and was wearing a black leather jacket and dark pants. He was scowling, but then, he usually was.

Weird, seeing the two of them together like this. They were usually polite enemies, sometimes right at each other's throat (literally). Not tonight, though. Not here.

Amelie glowed in the moonlight, ghost-bright, and when she smiled, she didn't look cold at all. She inclined her head to us. "Michael. Eve. Thank you for doing the little demonstration today. It was much appreciated."

"Ma'am," I said, and returned the salute. Eve waved. We would have kept on walking, but Amelie stopped, and Oliver was a solid block in front of us, so we stopped as well. I said, "Hope you're enjoying the walk. It's a nice night."

Lame, but it was all I had for small talk. I was aching to keep moving. I couldn't keep still, in fact, and I drummed my fingers against the side of my leg in a nervous rhythm. I saw Oliver notice it. His scowl deepened.

"It's turned quite cool," Amelie said. Like Oliver, she was zeroing in on my trembling fingers. "I heard you sampled the new product today."

"Yeah, it's great," I said. "I got another one to go." The can was heavy in my pocket, and I'd been thinking about it the entire evening. I'd found myself actually wrapping my hand around it inside my pocket, but I'd managed to stop myself from pulling the tab. So far. "Very convenient. You ought to think about selling them in six-packs."

"Well, the modern age seems to demand convenience." Amelie shrugged. "But we'll see how the single-can sales go. So many wanted access to the blood bank at odd hours that automation seemed the most logical solution. You don't mind the taste of the preservatives?"

"No, it's good stuff," I said. I remembered that I hadn't liked it at first, but now, for some reason, it seemed like that memory was wrong—as if it had actually been delicious, but I hadn't been ready for it. "It tastes better than the bagged stuff." I almost said *and better than from the vein*, but Eve was right there, and that would embarrass her on two levels, not just one. First, that I was telling people she was letting me bite her, and second, that somehow her blood wasn't good enough. I was able to stop in time, barely. "Has anybody else tried it?"

"Really, Glass, do you think we put it out for public consumption without testing?" Oliver snapped. "It's been tried, analyzed, and tested to death. I cannot imagine a more boring process. Two years, from concept to actual delivery. Half the vampires in Morganville have been involved in taste tests."

"Have *you* tried it?" I asked him. "You should. It's really—" I didn't know how to finish that sentence, once I'd started it. "Fierce," I finally said. An Eve word. I wasn't sure I even knew what it really meant in the way she used it, but it seemed right.

Evidently, Oliver didn't really understand the usage either, because he gave me a long stare, one that could have melted concrete. "Our major difficulty seems to be in convincing the elders to use it," he said. "Most of them are not familiar with the concept of identification cards, much less credit cards, and machines confuse them."

"I'll bet," Eve put in. "Not much call for Cokes among the fang gang, I guess."

"Well, I like Coke," I said.

Amelie smiled, very slightly.

"As do I, Michael. But I fear we're in the minority." There was something guarded in her eyes, a little worried. "Are you feeling all right?"

"Great," I said, probably too quickly. "I feel great."

Oliver exchanged a fast glance with her, and gave an almost invisible shrug. "Then we should be going," he said. "Matters to discuss."

It was a dismissal, and I was happy to grab Eve's hand and walk on while the other two headed the other way. Oliver always bothered me; partly it was his eviler-than-thou attitude, and partly it was that I could never quite shake the memory of how I'd met him . . . how he'd come across as a nice, genuine guy, and turned on me. That had been before anyone in Morganville knew who he was, or how dangerous he could be.

And he'd killed me. Part of the way, anyway; he hadn't left me much choice in becoming what I was now. Maybe he thought of that as a fair trade.

I still didn't.

A tremor of adrenaline surged through me . . . hunting instinct. It took me a second to realize that there was a complicated mixture of things happening inside of me: hatred boiling up for Oliver, well beyond what I normally felt; hunger, although I shouldn't have been hungry at all; and last, most unsettlingly, through our clasped hands I felt the steady, seductive pulse of Eve's blood.

It was a moment that made me shiver and go abruptly very still, eyes shut, as I tried to master all of those warring, violent impulses. I heard Eve asking me something, but I shut her out. I shut everything out, concentrating on staying me, staying Michael, staying *human*, at least for now.

And finally, I fumbled in my pocket and popped open the aluminum can of O negative, and the taste was metal and meat, soothing the beast that was trying to claw its way free inside. I couldn't let it out, not here, not with Eve.

The taste of the blood silenced it for a moment, and then it roared back, shockingly stronger than ever.

I dropped the can and heard it clatter on the pavement. Eve's warm hands were around my face, and her voice was in my ears, but I couldn't understand what she was saying.

When I opened my eyes, all I saw was red, with vague, smeared shapes of anything that wasn't prey. Eve, on the other hand, glowed a bright silver.

Eve was a target, and I couldn't resist her, I *couldn't*. I had to satisfy this hunger, fast.

I gasped and pushed her backward, and before she could do more than call my name in alarm, I spun and ran through the dark, red night.

I didn't know where I was headed, but as I ran, something took over, guiding me more by instinct than design. When I saw the shining, warm targets of human beings out there in the dark, I avoided them; it was hard, maybe the hardest thing I'd ever done, but I managed.

I stopped in the shadows, not feeling tired at all, or winded, only anxious and more jittery than ever. The run hadn't burned it off; if anything, it had made things worse.

I was standing in front of the Morganville Blood Bank. This was the entrance in the front, the donation part, and it was closed for the night. Blessedly, there weren't any people around for me to be a danger to, at least right now.

I turned and ran down the side alley, effortlessly jumping over barriers of empty boxes and trash cans, and came around the back. Unlike the front, this part of the building was hopping with activity—human shapes coming and going, but none of them had that silvery glow I'd become so familiar with. All vampires, this side, and none of them were paying attention to me until I got close, shoved a few aside, and made it to the withdrawal area.

The vending machine stood there in the center of the room. A few people were doubtfully studying it, trying to make up their minds whether or not to try it, but I shoved them out of the way too. I swiped my card; when it didn't immediately work, I swiped it again and randomly punched buttons when they lit up. It took forever for the mechanism to work, and the can to be delivered.

Working the tiny pop-top seemed impossible. I punched my fingers through the side and lifted the can, bathing in the gush of liquid. It no longer tasted like metal. Warm from the can, it tasted like life. All the life I could handle.

"Michael," someone said, and put a hand on my shoulder. I turned and punched him, hard enough to break a human's neck, but it didn't do much except make the other vampire step back. I grabbed my card again and swiped it, but it was slippery in my fingers, damp with the red residue from the can, which had gotten all over me. I wiped it on my jeans and tried it again. The lights flashed. Nothing happened. "Michael, it won't work again. You used all today's credits."

No. That couldn't be true, it couldn't, because the rush hadn't lasted, hadn't lasted at all this time, and I felt bottomlessly empty. I needed more. I had to have *more.*

I shoved the other vampire back and slammed both hands into the plastic covering of the vending machine. It held, somehow, although cracks formed in the plastic. I hit it again, and again, until the plastic was coming apart. I shoved my hand through, heedless of the cuts, and grabbed one of the warm cans.

That was when someone hit me from behind with an electric shock, like a Taser only probably five times as strong, and the next thing I knew, I was limp on the floor, with the unopened can of AB negative rolling on the carpet beside me.

I tried to grab for it, but my hands weren't working. I was still reaching for it, fumbling for the fix, when they picked me up and towed me out of the withdrawal area, into a steel holding cell somewhere in the back.

Days passed. They took me off of the canned stuff and put me on bags again, and finally, the frenzy passed. I won't lie, it was awful, but what was worse was slowly realizing how bad I'd been. How close I'd been to becoming . . . a thing. A senseless monster.

I wasn't sure if I ever wanted them to let me out, actually.

Music was the only thing that helped; after they got me stabilized, the woman who delivered the blood also delivered my guitar. I didn't feel like myself until I was sitting down with the acoustic cradled in my lap. The strings felt warm, and when I picked out the first notes, that was good, that felt right. That felt like me, again.

I don't know how long I played; the notes spilled out of me in a frantic rush, no song I knew or had written before. It wasn't a nice melody, not at first; it was jagged and bloody and full of fury, and then it slowly changed tempo and key, became something soothing that made me relax, very slowly, until I was just a guy, playing a guitar for the thrill of the notes ringing in the air.

From the doorway, a voice said, "You really do have a gift." I hadn't even heard him unlock it.

I didn't look up. I knew who it was; that voice was unmistakable. "Once, maybe. You took that away from me," I said. "I was going somewhere with it. Now I'm going nowhere."

Oliver, uninvited, sat down in a wooden chair only a few feet away from me. I didn't like seeing him here, in my space. Music was my personal retreat, and it reminded me of how it had felt when he'd turned on me in my house, in my *house*, and . . .

. . . and everything had changed.

He was looking at me very steadily, and I couldn't read his expression. He'd had hundreds of years to perfect a poker face, and he was using it now.

I kept on playing. "Why are you here?"

"Because you are Amelie's responsibility, and it follows that you're also mine, as I'm her second in command."

"Did you take the machine out?"

Oliver shook his head. "No, but we changed the parameters. The testing was done on older vampires, ones who'd had centuries to stabilize their needs. You are entirely different, and we'd forgotten that. Very young, not even a full year old yet. We didn't anticipate that the formula would trigger such a violent response. In the future, you'll only receive the unprocessed raw materials."

"So it's because I'm young."

"No," he said. "It's because you're young *and* you refuse to acknowledge what you are. What it means. What it promises. You're fighting your condition, and that makes it almost impossible for you to control yourself. You need to admit it to yourself, Michael. You'll never be human again."

Last thing I wanted to do, and he knew it. I stopped playing for a few seconds, then picked up the thread again. "Fuck off," I said. "Feel free to take that personally."

He didn't answer for a long moment. I glanced up. He was still watching me.

"You're still not yourself," he eventually said. "And you're speaking like your scruffy friend."

He meant Shane. That made me laugh, but it sounded hollow, and a little bit desperate. "Well, Shane's probably right most of the time. You are an ass."

"And even if you think it, you rarely say it. Which rather proves my point."

"I'm fine."

"Are you? Because you've not asked a thing about your girlfriend, whom you left on her own in the middle of a vampire district, at night."

That sent an electric jolt of shame through me. I hadn't even *thought* about it. I hadn't spared a single thought for Eve all the time I'd been in here; I'd been too wrapped up in my own misery, my own shame. "Is she okay?" I asked. I felt sick, too sick to even try to keep on playing. The guitar felt heavy in my hands, and inert.

"She's becoming annoying with her repeated demands to see you, but yes, otherwise, she's as well as could be expected. I made sure she got home safely." Oliver paused for a few seconds, then leaned forward with his elbows braced on his knees, pale hands dangling. "When I was . . . transformed, I thought in the beginning that I could stay with those mortals I loved. It isn't smart. You should understand this by now. We stay apart for a reason."

"You stay apart so you don't feel guilty for doing what it is you do," I shot back. "I'm not like you. I'll never be like you. Best of all, I don't have to be."

His eyebrows rose, then settled back to a flat line. "Have it your way," he said. "The canned blood had an effect on you, yes, but not as much as you might believe. That was mostly you, boy. And you need to find a way to control that, because one day, you may find yourself covered in blood that doesn't come from a punctured can."

The way he said it chilled me, because it wasn't angry, it wasn't contemptuous, it was . . . sad. And all too knowing.

I let it drop into the silence before I said, "Eve wants to see me."

"Perpetually, apparently."

"I think I'm ready." Was I? I didn't know, but I ached to see her, tell her how sorry I was.

Oliver shrugged. "It's someone's funeral, if not yours." He

moved fast, out the door before I could make any comeback, not that I could think of a good one anyway, and I clutched the guitar for comfort. My fingers went back to picking out melodies and harmonies, but I wasn't thinking about it anymore, and it didn't feel comforting.

I was afraid I wasn't ready, and the fear was a steady, hot spike that made my throat dry and, horribly, made my fangs ache where they lay flat. I didn't know if I was ready to see her. I didn't know if Oliver would care to stop me, if I went off on her.

But when Eve stepped through the door, the fear slipped away, leaving relief in its wake. She was okay, and back to her fully Goth self, and what I felt wasn't hunger, other than the hunger anybody felt in the presence of someone they loved.

The shine in her eyes and her brilliant smile were the only things that mattered.

I had just enough time to put the guitar aside and catch her as she rushed at me, and then she kissed me, sweet and hot, and I sank into that, and her, and the reminder that there was something else for me other than hunting and hunger and lonely, angry music in the night.

"Don't you do that again," she whispered, her black-painted lips close to my ear. "Please, don't. You scared the hell out of all of us. I didn't know what to do."

I relaxed into her embrace, and breathed in the rich perfume of her hair, her skin, the subtle tingle of blood beneath. I didn't like to think about that last part, but maybe Oliver was right. Maybe I needed to stop denying it, or I'd end up in an even worse place, in the end.

"I didn't know what to do, either," I whispered back. "I'm sorry. I could have—"

"Stop." She pulled back, staring at me fiercely. "Just stop it. You could have hurt me, but you didn't. You didn't hurt anybody, except that stupid machine. So relax. That's not you, Mike. That's some B-movie monster."

But I was the B-movie monster too. That was what Oliver meant, in the end; I was exactly that, and I had to remember it. It was the only way any of this would work.

I forced a smile. "I thought you liked B-movie monsters," I said. My girlfriend punched me in the arm.

"Like, not love," she said. "You, I love."

I held out my hands, and she twined her fingers with mine. Warm and cool, together. "I don't know how to do this," I said.

She laughed a little. "Dating? Because news flash, big guy: we've been doing it awhile."

"Being this. Being me. I don't know who I am anymore."

She stepped closer, looking up into my eyes. "I know who you are. More importantly, I know *what* you are," she said. "And I still love you."

Maybe she didn't know. Maybe she'd never looked into the heart of the red and black tormented *thing* that lurked deep inside me. But looking at her now, at her utter sincerity and fearlessness, I couldn't help but think that maybe she did, after all. Know me, *and* love me.

Maybe, in time, she'd be able to help me understand and love my monster too. Because, in the end, it was always Eve. And always had been.

And I bent close, put my forehead against hers, and whispered, "You make me real."

From the doorway, Oliver cleared his throat, somehow managing to make it sound as if he wanted to gag at the same time. "You're free to go," he said. "Congratulations. You've passed."

"Passed what?" Eve asked, frowning.

"They wanted to see if I'd hurt you," I said. I focused past her, on Oliver. "You were my test. And I won't hurt her, not ever. You can count on that."

He raised his eyebrows, without any comment at all, and left.

The vending machine suffered another accident the next day. And then the next. It wasn't just me. My best friend, Shane, took to the idea of vandalism with frightening enthusiasm. So did Claire (surprisingly), and Eve . . . but it wasn't just the four of us sabotaging the damn thing, because at least twice when I went to enact some mayhem, I found it was already nonfunctional.

The last time, I saw someone walking away from the machine, which had a snapped electrical cord. He was wearing a big, flaring coat, but I knew him anyway.

Oliver paused at the door, looked back at me, and nodded, just a little.

And that was the last time they fixed the machine. The next day, it was gone. I felt a little tingle of phantom hunger, of disappointment . . . and relief.

Because some things just aren't meant to come out of a can.

ABOUT THE AUTHORS

CLAUDIA GRAY (**"Giovanni's Farewell"**) is the pseudonym of Chicago-based novelist Amy Vincent, author of the *New York Times* bestselling Evernight series and the upcoming novel *Fateful*. Gray has worked as a lawyer, a disc jockey, a telemarketer, a journalist, and a waitress, and very much hopes this book-writing thing works out so she doesn't have to go back to any of those jobs. Ever. You can visit her online at www.claudiagray.com.

CARRIE RYAN (**"Scenic Route"**) is the *New York Times* bestselling author of several critically acclaimed novels and short stories set in the same world as "Scenic Route," including *The Forest of Hands and Teeth*, *The Dead-Tossed Waves*, and *The Dark and Hollow Places*. Her first novel was chosen as a Best Book for Young Adults by the American Library Association and a Best of the Best Book by the Chicago Public Library.

A former litigator, Carrie now writes full-time and lives with her writer-lawyer husband, two fat cats, and one large Rott-Lab in Charlotte, North Carolina. They are not at all prepared for the zombie apocalypse. You can visit Carrie online at www.carrieryan.com.

KAMI GARCIA ("Red Run") is the *New York Times* and internationally bestselling coauthor (with Margaret Stohl) of *Beautiful Creatures* and *Beautiful Darkness*, Books One and Two in the Caster Chronicles. Kami draws heavily on her Southern roots for her Southern Gothic paranormal novels. She is very superstitious and lives in Los Angeles, California, with her husband, two children, and her dog, Spike (named after her favorite character in *Buffy the Vampire Slayer*). You can visit her online at www.kamigarcia.com.

JACKSON PEARCE ("Things About Love") is the author of *Sisters Red*, *Sweetly*, and *As You Wish*; the story she penned for this anthology is set in the *As You Wish* universe. She currently lives in Atlanta, Georgia, with a lot of secondhand furniture and pets who like to sleep on her keyboard when she's trying to write. You can visit her online at www.jacksonpearce.com.

RACHEL VINCENT ("Niederwald") is the author of the Soul Screamers series, where the characters from "Niederwald" originate, as well as several other stories in that world. She is also the author of the *New York Times* bestselling adult series Shifters. Rachel lives in San Antonio, Texas, with her husband, two black cats, and a large cast of fictional characters, including *bean sidhes*, reapers, and cat shape-shifters. You can visit her online at www.rachelvincent.com.

MELISSA MARR ("**Merely Mortal**") is the author of the *New York Times* and internationally bestselling Wicked Lovely series (a film of which is in development by Universal Pictures). She has also written a three-volume manga series (Wicked Lovely: Desert Tales), a number of short stories, and her adult novel, *Graveminder*. All of her texts are rooted in her lifelong obsession with folklore and fantastic creatures. Currently she lives in the Washington, DC, area with one spouse, two children, two Rott-Labs, and two Rottweilers. You can visit her online at www.melissa-marr.com.

KELLEY ARMSTRONG ("**Facing Facts**") has been telling stories since before she could write. Her earliest written efforts were disastrous. If asked for a story about girls and dolls, hers would invariably feature undead girls and evil dolls, much to her teachers' dismay. Today, she continues to spin tales of ghosts and demons and werewolves while safely locked away in her basement writing dungeon. She's the author of the #1 *New York Times* bestselling Darkest Powers young-adult trilogy as well as the Otherworld and Nadia Stafford adult series. Armstrong lives in Ontario, Canada, with her family. You can visit her online at www.kelleyarmstrong.com.

SARAH REES BRENNAN ("Let's Get This Undead Show on the Road") is the author of the Demon's Lexicon trilogy, a series about demons, magicians, urban England, and two very troubled brothers. The first book was named a Top Ten Best Book by the American Library Association, was among the top ten for Best British Children's Fantasy, was long-listed for the Carnegie Medal, and received three starred reviews. She was into literary fiction until at the age of thirteen she stumbled across the combination of magic, teenagers, and city life that was Margaret Mahy and Diana Wynne Jones in her library, and she's been writing books like that ever since. She lives in Dublin, Ireland, which she uses as a base for many strange adventures, and she can always be found online at www.sarahreesbrennan.com.

Award-winning author JERI SMITH-READY ("Bridge") lives in Maryland with her husband, two cats, and the world's goofiest greyhound. Her novels include the Shade ghost series for teens, where Logan's story begins and continues. She has also written several novels for adults, including *Wicked Game* and *Eyes of Crow*. When not writing, Jeri can usually be found—well, thinking about writing, or on Twitter. Like her characters, she loves music, movies, and staying up very, very late. You can visit her online at www.jerismithready.com.

KIMBERLY DERTING (**"Skin Contact"**) lives in the Pacific Northwest, where the gloomy weather is ideal for writing anything dark or creepy, leading to her debut novel, *The Body Finder*, and its follow-up, *Desires of the Dead*. She lives with her husband and their three beautiful (and often mouthy) children, who serve as an endless source of inspiration. In "Skin Contact," you can find out more about Rafe, a character first introduced in *Desires of the Dead*. For more about Kimberly, you can visit her online at www.kimberlyderting.com.

ALLY CONDIE (**"Leaving"**) is the author of the *New York Times* bestselling *Matched*, a dystopian novel that is the first in a trilogy. She is a former high school English teacher who began writing because she missed being in the classroom and hearing her students' stories. In addition to writing she loves reading, running, and listening to her husband play guitar. She lives in Utah with her family and blogs at www.allysoncondie.com.

JESSICA VERDAY, *New York Times* bestselling author (**"At the Late Night, Double Feature, Picture Show"**), wrote the first draft of *The Hollow* by hand, using thirteen spiral-bound notebooks and fifteen black pens. The first draft of *The Haunted* took fifteen spiral-bound notebooks and twenty black pens.

The Hidden took too many notebooks and too many pens to count. When not searching for cannibal Girl Scouts, she spends her days and nights buying stock in pens and paper. The dedication for "At the Late Night, Double Feature, Picture Show" is: *For Lee, because you took me to my first Rocky Horror live show. For Tim Curry, because quite frankly, you are the shit. And to David: Sorry about the leg!* You can visit her online at www.jessicaverday.com.

MARGARET STOHL (**"IV League"**) is the *New York Times* and internationally bestselling coauthor (with Kami Garcia) of *Beautiful Creatures* and *Beautiful Darkness*, the first two books in the Caster Chronicles. *Beautiful Creatures*, named Amazon's Top Teen Title of 2009, is currently in development by Warner Bros. Studios. Studying American literature while living on Emily Dickinson's street in Amherst and earning an MA at Stanford, Margaret came to her love of the South much as she comes to her love of everything—through books. Margaret spends most of her free time traveling to faraway places with her husband and three daughters, who are internationally ranked fencers. You can visit her online at www.margaretstohl.com.

MARY E. PEARSON (**"Gargouille"**) is the author of several award-winning books, including *The Adoration of Jenna Fox*, which is being made into a movie by Twentieth Century

Fox. She is a native Californian and writes from her home in Carlsbad, where she lives with her family and two very spoiled golden retrievers. Her book awards and honors include the Golden Kite Award, the American Library Association's Best Books for Young Adults, the New York Public Library's Best Books, the International Reading Association's Choice Books, and the South Carolina Young Adult Book Award. Her other novels include *A Room on Lorelei Street*, *The Miles Between*, and her newest book, *The Fox Inheritance*. For more information on Mary and her books, visit www.marypearson.com.

JENNIFER LYNN BARNES (**"The Third Kind"**) is the author of eight books for teens, including *Raised by Wolves*, the Squad series, and *Tattoo*. She wrote her first YA novel when she was still a teenager herself, and since then, her books have been published in a dozen countries worldwide. Jen grew up in Oklahoma, lives in Connecticut, and generally tries to avoid road trips because she has no sense of direction whatsoever. You can visit her online at www.jenniferlynnbarnes.com.

RACHEL CAINE (**"Automatic"**) is the internationally bestselling author of the Morganville Vampires series as well as the Weather Warden and Outcast Season adult urban fantasy series; "Automatic" is based on the Morganville Vampires series and features Michael Glass and his Goth girlfriend, Eve. In 2011, Rachel premieres a brand-new adult urban fantasy series, the Revivalists, with the release of *Working Stiff*, the story of a young funeral director who discovers her new bosses have an illicit business in reviving the dead . . . for profit. Rachel lives in Fort Worth, Texas, with her husband, award-winning fantasy artist R. Cat Conrad, and their ginormous iguanas, Darwin and Popeye. You can visit her online at www.rachelcaine.com.